Praise for Jamie James and
ANDREW AND JOEY

A Selection of the Insight Out Book Club

"Jamie James cleverly updates the epistolary novel to produce a *Clarissa* for the cyber global village. This is a comic novel, but it explores such wonderfully dangerous subjects as sex and love, art and gossip, race and money. *Andrew and Joey* is as entertaining and real as a year's worth of somebody else's email."

—Christopher Bram

"Jamie James crafts a tale that is in turns humorous, sexy, sad and always entertaining. An uncommonly good read. The story is engaging and the characters are interesting and always authentic."

—*The Lambda Book Report*

"A 21st-century *Pamela*—told entirely in email—this fascinating picture of the collision of western gay men with the culture of Bali is also a devastating comment on the problem of desire and commitment among gay men everywhere. A fast, fun, surprisingly stinging read."

—Andrew Holleran

"The epistolary novel gets a fresh jolt of verve and zest in James' comic novel."

—*Booklist*

ANDREW and JOEY

JAMIE JAMES

KENSINGTON BOOKS
http://www.kensingtonbooks.com

KENSINGTON BOOKS are published by

Kensington Publishing Corp.
850 Third Avenue
New York, NY 10022

All Kensington titles, imprints and distributed lines are available at special quantity discounts for bulk purchases for sales promotion, premiums, fund-raising, educational or institutional use.

Special book excerpts or customized printings can also be created to fit specific needs. For details, write or phone the office of the Kensington Special Sales Manager: Kensington Publishing Corp., 850 Third Avenue, New York, NY 10022, Attn. Special Sales Department. Phone: 1-800-221-2647.

Kensington and K logo Reg. U.S. Pat & TM Off.

ISBN 0-7582-0107-9

First Trade Paperback Printing: February 2003
10 9 8 7 6 5 4 3 2 1

Printed in the United States of America

Designed by Leonard Telesca

For Rendy

J'ai vu les moeurs de mon temps, et j'ai publié ces lettres.

—Jean-Jacques Rousseau
Preface to *La Nouvelle Héloïse*

Subj: POF Grant
Date: 2/17 8:42:38 AM Eastern Daylight Time
From: jahull@POF.org
To: Danzguy@NYAN.net (Joseph Breaux)

File: POFgrant.mim (31588 bytes)
DL Time (32000 bps): < 1 minute
This message is a multi-part MIME message and will be saved
with the default filename POFgrant.mim

Dear Mr. Breaux:

As Executive Director of the Pullman-Oliphant Foundation, I am very pleased to inform you that you have been selected as one of the recipients of this year's Artistic Endeavor grants. The review committee was enormously impressed by the clarity and passion you conveyed in your description of the dance project you wish to create in Bali. Your proposal embodied the essence of what the Foundation is looking for in the Artistic Endeavor Program: an established artist with the vision and courage to try something completely new in mid-career. I sincerely hope that this grant will enable you to create some great work in Bali.

As you know, the grant comes with no conditions attached, although I do hope that you will keep us informed about the progress in your work. I have attached the press release, which was sent to the nation's major newspapers this morning.

Ernest Moss, the Program Director of the Artistic Endeavor Program, will be in touch with you soon about the financial details.

Congratulations, and best wishes for success in your endeavors.

Jeremy A. Hull, Executive Director
Pullman-Oliphant Foundation

P.S. Joe, it isn't possible to scrawl a hand-written P.S. on an E-mail message, but I do want you to know how personally pleased I am about this. You deserve it, and I know you'll make us proud.

Subj: Re: POF Grant
Date: 2/17 3:38:27 PM Eastern Daylight Time
From: Danzguy@NYAN.net (Joseph Breaux)
To: jahull@POF.org

Dear Jerry,

I am so thrilled and honored I can't even begin to tell you. Thank you, thank you, thank you. Of course I'll stay in touch about how the work is going. I hope we'll have a chance to get together before I leave for Bali.

Best wishes,

Joe

Subj: Yippee!
Date: 2/17 3:38:31 PM Eastern Daylight Time
From: Danzguy@NYAN.net (Joseph Breaux)
To: RayjnKayjn@labell.net

Hi,

Are you sitting down? I have some GREAT news – I got that grant I was telling you about! $155,000 for a year in Bali. I'm so

excited – it's not just the money, it really means I've "arrived."
Some of the biggest names in dance got one of these Pullman-
Oliphant prizes at this point in their career. It's sort of like the
bush-league tryouts for the Guggenheim and the MacArthur.
And it means that almost for sure I'll be able to find a venue for
whatever I come up with in Bali. Next step: my own company.

They just sent me the news. The announcement will be
published in the New York Times tomorrow – look and see if
the Times-Picayune picks it up. You might call Marge
Livingston at the culture desk there, and tip her off, "Local Boy
Makes Good." I'm sure she has the story from the wire service,
or will soon. Meanwhile, they sent me the press release – I
won't send you the whole thing, but here's what they said about
me:

<<Joseph Breaux was the sole grant recipient in the field of
dance. Mr. Breaux has been a leading figure in American dance
since 1992, when he debuted as a soloist with the Tim Winner
Dance Group, in Mr. Winner's "Endymion." He has danced the
role of Endymion to great acclaim throughout Europe and in a
tour of Asia, in 1997. He has also danced leading roles in other
works by Mr. Winner, including the title role in "Candide," a
full-length solo piece based on the piano works of Heitor Villa-
Lobos, and the lead in Mr. Winner's controversial ballet of
Handel's "Messiah," which premiered in Stuttgart in 1998. Mr.
Breaux departed the Winner group in the summer of 1998, and
since then he has danced leading roles with the Miriam Chase
Dance Theater, Jorge Asturias' Grupo del Baile Nuevo, and the
Mikell Jones Group.

<<In January, with the Mikell Jones Group, Mr. Breaux made
his debut as a choreographer with a satirical reinterpretation of
Agnes De Mille's "Rodeo," set in his native Louisiana. When it
premiered, New York Times dance critic Quentin Trent wrote,
"Even as Mr. Breaux remains at the top of his powerful form as
a dancer, with this wicked, witty triumph he is poised to make

his name as a choreographer." Mr. Breaux's grant will fund a
year of study and dance in Bali.>>

Whaddaya think? Pretty grand, hunh? In the Times they'll cut it
way down, of course. That's all for now. Take care, Dad. Love
to Lu Ann.

Joey

P.S. You and Lu Ann have to come to Bali for a visit while I'm
there.

Subj: Yippee!
Date: 2/17 3:38:48 PM Eastern Daylight Time
From: Danzguy@NYAN.net (Joseph Breaux)
To: Philip_O'Donnell@bostonglobe.com

Hi,

Well, I got it. Jerry Hull just E-mailed me. I'm sure you've got
the press release at the culture desk at the Globe – you're so
clever with computers, you can pop it up on a split screen while
you read this. It's pretty glowing, although of course as the
dancer I came last, even after the Peruvian textile lady. Also, it
sort of sounds like I was invented by Tim. Which is pretty close
to the truth, I guess. What do you think of "departed"? Does
that sound bad? It should have said, "In 1998, after eight years
of screaming fights with Mr. Winner, who is an insane paranoid
alcoholic, Mr. Breaux told him he could go fuck himself, if he
ever gets sober enough to find his butthole." I'll be curious to see
what the Times does with it.

So, I'm going to Bali. Now that I've got the Pouf, I ask myself,
Why am I going to Bali? I have this terrible feeling that I
proposed it because I knew it would win. That, and Bali is such

a beautiful place. But if I was really going to do what was really the best thing for my career, I would go to Stuttgart to work with Remy. He sent me another message last week, promising me anything I asked for. Thing is, I know Remy would work my Cajun butt off, and my Cajun butt would rather be sittin' on the beach in Bali. I was telling Andrew last night – the main problem in dance is that by the time you finally reach the point where you really know what you want to do, your body isn't quite as good at doing it. That quote from Quentin is bullshit – I'm not at the top of my form, I'm at about 98 per cent of last year, and 95 per cent of three years ago, when I WAS at the top of my form.

I feel like if I can make a success of this Bali thing, it will be my best chance of making that transition. I never thought I wanted to be a choreographer, but now I realize there's not much choice: at this point, either you lower the level of excitement in the work, or you start using other bodies. Does the world need another choreographer? It seems like there are too many already. "Rodeo" was cute, but a one-off – I can't keep sending up Agnes De Mille, God bless 'er. Like the song says, "Ya gotta have a gimmick" – maybe Bali will be it. I guess we'll find out. Anyway, how bad can a year in Bali be? Andrew and I had the most wonderful two weeks of our life when we were there after the Asia tour.

Love ya,

Joey

Subj: Fabulous you!
Date: 2/18 7:54:34 AM Eastern Daylight Time
From: WitchBitch@camnet.net
To: Danzguy@NYAN.net (Joseph Breaux)

Il tesoro mio,

Ta tante is thrilled to the threshold of moistness by her favorite
niece's well-deserved good fortune, though dismayed that she is
not properly grateful to those who helped to make her la
Duncan of the new millennium – for shame, Tim loves you like
his own child. Petal, you must always be mindful of the wrath of
the gods. The fickle goddess Fortuna is constantly attended by
the avenging Furiae, who are played in this evening's
performance by all the dancers and choreographers who applied
for the Pouf and lost. Now that you're the Next Big Miss Thing,
everyone will be sharpening their knives for you.

Speaking of virtue, what about Andrew? Is he coming with you?
I don't mean to be bitchy (petite moi?), but there's not much to
keep him in New York, is there? Has the job search turned up
anything? Maybe this will somehow be a good opportunity for
him, too. Forgive ta tante if her encomia are not as prolix as
usual, but she's dreadfully fatiguée, after writing a poison-pen
review of a truly wretched performance of "Two Noble
Kinsmen," the dullest play Shakespeare never wrote, when what
she really wanted to do was to compose a masque in blank verse
representing the apotheosis of La Nouvelle Terpsichore – fabulous tiny you!

Phyllis

P.S. Really, Joey, I'm so proud of you. Who knew that that crazy
Cajun dancer who answered my "Roommate Wanted" ad in the
Voice twelve years ago, with his skinny Chinese boyfriend in
tow, would turn out to be a great artist? I did, that's who.

Subj: Joey's grant
Date: 2/18 10:24:29 AM Eastern Daylight Time
From: AndrewTan@wol.com
To: etan@MIT.edu (Eric Tan)

Hi Eric,

Sounds like you have your hands full interviewing applicants.
Are you more interested in their research or their teaching? I
suppose at a place like MIT, they have to have both, big time.
Sounds pretty boring, actually. Doing the interviews, I mean.

If you read the arts page in today's New York Times, you saw
Joey's Big News. Joey tries so hard not to gloat around me; he
always tries to downplay his good news. But this Pullman-
Oliphant grant is a majorly big deal . . . the paragraph about
"previous winners include" was like a who's who of the arts.

I'm *so* happy for him. I can't believe this is my Joey, winning
such an important award. It's hard for him to understand this,
he's so ambitious, but I really don't feel any sense of jealousy or
rivalry or anything like that. Ever since I got laid off at Morgan
last year, he has been so solicitous of my feelings, always making
sure to ask if I've heard from Chase or Citibank . . . as if I would
forget to mention that I got a new job. If it had been the other
way around, if I had been promoted to vice president at
Morgan, and he was still dancing in the corps with Tim
Winner's group, I doubt if we would still be together. Joey *has*
to be number one; that's just the way he is. But I really don't
need that. Not to get overly psychoanalytical about it or
anything, but maybe it's because I grew up with you as my big
brother. I got used to you being the valedictorian in high school,
winning all the prizes at Stanford while I made B's, etc.

I've been lucky with the men in my life. I'll never forget what a
big deal you and Joey made when that little magazine in Palo

Alto published my short story, throwing that party at the Burrito Loco; meanwhile you were winning the Rhodes and Joey's performances were getting written up by the dance critics from the Examiner and the Bay Guardian! It was kind of embarrassing, actually.

Sorry to be so mushy. I can't really say any of this stuff to Joey; he just changes the subject. Anyway, he wants to know if it's okay if we invite his friend Phil, the theater critic at the Globe, to come with us to Lenox this weekend. Is that okay? He's so campy, but he has a heart of gold, and helped us both a lot when we first came to New York, etc. He'll probably say no, anyway. It will be great to see you and Sophie.

See you Friday night.

Andrew

Subj: Bali bound
Date: 2/18 3:11:53 PM Eastern Daylight Time
From: Danzguy@NYAN.net (Joseph Breaux)
To: BBlankenship@indonet.net.id

Dear Bob,

I got the news today: I won the Pullman-Oliphant, thanks in no small measure to your help. Now all we have to do is see if I can come through with half of what I promised in the proposal! In terms of my participating with the dance corps at the temple you're fixing me up with, does it matter when I come? Is there anything like a season, or a particularly important performance that I ought to be sure not to miss?

Andrew and I haven't yet decided whether he's going to stay there for the whole year, but he's almost certainly coming out with me in the beginning. You've been very generous about inviting me to stay with you, but I think we'll probably want to go back to the same bungalow at the Hotel Tjampuhan where we stayed the last time, at least for the first week or two. Then, if he stays, we'll start looking for a house. I hope I can find a nice house, maybe with a pool, with the budget I've got. If possible, I would like to keep it under $2,000 a month. Is that reasonable?

Again, thanks for all the help. I can't wait to get there and get to work. Please let me know if there's anything I can bring you from the States.

Best wishes,

Joe Breaux

Subj: Re: Yippee!
Date: 2/19 3:23:35 PM Central Daylight Time
From: RayjnKayjn@labell.net
To: Danzguy@NYAN.net (Joseph Breaux)

Dear Son,

Well, that really is great news. I'm so proud of you, you little dickens. We're sure going to miss you. I hope we're going to get a chance to see you before you leave. You'll have to stop by Covington on your way to the Far East, or else maybe we can come see you. We're about the same around here. Lu Ann and I put up some blackberry jam, about 20 pints, which is a lot. That's about all we have in the way of news.

Love,

Dad and Lu Ann

Subj: Re: Fabulous you!
Date: 2/21 3:49:51 PM Eastern Daylight Time
From: Danzguy@NYAN.net (Joseph Breaux)
To: WitchBitch@camnet.net

Hi,

Gee, Phil, I can't imagine why the guys at the Globe think you're
a big fag. <<the apotheosis of La Nouvelle Terpsichore – fabulous tiny you!>>??? Anyway, the muses already live on Mt.
Parnassus. They don't really need an apotheosis, do they? I
mean, we don't.

Andrew and I are going to the Berkshires for the weekend with
his brother and sister-in-law – why don't you come? You could
hitch a ride with Eric. It's a huge house. G&T's on the porch?
Barbecue? Andrew's blueberry pie?

Love ya, and thanks for the kind words.

Joey

P.S. I thought there were only three Furies.

Subj: Re: Joey's grant
Date: 2/21 5:50:02 PM Eastern Daylight Time
From: etan@MIT.edu (Eric Tan)
To: AndrewTan@wol.com

---

hi,

fine about inviting philip o'donnell. tell him to call if he needs a
ride. we'll expect you by eight o'clock – i invited andrea rudner
for dins, i hope that's all right.

e

Subj: Wicked saucebox
Date: 2/22 7:26:44 PM Eastern Daylight Time
From: WitchBitch@camnet.net
To: Danzguy@NYAN.net (Joseph Breaux)

Wicked saucebox,

Oh, how sharper than a serpent's pee-pee it is to have an
ungrateful niece. First she casts asparagus on auntie's classical
erudition, then she invites her to ride for three hours in a Volvo
with a physics professor and his lady wife to spend the weekend
posing for Norman Rockwell covers. As Titania said to Oberon,
Not for thy fairy kingdom. (But you were kind to invite me.)

Child, everybody needs a good apotheosis every once in a
while. And as for the Furies: the Greeks only had three of them
because that's all it took to get the job done in those days. A lot
of bad shit has come down since then. The Furies have been recruiting.

Phyllis

S.P.A.

Subj: Your Bali plans
Date: 2/24 3:55:02 AM Eastern Daylight Time
From: BBlankenship@indonet.net.id
To: Danzguy@NYAN.net (Joseph Breaux)

Dear Joe,

Congratulations! That's great news. Actually, I already knew,
Erica Golden at the Institute for Dance Studies was one of their
"secret" consultants. She said that after the reviews you got
from her and the others, she was reasonably sure that you would
win.

Now, first of all, you have to completely forget about concepts like "seasons" and "the corps." The Balinese don't really consider what they do here "dance," in the sense that we do. It's not art for art's sake; it always fulfills a ritual function. I can't explain it in an E-mail message. I do hope you'll read the manuscript of my book while you're here. I don't claim it's a literary masterpiece, but it will save a lot of time answering questions. As for when you come, it really doesn't matter. After you've been here for a while, you'll realize that a red-letter day in Bali is one that *doesn't* have some festival or other. The Balinese spend half their money and most of their time on their religion, and dance is at the very essence of the whole system. It's incredibly complicated: after twelve years here, I still don't understand it all. You'll see.

Having said all that, Galungan and Kuningan, sort of Christmas and Thanksgiving rolled into one, are coming up in less than a month. They really go all out, so maybe you might want to come sooner rather than later. This morning, I informed the leaders of the seka in Kerobokan about the good news, and they're ecstatic. I'm not sure they understand exactly what it all means, but they certainly understand the $30,000 donation you're making! Here in Indonesia, money talks just as forcefully as it does in America.

Would you mind bringing a few books for me? It's so difficult getting them here, especially scholarly books. If it's all right, I'll ask Erica to put together a *small* package. Do you know her? It would give you two a chance to meet. She's a big, big fan of yours.

Well, congratulations again. Of course I understand that "your little grass shack is calling you back," but after a few days, if you want to stay here while you're house-hunting, with or without Andrew, you're very welcome. As for your budget: for $24,000, which you say is your budget for the year, you could *buy* a house.

So, as we say down South (I'm from Tennessee, did you know that?) . . . Y'all come!

Best wishes,

Bob

Subj: Thanks
Date: 2/28 9:12:36 AM Eastern Daylight Time
From: Danzguy@NYAN.net (Joseph Breaux)
To: etan@MIT.edu (Eric Tan)

Hi Eric,

Hey, man, thanks a lot for the weekend. It's always so weird to come back to New York after a weekend in the Berkshires. I love New York, I just wish they would turn the volume down a bit. Whenever you hear people talk about the excitement and street energy of the city, you know they live in the suburbs.

It was really great to have a chance to thrash out what Andrew and I are going to do this year with you and Sophie. I mean, it was good for Andrew. I know I overpower him sometimes – I can't help it. When he starts agreeing with everything I say, I know it's time for me to shut up, time to start asking questions instead of making suggestions. It's part of the artistic personality – I know that sounds pretentious, but in a dance group, that's all you do, constantly make suggestions to each other about how to do it better.

I think it's the right thing for him to do. We had one of the best times of our life together those two weeks in Bali. I know there's the risk of the boredom factor taking over, but where/when is that not the case? Andrew always says he wants to get back to his writing again – now he'll have a chance to try. And as I said on Saturday night at some point after you opened the third bottle of wine, I'm really not sure that I want to come back to New York, anyway. I mean, obviously I'm not suggesting that we emigrate (unless leaving New York counts as emigration). I love New York, but it's starting to wear me out. I'm ready to try something new – if Andrew is willing. Maybe we could go back to the Bay Area, it's a much more interesting scene now than when we were at Stanford.

So, thanks again. Talk to you soon.

Joe

Subj: Outta here
Date: 2/28 9:12:42 AM Eastern Daylight Time
From: Danzguy@NYAN.net (Joseph Breaux)
To: RayjnKayjn@labell.net

Hi Dad,

Well, I think we're going to leave sooner than I thought – there's some special holiday coming up that my man in Bali says I should really be there for. Here's the deal: since both Andrew's parents and Chrissie are in northern California, we thought we would all meet out there for a little going-away bash. I just called Chrissie, and she's up for it. I know you're not that wild about the Tans. I agree the old man's pretty crusty – he has all the humility and great sense of humor you would expect from a world-famous surgeon. But he's not really that bad. I don't think he means to be pompous; he just can't help himself. Does that sound as lame as I think it does? I guess he has reason to hold such a high opinion of himself after saving so many people's lives and inventing all those machines. Anyway, he's Andrew's father, so I have to get along with him, but that doesn't mean that you do – if you don't want to do this, it's OK, I'll swing by Covington on my way out to San Francisco. But I thought it might be fun if we had a little Breaux family reunion. We could spend a day or two with the Tans at their house in the city, and then maybe all us Breauxs can go to Santa Cruz for a day or two. Whaddaya think? Love to Lu Ann.

Joey

Subj: Thanks
Date: 3/2 11:02:51 AM Eastern Daylight Time
From: AndrewTan@wol.com
To: etan@MIT.edu (Eric Tan)

Hi,

Great weekend, bro'. Isn't that funny? I have bro' and Breaux. As these semi-annual "What are we going to do about Andrew" seminars go, it was a pretty good one, I guess. Is it weird for me to be so apathetic about my "future," at the age of thirty-five? After all, I'm Chinese; I'm supposed to be working twelve hours a day, making piles of money to pay for all those gold chains and cell phones and the fully accessorized Beemer. Actually, if I were blind, and I couldn't see my slitty eyes and straight black hair, I don't think I would even know I was Chinese. Do you feel Chinese? Neither of our parents speaks a word of the language. Dad's porcelain collection was the only Chinese thing about our childhood, and there's nothing really "Chinese" about that . . . he could just as easily have collected Roman coins or Shaker chairs as celadon.

Anyway, Eric, do you think it's weird that I'm not really pursuing a career of my own? I hated it at Morgan . . . I was actually relieved the day Skate Campbell called me into his office and gave me the heave-ho. I never got the basic concept, that making money was the only reason we were there. It's not that I don't like money. Money's great, but we've got plenty of it, between my stock income and Joey's fees. Last year he earned exactly double what he did two years ago. What's the difference between $200,000 a year and $500,000 a year . . . or $5 million? The maintenance at Horatio Street is a fraction of our income. I suppose we could get a bigger apartment in an elevator building, but I don't want to move. Neither does Joey. We like it here. I'm glad we don't have a car, and we don't need a house in the country, thanks to you.

Anyway, as I said in Lenox, I already have a career, as the unpaid secretary and P.R. representative of the soon-to-be-formed Joseph Breaux Dance Company. Joey has no idea how much time it takes to do all the stuff I do for him. He doesn't get that much fan mail, but there's some, and just saying no to everything he gets invited to takes time. He hands me the letters and says, "Say something nice to them." And when the bill comes in for the rehearsal space, and the invoices from the dancers, who writes the checks? That's a job, isn't it? Joey jokes about me being his wife, but in some ways I am Mrs. Joseph Breaux. Sometimes I wonder what Dad really thinks. Mom's okay with everything; she still thinks I'm twelve years old, I think, but I know Dad is disappointed. He really wanted me to be a doctor, but after I got a C in molecular biology freshman year, that was the end of that, even if I had wanted to go to med school, which I didn't. Enough! That was more than fifteen years ago. Why do I still do this to myself?

The other thing is, nobody believes me when I say this, but I really do want to get back to writing. If I had been accepted at Iowa, I would never have applied for that program at Morgan, and who knows what might have happened. After all, I *have* published three short stories in my life, even if no one's ever heard of the journals. That novel I was working on before I got the job at Morgan is probably not worth going back to. Nobody wants to read about a sensitive gay adolescent coming out any more; there have been about a hundred of them published since then. Maybe a torrid behind-the-scenes potboiler about the debauched world of modern dance? Just kidding. I have no illusions about this, but maybe Bali will awaken my dormant muse.

Well, an overlong message, as usual. I suppose if I have the time to write a message this long, it proves that I really do need a job . . . or that I should start writing something serious. Anyway, here's what's happening. I think we're going to just go. Joey's main contact in Bali said they don't really have seasons or schedules over there, or rather they have so many special events that it doesn't really matter when we come, but there's some big holiday coming up, so I think we're going to go sooner than we thought. Joey suggested that maybe we could all meet out in San Francisco to say good-bye to everybody. Joey's sister lives in Santa Cruz, you know, so his father and stepmom can fly up from Louisiana, and then we can all have a little going-away get-together. I hope you and Sophie can come. Dad is always so much jollier if you're there to talk about the poetry of molecules and all the other boring crap that the rest of us can't understand. Besides, we need protective cover . . . it's so painful to see Dad trying to talk to Joey's father. We were thinking maybe the first or second week of May? What works for you?

Your long-winded brother

Subj: Re: Thanks
Date: 3/3 6:24:17 PM Eastern Daylight Time
From: etan@MIT.edu (Eric Tan)
To: AndrewTan@wol.com

---

hi,

sorry, kid, this is the worst time of the year for me: honors presentations due soon, gearing up for finals, more interviews for the new post. as if that weren't enough, sophie informs me that we're going to completely redesign the garden. she wants a deck, yes, fine, but the koi have to go – why? i like the koi. but I've learned to smell a losing battle from a mile away. Anyway, the garden's her baby. better for us to try for another weekend in lenox before you leave.

don't worry about what dad thinks. you're 35 years old.

e

p.s. the structure of the universe is boring crap? tsk-tsk.

Subj: Re: We're outta here
Date: 3/4 8:21:40 AM Central Daylight Time
From: RayjnKayjn@labell.net
To: Danzguy@NYAN.net (Joseph Breaux)

Dear Son,

It will be an honor to be permitted to be in the presence of the great man again. Just because he makes me feel like Li'l Abner every time I open my mouth, that's no reason not to come out for a really fun visit with him and his butler and maid in that beautiful old mansion full of priceless antiques. I promise to drink too much and tell a whole bunch of really tasteless doctor jokes, how about that? Maybe break a few of those 500-year-old teacups.

I'm just joshing with you, son. Of course, we wouldn't miss it for the world. You know how much we enjoy seeing Andrew, and I think Mrs. Tan is a very nice lady. The doctor don't scare me none. He's always been polite to me, just, like you say, pompous. I haven't been to see Chrissie's new house yet, you know, so it's a good excuse. I wish she would get on-line, it's so tedious trying to catch her on the phone.

Let us know when. Lu Ann and I have our frequent flyer miles on American, so we can go any time.

Love,

Dad and Lu Ann

Subj: Steam
Date: 3/7 12:30:52 PM Eastern Daylight Time
From: AndrewTan@wol.com
To: etan@MIT.edu (Eric Tan)

Hi Eric,

Can I blow off a little steam? Joey and I just had the biggest fight we've had in a long time. Last night, while we were talking about what we would take with us to Bali, he casually mentioned that he had made some calls to real estate agents about subletting the place. He hadn't said one word about it to me! I said, why are we subletting? It can't be for the money . . . you just won a grant for $150,000! I don't want some strangers living here, with all these antiques from Jones Street. Can you imagine what Dad would say if someone scratched or stained that marble-top Queen Anne dresser? Of course that wasn't the point, neither was the money . . . it was the fact that he didn't ask me. Then he said, Was I making a commitment to the year in Bali or not. So I said, my commitment was to him, not to an island. What if after two months I'm bored out of my gourd over there and want to come back here, even just for a visit . . . am I supposed to stay at a hotel? No matter how much we sublet it for, it wouldn't cover that. We were the closest to shouting we've been in a long time. He slammed his fist into the wall in the kitchen at one point, and I was *not* impressed. I think we were both thinking about sleeping in the guest room, but finally we went to bed, without so much as a "good night." But the guest bedroom would have been too much of a symbolic step.

This morning, there was stony silence all through breakfast, and then he proposed his compromise: find one or two dancers, women, from a group he has some connection with, to stay here for a small rent, with the understanding that they would have to move out at a week's notice. He made the excellent point that an apartment left unoccupied for that length of time would be sure to be burglarized. Then he said the most important thing: he apologized for calling the agents without consulting me first . . . it was a real apology, not the usual collection of excuses disguised as an apology. I accepted all that he said . . . actually, he was right, it was a stupid idea to suggest leaving the place empty for so long. I was just so mad! I kept on acting like I was mad for a while . . . I love his expression when I finally relent and smile at him. His face lights up like a little kid on Christmas morning.

So that was that. It was kind of scary . . . we hadn't had a real fight like that in ages.

Love from your pugnacious kid brother

Subj: Re: Steam
Date: 3/8 10:00:02 AM Eastern Daylight Time
From: etan@MIT.edu (Eric Tan)
To: AndrewTan@wol.com

---

hi,

if a woman does that pretending to still be mad stuff, she's called a manipulative bitch. we guys get away with a lot. don't worry, kid, a little row every now and then is good for a relationship, really. and it's so much fun making up!

e

Subj: Jones Street Blues
Date: 3/19 12:15:45 PM Eastern Daylight Time
From: Danzguy@NYAN.net (Joseph Breaux)
To: Philip_O'Donnell@bostonglobe.com

Hi,

Sorry I've been out of touch for so long. The last few days in
New York were so crazy, getting packed and ready to go, and
we had to figure out what to do with the apartment. I assumed
we would do the obvious thing and sublet it for as much as we
can get – I'm sure we could clear a coupla thou a month on the
place. But I think Andrew has a case of cool feet – he wanted to
leave it empty, in case he decides he wants to leave Bali and
come back. I told him, you might as well mail out invitations to
the burglars. We had kind of a rumpus over it, a pretty big one,
actually. In the end we compromised – I found two girls from
the corps of the Jones group who are staying there for the main-
tenance, with the understanding that they have to move out at a
week's notice. It seems ridiculous to me. Andrew says we have
plenty of money – that may be true, but $2000 a month free and
clear is pretty good walkin'-around money where I come from.
But I didn't want to spend our last few days in New York quar-
reling.

At least I know I can totally trust the girls – if they trash the
place, they'll have to answer to Mikell! They're nice,
hardworking Midwestern farm girl types, thrilled to be in the
Village and out of their illegal sublet in deepest, darkest
Brooklyn. I told them, no parties, no house guests, no pets, no
boyfriends, no girlfriends, no eating, no drinking, no breathing. I think they got the message. They've got the deal of the
century – a two-bedroom in a landmark building in the Village
for $600 a month. I also told them they have to put you up
when you're in New York – I realize it's not the same, but if
you don't have another place to go, at least you won't have to
pay for a hotel.

God, Phil, why did I ever think this was a good idea, for us all to come out here? Andrew should have come here by himself, and I should have gone to Louisiana and then met him for the flight to Bali. Everybody's being so damn polite it makes me want to puke. My cheek muscles are aching from smiling. Dr. Tan can actually be charming (sort of) when it's just the two of us. He has a ballet subscription (OF COURSE), and wants to talk to me about Fokine and Balanchine, so I pretend like they actually have something to do with what I'm doing – at least it's something to talk about. But when his wife is around, he turns into such a pompous asshole. She's kind of a space cadet, I have to admit, but he's so horrible to her, in this mild, bland way, and she doesn't even seem to notice. He's always apologizing for her, calling her his wife, as in, "My wife fails to comprehend the importance of a carefully planned menu in order to choose wines properly." He actually said that at dinner the first night. Can you imagine that being anybody's notion of dinnertime chat? He was apologizing for having a Merlot with a leek sauce, some shit like that. I've got to hand it to him, though, he's really made his fantasy come true – the mansion on Jones Street, the staff of servants, the fabulous wine cellar, the chauffeured Jaguar sedan, even a little formal garden, here in the middle of the city. (The gardener came today, a hot Filipino boy in a stretch T-shirt and running shorts – mercy!)

Dad is being great. I can see that he's dying to say something like, "Well, when Lu Ann turns in a sloppy menu, I just smack her upside the head," but he lets it roll off his back. Lu Ann doesn't get it: "Well, Ah think thayat wahn is jist delicious, Doctor Tayan." It's terrible for Andrew. He worships the guy, but he knows that no one can stand to be around him. It's been a long time since Mama died, but I know just what she would have said about him: "He's his own worst punishment." Why am I talking so much about Dr. Tan? That't always the way it is out here – he becomes the center of everything.

It's hard for Andrew and me to get into the going-away spirit – everyone keeps telling us morosely how much they're going to miss us, but we're thinking, "We're outta here!" It's not that I'm not going to miss everyone, but I'm about to have an adventure – I don't feel morose at all, I'm excited. It's almost over – we leave tomorrow afternoon. I'm ready to get to Bali and have some FUN.

Love ya,

Joey

Subj: Re: Jones Street Blues
Date: 3/22 1:21:55 PM Eastern Daylight Time
From: Philip_O'Donnell@bostonglobe.com
To: Danzguy@NYAN.net (Joseph Breaux)

Dear Joey,

I'm leaving in a few days for London, my annual fourteen-plays-in-twelve-days whirlwind tour, so I may be out of E-touch for a while. Maybe I can check in at a cyber-cafe over there. First, I can't tell you how cheering it was to hear that you and Andrew had a real fight. Nobody knows you two better than I do, but I've never understood that Ozzie and Harry, perfect gay couple thing you two have going. How do you do it? You're so totally different. I suppose the apt cliche here is, opposites attract. Only someone as cool and even-tempered as Andrew could put up with your wild Cajun moods. (By the way, there's no extra charge for the psychoanalysis.)

My only comment about Dr. Tan is that he obviously has a deep theatrical streak waiting to be tapped. That house sounds like a set for a Charlie Chan mystery: "Murder at Bayside Manor," with the doctor as Charlie, rounding you all up in the library to check out your alibis: the dotty millionairess, the temperamental ballet dancer and his mild-mannered Chinese traveling companion, the eccentric Southern colonel with his lively young wife and his daughter, the mannish veterinarian. (I'm sorry, angel, I know there's an alleged boyfriend, but when I met Chrissie I could almost smell the Old Spice aftershave. All those dogs? In SANTA CRUZ? As Charlie Chan himself would say, "Contradiction, please?") Then the swarthy, taciturn butler reveals that the ballet dancer had a midnight tryst in the conservatory with . . . the hot-blooded Filipino gardener! You and Andrew have been together so long, I've never really thought of you as a rice queen – you don't have that evil streak. But you'd better watch yourself over there, darling. I can see an attack of yellow fever in your future.

It was sweet of you to tell the dancing dairymaids that I can stay at your place, but without you there it would be too too melancholy. I can always force myself on David and Michael – they have a sofa-bed.

Bon Voyage and lots of love,

Phil

Subj: Home, damn it
Date: 3/22 3:42:29 PM Eastern Daylight Time
From: AndrewTan@wol.com
To: etan@MIT.edu (Eric Tan)

Hi Eric,

Thank god this is almost over. What a bad idea this turned out to be. Dad's being such a pill. The way he treats Mom is getting worse and worse . . . but only if he has an audience. That's what's so strange. Sometimes I hear them talking when they're alone, and they're completely normal. But especially when Joey's around, he treats her like she's a moron, and she sits there and takes it, with that little smile. It's so pathetic: he thinks it makes him look cool, and of course everyone is totally disgusted. As for

me, he basically acts as though I'm not there. I told him I
wanted to get some writing done in Bali, and he just gave me a
vacant little smile, which anyone who didn't know him would
call a sneer, but I knew that he just wasn't paying attention. I
could get pissed off about it if I wanted to, but as you said, who
cares what Dad thinks?

I said I'm glad it's almost over, but I'm not sure I am, really. I'm
starting to get nervous about going to Bali. I couldn't sleep last
night, thinking about it. I mean, what will I actually do there?
It's fine for me to say I'm going to write, but write what? Joey
said start off with a journal, till you discover what you want to
write about. I know he means well, but how lame is that? It's the
advice you would give a college kid on his first trip to Europe.
Of course, part of me is excited. I made Joey promise we'll have
a garden. It's funny, but the one thing I missed most in New
York, after California, was the garden. I need something to stay
busy. In Bali I'll know exactly one person, and he's going to
be busy himself. There, you see all the good stuff I have to worry
about?

The one thing I keep reminding myself is that those girls staying
at Horatio Street have to clear out with one week's notice. Come
what may, I can always go back to my little life in New York . . .
though what that would be if Joey were in Bali I can't imagine.
But Eric, as soon as I say things like that, I immediately start
thinking about how good it might be. For one thing, it will be so
interesting to experience all that Bali has to offer. It really is, in
some ways, a once-in-a-lifetime opportunity. All that free time to
see if I really can write fiction that other people might want to
read. And even though it's such a long flight, if wanted to I
could sort of commute, right? A month or two there, a month or
two back in New York?

Does this message sound as mixed-up as I think it does? Once I
get to Bali, to that cute little bungalow where Joey and I stayed
before, I'll be fine. It will be a great vacation for a few weeks,

anyway. Sitting by the pool at the Hotel Tjampuhan, sipping all those fabulous juices, actually having enough time to get some reading done. I brought some Big Books: Bleak House, War and Peace (don't laugh), and all of Jane Austen, but I'm sure I'll end up (or start out) reading the fun junky stuff I brought.

I'm sorry this has been such a dumb message.

Your dithering brother

Subj: Re: Home, damn it
Date: 3/24 7:38:11 PM Eastern Daylight Time
From: etan@MIT.edu (Eric Tan)
To: AndrewTan@wol.com

───────────────────────────────────────

hi,

the only part of your message that was dumb was the apology at the end. the best part: <<I could get pissed off about it if I wanted to, but as you said, who cares what Dad thinks?>> not what i said, the part about choosing not to be pissed off.

OF COURSE you're feeling mixed-up and stressed-out and all that millennial good stuff. i told you in lenox, this was not going to be as simple as you and joe seemed to think. you have to somehow make this YOUR year in bali, not just you coming along with joe on HIS year there, or else it won't work. and re-member, if it doesn't work, that's ok, too. as you pointed out, you can go back to horatio street any time you want, you've al-ways got family with me and sophie, and you'll never starve. you're one of the lucky ones, kid – you've got CHOICES. take a few weeks for a vacation, sip your mango juice and read a few junky books by the pool, and when the time comes to do some-thing, you'll do it.

i'm sorry to hear your report on dad. dad is a strange, cold man, i admit, but never forget, he is a great scientist. i've never met anyone with a better mind. we have to remember that mom chose to live her life with him. this isn't china, and mom doesn't have bound feet. I hope that doesn't sound cruel. and, as we have often observed, she has that lucy ricardo way of getting dad to do what she wants, and think it's his idea. it's their marriage. if i ever treated sophie the way dad treats mom, she would smack me. for that matter, if joe treated you like that, you wouldn't put up with it, either – look at your fight over the sublet. but we CHOSE to be with them. if i had wanted a submissive chinese wife, i would have had no trouble finding one, and if you . . . oops, the parallel is getting too complicated here. i better stop while i'm ahead.

i'm still at the office grading finals. gotta run.

love from eric

ps send a message as soon as you get to bali.

Subj: Howdy from Bali
Date: 4/2 8:52:14 PM Eastern Daylight Time
From: Danzguy99@wol.com
To: RayjnKayjn@labell.net,
Philip_O'Donnell@bostonglobe.com, etan@MIT.edu (Eric Tan),
jahull@POF.org, cseligman@saloon.com, Cneuville@wol.com,
Nedt23@wol.com, Pawley@athena.com,
RSW@dovecott.demon.co.uk, dschwartzman@timeequities.com,
rciochon@blue.weeg.uiowa.edu, cnwalker@zotmail.com,
Jruggia@advanstar.com, rhythmt@ecom.net, SRIPPS@wol.com,
spikerk@wt.net, mlivings@library.berkely.edu,
jstiles@ix.netcom.com, lontar@IBM.net, Pkennicott@wol.com,
norman@joyce.org

Hi,

I don't approve of mass E-mailings like this, and I promise that
this is the only time it will happen, but everybody who's getting
this message said some variation on, "Let us hear from you as
soon as you get to Bali." Well, if I sat down and wrote a nice little personal note to everybody on the list, it would take me a
week, and by then it wouldn't be "as soon as I got to Bali."
Besides, I don't want you comparing notes with each other
about who got a message from me first. You're all first! I also
wanted to make sure everyone got my new address – I can't use
my ArtNet address in Bali, so I'll be Andrew's "guest" on WOL
while we're here.

We had a nice big Breaux-Tan family reunion in San Francisco
last week at Andrew's parents' house – my father and his wife,
Lu Ann, flew up from Louisiana, and my sister Christine came
up from her home in Santa Cruz. Andrew's brother Eric and his
wife Sophie were incapacitated by an attack of final exams and
couldn't join us (and were sorely missed). The highlight was a
delicious roast goose dinner, supervised by Mrs. Tan, accompanied by a spectacular Petrus that Dr. Tan had been saving for a
special occasion.

The flight was horrendous, as expected – next time, we are definitely going to spring for business class! We were met at the airport by my main contact here, a dance scholar from Tennessee named Bob Blankenship. Bob's a great guy, who has supported this project from the very beginning. He helped me dream up all the happy bullshit that was in my proposal to the Pullman-Oliphant Foundation (oops, you didn't hear that, Jerry). He's one of the world's leading authorities on Balinese dance, and is writing a big book on the subject, so I'm in good hands. Tonight he's having a dinner for us, our official welcome to Bali.

We got in at midnight two days ago (or that's what the clock said – somehow time measurements don't mean much after flying halfway around the world). We've spent most of our waking hours since we got here either lazing by the pool or in the spa, having our jetlaggy limbs massaged. We're staying in the same bungalow where we stayed the last time we were here, at a funky old hotel in Ubud, in the central mountains of Bali. It's the most gorgeous, romantic place on earth – I'm sure you've all heard us mention it one time or another. On Bob's advice, I'm not planning to do anything in the way of work except read for the first week. In a couple of months the Balinese will celebrate the holidays of Galungan and Kuningan, sort of like Christmas and Thanksgiving rolled into one, when they perform several special dances. I'll get started in earnest on the project when the dancers here begin rehearsing for that.

Bottom line: Andrew and I are fine, having a wonderful time, wish you were here – and the next time you hear from me, it will be a personal message, I promise.

Big hug from Joe

Subj: Checking in
Date: 4/4 3:41:10 AM Eastern Daylight Time
From: thumbelina@indonet.net.id
To: Erica_Golden@IDS.org

Hi there,

Just checking in. Things are as poky as ever here in paradise. I
was in Singapore for the weekend. They were having big sales at
the malls on Orchard Road, so I did a ton of shopping. You
know you've been living abroad for too long when you hear
yourself actually squeal because you found something your size,
your color, on the "40% off" rack at Donna Karan.

The big news here is the arrival of Joe Breaux. Bob had a dinner
for him last night. All I know of his work is "Endymion," which
I saw in L.A. just before I moved out here. That was quite wonderful, but that's been a few years. I heard good things about
"Candide," and very mixed (i.e., bad) things about that Messiah
in Dusseldorf or wherever it was. I had a nice long chat with
him. He wasn't at all what I expected. I mean, he's not really like
a dancer. For one thing, he's smart. (Nobody loves dancers more
than I do, but let's face it, most of them are better off not talking
too much.) For another, he doesn't have that Fabulous Me attitude, which they all have, even if it's disguised as "Fabulous?
Little ol' me? Aw shucks, I'm just a girl from Little Rock," if you
know what I mean. He's so cute (that IS like a dancer), or at
least I think so. Not movie-star cute but like a cute normal guy,
with those lustrous green eyes and pretty white teeth and that
hairy chest, though that seems to be out of style these days. And
he's just bursting with vitality, though apparently it's all for the
boyfriend. Chinese, from San Francisco. I didn't quite catch
what he does, not a dancer for sure. They're a weird couple –
Joe is so lively, while the boyfriend is sort of . . . distinguished.
You could see him running for mayor. It was the usual bizarre
crowd at Bob's, the rice queens with their tarty little boys, the

art dealers with their blonde wives, the rich Americans who have mysteriously developed European accents, and the Balinese, who always keep to themselves.

When are you coming for a visit? We would love to see you here. Send news – what's happening at the institute?

Big kiss from Pam

Subj: Bali High
Date: 4/4 4:05:06 AM Eastern Daylight Time
From: AndrewTan@wol.com
To: etan@MIT.edu (Eric Tan)

_____

Hey bro',

Sorry about the stupid title, had to get it out of the way. God, what a relief to be here! You've received Joey's mass mailing, so you know all the facts. Actually, I thought his message was kind of dopey . . . it didn't really sound like him. "You're all first!" sounded more like Mickey Mouse. I have to say, after all the fretting I was doing, it has been absolutely wonderful so far. This is the most *romantic* time (wink, nudge) Joey and I have had together in years. You're as good a sport about gay life as any straight person I know, but even so, I won't go into any of the details, except to say that Joey and I have been together for what, five years longer than you and Sophie . . . forever . . . and inevitably, at a certain point, sex loses its excitement, no matter how much you love the person. I'm not saying it's not as good, it's just that it gets to be predictable . . . choreographed, you might say (no joke intended). But there has been a certain amount of . . . improvisation, shall we say, going on here in the Walter Spies bungalow at the Hotel Tjampuhan. Also, jet lag is a great aphrodisiac: there's not much else to do in Ubud at 4 a.m. (Sorry about the gloating tone, but it's fun to have something to gloat about.)

That's enough about that. But we haven't really been out that much, walking around the town a bit, which is overrun with tourists. We already feel snobby about not being tourists. The main news is the big party Bob Blankenship gave for us (for Joey, let's get that right). He's really nice, a very serious scholar. He lives in a gorgeous old house in the middle of a rice field. We arrived at dusk, mist swirling across the valley, Chinese lanterns hanging on the porch, the servants in golden silk sarongs, bowing when we walked in. It was like a dream. As I said, he's really nice, very serious and soft-spoken, but the crowd was kind of . . . weird. There seems to be a big "rice queen" subculture here. There was a group of chubby, sort of sexless-looking middle-aged men, mostly American and British, all with these adorable Indonesian boys, skinny and giggly and cute as a row of copper buttons. I'm sure they weren't as young as they looked, but some of them looked *really* young, like teenagers. Bob didn't seem to be a part of it. There were a lot of other people there, the world traveler set, if you know what I mean, the too tan, too blond, too much silver jewelry club. (Is that bitchy?) There were some interesting people there, I guess, but Joey and I agreed afterward that in terms of making friends, it won't be easy. He wants to keep his relationship with Bob mainly professional, which I think is a good idea.

We've gone to a couple of dance performances at the palace here. It's really quite a spectacular show they put on, but I have to confess, I'm already pretty close to having my fill of the music. It's totally repetitive, like a bunch of madmen banging on cans and bamboo sticks, and it's too damn loud. I haven't worked up the nerve to tell Joey yet, but I don't think I'm going to do this more than once a week, if that. Maybe I'll get to like it.

That's all for now. I know you're too busy to write back long messages, but send some news.

Love to you and Sophie from Andrew

Subj: Re: Checking in
Date: 4/6 9:01:52 AM Eastern Daylight Time
From: Erica_Golden@IDS.org
To: thumbelina@indonet.net.id

Dear Pam,

I'm so glad to hear from you, and thank you for the report on
Joe Breaux. I meant to write you before his arrival, to tell you he
was coming. He's sort of a little project of mine. I don't know
him at all well personally – we met just before he left – but I
campaigned pretty hard for him to get the POF grant. Of course
he's fabulously talented, but as we all know, that's just one in-
gredient of a successful career in dance. He's temperamental,
which is good; he doesn't seem very disciplined, which isn't necessarily bad. Quentin was here for dinner a few nights ago, and
he agreed with me: Joe is at an interesting juncture. He's making
the transition to choreography not out of necessity, the way
most dancers do, and usually fail, but because it seems to be
what he really ought to be doing. And this Bali business is so . . .
original. Fusion can be a disaster, but it can also be invigorating.
I'm *so* curious to see what he comes up with. Will you keep
an eye on him for me, send me a report about him from time to
time? I think Bob is sort of using him, to a certain extent, not in
a bad way, but to have a rising star from the world of "real"
dance associated with his research is a very good thing for him.
I'm not sure that the association is as good for Joe. I can't
believe that Joe Breaux will care very much about the 27 different finger movements associated with the Legong, Ubud district.
We shall see.

You ask for news about the institute – it's the same ol' same ol',
trying to raise money in a country where the government hates
art and the corporate sponsors think art is a business. It's so de-
pressing sometimes. As for my so-called personal life, don't ask.
I think I went on a date once, when George Bush was president.
The first one, I mean.

I would love to come to Bali. But when? Make the Rockefeller Foundation approve our main grant proposal, and I'll come for a month. Deal?

Love from Rica

Subj: Re: Howdy from Bali
Date: 4/6 11:08:42 PM Eastern Daylight Time
From: Philip_O'Donnell@bostonglobe.com
To: Danzguy99@wol.com

Provoking creature,

That's it? My favorite niece, who will some day inherit my flaw-less vintage Hawaiian shirts, my definitive Ella Fitzgerald record collection, my autographed portrait of Miss Loretta Young, in-scribed to me by her own hand in the lobby of the Beverly Wilshire Hotel on May 27, 1972, my darling pet moves halfway around the world, and all I get is a form letter? I can see that I've lost you to this Bob person, such a great guy, who has sup-ported your project from the very beginning. Petal, I quiver with joy to know that you're in such good hands, with one of the world's leading authorities on Balinese dance. Whatever you do, be sure to follow Bob's counsel in all things – oh yes, by all means spend the first week reading, what brilliant advice – who ever would have thought of that by herself? I hereby resign all claims to aunthood in favor of this artful Svengali. Someday you'll come crawling back to ta tante Phyllis, begging for forgiveness, but she will cast merry giggles in your face and send you straight back to The Bob.

Joey, what a ridiculous letter. For those of who know that your father-in-law is a twisted sadist and your mother-in-law a bor-derline cretin, the San Francisco paragraph was particularly en-tertaining. Of course I was joking, but isn't the cult of Bob laid on a bit thick?

My London trip is going very well, thank you for asking. I won't bother you with the details – there's nothing more boring and useless than reviews of theatrical productions one won't see. There, you see? – your ex-auntie is merciful even in defeat. I am writing this at my friend Geoff's bijou maisonette in Camden Town. I had such a crush on him twenty years ago. He was so divine, one of those gilt, willowy English lads. He's gilt and willowy no longer, more like silvery and oaken. It's so gratifying to see one that got away turn into a troll. I know that sounds bitchy, but in a few years you'll understand, child. Maybe you won't, with that perfect marriage of yours. It's an act of Christian martyrdom to be your friend.

I'll be home in two days but not back in the office until Thursday or possibly even Friday, so if you can tear yourself away from Bob's Big Book long enough to answer, send it to the home address.

Ta tante Phyllis

S.P.A.

Subj: Re: Bali High
Date: 4/7 4:43:20 PM Eastern Daylight Time
From: etan@MIT.edu (Eric Tan)
To: AndrewTan@wol.com

---

hi yourself,

you're right – i don't have time for a long message. or a short one. i just wanted you to know we're thinking about you – have some fun! work on that tan. drink too much wine for once in your life.

c

p.s. what were you doing up at 4 a.m.? was it before or after the . . . wink, nudge.

Subj: Yeah, yeah, yeah
Date: 4/8 2:31:27 AM Eastern Daylight Time
From: Danzguy99@wol.com
To: WitchBitch@camnet.net

Hi,

Yeah, yeah, yeah. I was holding off getting in touch because I knew you were in London. How was I supposed to know that you were going to check in at the formerly-gilt-and-willowy Geoff's bijou maisonette? Jesus, Phil, if I hadn't know you for so long, I don't think I could unravel all the encrustations of fag-bitchery in your messages. The combination of homosexuality, two years of high-school French, and meeting Loretta Young when you were twenty years old wreaked life-long havoc on your prose style. You should try writing one of your reviews for the Globe in Tante Phyllis style.

The idea of you being jealous of Bob Blankenship is so hilarious. He's the quietest little man in the world (but I remember my mother always said, "Watch out for the quiet ones"). I think he's actually a closet queen, mind-boggling in a place where most of the expats are flaming fags. And it's mostly a matter of cultural differences, I realize, but Balinese men are the flittiest people I've ever seen, especially the young ones. The boys are always holding hands and sitting in each other's lap; you never see them with girls. There was a whole corps of rice queens at the party, either short and pudgy or tall and skinny, with really cute young Indonesian guys (although most of them were Javanese, according to Bob, my new mentor). None of them were what you would really call chicken, but even at thirty a lot of the men here still have that boy look, the tiny waist and long neck. I've never been into that, but the boys here really are so goddamn PRETTY.

Anyway, Bob, my guru, who gives me really great advice, told me that there's a pedigree for "boy love" in Ubud. That was his quaint phrase. Andrew's and my bungalow at the Tjampuhan Hotel is named after Walter Spies, a German artist who lived here in the twenties and thirties. The hotel is built on the site of his house. His paintings are interesting. Bob showed me the book – Balinese myths in nightmarish perspective, lots of chiaroscuro. He was also a photographer and a choreographer. He choreographed the kecak, the most famous Balinese dance, where the men lie in a circle chanting "chak-a-chak-a-chak" while the soloists act out the story, some Hindu myth. You've probably seen it. Walter built the bungalow we're staying in for Barbara Hutton, the Woolworth heiress who married Cary Grant. I didn't really know who she was, but apparently she was a famous jetsetter in the days before they had jets, and sort of a Judy Garland type, only dated gay men.

Well, the Dutch colonial authorities busted that rascal Walter for poking underage boys. The funny thing was the way Bob told me the story. The first few times he said the word "gay," he got all pink in the face and lowered his voice. Kind of bizarre, really, with the rice queens slinging camp all over the place, but he must be close to 65, and comes from Lookout Mountain, Tennessee, which explains a lot. That be real Bible-thumpin' country, son. Anyhow, the Balinese were incensed about Walter's arrest. They loved him, thought he was a great guy. The boy's father testified on his behalf at the trial. And the great part is, when Spies was in prison, his favorite gamelan orchestra came down and played outside his cell window, and the boyfriend sang for him. Isn't that the sweetest story? It's such a great story, you gotta wonder if it's true.

So, yeah, great so far. Andrew seems to be relaxing and having a good time, which is a relief. We've had a sort of sexual renaissance, doin' it in the sunken marble tub under the stars, all that romantic fantasy stuff. Actually, Andrew is livelier in that department than he's been in years. I've never had anything to complain about, exactly, but sometimes I know he's just being a good sport, that he'd rather be in the kitchen making blueberry muffins or something. This idea you have that we're Ozzie and Harry, with the perfect marriage, is so . . . ridiculous. I think people who are alone idealize couplehood, and people who are in couples remember what it was like to do whatever you wanted, whenever you wanted – with whoever you wanted to do it! There are a dozen conversations that Andrew and I have had, verbatim, a thousand times. I'm not exaggerating. There's "I don't hate your father" (me), "I'm not jealous of your success" (him), "What's the use of having money if you don't spend it?" (me again), and the ever-popular "I'm your boyfriend, not your maid" (pas de deux). God, what am I doing! telling you, of all this people, such private stuff. I can already see the blackmail letters. I'd better stop before I get into trouble.

Love ya,

Joey

P.S. What does S.P.A. mean?

Subj: S.P.A. & proud, baby
Date: 4/11 6:34:52 PM Eastern Daylight Time
From: WitchBitch@camnet.net
To: Danzguy99@wol.com

Il tesoro mio,

S.P.A. stands for "Sola, perduta, abbandonata," an aria from Act IV of Giacomo Puccini's immortal "Manon Lescaut," which is the only scene in Italian opera, as far as I know, set in your native state. It is a number of exquisite pathos, sung by the eponymous heroine as she lies dying "in a desert in Louisiana" (geography wasn't piccolo Giacomo's best subject). "Sola, perduta, abbandonata," roughly translated, means, "Fucked over,

fucked up, and never to be fucked again," and it is the anthem
of fallen women everywhere.

Joey, I was touched by your comments. It's true, I think that
most lonely people like me think that couples like you and
Andrew live in a sort of conceptual cottage with a white picket
fence, where you continually prune the roses and bake cookies
(you can't deny it, Andrew does a LOT of baking), and I think
that people who are happily coupled imagine that single men are
out having tons of fabulous sex all the time. In fact, most of the
fabulous sex I hear about is being had by married boys who are
cheating on the cookie-bakers. But I must tell you that it's better
to have those dozen conversations with another person than
with yourself. I've tried it both ways. Now I find myself in the
scary situation of getting into shouting arguments with
Republican lawyers on CNN.

It's impossible NOT to be lonely in this dreary place. God, how
I hate Boston. Cotton Mather is still the chairman of the enter-
tainment committee here. Their idea of fun is turning down the
thermostat. Remind me again what a great career move it was to
take this job, because frankly, if I were offered my old job at the
Voice again, I would leap like Tarzan. For a theater critic to be
in Boston is like . . . what, like being a hockey correspondent in
Havana. These people don't care about the theatah – what's the
point of writing about a brilliant Terence Rattigan revival in
London, when the culture desk editor asks, Is that the guy who
wrote "Master Class"? Really. But if the Handel & Fucking
Haydn Society does the bloody Messiah for the umpteen
millionth time, it's on the fucking front page with a bloody
photo. Bitter, moi?

Well, time to cast pearls before swine.

Cuddles,

Phil

P.S. I ran into your brother-in-law at my favorite little book-
store on Newbury Street yesterday. He really is a divinely handsome man. And such lovely manners. I feel a bit uncouth around
him.

Subj: House-hunting
Date: 4/11 10:36:25 PM Eastern Daylight Time
From: AndrewTan@wol.com
To: etan@MIT.edu (Eric Tan)

Hi,

We've been ensconced in the Walter Spies bungalow for a week
now, wallowing in sybaritic luxury . . . not really, the Hotel
Tjampuhan is a little funky around the edges. The staff's better
at apologizing sweetly than getting it right the first time, and the
food's merely okay. Early this morning I went up to look at the
bill, and we're already almost up to $2,000! We've been having
room service every night, with wine, which is incredibly expensive in Indonesia. Also, they have something devilish here called
the "plus-plus," which means that everything gets charged 10
percent tax and 5 percent service, so it's not as cheap as it looks.
It *is* cheap . . . we've got a beautiful two-story bungalow with
a private garden for $175 a night . . . but I told Joey just now, it
was a great idea to do nothing the first week we were here, but
guess what? The week is up.

So I'm going to start house-hunting. We're not going to stay in
Ubud (even though it is the most beautiful place on earth, and
the rice fields at twilight make you want to weep they're so romantic), but in the south. The company (they call it a seka) that
Joey's going to be associated with, at least to start, is in a town
called Kerobokan, just north of the Legian beach area, the center
of the expat scene. That's where we're going to stay. The farther
south you go, the more surfers and lager louts and T-shirt sales-
men there are, and by the time you get to Kuta, the big surfing

beach, it's hellish, unbelievably crowded, horrible traffic, etc. But Kerobokan (you need to get a map of Bali) is still relatively un-touristy. This is all according to Bob. He and Joey are going down to the seka today, so Joey can meet everyone, and I'll drive around and look at houses (or rather Bob's servant is going to drive me around). Bob is calling up some of his friends in Legian, to ask around. I should have waited till I got back from Kerobokan before I wrote you.

Andrew

P.S. Four in the morning Eastern time is . . . guess what?, four in the afternoon in Bali. Duh. What line of work did you say you were in, Mr. Rhodes Scholar? I think WOL puts everything out-side the U.S. into Eastern time.

Subj: House hunting 2
Date: 4/12 7:03:12 AM Eastern Daylight Time
From: AndrewTan@wol.com
To: etan@MIT.edu (Eric Tan)

Hi,

Tsmee again. What a day! Everyone here is certainly nice to you when you want to rent a house for the year. I've found several good prospects. I don't know why I thought I could find a "real" house, by that I mean a furnished house belonging to a regular Balinese person, for rent. There are lots of furnished houses, available by the month or the year, catering to foreign-ers. The problem with these rental villas, as they call them, is that they are clustered in little "villages," and seem to be mostly populated by cute, dumb-looking Japanese surfers with bleached hair and their cute, dumb-looking girlfriends. I don't want to live with a bunch of Japanese surfers. Is that racist? Remember Manchukuo!

Bob was right: Kerobokan isn't terribly touristy. It's also isn't terribly interesting. There are some pretty rice fields, but it's mostly a middle-class suburb of Denpasar, the big city to the east. I had to go a little south, toward Legian, to find anything. Some of the villas are out in the fields, which is nice, but they have more of a tourist compound feel to them; it's just you and the surfers, out in the middle of nowhere. (Am I dwelling on minutiae? Whey am I telling you about the places I *didn't* like? But the choices for Stuff To Do around here are limited, and writing these messages to you is one of the good ones.)

Anyway, to make a long story a bit shorter, I found a place that I really liked just outside of Kerobokan, on the outskirts of the expat "scene." It's not far from the Oberoi, the fancy resort around here. It's owned by a guy who has villas and bungalows all over Legian. His name is Swastika. Is that bizarre or what? Rai Swastika. Everyone has carefully explained to me that the swastika is an ancient Hindu symbol that existed for thousands of years before the Nazis, and it's a common name in Bali, but I'm sorry: I'm from California, and Rai Swastika is a *weird* name.

Anyway, this particular villa is not part of a "village" but all by itself, down a little alley off the main drag. Quickly, here are the details: two huge bedrooms, each with open-air baths, an open kitchen/dining area in between, with a wide tiled porch wrapping around. And the main thing is the garden, a really nice walled garden, L-shaped, with lemon, coconut, and papaya trees, ginger and hibiscus, big beds of bird of paradise, a koi pool, and a thatched mahogany pavilion in the middle. The house, including the porch, is about 4,000 square feet, the gar-den the same. Joey didn't want to come look at it tonight, as it was already dark. It's not exactly "tasteful" . . . the colors are sort of psychedelic, you can almost see the surfers getting down with their bongs . . . but it's way below our budget, and we can repaint and refurnish for next to nothing, according to Mr.

Swastika. I won't describe the other houses I found. They're
nicer, newer, more fixed up, but it will be fun to do some fixing
up of our own, and the garden chez Swastika is by far the
biggest. I already have some ideas.

I hate to leave Ubud, but as Joey points out, Bali's a small island.
It's an hour from Kerobokan to Ubud. And as lovely as Ubud is,
it's slooow. That's part of why it's lovely, but for living year
round, we might actually want some "scene." Bob showed us a
really pretty Italian restaurant on the beach, about a mile from
the house, there's a decent French bakery within walking
distance, etc.

Well, as you can see, I've got a lot to report. You know, it
wouldn't kill you to pass along some news once in a while. Have
you started on the new garden?

Your brother

Subj: Re: House hunting 2
Date: 4/13 9:41:44 AM Eastern Daylight Time
From: etan@MIT.edu (Eric Tan)
To: AndrewTan@wol.com

hi,

sounds to me as though joe better say yes to swastika manor, if
he's knows what's good for him. don't ask me about the garden
– all i do is sign the checks.

e

Subj: Swastika Manor
Date: 4/14 9:45:55 PM Eastern Daylight Time
From: AndrewTan@wol.com
To: etan@MIT.edu (Eric Tan)

Hi,

Well, it's all set. As you said, Joey knew what was good for him
and agreed to Swastika Manor. Actually, I think he really does
like the place. As they say in New York, what's not to like? I've
been so busy. We signed the contract on the spot, and since then
I've been busy with Mr. Swastika's hired hands, who seem to
come with the place, cleaning and getting ready to paint. Also
getting the garden into decent shape. I've discovered the secret of
gardening is to have a gardener, a strong lad like Agus, my 18-
year-old Javanese gardener, who, as Joey says, is a working fool.
I point to a bare patch along the wall, and say, "Let there be ginger," and a few hours later, after Agus hops on his motorcycle
and scoots down to the nursery . . . voila, there is ginger.

I've hardly seen Joey except at meals. He has been so busy at the
seka, working with the dancers. They rehearse late into the
evening, because of course the dancers aren't paid, and they all
have jobs. And then during the day he's working with Bob
Blankenship, who knows everything about Balinese dance. I'm
glad to see him working; the last few weeks in New York, he
was driving me crazy. When he's idle, he literally rampages, fid-
geting and stomping around. I think it's what they mean when
they talk about raging Cajuns. But when he comes in at night,
he's so tired. He keeps inviting me to come to the seka, raving
about how great it is, but (entre nous) I really can't think of anything more boring than watching Balinese dancers rehearse. I
can't quite figure out what he's doing with them. I don't think he
knows, either. He is certainly going to perform with them at the
big temple in Kerobokan on this holiday that's coming up, and I
think he eventually wants to use some of the dancers in the seka
to create his own ballet.

We went out for some nightlife for the first time last night. Bob took us to Cafe Luna, the big watering hole around here, a couple of miles down the street. I was amazed at how gay it is. It's not a gay bar, per se, it just seems like . . . there are a lot of gay people here. There were lots of gay foreigners like us, of course, but there were also a lot of gay Indonesians. Bob said many of them were from Java. It seems that if you're gay in this country, your choice is either to go to Jakarta or Bali and hang out with the gay foreigners, or else stay in your village and become a professional banci, as they call homosexuals here. Bancis dress like women and their main job, traditionally, is to work as stylists for the brides in the village. Seriously. So the gay boys who aren't into cosmetology either go to Jakarta or come to Cafe Luna.

I also found out where I fit in in the social hierarchy here: I don't. As an ethnic Chinese, I'm either hated or invisible. Whenever Joey and I are out together, people invariably speak to him and ignore me. People in the shops speak to me in Indonesian, assuming from my overgrown-Stanford-boy clothes that I'm a rich Chinese-Indonesian businessman. And they do *not* like rich Chinese-Indonesian businessmen here. We knew that; whenever there are any political problems here, the first thing they do is get a mob together to go burn down the Chinese shops. It's amazing how open they are about it. A place like Cafe Luna is okay, but in more "Indonesian" places, I get dirty looks. Living all my life in San Francisco-Stanford-Greenwich Village, I've been sheltered from all that. These people look at me like they really hate me.

Joey, on the other hand, is a god here. At the cafe, I was sitting next to Bob, with Joey across the table, so it looked as though he might have been on his own, and it was literally like the honeypot drawing flies. It was amazing. At least half a dozen boys, very pretty they were too, sidled up to him and said, "Hello, what's your name?" And lots more smiled at him. Joey is handsome, but he's not *that* handsome, is he? It's a strange sensation; at home, frankly, I'm accustomed to drawing more notice from strangers than he does. But here, I just blend into the woodwork, while Joey is like a movie star. Really, it's like James Dean walked into the room. He tried not to show it, but he was enjoying it just a little too much.

The aura of sex was so thick you could almost smell it. There was a guy there selling pot, Viagra, and poppers . . . a complete kit! It seemed as though most of the boys were "available," and not only gay, by any means. There were several very handsome young guys with dumpy-looking Australian girls, and it was clear that they were there on a salary.

Well, enough about the seamy nightlife of Bali. I could tell you about the unbleached linen wall coverings I've picked out for the bedroom, or the gorgeous leather sofa I've ordered (about $300, beautifully made, would be at least $5,000 in New York), but I know you're one of these macho straight guys who doesn't have time for interior-decorator queer crap like that, and you've probably got to go grade papers or whatever it is that physics students turn in.

Love from Andrew

Subj: Change of Address
Date: 4/16 9:46:01 PM Eastern Daylight Time
From: AndrewTan@wol.com
To: RayjnKayjn@labell.net,
Philip_O'Donnell@bostonglobe.com, etan@MIT.edu (Eric Tan),
jahull@POF.org, cseligman@saloon.com, Cneuville@wol.com,
Nedt23@wol.com, Pawley@athena.com,
RSW@dovecott.demon.co.uk, dschwartzman@timeequities.com,
rciochon@blue.weeg.uiowa.edu, cnwalker@zotmail.com,
JRuggia@advanstar.com, rhythmt@ecom.net, SRIPPS@wol.com,
spikerk@wt.net, mlivings@library.berkeley.edu,
jstiles1@ix.netcom.com, lontar@IBM.net, Pkennicott@wol.com,
norman@joyce.org

New address and contact information for Joseph Breaux and
Andrew Tan:

Jalan Kerobokan Raya 54X
Kerobokan
Bali
Indonesia
Telephone and fax: 62 361 2930203
E-mail remains unchanged.

Stay in touch!

Subj: A real howdy
Date: 4/20 7:52:43 PM Eastern Daylight Time
From: Danzguy99@wol.com
To: RayjnKayjn@labell.net

Hi,

Just a quick note to let you know that we've found a really nice
house (actually, Andrew found it), on a quiet little alley off the
main drag in this part of the island. It has a big walled garden,

really pretty. Your and Lu Ann's room looks out on the little fish pond, full of giant goldfish. The house is a wee bit funky around the edges, but Andrew has already started fixing it up. Actually, it's good to be in a place that Andrew can work on – I've been so busy, I don't have time to take a pee.

Work is going great. I promise I'll write a longer message soon.

Love ya!

Joey

Subj: S.P. Double A
Date: 4/29 8:13:12 PM Eastern Daylight Time
From: WitchBitch@camnet.net
To: Danzguy99@wol.com

Hel-lo!

Is anybody home? You promised, once a week, come what may, that you would let me hear from you, even if it was only "Hi, I'm okay." But you haven't done that, have you? No, you have not. And you know what that makes you, don't you? That makes you an L.C. Figure it out. I'm going to New York for the weekend, to see that revival of "South Pacific" that had London dripping desperate droplets of mad desire last year, which I missed when I was there. It'll be better here – in London, they don't know from a chorus line. Aiyand those fike Amurican ax-ints.

Write me soon, you wicked, wicked child.

Aunt Phyllis

S.P. Double A

Subj: Update
Date: 5/2 11:50:21 PM Eastern Daylight Time
From: thumbelina@indonet.net.id
To: Erica_Golden@IDS.org

Dear Rica,

You asked for periodic reports on your little project, as you call
him. Well, I saw Bob last night, and he was just bubbling over
with enthusiasm about the wonderful Joe Breaux. Bob is such a
funny little man, he has such flights of rapture, and then he stops
himself, gets embarrassed and turns all pink. He's like the
world's oldest teenager. I think I'm getting sidetracked. Anyway,
he says that Joe is catching on to Balinese dance like a house on
fire. Apparently everyone in the seka adores him, and he just instantly picks up every move they show him. Bob was saying how
miraculous it was, going on and on about the cultural gulf between East and West, the spiritual approach to dance here and
the rigorous aestheticism of modern dance (his words). I tried to
explain to him, spiritual or not, it's body movement, and someone like Joe Breaux is physically trained to the point of perfec-
tion. It's not a miracle at all. He would quickly become a star at
a czardas tavern in Budapest or a tango club in Buenos Aires,
too. Bob wasn't buying it. These professional expats are such
snobs: If you haven't been here for twenty years, they don't even
listen to you. They don't realize that for the rest of the world,
Bali is not the center of the universe – it's a beautiful, fascinating
island in Indonesia, period.

I keep saying it's time for me to move back to the States, but I
never quite book the flight. You know why? the main reason I
can't leave this place? Nyoman, my maid. I can't face life without servants. In five years, I think I've washed maybe a dozen
glasses, and done exactly no laundry. When did Americans stop
having maids? Even the Brady Bunch had a maid. What
happened? Now, the millionaires I know in New York and

California do their own cooking and washing up. OK, most
people have a Jamaican or Guatemalan lady who actually scrubs
the toilet, but Nyoman does everything: she shops, she cooks
much better than I ever could, she sweeps, she scrubs, dirty
clothes miraculously appear cleaned and pressed in the closet. I
even taught her how to make a proper martini. She does far
more for me than either of my husbands ever did.

All right, now I know I'm sidetracked. I have no news, of
course, but I thought you would be interested in that rosy report
about your "little project."

Kisses from Pam

Subj: I'm in love
Date: 5/3 11:38:20 AM Eastern Daylight Time
From: Danzguy99@wol.com
To: WitchBitch@camnet.net

Hi,

Don't even start wid me, bitch. You can't imagine how busy I've
been. Where shall I begin? First, let me guess . . . Lousy Creep?
Lordly Cajun? Honey, when the feminist thought police catch up
with you, you're going to be in deep shit.

Oh god, Phil, I'm in love! This is the most exhilarating experi-
encee of my life, truly. I LOVE Bali. I love everything about it. I
love the land and the sea and the sky. I love the men and the
women. I love the clear honest gaze of the children, the fiery
candor of the food, the majestic temples, the hundred high-flying
kites that twinkle in the last rays of the setting sun every
evening. The offerings they make to the gods, little bamboo
trays with flowers and rice and silver coins and incense, are exquisite works of art. But most of all, I ADORE Balinese dance. I
don't know how else to put it: the people here move perfectly. I

know you'll think I'm crazy, but I swear to you, the dance here
is the best in the world. New York is full of bumbling rank amateurs compared with Bali. No, that's exactly wrong: the creeping
professionalism of Western dance in the twentieth century is
what has killed it. Diaghilev and Nijinsky, and even Fokine, in a
way, were basically amateurs, making it up as they went along.
Isadora and Ruth St. Denis and Ted Shawn were total, funky,
visionary amateurs, who were willing to try anything but established technique. The more I think about it, Balanchine is to
blame: even the so-called revolutionary figures were cowed by
him into thinking that the most important thing was to maintain
a mythical essence called "performance standards." Instead of
fresh ideas we have the Perfect Movement. I hate the Perfect
Movement! (Of course, Mark is exempted from all of this, but it
goes double for the Germans. To think that I almost ended up in
Stuttgart – god, what a disaster that would have been.)

In Bali, they have no standards: Hallelujah! For example, I'm
going to dance in the Kuningan celebration at the temple in
Kerobokan in a few weeks. When Gde (pronounced like the
Australian greeting), the master of the seka I'm working with,
invited me to perform one of the solo parts, I couldn't believe it.
It was obvious that I was catching on quickly, but there was no
way I was ready to dance a lead role. I thought he was just being
polite, and I turned him down as nicely as I could, but he
insisted: "Everyone has heard about the famous American
dancer visiting us, and they want to see you. It will be an honor
for the seka. Don't worry about making mistakes, they don't
matter if you have a strong spirit. And the next time you dance,
people will see how much you have learned." That was the
essence of it; I sort of fixed up the English.

You should see Gde at work. I don't know what the Balinese call
him – to call him a dance master in the Western sense is all
wrong – anyway, he's the guy in charge. He's always so clear and
firm with the dancers, sometimes a little harsh, but never any
bullshit. When I think of all the neurotic mind games I've gone

through with Tim, and even Remy and Mikell, that "I don't know what I want, but I'll let you know when you get it right" crap, it pisses me off. Here they understand: IT'S ABOUT THE PROCESS. The work is always growing, like a healthy plant. I tried to explain the concept of an opening night to Gde, but he couldn't understand it. Why should he? It's nonsensical, the idea of the artists rehearsing for months to prepare the piece, and then a bunch of professional sourpusses who don't actually know how to do the foxtrot decide whether it's any good or not. (Sorry, Phil, but you're the one who always used to say, "Artists need only praise and money.")

The perfect performance has nothing to do with the choreography, matching the movement to some ideal template; it's the one in which the dancer is completely possessed by inspiration. In Bali they put a religious construct on it, just as they did in ancient Greece, but it's really indistinguishable from what Nijinsky and Isadora were doing. They don't have anything like a star system here, of course, but they have a boy at the seka named Wayan Renda, who is one the most brilliant dancers I've ever seen perform. I won't go into the aesthetic issues of Balinese dance, since I don't really understand it (and frankly, I find it a bit boring), but the performances I've seen over the past few days are more exciting, more moving than nine-tenths of the stuff I've seen at City Center or the Joyce or BAM, and certainly more so than anything at Lincoln Center. I don't say that lightly – I've seen some great performances in my life. But the way the music and the dancers and the audience unite in a kind of rapture is just . . . it's like entering a new world.

I don't think I realized how pissed-off and burnt-out I was until I got here. It will be hard for me to come back to the twisted, self-thwarting way we do dance in New York. Phil, please don't piss on my parade. I know I sound goofy, but I don't WANT to come down to earth. Anyway, I'm not as far gone as this message makes it sound. I'm getting off on writing this – it's like I'm, yew know, on, like, a natural high. Yew know?

I haven't told you any actual news. The house is starting to look good – Andrew's working really hard on it. There's not much to do here, really, except the beach. He hasn't said anything, but I don't think he's really that into the dance here. It's like what Glenn Gould or somebody said about Bach – it makes more sense if you're playing it than if you're listening to it. I was supposed to be telling you news – we've gone out a couple of times to a cheesy, semi-gay bar called Cafe Luna, just down the road a piece, the big hang-out for the expats and "cool" Indonesians. Phil, you can't imagine what happens when I walk into that place. I've never thought of myself as a beauty – of course the bod is great, that comes with the territory. But when I walk into Cafe Luna . . . they say that when Nureyev went to the International Baths in Paris, the boys would literally line up, and he would pick the ones he wanted with a nod, and they would follow him and wait for their turn in the cubicle. That's basically what it's like for me, except without the cubicle (damn!). It's not just me – even the homeliest old gringos have a couple of cute young twinks hanging around them. It's hard to know who's on the game, and who's just into white dick. Andrew, on the other hand, doesn't get a second look. I think it pisses him off, but he's being a good sport about it. So far.

This is the longest message I've ever written anybody – I don't want to hear any more of that S.P.A. shit. But that's enough – my fingers hurt.

Love ya,

Joey

Subj: Re: I'm in love
Date: *5/6* 12:02:46 AM Eastern Daylight Time
From: WitchBitch@camnet.net
To: Danzguy99@wol.com

Poetical poppet,

I'm quite overwhelmed. I had to towel off my computer after
reading your effusions. Aren't you the budding Walt Whitman!
<<The hundred high-flying kites that twinkle in the last rays of
the setting sun>>? Petal, the word "twinkle" was made forever
disreputable by that little star. You must expunge it from your
word hoard forever. And to think that you have reproached auntie for her occasional floral flourishes.

I am truly glad that you have found so much to rejoice about in
your new home, but frankly, I'm a little worried about you.
Before you convert to Buddhism, or whatever heathenish idola-
try they practice down there, and get an Indonesian passport,
may I remind you that you've been in Bali for less than two
months? And now you suddenly realize <<how pissed-off and
burnt-out>> you are? that your chosen profession in your native
land is <<twisted and self-thwarting>>? Is this not just a wee bit
rash? Joey, you have always been impetuous and enthusiastic,
and I'm sure that's one of the reasons it's so wonderful to watch
you perform, but what concerns me here is the negative spin –
not only do you love Bali, but everything that you've known all
your life until two months ago is total shit. After you know a bit
more about the Balinese, I'm sure you'll have a few complaints
about them, too.

Darling, take a deep breath into those manly lungs of yours, and
try to remain calm. We may be twisted and self-thwarting here,
but we love you.

Phil

Subj: Update from Paradise
Date: 5/13 11:24:11 AM Eastern Daylight Time
From: AndrewTan@wol.com
To: etan@MIT.edu (Eric Tan)

Hey bro',

I will keep my promise not to lecture you for being a lousy correspondent; you always were one, and it would be unreasonable
to expect you to change. I could explain how frustrating it is to
be in a country where you don't know anyone except your over-
worked boyfriend, and to send off messages to your dearly
beloved family and hear nothing in reply. I understand that
you're always busy discovering new galaxies or whatever it is
you do, but you *could* call me on the phone . . . I know it
costs a fortune, but I don't think $30 for a little chat once in a
while is going to bust your budget. I could say all those things,
but I promised not to, and you know I always keep my promises
(you dirty rat).

Just kidding, sort of. I'm not getting bored, exactly . . . there's
too much going on, getting the house and garden into decent
shape. But I can see that it will get to be a problem, not having
anyone to talk to all day. And while Joey is taking an interest in
the house, he's getting so wrapped up in his new dance group
that when I am favored with a brief visit from him, that's all he
wants to talk about. I'm starting to feel too much like the wifie,
listening to the hubby talk about the office, and then showing
him the swatches for the new kitchen curtains. I've got to somehow prevent this from happening.

I finally found some servants. A sister of one of Bob
Blankenships's servants and her husband, from Java. Her name
is Sri, sort of a sultry sexpot type, like a Malay version of Anna
Magnani. Her husband is much younger, a bit sullen. His name
is Mul, short for something or other. Joey said, short for Mulish.

He's her second husband; I would guess she's 33 and he's 25.
they live in a tiny room in the house next door, which is a sort of
dormitory for Mr. Swastika's employees. I feel very weird about
having servants. Remember how embarrassed we were about
Jorge and Veronica when we were kids? How we always invited
our friends to come over on Sunday night, when they were
off . . . but Dad would say no, we're going to the St. Francis for
dinner? But I have to admit, it's nice never having to clean up
after yourself, and Sri is a good cook. She's a little heavy-handed
with the spices, but I'm getting used to it.

Now Joey wants to buy a car. Personally, I'm opposed to the idea.
You simply can't imagine how insane the drivers are here. Makes
Rome look like Palo Alto. I'm not kidding, just unbelievably reckless. Not really reckless . . . it's like nobody knows how to drive.
But I can't put up too much resistance, we're a little too far out of
town to have ready access to street taxis, and of course we don't
know how to talk to them. I suppose we'll just have to learn how
to drive here. At first Joey said he wanted to get a motorcycle, and
that really scared me! I put my foot down about that.

Okay, that's enough for now. I was just kidding before, but it
would mean a lot to hear some news from home.

Love from your brother

Subj: No no no
Date: 5/14 9:27:46 PM Eastern Daylight Time
From: DanzGuy99@wol.com
To: WitchBitch@camnet.net
_____

Hi,

No no no, really, you've got it all wrong. How can I explain?
Actually, maybe you're right, maybe I am going bonkers. How
can I explain it without sounding pretentious? Phil, I'm an artist,

I thrive on change. OK, I was a little exaggerated in my last message, but really, now I see that although I wasn't consciously aware of it, I was going stale, feeling restless in New York. The so-called avant-garde of the West Side of Manhattan has become so lifeless and – what's the word? – ossified (I looked it up on my computer's dandy little built-in thesaurus). So smug, so seeerious. Art is supposed to be ecstatic, not carrying out some dogmatic mission. And they've got ecstasy big-time in Bali.

What I'm doing now is the most exciting experience of my artistic career. I've never had a partner that I connected with the way I do with Wayan – it really is like telepathy. It's like – what is it like? It's hard not to fall back on cliches. We're on the same wave length. We're in a total groove, man. In the dance we're doing for Kuningan, I'm the good queen and he's the evil mistress who's trying to steal the king away from me (all the obvious witticisms have already been made, so you can save yourself the effort). When Wayan was showing me his part, I actually knew what he was going to do next before he did it, even though I had never seen the piece performed before. And the really weird thing is, Wayan didn't think this was at all strange. That's just the way they do things here, by magic.

I wish you could see him. He is divinely beautiful, literally like a god – a perfect body, slim and strong, with this wild, animal fire in his eyes. Debussy could have been thinking of him when he composed the "Faun." He moves with fierce, economical grace, nothing fussy, just beauty and power, purely and elegantly expressed. There's a joy and a transcendent spirituality in his every movement, the way he turns his head and splays his fingers, the symmetrical balance of his attitude at rest, that's so strange and yet you immediately know it's just right.

I shouldn't be going on about Wayan so much – he is only the most exceptional example of what I'm talking about – but if he performed in New York, he would create a sensation. Maybe I AM going bonkers, but that doesn't mean that this isn't what I ought to be doing, ya dig? Just because I was born in Louisiana, educated in California, and have lived my adult life in New York doesn't mean that Bali isn't the place I was meant to be, to live and work.

Also, I like the way they do things here. Here, I am tuan. Do you know the word? It means lord. Conrad's original title was "Tuan Jim." When the servants walk past me, they dip their heads deferentially. Being tuan is FUN. I just realized, I haven't told you about the servants. I'm not being very good about sending news, I know. Sorry. Anyway, we have servants now, a young married couple. Seem nice enough. She's a good cook if you like oily, spicy food, which I, of course, was raised on. I think it's a little too much for Andrew. It's ironic; supposedly he's the ethnic one, but he's much more of a honky than I am. Also, I bought a car (an essential attribute of modern tuanhood), a neat BMW, '92 four-door sedan. Dark blue. Powerful as fuck. It's a little terrifying to drive here; you have to sort of conceptually close your eyes or you get too scared to keep going. Actually, I'm starting to get off on the anarchy here. What I love about Bali is that you can do whatever the hell you want as long as you don't hurt anyone else. America is getting to be like Germany – too many goddamn rules and regulations. Here, nobody cares. The only rule is, do it.

So . . . that's about it for now. Andrew's fine, busy as a bee fixing the place up. He's working out in the garden so much, he's getting to be as dark as a Mexican. I told you before, but we would LOVE it if you came to visit. I realize that it wouldn't be a typical vacation for you – god forbid, no theatre! – but just once in your life you should visit a part of the world that is completely alien to you. It's exhilarating like no other experience can be. I don't say it's better than the European culture vulture tour, but it's more exhilarating. Truly.

Love ya

Joey

Subj: O Mighty Tuan
Date: 5/16 7:21:09 PM Eastern Daylight Time
From: WitchBitch@camnet.net
To: Danzguy99@wol.com

O Mighty Tuan,

Servants, how divine! I've always dreamed of having servants, so
Nick and Nora Charles. Are you allowed to beat them? Does
tuan have droit de seigneur with the gardener? Now I'm going
to play the dangerous game of claiming to know you better than
you know yourself. The divine Wayan: have you fucked him yet?
(not to put too fine a point on it). If the answer is no, please do
so immediately, and get it over with. Better to squirt a few blobs
of baby batter now than to let all this panting and pining for the
perfect faun seep into your soul. Take my word for it, he's not
divine. He may be a fabulous dancer and a hot piece of tail, but
he is certainly human. As your spiritual adviser, I give you absolution in advance for a quickie behind the woodshed with this
child. That's my next question: you call him a boy without actually mentioning his age. Does he wear long pants and stand up
when he pees?

I give you this advice with a heavy heart (or is it a heavy hand?).
You well know that ta tante doesn't approve of or even understand marriage. The closest I came was those two years with
Steve, but we both knew it wasn't the real thing from the beginning. Yet you have chosen the estate of matrimony, and while
your record isn't exactly spotless (unfortunate metaphor, but
that's what it comes down to, doesn't it? stains on the linens?),
you've been a better boy than anyone had a right to expect.

I have a little book under lock and key, which contains the cata-
logue of your tiny adventurettes, and there it shall remain, with
the key ever clasp'd in mine bosom. I salute you for having had
the decency to conceal your indiscretions from Andrew, who
probably knows more than you think and doesn't care as much

as you fear. Did he ever find out about the Brazilian stewardess? or the Korean window dresser? (Just fancy, in the window dressers' prop room at Bloomingdale's! I get a vicarious tickle Down There when I think of it.) But I suppose you never really know if he knows: Andrew would be too polite to bring it up, and you can't very well ask him.

However, even as I wickedly abet your libertinage, it is my duty to point out that South American stewardesses and window dressers at Bloomingdale's are more accustomed to the adventurous life than are the temple boys of Bali (or so I assume). So beware! Perhaps I've got this all wrong, and your devotion to young Wayan is a pure and noble passion, untinged by the baser appetites of the flesh, but me don't tink so. Oscar tried using that line, and look where it got him. When I read about the wild, animal fire in his eyes, and the adorable way he splays his fingers, it was a Western Union telegram: SARONGS WILL FALL STOP ONLY QUESTION WHEN STOP

Thank you for inviting me to visit, but I'm certain that if I came to Bali I would fall sick with one of those rare tropical diseases one reads about in Somerset Maugham's stories. But you were very kind to invite me.

I shall click on "Send" with great trepidation, Joey. Seriously, I may be all wrong about this, but I don't think so. You are in the middle of a great emotional event in your life, and I'm afraid for you. I don't want to be a goody-goody, because I truly don't understand any kind of marriage, much less the gay kind, but you and Andrew have something precious, and I don't want to see you imperil your happiness on a whim. Promise me you'll be careful!

Love from Phil

Subj: Sorry!
Date: 5/22 7:39:01 PM Eastern Daylight Time
From: Danzguy99@wol.com
To: RayjnKayjn@labell.net

Hi Dad,

I'm so sorry I've been out of touch. I hope you don't think I've
ignored your messages, but (as you used to say when we were
kids) I've been as busy as a one-armed paper-hanger (and now
that we're all grown-ups I can add the part you used to leave
out) with a bad case of crabs. Everything here is just fine – great,
in fact. I'm so excited about my work. It's too soon to say anything about it, but I think it may become the best work I've ever
done. I've got so many ideas! – the trick will be to get them
down in performance. Ideas are no good just buzzing around in
your brain.

I bought a car last week, a quick little '92 BMW four-door
sedan, dark blue. It's really fun – I haven't had a car since the
Toyota I had at Palo Alto. You can't believe how crazy they
drive here. I think they just buy a driver's license, then hit the
road. Every kid over the age of fifteen has a motorcycle. Andrew
is fine, working in the garden so much he's dark as a Mexican.
He's having a little trouble, because it seems that they don't like
Chinese people here. We knew that before we came. Nothing
serious, just dirty looks.

Well, that's about it. I promise I will try to keep in better touch.

Love to you and Lu Ann from

Joey

Subj: Long-lost friend
Date: 5/25 8:23:21 AM Eastern Daylight Time
From: AndrewTan@wol.com
To: etan@MIT.edu (Eric Tan)

Dear Prof. Tan,

It was a long time ago, but I hope you will remember me. I am a few years younger than you, but I grew up near you in San Francisco, and we both attended St. Christopher's Academy and Stanford University. In fact, I also lived on Jones Street, where you lived. Now that I think about it, I believe it may have been the same house. Three-story Italianate town house? with a small formal garden in the back? My name is Tan, too . . . are you by any chance the son of Dr. Raymond Tan, the surgeon? I think it's very possible that we're related.

Ha ha ha, but really, man, you have to at least answer one out of four of my messages. Enough scolding. Maybe the cat ate your computer.

So much news here, I'll kind of quickly run it down. A few days ago I ordered a suite of leather-upholstered furniture, a big sofa and two easy chairs. Really beautiful, teak and cordovan-colored leather. They arrived today. We sent some of the junkier stuff that came with the house back to Mr. Swastika. (Actually, I have since found out that we're supposed to call him Mr. Rai, which to me is a bit too much like Miss Scarlett and Mr. Rhett. As far as we're concerned, he will always be Mr. Swastika.) Joey bought his car, a '92 BMW. Blue. I haven't been brave enough to drive it yet.

The main problem we have, just as we expected, is a severe shortage of smart English-speaking people to talk to. In terms of foreigners, the choice seems to be between dumb kids, the big blond muscle-bound surfer types, and the jaded, druggie expats, the wizened old hippies. Bob is very nice but a little dull. We've met a wild Scottish guy named Angus who seems to turn up everywhere. Last night he arrived here at seven o'clock, without calling. I think he's basically a big mooch. He drank a lot of wine, opened a second bottle without even asking. After dinner he produced a joint. I hadn't smoked pot in ages. I never really stopped, I just sort of . . . stopped, if you know what I mean. It was sort of fun to get stoned again. Anyway, this Angus guy talks a blue streak, and most of it is just sexual braggadocio (thank heaven for spell check). I was a little shocked . . . he was talking about all the Indonesian boys he had screwed as though he were a big-game hunter or something. He is very clever, I have to admit. Joey was in hysterics. I'm a little bit worried about this idea of him turning up all the time, but Joey said I should loosen up, we're in Bali.

Joey is so excited about his work. His Big Debut is coming up in a couple of weeks. I remember what this is like, when he's starting a new piece and really getting into it. It's a little frustrating, because his mind is always on the work, but he's so happy, like a little kid. Of course he's always sort of like a little kid. But we hardly ever see each other . . . the rehearsals don't start till after dinner, and go on until really late. Over the past couple of weeks Joey and I have spent only two or three evenings together, watching videos (and he usually falls asleep ten minutes after it starts).

But my main news is, he's not the only one whose work is going well . . . or going, at least. I've started working on a story, which I think will eventually become a short novel. I'm not sure yet. It's based on me and Joey, though I've made the characters entirely different. It's about a relationship between a rich Chinese kid who isn't really Chinese, except in the slitty-eyed department (guess who?). He's an artist in New York who falls for a struggling photographer from Texas, who comes from a "poor white trash" background. That's not Joey, of course; his family were regular middle class, and both his parents had college degrees. But in some ways the problems we have had have been because his background was more . . . normal, I guess.

Mom and Dad didn't spoil us, but it was just understood from the time we were born that everything we wanted or needed would be provided, and we would have the best. Remember how much we wanted to go to public high school? Dad would-n't hear of it; it had to be St. Kit's. Now I'm glad that he made us go there, but at the time, it seemed so embarrassing. Well, when we were up at the Hotel Tjampuhan, Joey told me that he almost didn't get to go to Stanford, because the scholarship was-n't really that generous. I still remember junior year, Joey having to get up at six o'clock in the morning to prep breakfast at the dining hall. It has never quite been a big deal for us, though whenever we have a fight, his killer line is always, "At least I earn my money, it wasn't handed to me on a silver platter." In my story I exaggerate the differences, to make it more dramatic. I've already written twenty pages, and I think it's off to a pretty good start. This is a deliberate strategy, by the way. I've noticed that most serious first fiction that gets published addresses the writer's own life and background, however much it's fictional-ized. It's not a question of "Write about what you know," but more what you care about. Maybe the editors in New York will think I'm Amy Tan's son! I'm getting carried away. But at least I'm enjoying myself.

Another long message from your brother

Subj: Re: Long-lost friend
Date: 5/27 9:16:29 PM Eastern Daylight Time
From: etan@MIT.edu (Eric Tan)
To: AndrewTan@wol.com

File: garden.jpg (79764 bytes)
DL Time (32000 bps): < 1 minute

---

hi,

very funny. sorry, kid, you can't image what a time-consuming
process it is, discovering new galaxies. actually, the problem is
more like discovering new grants to pay for discovering new
galaxies, not to mention discovering new faculty – even more
difficult than new galaxies. i know i've been a lousy correspondent, but we've filled the position, and i'm actually more or less
caught up now, so i promise i'll do better. i'm so glad that you've
started writing, andy. you didn't say anything about letting people read it, but as soon as you're ready to show it, i would
LOVE to read it.

pot, eh? you wild man.

sophie and i have been busy trying to get pregnant, a very plea-
surable project, but so far it's only been practice, practice, with
no pay-off. i'm afraid that one of us is sterile. there are so many
new fertility drugs now that we're not really worrying yet, but
sophie has a problem with that, i'm not exactly sure why. i think
part of it is that she doesn't want to have a litter, i don't blame
her. twins would be okay. you knew we were trying, but it's been
a while now.

so, there's some news for you, or rather non-news. the house is
an absolute wreck with the new garden coming in. you should
meet the designer sophie found, he's a very intense, glamorous-
looking italian guy. i suppose he's gay, i don't know. he gets paid

a bundle, that's for sure. i've attached some snaps of the garden-in-progress. you really need to get a digital camera, so you can send us some pix of your place.

big hug

e

Subj: Fw: Joe Breaux
Date: 5/30 12:16:15 PM Eastern Daylight Time
From: jahull@POF.org
To: quentin.trent@nytimes.com

Dear Quentin,

Bob Blankenship agrees with me that you should see this. By the way, I thought your Critic's Notebook about the perils of putting the arts on the Internet was brilliant – I'm glad someone is saying these things.

Best,

Jerry Hull

– – - Original Message – – -
From: BBlankenship@indonet.net.id
To: jahull@POF.org
Sent: 5/27 1:29:55 PM Eastern Daylight Time
Subject: Joe Breaux

>Dear Jerry,

>Now seems like as good as any to send you a brief interim re-port on the

>progress that
>
>Joe Breaux is making here. Actually, it is truly sensational. I've been here
>
>for twenty years, and I've never seen anyone who had such an
>
>immediate, intuitive grasp of the dance here. I realize that he's an
>
>enormously gifted dancer, and
>
>that one would therefore expect him to catch on quickly, but he
>
>has made more progress in a few weeks than most Westerners do in years.
>
>And the way he communicates with the Balinese is
>
>uncanny: of course
>
>he doesn't speak Indonesian, much less Balinese, but he seems
>
>to understand what they want immediately. A friend of mine here in Ubud,
>
>an American woman who used to work for Twyla Tharp, explained to
>
>me that a dancer thinks
>
>with his body; just as a linguist will pick up any new language more quickly than
>
>someone studying

>a foreign language for the first time, so a trained dancer will quickly learn

>

>the vocabulary of any dance tradition. That may be so: I'm just a

>

>dreary old academic, and

>

>all I know is theory, not performance. But I do know that what I'm

>

>witnessing with Joe is something really extraordinary.

>

>It seems all the more exceptional to me because he has taken absolutely no interest in

>

>studying the aesthetics of Balinese dance, much to my disappointment.

>

>The first few days he was here, we set up some tutorials here at my

>

>house, but he was literally falling asleep. He claimed it was jet lag, but I know a bored

>

>student when I see one.

>>

>He's preparing his first part with a young dancer named Wayan Renda.

>

>They're performing the Gambuh: I'll spare you the details,

>

>but essentially it's a comedy of court intrigue, one of the

>

>oldest pieces in the Balinese repertoire, dating to six hundred years ago

>(which makes it older than the ballet in Europe, by the way).
I've
>
>never seen such a potent chemistry between
>
>two dancers. Everyone is talking about it. It will be the Balinese
equivalent of a hot
>
>ticket, meaning people
>
>are coming
>
>from all over the island to see it. The interesting
>
>thing is, it's not simply that Joe has picked up Balinese
techniques so quickly,
>
>but he's also influencing the Balinese in subtle
>
>ways. I see Wayan appropriating aspects of Joe's movement
>
>in his performances, too. Joe has a way of pausing for just a
>
>moment before he executes a turn, which gives it a dash of
edgy, Western
>
>excitement, if I may put it that way. Now I see Wayan doing
the same thing.

>>

>I am so glad that Joe thought of this, and that you agreed to
support
>
>him. Thus
>
>far, I would call it a complete success: a triumph, in fact.

>>

>Best wishes to you and Alexandra,

>>

>Bob

Subj: Only the best
Date: 6/1 1:02:01 AM Eastern Daylight Time
From: AndrewTan@wol.com
To: etan@MIT.edu (Eric Tan)

Hi,

Are you sure? It's probably not ready for anybody to read it yet, but I'll send you the first few pages, as much as I can paste into this message. Maybe it's better to have an objective opinion from the beginning . . . you can let me know if something seems really wrong. Here goes:

Only the Best
By Andrew Tan

If the Woo family had an escutcheon, the motto underneath would read, "Only the best." Long before luxurious brand names became the mark of prestige they are today, Leslie Woo set his table with Royal Derby, Georg Jensen, and Waterford. His wine cellar was better than those in most of the restaurants in San Francisco. He drove (or rather was driven in) a Jaguar sedan; as he liked to say, mechanically every bit as good as a Rolls, yet much less ostentatious. His wife was a charming lady from one of the oldest and best Chinese families in northern California. Leslie Woo's children, his two sons and daughter, were sent to the finest private schools. They desperately longed to go to public high school, where the kids had fun and didn't have to study so much, but being Chinese children they submitted dutifully. Their dutifulness, however, was almost their only Chinese quality. They never heard Chinese spoken until they were old enough to go to cheap Chinese restaurants on their own; neither of their parents spoke a word of the language, and when the family went out for dinner (always on Sunday, cook's night off), it was either to the grill at the Fairmont Hotel or to dim French restaurants where Mr. Woo and the waiters spoke to each other in murmurous French.

Leslie Woo was one of the richest men in San Francisco. It was always mysterious to his children how he had made his money, because by the time they were old enough to take any interest in the subject, he was devoting most of his time to the boards of the opera and the art museum, and organizing charity balls. His oldest child, Cynthia, was a gawky adolescent; at her coming-out ball, she was beet red, refusing to dance with anyone but her father; and even the best dressmaker in San Francisco couldn't disguise the fact that her body was indistinguishable from that of a twelve-year-old boy. She went to Stanford, where she developed a bosom and married a lawyer, the son of a business associate of her father's. The middle child, Sean, played tennis at Stanford and went to medical school, where he specialized in pediatrics. He also married a lawyer, the daughter of another of Leslie Woo's business associates.

The youngest son, Georges, was the blot on the Woo escutcheon. He was christened George, but the year after he graduated from Bennington, he went to Paris, where he added the "s" to his name and became a homosexual. When he turned twenty-five, he came into enough money to live decently without working, which is what he did. He moved to New York, where he tried to be a real artist and failed. Then he decided to make an art of being a dilettante: in other words, he hopped on the post-modernist bandwagon. He wrote stories that didn't make sense, and illustrated them with crude drawings that had nothing to do with the stories. Soon he was a famous denizen of that strange, opulent village called the New York art scene, and made pots of money. Georges spent every cent of it on clothes, restaurants, and boys. He was a true Woo as far as the clothes and restaurants went, but his boys belonged to the class known in gay argot as "trade," handsome young men with no money and no skills that polite people talk about. Georges's boys were a bit dangerous: not prostitutes exactly, but when Georges grew tired of giving them gifts, they stopped coming around.

Then he met the man of his dreams. Heath Tucker was tall, handsome, white, and poor. He was in no sense trade, but he was [italic] a bit dangerous. He was from Galveston, Texas, where his mother lived in a trailer. Heath had a picture of the trailer tucked into the frame of the mirror in his tiny, squalid, mattress-on-the-floor apartment on Avenue B. On the night Georges met Heath, he saw the picture and asked him what it was. When Heath responded, "That's my mother's trailer in Galveston," Georges was overwhelmed with lust. For the first time in his life, he thought, if I don't get that man, life won't be worth living. It was already a dead cinch that they were going to have sex: they had met at an art opening in Chelsea, gone on to drink metropolitans at a louche bar in Tribeca, and by the time Heath invited Georges back to his place, the handwriting was on the wall. No, sex wasn't lacking in Georges's life, but true companionship was.

After a few hours of rapturous dalliance, Heath lit up a Salem and told Georges his life story. It was an appalling tale. Heath's father was in prison for murdering Heath's mother's boyfriend. Now his mother was shacked up with the trailer park's Mexican handyman, though he didn't speak English and she didn't speak Spanish. Her hobby, Heath said, was to go to K-Mart and steal things. Anything, it didn't matter whether she needed it or not. With a grin that showed off his flawless white teeth, his Texas accent dripping like honey from a spoon, Heath said, "I keep trying to convince her to steal some new clothes. She dresses like a tramp." Georges was so overcome with desire, their previous

exertions notwithstanding, that he tore the cigarette out of
Heath's mouth and threw him back on the mattress. When they
had breakfast the next morning at a diner, Heath paid the bill.
When he picked up the check and said, "It's on me," with
another big grin, Georges realized that the night before had been
the first time since he moved to New York that he had had sex
anywhere except his stylish, smallish penthouse apartment, in an
elevator building on Jane Street. Trade never let the client see
their squalid abodes. Trade visit.

The courtship was, for Georges, a painfully drawn-out affair.
Heath liked him a lot, or so he kept saying. He was eager to
prove to Georges that he was an honest, decent person, despite
his criminal family background. Georges did his best to conceal
his own background. It had been a powerful attraction for most
of the men who had drifted through the apartment on Jane
Street, but Heath was different. From the start, it never occurred
to Georges to buy him a Cartier lighter or a manly silver bangle
from Tiffany's, his standard gifts. But Heath was bound to find
out, and when he did, it made him nervous. He insisted that they
alternate picking up checks at restaurants, and that didn't
include Georges treating him to dinner at Le Cirque after he,
Heath, had taken Georges to the New Cosmos Diner again.

Heath Tucker put bread on the table by working as a waiter at a
restaurant on Eighth Avenue, where all the waiters were tall and
cute, but by profession he was a photographer. When Georges
saw his work, he knew at once that he was talented. He took
pictures of lower-middle-class people in Texas, Queens, and the
New Jersey shore, magically transforming them with the lens of
his beat-up old Pentax. Children dressed for Halloween were
genuinely frightening; an old, obese woman with smoker's face
looked radiantly beautiful. Georges was impressed by the fact
that Heath had chosen not to shoot in Manhattan. "There are
too many pictures of the City already," he said, and Georges
was inclined to agree with him. When Heath moved to New
York in search of fame and fortune, he found his subjects by rid-

ing out to the ends of the subway lines, searching for the dreary, run-down milieux he was familiar with. In the summer, he took the bus to run-down resorts on the Jersey shore like Long Branch and Asbury Park, where he stayed at cheap motels and made friends with the people who ran them.

He had had a few of his photographs exhibited in group shows, and he had even sold some of them, making enough money to buy a new enlarger. But Heath believed in himself, and he persevered. He indignantly spurned Georges's offer to buy him a new camera, but actively encouraged his efforts to find him a dealer. It wasn't easy: Georges's own gallery didn't represent photographers, and art dealers in New York are experienced at dealing with artists trying to find galleries for their lovers. Nonetheless, there were nibbles. Georges wasn't a blue-chip artist yet, but his name helped. And Heath's photographs were good.

Their romance was cemented when the two men went to Galveston together, to visit Heath's family. He and Heath's mother hit it off at once. They spent hours together, drinking iced beer and smoking cigarettes and watching talk shows on television while Heath was out shooting his old haunts. The men stayed at a motel near the trailer park. It was deliriously exciting for Georges: Heath obviously felt a strong physical attraction for him, unlike the trade, who had been somewhat perfunctory in their bedtime affections. Georges was experiencing pleasure unlike anything he had ever felt before, and it was getting to be addictive. Heath, for his part, was growing deeply attached to Georges. He was the first man he had ever dated who accepted him as he was, who didn't try to smarten up his appearance and manners. Growing up in Galveston, he had always been open about his sexuality: in a family of murderers and kleptomaniacs, a gay son is hardly worth making a fuss about. But he never dreamed that he would meet a man of Georges's intelligence and sophistication, who would want to stay with him after meeting his family.

Then Heath began to ask when he was going to meet Georges's family, and that's when all the trouble began.

* * *

That's more than 1,600 words, and I wanted to add a few comments. I seem to be stuck in a dry storyteller's voice . . . somehow I need to get more into the moment. I don't know what the right word is, but with action and dialogue. But it's easier for me to be funny (I hope) when I'm in the storyteller's voice. I ended it just at the point where it's starting to get more difficult. I've made several attempts to make the transition, but you can't just suddenly say, "Sweat poured from his craggy brow as the hot Texas sun beat down on him, cruel and relentless as a cattle driver's whip." So I've skipped ahead to the scene in San Francisco, where the father tries to run off Heath, giving him the full Raymond Tan treatment. That part is coming along pretty well, but it's completely different in style.

Anyway, Eric, I want you to tell me what you *really* think. You won't say it's horrible, because it's not. I also know it's not great. Anyway, I'm having fun doing it.

Nervously,

Andrew

P.S. The garden looks great, at least what I could make out. Send more pictures after some of the piles of dirt are gone.

Subj: Your Bali project
Date: 6/2 11:57:04 AM Eastern Daylight Time
From: quentin.trent@nytimes.com
To: DanzGuy99@wol.com

Dear Joe,

Jerry Hull has forwarded to me a glowing report from Bob
Blankenship (with his approval, of course) about your project in
Bali. Jerry also gave me your E-mail address; I hope you don't
mind. With your permission, I would like to plan a visit to Bali
some time over the next few months, to write a story about your
work there. I would be less than honest if I didn't admit that I'm
also looking for a place to spend a couple of weeks of vacation
time, and I've always wanted to visit Bali. Please let me know if
you are agreeable to do two in-depth interviews with me, and to
let me attend a few rehearsals. The story will be a major feature
for Arts & Leisure. Please tell me when might be convenient,
when you might be doing something of particular interest – and
please choose a time when the weather is good!

Looking forward to meeting you in Bali.

Best wishes,

Quentin Trent

Subj: Re: Only the best
Date: 6/4 11:35:21 PM Eastern Daylight Time
From: etan@MIT.edu (Eric Tan)
To: AndrewTan@wol.com

---

hi,

you know i'm an astrophysicist, not a literary critic. (though it
seems i've now been transformed into a tennis-playing pediatri-

cian, with a sister!) however, unlike most of my colleagues, i do read novels by writers other than john grisham and stephen king, and i have to say that i enjoyed reading "only the best" enormously. really, andy, i did. it's very clever and well-written, and by the end i was curious to know what would happen to these two guys. a lot of it is very funny – i loved<<the man of his dreams. Heath Tucker was tall, handsome, white, and poor.>> also <<a manly silver bangle from Tiffany's>>. i don't know why, that made me laugh. but you're right about one thing – you did leave off at a crucial point. and i agree that the "dry story-teller voice," as you put it, can't go on much longer without it beginning to seem too artificial. maybe it would be INTEREST-ING to have a complete change in tone, to go from the dry sto-ryteller to the sweat dripping from the craggy brow. maybe the critics will think it's a daring post-modernist touch. that's another point – i'm not sure it's such a good idea to knock post-modernism. i think it's sort of accepted now, isn't it? but as i said, i'm not a literary critic.

i have a few comments about language: it seems to me that you are a little bit prissy about sex. i think <<rapturous dalliance>> is just too quaint, also <<somewhat perfunctory in their bedtime affections>>, although i know you meant it to be tongue-in-cheek. i think the storyteller sounds a little too horny, telling us they have sex for a few hours, and then georges throws heath on the mattress <<their previous exertions notwithstanding>> (ditto above). also, isn't "milieux" a little weird?

finally, i probably shouldn't say this, but you're pretty hard on dad, and mom is just a paper doll. i mean, assume your fantasy comes true and they publish this in the new yorker, he'll be pretty hurt. can't you make it in florida or something? (i realize that you made him not a surgeon.) and aren't you at all concerned that joe might think it portrays his family as white trash? i know you changed almost everything, but it's pretty clear who all the players are. i know, i know, it's art. forget i mentioned it.

well, i think you're off to a good start, but it will get more and more complicated the more you write. but stick with it, kid! you know, the literary editor of the new yorker has a place in lenox, and we've been back and forth for dinner with them a couple of times. not that he'll publish your story because your brother is a genius at the barbecue grill, but hey, you never know.

keep up the good work.

e

Subj: FUCKING
Date: 6/5 1:57:40 PM Eastern Daylight Time
From: DanzGuy99@wol.com
To: Philip_O'Donnell@bostonglobe.com

hi Phil, god yes I'm fucking him. almost every night, practically since we met. It's incredible. I don't mean the sex, which is like a vision of heaven, I mean how much I'm feeling. I look into his eyes and I get lost in some place I've never seen before, and I never want to leave. He's so beautiful, so innocent yet so amazingly sensual, like a beautiful wild animal. Every night. I've made friends with this crazy Scottish guy named Angus Gray, he's actually kind of a lout but a very funny, clever guy who lets me and Wayan use his place. He's always out partying, never comes home until the clubs close, so when seka finishes I meet Wayan there. You know Andrew, soundest sleeper in the world – I sneak into bed, get up a couple of hours later with him and have breakfast, then go back to Angus's to sleep on couch, or sometimes Wayan comes back, but he most days he has to work at his father's shop, selling fake antiques. A thinks I'm working with Bob during the day. I spend one or two evenings a week with him, watching videos or talking about what to do in the garden. makes me crazy, i can't concentrate, I'm thinking of Wayan the whole time. We haven't had sex in two weeks and he hasn't even noticed. thank god, I could never fake it. God, that sounds horrible. of course I

feel guilty as hell but that's part of what makes the experience
with Wayan so intense. Angus's little bungalow is so dingy and
squalid, like a Mexican motel. I feel like I'm being wicked and i'm
going to hell anyway, so I might as well just let 'er rip. I've been
smoking pot a little, that's not good. Wayan's so naive, he's met A
but thinks he's just my friend. What am I going to do? tell me
what to do. Thing is the performance is Tuesday, and Andrew's
already talking about we have to do something, go back to Ubud
or go on trip to another island after the performance. I can't do it.
Of course I have to tell him, not just because that.

What do I tell him? phil, Andrew is my family, my homestead,
he's always there. But I have to tell you, i don't want to stop seeing Wayan. I can't. I want to spend MORE time with him. I
can't stop thinking about him. I've got this fabulous idea for a
new piece, for him and me, i want to get started on it NOW. But
life without Andrew? I can't even imagine it. It seems impossible. I rack my brains and I can't come up with solution. Don't be
mad that I haven't told you. I was sending you hints, at least I
didn't lie. Just now I tried writing a message that didn't mention
Wayan, but it was even more obvious than screaming YES I'M
FUCKING HIM. Phil, he's nineteen years old. I don't know
what to say. You know I've never been into that, but it really is
like two souls connecting ya dig? there's no clear boundary between the dancing and the sex, they're sort of blending into each
other. But I have to admit, his youth is part of it. he's the freshest
tenderest creature I've ever seen. He's so beautiful, so soft and at
the same time so strong, so elegant and perfectly made I can't
believe he's mine. He doesn't speak much english, but it doesn't
matter, the sound of his voice is so sweet, it's like a strange new
kind of music. When the first light peeks into the sky I want to
cry because I have to leave him. When we're making love I feel
like I'm melting and pouring into him and him into me like two
rivers flowing together. Please don't make fun of this phil. Please
don't hate me. I had to tell someone. i had to tell you.

Joey

Subj: i'm here
Date: 6/6 10:32:05 AM Eastern Daylight Time
From: etan@MIT.edu (Eric Tan)
To: AndrewTan@wol.com

---

hey there kiddo

can we hug on-line? it's a few hours after you called. you're
right, don't even think about what it costs. if it costs $200, who
cares, that's a nice little dinner in new york. i'll call you tomorrow, just tell me when. i wish i could give you better advice. i
wish i knew what to say! i guess i'll start with, i love you, kid. if
you want to hop on a plane to boston today, i'll meet you at
logan and we can drive straight out to lenox, just the two of us.
get drunk on the front porch. but i don't want to patronize you.
i won't say everything is going to be all right – it's obviously far
from all right! but remember, you and joe have been together for
fourteen years, right? i remember there was a period in the beginning when it was sort of off and on again, but you came to
new york together twelve years ago – andy, that kind of commitment doesn't just disappear overnight.

it's hard for me, as your brother, not to simply be totally pissed
off at him, and i have to admit, i was pretty grossed out when
you told me that the kid is just 21. but it's ridiculous for you
even to think of some boy with a pretty face that your shit of a
boyfriend has been screwing for a couple of weeks as a rival.
who cares how cute he is? you've given joe your whole life. it's
natural for you to feel this as a rejection, it IS a rejection, but
please try not to think of this wayne guy as a rival. this is all
about glands and hormones and nerve endings. and racial traits,
if i can put it that way. you're chinese and it's in your nature to
nest and make a family. joe's of french origins, and it's in his nature to fool around (not that plenty of chinese married men
don't fool around, but you know what i mean). he's a wild man,
he always was. you told me about his little fling with that

korean fashion designer – i'm just surprised that there haven't
been more of them.

the real question is, what do you say to joe when he comes
crawling back to you? you've got to figure out what you want to
do for YOU. i know we're supposed to pretend that there's no
difference between gay and straight relationships, but i'm sorry,
aside from you and joe (until seven o'clock this morning, boston
time) and willie and stefan, all the gay couples i know do a certain amount of fooling around. in some cases a lot of it. it
always seems that one guy is the faithful one, and the other one's
the slut. now i am not by any means saying that you should get
into a so-called open relationship with joe, not by any means.
you deserve a loyal, faithful lover. i'm only saying it's in the nature of most men to be attracted to more than one person in
their lives. what i really mean is, most guys are on the look-out
for some strange ass once in a while. i would be lying if i didn't
admit that there haven't been a few times since i married sophie
when i looked at a beautiful woman, and she looked at me, and
i thought, "hmm, i wouldn't mind giving THAT a whirl." of
course i only thought it – joe has gone out and done it, and flung
it in your face, in the name of "being honest with you," and furthermore told you he's not ready to quit. what an asshole!

but all i'm saying is, don't make any big decisions today or tomorrow or the day after. wait till you're feeling calmer. the one
thing joe did right was to clear out of the house. you asked me
what you ought to do now? i hate to advise you – what if i say
the wrong thing? but i think you should definitely not call him
or have anything to do with him, give him three days or so to
come to his senses, to apologize and try to make it up to you –
at which point you're on your own, no advice from me what to
do. at the end of the three days, or however long you think you
want to wait, come to boston. forget about the girls in the place
on horatio street, you need a neutral, non-joe place. come here.
but my main advice is, do NOT go storming over to his hotel

and announce that it's all over. it's too soon for that. even if you hate him now, you may feel very differently in even a few days. these are the certainties: 1. joe still loves you, 2. he has made a colossal mistake, which he'll regret for the rest of his life (though when he will realize that is one of the uncertainties), and 3. it will ultimately be up to you to decide whether your relationship with him will survive. you may feel powerless, but in fact you have all the power.

i wish i had the power to make this all ok for you, but i don't, so i'll just tell you again, i love you, kid. go ahead and feel miserable for a while. all you have to do is e-mail me the details about your flight.

eric

Subj: A deep breath
Date: 6/6 11:01:54 AM Eastern Daylight Time
From: WitchBitch@camnet.net
To: DanzGuy99@wol.com

Dear Joey,

It's time for you to sit down, take a deep breath, and listen to your old friend. Of course I don't hate you – you knew that – and I'm not mad at you. I love you like my own brother. You also knew that. But I am very frightened for you, Joey. Your message was wild and incoherent, but I think I understand what's happening. I want to write it down for you in English prose: You are endangering the most important relationship of your life, with the possible exception of your relationship with your father, for the thrill of fucking a nineteen-year-old boy you met two months ago, with whom you can't communicate. I can see there's no point in sternly telling you you must drop this boy immediately and go running back to Andrew, though of course that's exactly what you should do. But whatever you do,

DON'T tell Andrew. However dishy this kid may be, you can't talk to him, and with the cultural and age differences between you, the chances that you will ever have a meaningful relationship with him are nil. You WILL get tired of him, and he of you, and it will happen much sooner than you think.

I always thought that you and Andrew settled down too young. You met him when you were twenty and he was nineteen, and you've been together almost ever since, solidly so since you were 23 (right?). No healthy 23-year-old man, regardless of his sexuality, should be expected to swear eternal loyalty and fidelity to one person. In my last message, I made some satirical comments about your casual affairs, but in fact you are really quite innocent. If my calculations are correct, and you haven't held out on me, over the past twelve years, since you and Andrew have officially been a couple, you have had sex with only four other men, including the Balinese child, who is, I suppose, technically speaking a man. Andrew, as far as I know, has never slept with anyone but you, though I would assume there must have been a couple of wild weekends in San Francisco when he wasn't with you.

What you are experiencing, my dear, is the mad, delirious pleasure of being loved by a beautiful boy. The only problem is, it should have happened fifteen years ago, when YOU were a beautiful boy. These flings based on the flesh have a very short shelf life. It's been a while for me, but I do remember what it's like. Someday soon, in a matter of days or weeks, something will go wrong. He'll be three hours late, or the sex for some reason will be lousy, and you'll look at him and suddenly he won't be beautiful. Those gorgeous, dreamy eyes will look vacant. His lovely, slender limbs will look merely skinny. You won't believe that it's the same boy you were lusting after a few hours before.

I know you will say it's not just the sex, and how great a dance partner he is, and physical communication is just as powerful as the verbal kind. That's all true. But it's also obvious that the intense emotions you're feeling are being aroused mostly by the sex. You're thinking with your cock, which is another way of saying you're not thinking. The reason you can't figure out a way to fuck this boy to your heart's content and keep Andrew is because it's impossible. I repeat, DON'T TELL HIM. Be as devious as you need to be, but don't tell him. Don't delude yourself with the false notion that you're doing him a favor by "being honest" with him – he will hate you just as much if you tell him as if he finds out on his own. Meanwhile, try to come to your senses. I know that's absurd advice, you think you're having the time of your life. But Joey, if you lose Andrew because of this boy, you will never forgive yourself. I will love you and support you no matter how foolishly you behave, but you still have to live with yourself. Remember what you said in your message: <<life without Andrew? I can't even imagine it. It seems impossible.>>

How foolish I felt, advising you to give him a preemptive poke. As the days lagged by without a reply, I knew what was happening, and that you were trying to figure out a way to tell me. I was hoping for a sheepish message begging for absolution for losing your head and having a fling with your cute young dance partner. I would have given you an astringent lecture about the frailties of the flesh, and rubbed a bit of salt into your guilt-wounds, and it would have gone away. But instead you wrote me an incoherent rave, a clear blueprint for disaster, perfumed with marijuana smoke. Just stop that, Joey. There's no such thing as hell, that's just something the nuns made up to stop us from masturbating. You're too old to be smoking pot and acting like a crazy teenager.

End of lecture. For your homework, compose the message you will write me three months from now, saying what a fool you've been. And Joey, you must NEVER send me a message at work with a headline like "FUCKING." They're such Nazis about the Internet over there. I could be fired for something like that, really. Why did you send it to me at work, anyway?

Phil

Subj: Re: i'm here
Date: 6/7 2:59:46 PM Eastern Daylight Time
From: AndrewTan@wol.com
To: etan@MIT.edu (Eric Tan)

Dear Eric,

Thanks for your great message. It's the middle of the night here; I can't even pretend to sleep. I still can't believe this is happening. What a horrible, sick feeling it was, to wake up in full daylight, reach across the bed, and find no one there. In that moment it was all so clear . . . I knew everything. I think I knew all along, or at least for the past few weeks, but unconsciously turned a blind eye. When I would wake up in the middle of the night to take a pee, I wouldn't look at the clock, secretly afraid it was closer to morning than late at night. I could smell pot on his breath sometimes when I woke up, and he was so hard to rouse. This morning, when I saw his half of the bed still made, his pillow so crisp and plump, I knew everything.

Oh god, Eric, I know I'm repeating myself, but it just goes round and round in my brain, like a nightmare that keeps waking you up. He was sitting in the garden, wearing the same clothes he had had on the night before, drinking coffee, obviously waiting for me. He looked so tired, his eyes kept drooping. It was a little speech . . . he might as well have been reading from index cards. The third time he said "I know how hard it must be for you to understand this" I told him to stop it, to skip to the bottom line. He sighed theatrically and said he needed some time apart from me, that he wanted to move out. I couldn't believe it. Nothing seemed real . . . the garden looked as fake as an old Hollywood set.

I can't stop asking the same stupid question: What did I do wrong? It's not as though I let myself turn into a fat slob; I've kept myself in good shape. Most people think I'm ten years younger than I am . . . though not 21, sorry, Joey, I'm a grown-up. Oops, now we're getting into the Howl of Wounded Vanity Department . . . sorry. The other stupid question is, Why did he have to tell me? He told me about that Korean fashion designer, but it was in the context of an apology, a solemn vow not to do it again. Not that that was the only time. I never spied on him, but when you're the one in charge of the laundry, you have to go through the pockets . . . I never told you, but a few years ago I found some matches from an airport hotel in his jeans, with a Latin name, I forget, and a room number written inside. That week he suddenly had some important meetings that started early in the evening and lasted till late at night . . . "important out-of-town donors, gotta go out on the town with them," exactly the sort of thing I would ordinarily have been dragged to. Every once in a while I would find a receipt from the Wall Street Sports Club, which is better known for the activity in its sauna than for its sports facilities, but I didn't really care. I trusted him to play safe, and anyway, maybe he just went there to work out. What would be the point of making a fuss? He was so much my partner; our lives were so deeply intertwined. It just didn't matter to me, because I never once doubted he was mine, that I belonged to him. It's not as though I never thought about it myself . . . I had plenty of opportunities. I was just never interested.

But this isn't about sex, it's dumping his and my life together down the garbage chute, swapping me in for a kid he can't even talk to. He tried to say something about it, and that was when I completely cut him off. I just said, "I thought you said you were leaving," and turned around, so he wouldn't see me cry. Anyway, I've decided to come home as soon as I can book a ticket. This house is so empty now . . . the servants act like somebody died . . . looking at my beautiful linen wall coverings, the new furniture, everything, my little tropical retreat with Joey, it makes me so angry I want to burn the place down. I'll let you know.

Love from me

Subj: I'm still me
Date: 6/8 10:10:22 PM Eastern Daylight Time
From: jbreaux@denpasar.wasantara.net.id
To: WitchBitch@camnet.net

Dear Phil,

I just reread the message I sent you before. You're right, it is
pretty insane. And you were also right, I was stoned when I
wrote it. And yes, I did flush the rest of the pot down the toilet.
I'm sorry about sending the message to the Globe – I went to the
address book instead of replying to your last message. You may
be right about a lot of things, but you're wrong about the attraction between me and Wayan being just physical. I'm not doing
this just <<for the thrill of fucking a nineteen-year-old boy.>> Of
course I realize what it looks like: it looks like I'm a selfish bastard who is dumping the perfect boyfriend for a hot piece of tail.
Maybe I am a selfish bastard, but do you really think I'm so
naive that I don't know the difference between a sexual escapade
and a deep emotional bond? On the contrary, I think the appar-
ent total inappropriateness of my relationship with Wayan is
proof that it must be more than a sexual romp. I don't deny that
the sex is a powerful part of it – sex is always the fuel that feeds
the fire – but if that's all there was to it, I wouldn't be doing
what I'm doing.

Phil, I appreciate everything you said in your message, I really
do. And to a certain extent, you're right: I'm doing this blindly,
the risks are so great I can't even think about them. But I've got
to go through with it. Anyway, it's too late – I've already
jumped. A lot of your advice was already out of date by the time
I got it – I had already told Andrew and moved out of the house.
I asked him for a trial separation of two months. I'm not going
to stop seeing Wayan, and no matter how much of a shit everyone thinks I am, I'm not so evil as to carry on a love affair with
someone else while we're still living under the same roof, sleep-

ing in the same bed. I may be making a huge mistake, but you
just have to take my word for it that my motives are much
deeper than you think. I'm sorry about all the rapturous crap I
wrote about how beautiful he is – that's embarrassing in hind-
sight, and I think a little misleading. Phil, I'm in love with that
boy. I am madly, passionately in love with him.

I tried to be gentle with Andrew and tell him how sorry I was,
how much I loved him, but he cut me off – of course I don't
blame him. I felt like a barbarian vandalizing something beautiful. The hurt, fearful look in his eyes made me panic for a moment. I could read it so clearly – he saw his life falling apart. I
wanted to say, "No, forget it, it's all a mistake," but it was too
late. Of course I realized he would be just as devastated if I told
him as if he found out on his own, but I had to tell him – the de-
ception was getting harder and harder to maintain. I kept pushing it, staying with Wayan later and later, sleeping less and less,
till I was a wreck.

Don't ask me what the two months are supposed to accomplish;
I guess what I'm secretly hoping is that Andrew will eventually
realize that even if I am a deceitful, philandering jerk, he still
wants to be with me. I know it's selfish, I know it's wanting to
have my cake and eat it too, but it's not as though I'm the first
gay man who has ever done that. Andrew jokingly calls himself
my wife, but he isn't really. We aren't married.

You're right, I have been a pretty good boy. I may have failed to
mention a few fleeting encounters that hardly deserve to be
called even tricks, but basically you're right, and none of them
ever posed any threat to Andrew. If only he had some tiny im-
pulse to trick himself! Before you open your mouth, I realize this
isn't a trick, "a quickie behind the woodshed," as you put it. I'm
dumping Andrew for Wayan – there's no way around it. But I
refuse to believe that in the end, he won't come around. God,
does that sound egotistical.

Time will tell whether I have made a horrible blunder. I feel sorrier about Andrew than I can ever say: I'm sure I don't even know yet how sorry I am. But I believe it's always a mistake not to follow the dictates of the heart. Remember that summer we all read Walker Percy's novels? His house was less than a mile from ours in Covington, though I never met him. In one of his novels, he says something to the effect of, "Sometimes there's nothing like a little disaster to sort things out." Maybe that's just demented Louisiana optimism, but something tells me that while this may not necessarily be a good thing, it was a necessary thing. Remember what you said in your message a few weeks ago, about me and Andrew living in a conceptual cottage with a white picket fence, baking cookies and pruning roses? That's where Andrew has been living for years, but I ask you, does that sound like the place for Joe Breaux?

I know you're mad at me, Phil, but please get over it quick, as I have a new piece I'm working on which will be the best thing I've done, and I want to tell you about it. I'm staying at a crummy little tourist hotel until Andrew clears out. He's leaving on Monday, he said. I guess he wanted to leave the island before I perform in public with Wayan. He's going to Boston to see his brother – I'm sure he'll call you, so he can come over and you two can talk about how horrible I am.

Listen, babee, you're the one person in the world I can't afford to let stay mad at me. Your E-mail messages have been like a lifeline to me out here. It may seem to you that I'm acting crazy, but I'M STILL ME. I was always a little bit crazy, you know that.

Love ya,

Joey

P.S. Please note the new E-mail address.

Subj: Y'all come
Date: 6/8 10:10:45 PM Eastern Daylight Time
From: jbreaux@denpasar.wasantara.net.id
To: quentin.trent@nytimes.com

Dear Quentin,

Sure, y'all come on down, as we say here in Bali. I would be delighted for you to have a look at what we're doing. I am making my Bali debut, if so grand a word applies, next Tuesday, in a performance of the Gambuh. It's a stately drama of romantic intrigue in the royal court, one of the oldest works in the Balinese repertoire, which dates back to the fifteenth century. It has been an amazing experience for me, discovering Balinese dance, and I'm happy to do anything I can to make it better known in the West.

I have just begun work on a new full-length work, a narrative piece about the German artist Walter Spies and his tragic love affair with a Balinese boy in the 1930's. The score will be a pastiche of works by Colin McPhee (who was a friend of Spies'), written for full Western orchestra, based upon Balinese musical concepts. The principal roles will be danced by myself and a young Balinese dancer named Wayan Renda, who is also my partner in the Gambuh. He is one of the most exciting, gifted dancers I have ever seen perform. I am delighted that you're coming here and will be able to see him. Members of the Seka Kerobokan, the group with which I am associated, will dance the smaller roles and form the corps. It is my hope, if the piece is a success, to bring Wayan Renda to New York to perform it. I realize that that's a bit premature, but there's no harm in being an optimist, is there?

I've just finished the first rough sketch, and I anticipate that it will be two or three months before there's much to see. They say that the weather is still good here in October: Why not plan a visit then?

I look forward to welcoming you to Bali.

Best wishes,

Joe

P.S. Please note my new E-mail address.

Subj: Flight details
Date: 6/8 11:01:21 PM Eastern Daylight Time
From: AndrewTan@wol.com
To: etan@MIT.edu (Eric Tan)

Hi Eric,

Arriving Logan June 24 at 4:00 p.m., on Singapore Airlines,
flight SQ 007. Thanks for calling this morning, man. Joey
wanted to come see me again today, but I told him no. I didn't
want him to see that I'd been crying. Anyway, I'm all talked out.
I will be *so* glad to see you. Of course it's okay for Sophie to
come. I would love to see her.

Andy

Subj: Your Bali project
Date: 6/12 9:52:30 AM Eastern Daylight Time
From: quentin.trent@nytimes.com
To: jbreaux@denpasar.wasantara.net.id

Dear Joe,

Thanks for your prompt reply. It sounds as though you've chosen a juicy subject for your piece – a long way from "Rodeo,"

anyway! I confess that I had never heard of either Spies or McPhee, but Walt McCoy, our contemporary music man here, says that he's one of the most brilliant twentieth-century composers, an eccentric unjustly neglected because he didn't follow the atonal orthodoxy. He's promised to get me some recordings of his music. Spies is proving more elusive.

Thank you for your kind invitation. I'll tentatively plan on a visit in October. I'll be in touch again in a month or so, to see how the work is coming along.

Best,

Quentin

Subj: Breaux scandal
Date: 6/13 3:15:20 AM Eastern Daylight Time
From: thumbelina@indonet.net.id
To: Erica_Golden@IDS.org

Hi there,

Well, sit down and prepare yourself for the clatter of falling hairpins. Here's the dish: your buddy Joe Breaux has kicked out his boyfriend of fifteen years, the Chinese millionaire, for a nineteen-year-old Balinese boy! He's the star of the seka, Wayan Renda, a very cute kid, tall and slender, with huge liquid eyes and long fluttery eyelashes, and a smile sweet as a mango. Hair down to his shoulders, the way the boys wear it here. Joe, it seems, has no idea what a scandal he has created. Wayan moved in with him, in his swanky villa rental, the same day that the boyfriend flew back to the States. (I really feel sorry for him, he seemed like such a sweet guy.) His father told him it was okay – he had been living in a tiny little rented room, so it's not like he was still at home.

I have to admit, they make a stunning couple. Joe doesn't look a day over thirty, though he has developed a suggestion of a belly, and Wayan's so tall and pretty, with not the vaguest suggestion of hips, he could be a runway model in Paris. (For women's clothes, I mean.) But it's just that he's SO young. You see, he's a brilliant dancer, he really could be one of those legendary performers they remember forever here. They're so afraid that Joe is going to corrupt him – I don't mean the gay part of it, though they don't like that either, but Wayan is just gay, that's all there is to it. Everyone knew that. What they're worried about are all those sinful Western ways. When these young Indonesian boys take up with foreigners, they get spoiled – "Honey, take me to Singapore, the new Prada line is out," that sort of thing, when he should be devoting himself to his sacred calling.

It's a little unclear how it will affect Joe's standing with the seka. Bob was over here last night, he's really freaking out. When word got out that Wayan was shacking up with the evil foreign banci, some of the elders in the seka wanted to kick Joe out immediately, but they couldn't, as that would have ruined the big performance for Kuningan, the holiday that just finished. Joe and Wayan had the lead roles. They gave such a stunning performance, I don't want to get sidetracked, but it was really electric the way they danced together. Anyway, everyone was so knocked out that they decided it was better just to let everything go on as before, at least for now. It's obvious that, as far as the dance goes, Joe has been a great influence on Wayan. Bob said that Joe was completely unaware of all this. He thinks it's just grand that the Balinese are such lovely people and so tolerant – totally clueless.

And here's the REALLY good part. Rica, this is total gossip, and I will be really mad if you ever tell anyone like Jerry Hull about this. I'm sure he'll hear about Joe and Wayan, but not what I'm about to tell you. Well, Nyoman, my maid, told me that her brother Putu, who is also a dancer, has a good friend who is a member of Joe's seka, who told him that Wayan put a love spell on Joe! Putu's friend is also gay, deeply closeted, with a wife (same as in the States, they're total hypocrites about that here), and he says that Wayan was after Joe the minute he set eyes on him, flirting like mad. And at the end of Joe's second or third rehearsal with the seka, when he went to change he couldn't find his underwear! Every Indonesian knows exactly what that means. If you want to make someone fall in love with you, you steal something personal and take it to your dukun, the wizard, and he puts a spell on them. Isn't that wild? No one can prove that Wayan was the one who stole Joe's underwear, but Joe has been acting exactly like someone under a spell. He is absolutely besotted.

You can stop rolling your eyes. Remember, Nancy Reagan's astrologer was in charge of the travel schedule of the President of the United States. If you don't believe in spells, fine. I'm not saying that I necessarily believe in spells. But I could tell you stories. . . . So that's my big scoop. From the friend of my maid's brother – now that I'm telling you, we're up to fourth-hand gossip. Bob told me that Joe's choreographing a new piece for himself and Wayan, based on the life of Walter Spies, the German artist who was convicted of buggering underage boys here in the 1930s. Did you ever hear anything so outrageous? They still worship Spies here, but you will never get most Balinese to admit that he was a homo. They just say, "I don't know," and blush.

I'll keep you posted on any further developments. I'll write again tomorrow or the next day to answer your last message. Of course I'll be happy to read your grant proposal, just post it along, and then I'll send you my comments. But I had to pass along the dish while it was hot!

Love from Pam

Subj: Joe Breaux
Date: 6/20 5:56:12 AM Eastern Daylight Time
From: BBlankenship@indonet.net.id
To: jahull@POF.org

Dear Jerry,

I have some rather strange news about Joe Breaux. It's nothing
to be terribly alarmed about at this point, but I thought I should
let you know. Joe has broken off his relationship with Andrew
Tan and taken up with a young Balinese man. In fact, he's nineteen years old. His name is Wayan Renda, and he is one of the
most talented dancers in Seka Kerobokan (or all Bali, for that
matter). There's nothing illegal about it, and the boy's father is
aware of the circumstances. Wayan moved to Joe's house after
Andrew left Bali.

Ordinarily, I wouldn't dream of spreading reports about an
artist's personal life (or anyone's personal life, for that matter).
But this incident has ruffled a lot of feathers at the seka, I can tell
you, and it has put Joe's project here at some risk. Several of the
elders were so angry they were talking about asking Joe to leave
the seka immediately. But a few days after everyone found out,
Joe and Wayan danced the lead parts at a major festival, Joe's
first public performance. They were simply sensational, a truly
breathtaking performance. So the grumbling appears to have
been quelled, at least for the moment. I presume you will realize
that I am not sending you gossip about Joseph Breaux's personal
life but rather informing you about a somewhat delicate develop-
ment pertaining to his project here, which your foundation has
so generously supported, and which we would all like to see succeed. As I said, the situation seems to be stable at the moment,
but I'll keep you informed of any further developments.

Best wishes,

Bob

Subj: My new piece
Date: 6/22 8:22:33 AM Eastern Daylight Time
From: jbreaux@denpasar.wasantara.net.id
To: WitchBitch@camnet.net

File: Spies.mim (29537 bytes)
DL Time (32000 bps): < 2 minutes

This message is a multi-part MIME message and will be saved
with the default filename Spies.mim

Dear Phil,

Well, since I haven't heard from you, I assume you're still mad at
me. I don't know about everybody else, but I'm going to move
on and live my life. Are you still mad at me? That was a pretty
starchy message you sent me – it was terrifying to receive a letter
from my Aunt Phyllis without a single feminine pronoun or one
word of French or Italian. This really is between me and
Andrew, isn't it? I don't mean that you aren't entitled to your
own views, and after all, I did ask for your advice (rather hyster-
ically, as I recall). But look at it from my point of view. Assume
the worst, that I'm just in the middle of a mad infatuation: What
am I supposed to do, snap my fingers like Samantha and make
myself not be infatuated? By force of will pretend that
everything is normal? You've only ever known Andrew and me
as a couple, so I know it must be shocking. But we were always
two separate people. Were you friends with me or with
Joey'n'Andrew, Inc.? At this point I've got to figure out some
way of making this up to him – I know I've made him
completely miserable. Maybe I'll never be able to make it up to
him.

I've been thinking about him a lot. I'll never forget the night I
met him. It was at that burrito joint we always went to in East
Palo Alto. He was with his brother. I can't remember exactly

how it happened, it's so easy at that age. I think Andrew just smiled at me and said, "Hi! I saw you at orientation." So innocent: I saw you, i.e. I noticed you, i.e. I think you're cute. It was sort of a tiny bond that we were in the so-called "bad" part of town, getting real Mexican food instead of going to the tacky places that catered to students. Eric gobbled his food up and said that he had go to the lab, wouldn't be back until late, winking at Andrew, but I could see. Maybe I was supposed to. Even though he was a freshman, Andrew got to live off-campus, because Eric was a junior. Anyway, the next thing we knew, we were back at his place, making out like mad. It was the first time for both of us – neither of us knew what to do, though it didn't take long to figure out.

Andrew wasn't so demure in those days, with long hair and ripped dungarees. We were both infatuated right from the start. He wanted us to live together off-campus when we were juniors, but I was the one who wanted to keep a little distance. The gay scene at Stanford was pretty open in those days, nothing like now, but I did a little shopping around. Andrew was so cool, he never got jealous. He went out with a couple of guys – one in particular, a really cute jock named Ronnie Holt. No one believed he was really gay, just like they did with me, until people began comparing dance cards. . . . Anyway, I realized later it was a classic Marcia Brady move, go out with someone else to make the guy you REALLY like jealous. And man, did it work – the thought of Andrew and Ronnie having sex made me CRAZY. I went over to his apartment late one night, pretty drunk, Eric was in England by that point, and banged on his door and did the 20-year-old version of sweeping him off his feet. Then we went to Italy after graduation, and that sealed the deal, at least in principle – his father tried to make him stop seeing me for the first year or two after graduation, which of course only made him more determined. He was so feisty then. Damn, how I loved him! Still do – I can't believe that this won't all come right in the end somehow.

Getting seriously sidetracked here. I've got work to do! For the first time in my career, I actually have the time and the money and the opportunity to do the best work of my career – to MAKE my career. Most important, I've found the ideal performer for my work. I hope I am at least allowed to mention him. Since the last time I wrote you, Wayan and I performed the Gambuh for Kuningan. You know I don't let praise go to my head, but you can't believe how everyone raved about our performance. And what everyone remarked the most was the chemistry between us, how perfectly we moved together. Bob Blankenship, who I know is appalled about me and Wayan, was ecstatic.

Anyway, I have the greatest idea for a new piece, with me and Wayan in the principal roles. When I was up in Ubud staying at the Hotel Tjampuhan I told you about Walter Spies, the German painter who went there in the twenties and got into hot water for boinkin' the local laddies? It's really a classic tragedy, true love thwarted by cruel society, the sensitive artist martyred by the grimly moralistic colonial authorities, can East and West ever meet, etc. Still relevant issues. The more I find out about Spies's life, the richer it seems in dramatic possibilities. Bob gave me an article about him that came out in the Atlantic Monthly a couple of years ago. I scanned it in and am sending it to you as an attachment. I only included the relevant portions, cut out all the flowery travelogue stuff. If you read that first, the rest of this message will make more sense.

The title is "Elegy for Walter Spies." The score will be a pastiche of music by Colin McPhee, a Canadian composer who was in Bali at the same time as Walter Spies, and a friend of his (also another friend of Dorothy's – she's a popular lady here). The pieces I'm using are scored for full Western orchestra, but based on Balinese musical concepts. You see? Even the music is about the mingling of cultures. I've got it all worked out. There's humorous, "sexy" music for the duet with Barbara Hutton, tender stuff for Spies and the boy, blustery brassy passages for the Dutch authorities, and a pure gamelan sound for the finale, when the boy comes down to the jail to sing for Spies. Wayan has a beautiful singing voice; I'm thinking of finding someone (maybe Wayan himself) to come up with a sweet little song he can sing for the finale.

Phil, this is just what I've been looking for: a big, complex piece, with the perfect parts for me and Wayan. And it's SURE to be noticed. It will be the first dance piece ever with Margaret Mead and Noel Coward as characters! Also, I'm not being calculating about his, but everyone will know about me and Wayan, and for us to perform together in a piece with this subject matter is sure to attract controversy. Controversy gets booked. Whaddaya think? Quentin Trent is coming to Bali to do a piece about me while I'm working on it.

It's all so clear in my head. I know I can do this. Now let me hear from you, Phil. I need you, babee.

Love ya,

Joey

<HTML><FONT SIZE=3 PTSIZE=10>Phil,

The story is called "Ubud, the Heart of Bali," by Jamie James, from *The Atlantic Monthly*, August 1999. Here's the first few paragraphs:

Tourism to Bali began in the early twenties, when the Royal Dutch Steam Packet Company added the island to its itinerary. By 1930, there were about a hundred visitors a year; a decade later, the figure had leapt to 250. The ships stopped off the north coast, where passengers were ferried to shore first aboard tenders and then on the backs of Balinese men. Most visitors would then traverse the island by motor car to the capital city of Denpasar, in the south, where they stayed at the luxurious Bali Hotel, which had opened in 1927.

Discriminating travelers, however, headed for the green hills of the interior, to visit the princedom of Ubud. There was no hotel in Ubud: one stayed in the bungalows that Prince Gde Agung Sukawati had built for the circle of artists he patronized. What was surely the most exotic art colony in the world at that time began with the arrival of Walter Spies, a Moscow-born German artist and musician who came to Bali for a visit in 1927 and stayed there until the Second World War, when he became a prisoner of war in the Dutch-controlled East Indies. In Ubud he encountered a culture as graceful and refined as any in Asia (or anywhere in the world, for that matter), where everyone, it seemed, was an artist of one sort or another, and child dancers in mystic trances enacted the fables of the *Ramayana* to the exuberant, clangorous accompaniment of a gamelan orchestra.

Charlie Chaplin was one early visitor to Ubud; another, Noel Coward, had him in mind when he wrote this bit of doggerel verse:

As I said this morning to Charlie,
There is far too much music in Bali.
And although as a place it's entrancing
There is also a thought too much dancing.
It appears that each Balinese native
From the womb to the tomb is creative,
And although the results are quite clever,
There is too much artistic endeavor.

[Me again. I knew you would like the Noel Coward poem. Now here's the part about Walter Spies.]

When Walter Spies arrived in Bali, he found a culture completely devoted to art, yet to whom the notion of art for art's sake was alien. The Balinese have no word for "artist"; painting, carving stone and wood, weaving, playing in the gamelan, and above all dance were just what one did when not fishing or working in the rice fields.

It is an axiom of art history that what used to be known as primitive art had a profound formative influence on the emergence of modernism in twentieth-century Europe. In Bali, Europe returned the favor: Spies had an uncanny affinity for the Balinese sensibility, and he totally transformed the arts of the island in the fourteen years he lived there. The famous school of painting in Ubud, one of the principal reasons people come from every part of the world to visit here, was virtually his invention.

Traditionally, the Balinese considered painting to be among the lowest of the arts; before Spies it was comparatively primitive, consisting mainly of astrological calendars and scenes from the *wayang*, the mythological shadow-puppet show popular throughout the archipelago. Painters were limited by convention and the natural pigments, such as bone, soot, and clay, that were available to them.

Spies, later joined by the Dutch pastelist Rudolf Bonnet, introduced Balinese artists to the wider range of colors of Western painting, and the greater range of effects possible with ready-made brushes and fine-woven canvas. More important, Spies and Bonnet introduced Western techniques, like perspective, and encouraged their students to venture beyond the traditional mythological subject matter and paint scenes from everyday life. Lest Spies and Bonnet be accused of tampering with an ancient tradition, it should be pointed out that Balinese art, while formulaic, was never opposed to individual expressiveness; the island's most famous artist, I Gusti Nyoman Lempad, had begun to innovate stylistically before Spies's arrival.

As far as I know, there has never been a case of one person's
having such a profound impact on the arts of a foreign culture.
The best-known dance of Bali, the *kecak,* in which a chorus of
men wearing checkered sarongs lie in a circle, loudly chanting
"chak-a-chak-a-chak" while elaborately costumed soloists act
out a tale from the *Ramayana,* was choreographed in its present
form by Spies in 1931. Originally, the chorus was much smaller,
and performed in a trance, but Spies wanted to create something
more dramatic for a film he was working on, Victor Baron von
Plessen's *Island of Demons,* an early effort to capture and export
the romance of Bali.

Ubud in the 1930s was one of the most chic bohemian destina-
tions in the world. Chaplin is said to have been disappointed
that Balinese girls were not as promiscuous as their bare-
breasted condition suggested. Margaret Mead and her lover,
Gregory Bateson, got married on a ship steaming toward Bali,
where they dropped in on Spies. Ruth Draper visited for a while,
no doubt reciting her droll monologues for everyone after dinner. Most flamboyant of all was the heiress Barbara Hutton,
who fell violently in love with Spies and dragged him off to
Cambodia to see Angkor Wat. With the money she paid him for
some paintings, he built her a bungalow and swimming pool
next to his own house, but by the time it was finished she had
moved on to Persia. (Guests at the Hotel Tjampuhan may stay at
this bungalow, which is named after Spies; the swimming pool is
now a lily pond.)

Spies, however, was sexually inclined in a different way, with
disastrous results. The Dutch authorities, scandalized at the general moral laxity of the foreigners in Ubud, and as part of a
crackdown on homosexuals throughout the colony, arrested
Spies on New Year's Eve, 1938, for committing sodomy with a
minor. According to his biographer, Hans Rhodius, the Balinese
were puzzled and shocked by the arrest, and brought Spies's favorite gamelan to play for him outside the window of his jail
cell. The boy's father told the trial judge, "He is our best friend,

and it was an honor for my son to be in his company. If both are
in agreement, why fuss?"

Spies was released from prison in September of 1939. While war
was breaking out in Europe, Spies began a passionate study of
insects and marine life, turning out some exquisitely observed
gouaches of his specimens. After Germany invaded Holland, the
following year, all German citizens living in the Dutch East
Indies were arrested. Spies, the last German on Bali, was sent to
a prison in Sumatra, where he continued painting and organized
an orchestra, which he conducted in performances of
Rachmaninoff. In 1942, fearful of an imminent Japanese attack,
the Dutch authorities put their German prisoners on a ship for
transport to Ceylon. The day after it embarked, the vessel was
hit by a Japanese bomb. The Dutch crew abandoned the sinking
ship, and left their prisoners to drown, slowly and
horribly.</HTML>

Subj: Melancholy weekend
Date: 6/24 7:52:31 PM Eastern Daylight Time
From: WitchBitch@camnet.net
To: jbreaux@denpasar.wasantara.net.id

Dear Joey (Oh all right, Il tesoro mio, if it makes you happy),

No, I'm not mad at you. If I sounded starchy in my last letter it's
because at the time I was so fearful that you were losing your
mind that I was seriously considering hopping on a plane to
Bali, rare tropical diseases be damned. I'm not joking – I was almost to the point of investing a month's salary in a phone call,
to see if you wanted me to come. Then I received, with great relief, your more rational message in reply to mine. I apologize for
being so slow to answer you. I have a sort of excuse: I had to go
out to Williamstown last week for the theatre festival, and I just
got back yesterday. But you and your little disaster are more important than that, and I should have gotten up earlier in the

morning to at least send you a message to tell you I was going
out of town.

I saw Andrew. He called me from Lenox just as I was leaving,
and when I told him I was going to Williamstown, he insisted
that I come for dinner. It's not that I didn't want to see him,
but . . . he wasn't quite ready for it. Neither was I. He sounded
very brave and cheerful on the phone, but the moment he saw
me, I won't say he burst into tears, but he got all misty and
couldn't speak properly. And you know me, I always land on
Water Works in Monopoly – when he started crying, I joined in.
it was a very melancholy evening. He is such an adorable, lovely
man, and he is so very miserable. It was not by any means a case
of "the two of us getting together to talk about how horrible
you are." Joey, what a tacky, bitchy thing to say! Deliberately
trivializing it. And telling Andrew the child is 21, that was pathetic, as if two years make any difference. You should have seen
his face when I set him straight about that – he couldn't conceal
his disgust. I guess I am a little bit mad at you. That business
about how some men get away with having their cake and eating it too is the original "But Mom, all the guys at school are
doing it." Just because New York is swarming with selfish, nar-
cissistic faggots doesn't mean you should be one of them. Don't
start, girlie – I'm not saying you are one, but you ARE using
them as your excuse.

It's not a question of me taking sides, but after seeing Andrew
this weekend it's impossible for me to be happy for you. He's SO
goddamn miserable. We really should have waited at least until
he had gotten over jet lag. That always makes one so over-
emotional. You must know that he never said one angry or bitter word about you. A few times he began a sentence that was
veering in that direction, but he stopped himself. Mostly, he
asked questions I couldn't answer: "Why?" "What did I do
wrong?" I hope I'm not making a mistake by telling you all this.
My purpose certainly isn't to make you "feel bad" – if you don't
feel bad now, your heart is carved from stone. Perhaps I've said

too much. I just thought you would want a report on him. The last thing I will say is that he's very fortunate to have that brother of his – he's as sweet and kind (and smart) a man as ever I met. And amazingly cool about faggotry. The wife's a bit hard-edged. Eric was very discreet and careful not to put me in an awkward position by attacking you, but she was obviously very angry.

I concede one point to you: when a man is in the throes of a carnal passion, he can't simply push a button and make it go away. And while I am by NO means granting you absolution yet, under those circumstances you had to tell Andrew. All that midnight sneaking over to the Caledonian fleshpots was too wicked for words. I think perhaps it might be better if I don't say any more on the subject at present. Your basic points, that I was friends with you and with Andrew, not with a corporate partnership, and that it's really between the two of you, are sound ones. I'm here if you need me.

Now, as to your magnum opus, the homage to buggery in Bali – it sounds davoon. You know I don't know a darn thing about dance, unless it's on the Broadway stage, and even then I have to fake it. But this sounds great to me, and you are right – it's sure to create a sensation. It's too soon for me to start being so nice to you – but I have to admit, if I didn't know you, and I read Quentin Trent's story in the New York Times about the noted dancer and choreographer Joseph Breaux, who went to Bali, dumped his boyfriend to shack up with a teenager, and then choreographed a ballet about a chicken-and-rice queen in Bali, and cast himself and his very own Chicken McNugget in the lead roles, I would be hooting with laughter. Joey, it's outrageous. I think you should lie to Quentin Trent and tell him that Wayan is twelve, just big for his age, and then hire some actors to play Indonesian policeman to come shut down your production. They would put you on page one.

I enjoyed the story about Ubud you sent me. Auntie Noelle's ditty was dear. My piece about the Williamstown festival is on the Globe's website today, if you're interested. Why would you be? Anyway, it was the lead on the Sunday arts page, with a tease box on page one.

Phil (OK, OK, ta tante Phyllis)

P.S. I said I wasn't going to say anything more about it, but I hope you will wait to hear from Andrew before you write to him.

Subj: Whew
Date: 6/26 10:34:21 PM Eastern Daylight Time
From: jbreaux@denpasar.wasantara.net.id
To: WitchBitch@camnet.net

Dear Phil,

Thanks for your GREAT message. Whew. I was getting pretty miserable, afraid that I had not only destroyed my "marriage" but also jeopardized by most important friendship. I'm sorry, I can't chat now – too busy to take a pee. I promise to write soon.

Love ya,

Joey

Subj: Me
Date: 6/26 10:34:36 PM Eastern Daylight Time
From: jbreaux@denpasar.wasantara.net.id
To: AndrewTan@wol.com

Dear Andrew,

Phil told me that he saw you – I'm glad you two guys had a chance to get together. He warned me not to do this, but there

are two things I HAVE to say: I will always love you until the
day I die, and putting you through the hell of the past few weeks
is the worst thing I've ever done in my life. I am heartily sorry
for it. I hope you can forgive me some day. I know you said
you're all "talked out," and I don't blame you. I don't expect a
reply to this message, but any time you want to open communication, I'm here. I will spend the rest of my life trying to make
this up to you.

Joey

P.S. Please note my new E-mail address.

Subj: Weeping in the Berkshires
Date: 6/28 11:20:01 AM Eastern Daylight Time
From: AndrewTan@wol.com
To: WitchBitch@camnet.net

Dear Phil,

It was great to see you last week. I'm sorry I was so weepy. I
don't think I'm wallowing in my misery, but I just can't seem to
stop feeling miserable. I'm not going to rehash any of the stuff
we talked about . . . one of the worst parts of this is always talking about it. I just wanted to tell you that even though I realize
that you and Joey have a lot more in common, I always did and
will continue to think of you as my friend. We probably should
have waited a few days before getting together, but you were so
near by, I thought it was a good opportunity. Actually, you were
a great help. I really appreciate some of the sweet things you
said.

I will stay in Lenox till the end of the summer, and then go back
to the apartment on Horatio Street, I suppose. I can't very well
go tagging along with my big brother forever. At some point I'll
have to sort out with Joey what's happening with the apartment.

He sent me a message yesterday. He said that you had advised him not to do it. You were right! It was a nice note, I guess. It was certainly contrite. Big Whoop.

This is perilously near Talking About It. Please come back for another weekend, and I promise we'll have fun. You said they were reviving some one-act plays by Pinter in Williamstown in August. I love him – take me as your date, and stay here. It's barely an hour's drive to Billsville.

Take care, pal.

Andrew

Subj: who's outrageous?
Date: 7/2 9:03:56 PM Eastern Daylight Time
From: jbreaux@denpasar.wasantara.net.id
To: WitchBitch@camnet.net

Dear Phil,

I'm sorry it has taken me so long to write, but I've been working on the piece night and day. It's coming together beautifully, but there's so much to do! The Balinese are way into it. When I told them that I wanted to do a piece about Walter Spies, they were thrilled. It's been fifty-something years since he died, but they still worship him here. Bob told me not to tell them about the gay angle, just say that Walter and the Boy (I'm not giving him a name) are friends, and the Boy is so sad his friend went to jail. Isn't that ridiculous? The story makes no sense unless you know they're lovers. But he has been very stern with me since you-know-what. I don't think he approves of my piece.

Everyone tells me it's outrageous – that's what you said – but I wasn't trying to be outrageous. I just thought it was a great story. However, he has convinced me that the Balinese aren't nearly as cool about the gay thing as I thought. It's so confusing – the boys here are SO swishy, and LOTS of the dancers here are gay, but they're way deep in the closet. So I've decided to follow his advice – after all, he's my official guru now.

The sketches are mostly done. The hard part will be to work out how to blend my movements with theirs. There has to be a clear distinction between the Balinese and the foreigners, but there also has to be some blending. They have to inhabit the same dance world. I've found an Italian gal for Barbara Hutton – we've already started working on our duet. She looks right, and can dance, but she's a total flake, stoned all the time. There's a comic quartet of foreigners – Margaret Mead, Gregory Bateson, Noel Coward, and Ruth Draper – who run around in a pack, like their hips are glued together. I've got some more-or-less adequate American dancers (actually Margaret Mead is Australian) to play them. At least they can understand what I'm saying. The Balinese parts are easy to cast, but getting them into the idea of doing something that's not part of their own repertory is hard. There has to be a dance-within-the-dance – the kecak, of course, since it was choreographed by Walter. Isn't that neat? The choreographer choreographing the part of a choreographer at work? The kecak is perfect, because it doesn't have any instrumental music, just the chanting of the men. I think it will be very dramatic, when the orchestral music stops and the chanting begins. Thank god for the Pouf – I have to pay these people, and even though I'm not paying them much, I'll be lucky to end up with ten dollars after this is all over.

I hope I'm not going into too much detail here. Of course, I haven't even mentioned what will make the whole thing work – my collaboration with You-Know-Who. He's the key to the theme of East-meets-West – our duets will be the nut of the piece. The other principal Balinese parts – the father, the prince – can just be Balinese. It's good for me to write all this out – I don't have anyone here I can really explain it to.

In fact, I'm starting to feel sort of alone here, in some ways. I'm never lonely, thanks to the beautiful friendship I have with my adorable lover, whom you insist on calling "the child" – Phil, his name is Wayan. The problem here, as I feared from the beginning, is finding other gringos to be friends with. As I said, Bob has become very frosty, and Angus Gray and his crowd are getting stale. Always stoned and chasing tail. No time for the former, and as for the latter . . . oops, never mind. The dancers I've hired are very standoffish, very puristic. I can tell they disapprove of "fusion" – so do I, for that matter. This is more like a mosaic.

Well, back to work. I won't be able to keep up the same pace of correspondence as I did before. I've decided to try to get the piece ready by the time Quentin gets here, in October, so I can maybe get a review. So don't give me any of that S.P.A. crap if I don't answer every single message right away. My father gets all impatient if I don't answer the very next day. All I ever tell him is how busy I am, anyway.

Love ya,

Joey

P.S. Did I tell you? I have a venue – the ballroom at one of the big hotels here. $300 a night, can you imagine?

Subj: My big news
Date: 7/6 9:32:11 PM Eastern Daylight Time
From: WitchBitch@camnet.net
To: jbreaux@denpasar.wasantara.net.id

O riddling sphinx,

I'll bite. You're dying to tell all the gory d's about the Infant Phenomenon, this tropical Bosie of yours – but I want detailed descriptions of the past thirty fucks (which I suppose will take us back to sometime late yesterday afternoon), and I want you to compose this epic in dactylic hexameters, laden with epithets – "honey-skinned Wayan, he of the magic booty," "stout-limbed Joseph, wielder of the mighty love-club," that sort of thing. I assume you're the gentleman and he's the lady? I want to know every filthy, lascivious detail. Keep a little log next to the bed, with a stopwatch and a tape measure, so you can jot down positions, trajectories, time elapsed, etc. I was lying to you before: You ARE going to hell, you wicked man. As the nuns used to tell us, you're making Jesus cry.

But you must get the Fuckiad to me within the next two weeks, because . . . I have REALLY big news: I have a new job. I resigned yesterday at the Globe, and as of September 1, I am the second-string drama critic of the San Francisco Chronicle. What do you think? Shirley, be frank. I don't know anyone in San Francisco, the Chronicle is basically a joke, with less clout than the Globe, and the drama scene in San Francisco looks to be even more dismal than it is here, but . . . I'm out of Boston! Forever! I'm going to live in one of the most beautiful cities in the world, where people heat their houses in the wintertime, and only eat beans at Mexican restaurants – and where it's possible to have a little fun once in a while. I didn't tell you I was looking, because I didn't think I had a Chinaman's chance. (I suppose one doesn't use that expression any more.)

The pay is only slightly better, but my other news will help out there – Playboy, of all places, called me up and asked me if could I go to London to interview Anthony Hopkins. They're paying me $15,000 for 8,000 words! I was floored. The calls from the Chronicle and Playboy came exactly 24 hours apart. The editor at Playboy is a guy I knew very slightly when I was at the Voice. Total woman. She was very grand: "I think you'll find that the magazine is generous about travel expenses," that kind of garbaggio. I have three weeks to get it done. It was obvious that the original reporter dropped out at the last minute, but

Hopkins had already said yes. So I was only able to give exactly two weeks notice at the Globe. It's still a tight deadline for Playboy, but it will be easy, a Q&A format. Actually, I was very flattered. He had obviously read a lot of my stuff. I don't expect much will come of it. I hate that kind of high-powered journalism, anyway – the more they pay you, the more stupid and evil the editors are. Give me the newspaperman's life, where everyone is always in such a hurry that they never notice if your copy's any good.

I'll soon be out of E-touch, until I get settled in San Francisco. I'm not quite sure what to do for August. As it happens, the lease on my igloo here expires in September – that was lucky. I've got a decent relocation budget, so I'll go out at the end of the month and stay in some flophouse while I look around. Maybe I'll stay in London a while – Geoff will put me up after I check out of my suite at the Savoy. I hate moving. I'm rambling. Talk to you later.

Love from Phyllis

Subj: Bored in the Berkshires
Date: 7/8 7:31:09 PM Eastern Daylight Time
From: AndrewTan@wol.com
To: etan@MIT.edu (Eric Tan)

Hi Eric,

When I woke up this morning, the first thing I thought of was you and your news. It was the first time I've woken up happy since . . . you know what. I am *so* glad for you and Sophie. Me too . . . Uncle Andrew. I like the sound of that. The phone bill came today, $107, so I thought I would send E-mail again, for a change. Of course there's no news. I had dinner at the Inn last night with Andrea Rudner. The second time this week. She's a smart, nice lady, but I can only talk so much about books and

movies and theatre. When I got home, it occurred to me: I've
only been single for a few weeks, but I'm not going to stay that
way. I don't want to end up like Andrea, with plenty of time and
money but nothing to do, and no one to do it with. She's a nice
lady, but in the emotional department, there's nothing there but
cobwebs. Obviously, it's way too soon to be worrying about that
. . . it will take a few months for me to get back on an even keel.
The worst part is bedtime, not having anyone to say goodnight
to. But I've realized, getting Joey back isn't the most important
thing in my life. I can live without him. It's an important realiza-
tion, y'know? You told me that in the beginning, but it's one
thing to hear someone say it, and another thing to know it.

I'm also starting not to hate him, or whatever it is I've been feeling. He was always so emotional, so high-strung; it was one of
his endearing qualities, but it was also like a time bomb waiting
to go off. I can't imagine doing what he's done . . . that kid is
so young. Joey was obviously embarrassed, adding a couple
of years when he dropped the bombshell. But I can understand it
now, a little bit. Who knows what we have lurking inside our-
selves? In my case it would be older, not younger. If some
debonair Cary Grant type wanted to take me off on his yacht
. . . who knows? This was some thrilling, taboo fantasy come to
life for Joey. I have to admit, the kid is really cute. Don't you
think it's good that I can say things like that? Sometimes I think,
maybe I don't want Joey back. I was so much in his shadow. I
always said I liked being Mrs. Joseph Breaux, but I don't think I
ever had much of a choice about it.

I don't know how it happened. In theory we were always equals,
but even in the beginning, he always ran the show. It wasn't that
he was bossy . . . he made everything into an adventure. If I said
I was going to the supermarket to buy a chicken for dinner, he
would say, "No, wait a minute, I have a great idea – let's go to
the Lower East Side for deli. Brisket at Bernstein's, then we can
go check out the record shops on Second Avenue. Whaddaya
say?" What *could* you say but yes? Phil was a little in love

with him, we all knew that, and everybody knew that everybody knew, but no one ever said anything . . . Joey was our little prince, our Peter Pan, always buzzing with ideas and projects, and we followed him happily. Yet he never gave me any reason to complain. I was truly never jealous of his success, and anything I ever tried to do, he supported me 100 per cent. When I got into that training program at Morgan, something I expected him to turn his nose up at, he said, "That's great! Get rich."

Somehow he just took over my life. You wouldn't understand this . . . you're more like Joey in some ways than me, but life is much less complicated when you have someone else calling the shots. I guess I looked at Joey's talent, and then at my own fumbling efforts to write fiction, and put my money on him. And now look what I have to show for it . . . an empty bed and a question mark for the future. I miss him all the time, but in some ways it feels good. I'm starting to love the quiet . . . it was never quiet with Joey around.

I've made a vague sort of decision: I have to use this as an opportunity. For what, I'll tell you in a few years. Better it happened now than when I'm 50, starting to run out of steam and losing touch with the culture. Andrea had an interesting idea: she thinks I should get into the philanthropy business. Not giving the stuff away, she knows I'm not that rich, but working for a foundation, helping them to give it away. Some place like the Rockefeller Foundation. What do you think of that? I think Dad might like the idea, and he's got all the right connections. Maybe go back to California. I reread that story I was working on . . . you were nice to encourage me, but it's like Andrea's pottery, a hobby for a rich, bored person. Well, I'm getting bored with being bored.

Speaking of which, I'm fed up with Lenox. It's great for the weekend, but by Wednesday, I'm already starting to fidget, wishing you and Sophie were here. If it's okay with you, I'm going to go back to Cambridge with you on Sunday. Tell Silvio I'll dig holes and haul manure for him.

See you tomorrow,

Andy

Subj: Congratulations
Date: 7/10 11:15:29 PM Eastern Daylight Time
From: jbreaux@denpasar.wasantara.net.id
To: WitchBitch@camnet.net

Hi Phil,

That's great – congratulations! Everybody needs a friend in San Francisco to come visit. Career-wise it's good too, isn't it? The Globe might have more clout, but still, it's San Francisco – obviously better than Boston. You'll be so much happier there. And as for friends, Andrew and I – oops! THAT was a Freudian slip, and I'm going to be brave and leave it in. Let's start over: I have a lot of friends in the Bay Area you can look up. Anyway, it's so much easier to make friends in California than in the East. If anything, it gets to be a pain in the butt, everyone always wanting to be your friend.

Phil, what a dirty old man you're turning into! Wayan and I have one of those profoundly spiritual relationships, like Heloise and what's his name – we're so deep in love we don't need to express it physically. We just look into each other's eyes and sigh, or pick a perfect hibiscus and contemplate it together. Yuck, of course I'm not going to tell you what we do. I will say, we have a lot of fun. He's so young, and I'm pretty sure he was a virgin, so it's like he's discovering a whole new world. Discovering life, I guess. He's incredibly passionate and affectionate. But that's all I'm going to say for now.

There's no news. The piece is coming along well; there's just so much to do. I'm obsessed with it, working ten hours a day.

Love ya,

Joey

Subj: Re: Dirty old man
Date: 7/12 10:53:11 AM Eastern Daylight Time
From: WitchBitch@camnet.net
To: jbreaux@denpasar.wasantara.net.id

Petal,

His name was Peter Abelard, and his love affair with Heloise went way past the hibiscus-contemplating stage – they had a love child. I suppose you and Lolita don't have to worry about that. When Heloise's uncle, the Canon of Paris, found out, he had Abelard's nuts cut off. Does Wayan have any ecclesiastical types in the family?

Me

Subj: Bali-bound
Date: 7/18 9:46:57 AM Eastern Daylight Time
From: quentin.trent@nytimes.com
To: jbreaux@denpasar.wasantara.net.id

Dear Joe,

I have booked a flight to Bali, arriving August 28. I realize it's a bit sooner than we had planned, but for reasons beyond my control, it's then or not at all. I'm afraid I can only stay in Bali for a week – I'm aware of how absurd that is, but there's something in L.A. on September 7 that I absolutely must cover. I hope we're still on – I am looking forward to seeing you again, and writing this piece for Arts & Leisure.

Best wishes,

Quentin

Subj: Re: Bali-bound
Date: 7/19 11:23:17 AM Eastern Daylight Time
From: jbreaux@denpasar.wasantara.net.id
To: quentin.trent@nytimes.com

Dear Quentin,

Your timing is impeccable – you should become a dancer! As it happens, I have had some scheduling problems of my own – the Western dancers I'm using for the piece are what we would regard as semi-professionals in New York, and I'm having trouble getting them to commit to a firm date at all distant in the future, the ballroom I want is getting booked up for weddings, etc. – too boring to go into, but the upshot is that the performances are now scheduled for September 1 and 2, so you will be able to attend the premiere as well as the dress rehearsal, if you like.

I look forward to seeing you in Bali.

Best,

Joe

Subj: Re: Bali-bound
Date: 7/21 11:14:27 AM Eastern Daylight Time
From: quentin.trent@nytimes.com
To: jbreaux@denpasar.wasantara.net.id

Dear Joe,

Excellent, excellent. That means I'll be able to review the piece
as well as write the feature. I've booked a room at a place called
the Legian, which has been recommended as a good hotel in the
Kerobokan area. I'll be in touch as soon as I arrive. I won't ask
for any of your time until after the performances. For the moment, can we pencil in lunch and part of the afternoon at my
hotel on September 3? I leave on the fourth, so if we are going to
do the interview, it really must be on the third. One good interview will be enough. I'm sure you have a lot to say. I hope this
meets with your approval.

Thank you,

Quentin

Subj: Re: Re: Bali-bound
Date: 7/22 8:11:27 PM Eastern Daylight Time
From: jbreaux@denpasar.wasantara.net.id
To: quentin.trent@nytimes.com

Dear Quentin,

That's fine. I won't schedule anything for the day of September
3.

Best,

Joe

Subj: Breaux scandal
Date: 7/24 2:53:29 AM Eastern Daylight Time
From: thumbelina@indonet.net.id
To: Erica_Golden@IDS.org

Hey,

In your last message, you asked for the latest scoop on the Joe
Breaux scandal. There's not much to report. As improbable as it
seems, their relationship appears to be for real. It's a little hard
to make out what's going on, because my only source is Bob,
who's a hopeless prude, and talks about it in impenetrable eu-
phemisms. I don't mean to imply that it's prudish to disapprove
of a relationship between a 36-year-old man and a 19-year-old
boy. I say live and let live, but that's pushing the limit. But I can
definitely see it – he's so cute, if he fluttered those long eyelashes
at me, I might flutter back.

The gay scene here is so complicated, I'm not sure I really understand it. it seems that the relationships are almost always
between older white foreigners and young Indonesians. It's usually a financial arrangement, to some extent – it's inevitable,
since the foreigners here are at least comfortably well-off, and
the Indonesian kids are always so poor.

I ran into Joe and Wayan at Made's Warung, everybody's
favorite little place to go in Kuta. There they were, at eleven
o'clock at night, Joe helping him with his English homework.
Very touching. Joe told me that he was working ten hours a day
on the piece, but he said it was coming along well. Bob confirms
that. I think Bob's pissed off because the scandal has taken the
shine off his association with Joe. But from an artistic point of
view, Joe's doing something amazing. Besides the choreography,
he's doing the costumes, the lighting, managing the whole business side of the thing. Wayan seems to be the key, the go-
between for Joe and the Balinese. It's all the more amazing,
considering the boy's English is so basic. They really do seem to

have this intuitive, almost telepathic communication. The piece
will be performed in early September, two nights at the Radisson
ballroom. And guess what – Quentin Trent's coming out! It's
hard to believe, the critic from the New York Times coming to
little ol' Bali.

Take care, sweetie.

Pam

Subj: Bye-bye
Date: 7/27 1:23:25 PM Eastern Daylight Time
From: WitchBitch@camnet.net
To: jbreaux@denpasar.wasantara.net.id

O Garboesque one,

I can't very well reproach you for not writing, as I have been
silent for so long myself. I hate moving, it's more stressful than
being in love. So many things to worry about. My instinct is just
to give everything away and buy it all new in San Francisco. It
seems like such a waste of time, packing up my collection of Star
Trek glasses from McDonald's, and towels so threadbare you
can practically read through them. Worst of all are the books – I
look at the shelves and I want to weep. I think I'll just throw the
jewels and furs and my autographed portrait of Miss Loretta
Young, inscribed to me in the lobby of the Beverly Wilshire
Hotel on May 27, 1972, into the Vuitton, and then torch this
place. I never had one happy minute here – I spent most of my
time huddling in front of a space heater.

Here's my plan: I'm flying to London (BA business class,
thenkyewveddymuch) on Sunday for my interview with Tones,
as we call him – Sir Anthony to you, fella. I actually am staying
at the Savoy – why not? The cheapest room, of course, but it's
still the Savoy. I've invited him there for tea, so everyone can

look at us and say, "Who is that old man with Phyllis
O'Donnell?" Then after three days at the Savoy, I'm staying on
for a week or so with Geoff. I can file my story to the titty magazine by E-mail, and there is absolutely no reason to come back
to Boston in August. Every reason to avoid doing so. By the time
I leave here, I'll have everything shoved into boxes, so when I
come back, I can head out to San Francisco and have a heart attack when I see how much it costs to live there. They say it's
worse than New York. Geoff wants to take me up to Edinburgh
for the festival for a few days – I've never done that, and he has
a place we can stay.

I may check out the possibility of getting a temporary E-mail address. I'm not sure if it's worth it. I hate being out of touch, but I
can call my parents on the phone once or twice, and you're obviously too busy to write. If you have time, send a report before I
go. Are you still in the thrall of Aphrodite? Is Terpsichore being
a cooperative girl? Tell all.

Big wet kiss.

Phil

Subj: Re: Bye-bye
Date: 7/28 1:51:53 PM Eastern Daylight Time
From: jbreaux@denpasar.wasantara.net.id
To: WitchBitch@camnet.net

Hi Phil,

I'm sorry I've been out of touch for so long, but as you say, between Aphrodite and Terpsichore, I don't have time left for mere
mortals. It's boring always to be saying this, but you just can't
imagine how busy I've been. Seems that Quentin Trent has to
come here much sooner than the time we'd agreed on, so I've
had to move the performances up by more than a month before

I'd planned. I told you, I always intended to schedule the performances for when he was here, so I could get a review in the Times. I cooked up a bogus tale for him about scheduling problems, and booked the ballroom for September 1 and 2. It's ridiculous the way we all bow and scrape and tug our forelocks to the New York Times, but if I don't get the review, this might as well not have happened.

Phil, I'm insane! The choreography isn't complete yet, and I haven't even thought about costumes or lighting. Sets are done, in a way – I'm using projections of Spies's paintings for the outdoor scenes, and they have these beautiful little fake-antique carved cabins (they're actually called opium beds), which will be perfect for the house and the jail, with different lighting. I shouldn't be chattering on about the piece. I don't mean that you're not interested in it, but you don't need to hear about all my boring problems, and there's so much I want to tell you. Mainly this: you know what? I think this piece is going to put my name on the map, move me from the "promising" category to Markville. It's a terrible thing, feeling hopeful. If this piece doesn't measure up, if Quentin comes out and writes a dismissive, sneering review of Joe Breaux's buggery ballet, I'm going to give up. Sell the apartment on Horatio Street and move to Bali. Grow a ponytail and ride around on a motorcycle, like the loser expats who live here. But I have a feeling that this is going to be the catapult. (Even as I write that, I can see the gods, thunderbolts poised.)

It's also turning into a financial investment – the Pouf money is running out. The grant was never meant to fund a full-length production; that's just my grandiosity. I'm having to pay everybody. I've also put Wayan on a salary, more than I should, probably – he's getting ten times more than the others, and of course he has no expenses. I know you'll disapprove, but it just seems like that's the way it's done here. Since it's Pouf money (in theory, at least), I think it's all right. Anyway, he's earning it – he's such a trouper. I couldn't do this without him. Since we shacked

up, the Balinese have sort of cut me off. I mean, they're polite
and cooperative, but if I stopped paying them they would disappear in a flash. Wayan is the main creative conduit between me
and them. I know he would like to go out and have some fun
once in a while, but he's so loyal. His little friends call him on
his hand phone, but he always tells them no.

I still can't believe this exquisite creature wants a hairy old
Cajun like me. I can't wait for you to meet him – you'll adore
him. He is SO excited about coming to America. He and his
buddies have such an exaggerated idea of what our way of life is
like. They think America is one big Disneyland. His favorite
movie of all time is "Grease" – he has all of Travolta's dance
moves down perfectly. His great ambition in life is to come to
America and star in Hollywood dance musicals. I've tried to explain to him that "Grease" was the last one they made. Can you
believe that "Grease" was made three years before Wayan was
born? I have to admit, that scares me. I was in high school. I'm
so sick of hearing that soundtrack, I can't tell you.

I know my relationship with him appears bizarre. I don't expect
you or anyone to understand. I can't really explain it, since it's
all new to me. It's not a partnership in the way that Andrew and
I were partners, sharing everything and making decisions
together. With Wayan, I have all the power. It's almost like fa-
therhood in a way: I want to help him so much, while he looks
to me for guidance, and desperately seeks my approval. There's
something so touching about the aspirations of young people.
I'll never forget the expression on his face the first time I told
him I wanted to bring him to New York. I can't think of
anything that could give me greater pleasure than to bring
Wayan to a place where his amazing talent will be appreciated.
No, that's stupid – of course his talent is appreciated here, but
artistically he's outgrowing the Balinese system. For one thing,
he's already too old for some of his best parts. I admire their
spiritual approach to dance here (how I blush when I think of
the gushy stuff I wrote you when I first got here!), but Wayan is

looking at a lifetime of selling fake antiques to foreigners, or maybe getting a job at a resort, making barely enough money to get by. Also, he told me that if I left Bali without him, he would probably have to get married – if his father could find a family that would accept him. The Balinese are much more conservative than I realized. Wayan's sort of like a "fallen woman" now. So in a way, I have an obligation to him. I can't leave him "S.P.A."

The thing is, I see no reason in the world why his dream can't come true, obviously not in film but on the stage. He can do anything he wants to do in dance, except classical ballet, which is out of the question. Of course I want him to go on with modern, but with some training he would be a fabulous Broadway dancer. Hell, he could do ballroom, though I wouldn't let him. I already have some ideas for the next piece I want to create for him, but no part for me this time. I'm ready to stop dancing, if I can make a go of it as a choreographer. How can I make Quentin Trent love this piece? Maybe I should get one of these witch doctors they have here on the case.

Yikes, what a long message this has turned out to be, it's nearly two a.m. But I had to tell all this to somebody – Angus and his crowd are so cynical, they would just laugh at me. Bob is hopeless; he thinks I'm going straight to Southern Baptist hell. So, babycakes, say hi to Tones, and have a great trip. You'll love the Edinburgh festival – when I did "Endymion" there, I had a ball. The Scots are wild men.

Love ya, get in touch when you can,

Joey

P.S. What am I going to tell Dad? He and Lu Ann are threatening to come out for the premiere. He still thinks Andrew's here. He's cool about the gay thing, but when he sees Wayan, he's going to flip.

Subj: Last goodbye
Date: 7/28 9:14:25 PM Eastern Daylight Time
From: WitchBitch@camnet.net
To: jbreaux@denpasar.wasantara.net.id

My dear Pinkerton,

I'm sitting in the posh departure lounge at the airport, plugged into one of their little businessman's cubicles with my free martini, feeling quite the jet-setting journalist. With this trip and my new job looming, I feel almost as though I'm setting off on my own little life-changing adventure, the way you did last spring. Maybe I'll meet some dreamy millionaire in the business-class cabin, who has an erotic fixation on slightly overweight drama critics – it seems vastly more probable than what happened to you.

I was wrong – it's such a delicious pleasure for a critic to be able to say that and not get into trouble. But I obviously misjudged your feelings for this boy. Under the circumstances, I don't think I was a cynic or a false friend to have reached the conclusions I did, but nonetheless, I was wrong. If it had just been a case of carnal attraction, you could never have written the lovely message I just received – you would be tearing your hair out and screeching, "What have I done?" In retrospect, I now see the persuasiveness of an argument you used early on: if it had just been about sex, even impetuous tiny you wouldn't have turned your life upside down the way you did.

You're right about something else – I don't understand it. It doesn't have the slightest appeal to me. It wouldn't matter if he was Donatello's David with permanent wood: I'm always the one who gets taken care of. Also, I think most American fathers might take issue with your premise that butt-fucking a heathen adolescent boy is like raising a son – but then, American fathers are confused about so many things. I do see the logic: instead of spanking him when he's naughty, you poke him when he's nice –

positive reinforcement, much more civilized. It's very Greek, what you're doing, playing Socrates and Alcibiades, you might say. It's about the same age difference, I think. You're taking the lad up at exactly the point where they begin to be amusing. The parents have dealt with all the dreary stuff like toilet training and how to tie shoelaces – now you can teach him some of the more interesting skills in life, like the importance of contrast and color coordination in choosing an ensemble, the proper way to open and pour a bottle of champagne, and techniques useful in another activity I have been chided for mentioning in previous messages.

I'm afraid the martini is beginning to affect my ability to type. Anyway, I just wanted to say goodbye for now. This E-mail address will expire while I'm in Angleterre, so you must wait to hear from me.

Me wuv oo.

Suzuki

Subj: Joe Breaux
Date: 8/10 4:52:26 AM Eastern Daylight Time
From: BBlankenship@indonet.net.id
To: jahull@POF.org

Dear Jerry,

I'm sorry it has taken me longer than usual to answer your last message. I understand your concern about Joe Breaux, and I'm glad you came to me about it. No, Joe Breaux's production isn't falling apart. Yes, he's having some problems, particularly with the Western dancers, who are unreliable and not very well-trained. But I saw him yesterday afternoon, and he has ironed all that out. He went to Jakarta over the weekend, and has found dancers to replace the ones who dropped out. He says they're

better than the ones he had cast before, and in any case they're
bit parts. I think I know who told Erica Golden about the problems Joe's been having, and I wish she would mind her own
business. With the Internet, it's now as easy to gossip halfway
round the world as it is over the backyard fence. This constant,
irresponsible gossip in the expat community is one of the worst
aspects of living in Bali.

Far from falling apart, Joe's progress on this production is astonishing. Of course he's having problems: he's trying to create a
new work of modern dance in Bali, where there is virtually no
precedent for such a project, and few resources to draw upon. I
am in awe of his energy no less than of his talent. Indeed, there's
something almost Herculean about what he's doing.

Jerry, we're old friends, and I will be frank with you. As I said, I
can't abide gossip, which is why I have thus far refrained from
expressing my views about Joe and the whole situation here. But
I must confess that personally, I find his conduct with Wayan
Renda to be deplorable. It may not be illegal, but I think it is immoral and irresponsible. As you know, I myself am similarly ori-
entated, but I believe that homosexuals (how I detest the
prevalent misuse of the word "gay"!) should adhere to the same
moral standards as the rest of society. However, I don't believe
that it is my place to judge his or anyone else's private behavior,
and furthermore, I strongly believe that his personal life should
have no bearing on how he is viewed as an artist.

I realize that he is pushing the boundaries of good taste with the
subject matter of his new piece. Indeed, when he first outlined it
to me, I was shocked. However, I now believe that he is quite
sincere in what he is doing, and has no cynical intention to create a scandal and get cheap publicity for himself. From a histori-
cal point of view, it is scrupulously accurate, as far as I know.
And I may tell you, I think it is going to be a brilliant piece. I
don't know much about modern dance; to be frank, I usually
find myself feeling perplexed and bored, wondering, What on

earth are those people doing? But Joe's piece is engaging on so many levels.

Now you know my thinking on this matter. I hope I have reassured you. Joe's undertaking may be a bit bizarre, but you and the foundation have no reason to feel anything but satisfaction for being associated with it. Even the Balinese are getting into the spirit: I think most of them don't really understand the homosexual theme, or turn a blind eye, and the idea of an American coming here to stage a piece about their beloved Walter Spies is a source of great pride to them. Their resentment about his personal affairs seems to be waning; the Balinese sometimes react violently, but they seldom hold a grudge.

If you have ever thought about visiting Bali, now is the time to do so. You and Alexandra are more than welcome to stay here with me.

Best wishes,

Bob

Subj: My new laptop
Date: 8/19 5:11:26 PM Pacific Daylight Time
From: AndrewTan@wol.com
To: etan@MIT.edu (Eric Tan)

Hey bro',

I went out to Oakland yesterday and bought myself the niftiest laptop. I decided that I couldn't go computerless any longer, and they're so cheap and powerful now . . . my new $1,900 Compaq is so much faster than your three-year-old Mac desktop, which cost a fortune, and the screen's almost as good as a real monitor. It's great to be back on-line, but it seems as though almost every

website nowadays wants your Visa account number. And there's
so much porn, it's disgusting. The thing came loaded with soft-
ware, ten times more than any sane person would ever need . . .
and *of course* it included the inescapable WOL, so now we
can get back into E-mail. The phone is great, but E-mail is more
fun, somehow.

I showed the computer to Dad last night, and he was very impressed. I can't believe he doesn't know how to use one. At the
institute, I guess he's so grand that everyone just does everything
for him. We checked out the City of San Francisco website,
which had a little video with Judy Garland singing "San
Francisco" on the soundtrack. Dad was giggling like a little kid.
Dad, giggling! Then we searched his name. There was a lot of
junk, of course, but we found an article in a British journal that
disagreed with something Dad wrote a few years ago. That
really impressed him. He said the guy was all wrong (big surprise), and he was going to write him a letter. I pointed out that
if he were on-line, he could send his letter to the guy by E-mail. I
think this was the first time in my life I ever did anything with
him that he didn't know ten times more about than me. I told
him I would go back to Oakland and buy a computer for him,
and he was horrified.

I think it was a good idea for me to come out here. It's great to
spend some time with Mom, and Dad has been nicer to me than
he has in ages. It's the first time I've been here in years without
Joey; Dad was always so busy trying to impress Joey that he forgot about me. But it's always the same problem when the three
of us are together, him putting down Mom with his nasty little
cracks. If she ever asks him to repeat anything, he SHOUTS – IT
– LIKE – THIS. Why am I telling you all this when you know it
perfectly well? I'm on Day 6, so I'm just reaching the point
where I to start to go batty. I still haven't worked up the nerve to
talk to Dad about my Big Plan.

You told me not to say it again, but you and Soph were great to take me in for so long. I don't know what I would have done without you. I miss you!

Love from your brother

Subj: Re: My new laptop
Date: 8/21 8:21:52 AM Eastern Daylight Time
From: etan@MIT.edu (Eric Tan)
To: AndrewTan@wol.com

---

hi,

your new computer sounds totally cool, dude. i think i'm about ready for an upgrade myself. but i'll kill you if you get dad on line. he'll pester me to death.

andy, don't let dad get to you, he's just a grouchy old guy who's getting to be an older and grouchier old guy. don't forget, he's facing retirement next year, though i'm sure he'll get around it. he'll go on forever, like de bakey. nothing much going on here, sophie's getting over her morning sickness, thank god. she's doing fine now. hey, we miss YOU. sophie said the other day how much fun it was having you around.

e

Subj: I'm back!
Date: 8/23 5:36:12 PM Pacific Daylight Time
From: podonnell@sfchronicle.com
To: jbreaux@denpasar.wasantara.net.id

Hello, World – I'm back!

Yes, it's me. Actually, I've been back for a week, and every time I passed a cybercafe I felt a twinge of guilt for not sending you a message. This is going to be a quick blast of news. Tones was adorable, told me all her deepest darkest, the titty magazine loved the piece, the Savoy was beyond dreamy. Sophia Loren was staying there at the same time – I pounced on her while she was waiting for the elevator and got an autograph. Edinburgh was a hoot, mon. Geoff and I stayed with some boys – I call them that because they were all in their twenties. Geoff used to date the older brother of one of them. It was basically a gay crash pad, little tiny bedrooms all in a row. They were nice wee lads, to be sure, but ach, were they nae wild! Every night was a party. The festival was fabby. I saw your buddy Mark's new piece, a pretty rotten early Verdi by the Scottish Opera, and tons of theatre of course, but I won't go into that, it was all British.

And now San Francisco has opened its Golden Gate for me. Yesterday I signed the lease on a bijou ground-floor apartment with a pretty little garden on Larkin Street, just off Polk Gulch. Conveniently located near all the camp memorabilia and used record stores, not to mention the city's most distinguished wrinkle rooms. I don't start work for a week, but I came in this morning for what they called orientation. Part of it was to get my E-mail address, so now I'm back in communication with tiny you. The great thing is that unlike the Globe, here I can check my mail at home.

I really can't chat for long – the only thing that's unpacked is the computer. I am so excited to be here, I can't tell you. I have money in the bank, I have a garden apartment in a neighborhood seething with sissies, and the Chronicle is treating me like royalty (which is only appropriate). It was great fun there this morning, modestly saying I had just come back from London, where I interviewed Sir Anthony Hopkins (pronouncing it "Antony" to show them how swave and cosmopolitan I am) for Playboy. And how thrilling that the culture editor asked me where I stayed in London! I'll pay for this. Vanitas, vanitas, omnia vanitas. That's your actual Latin for "Che sera, sera."

Send me Chrissie's phone number, and I'll invite her up for a lunch. And how about all those friends you were going to introduce me to? I realize you're insanely busy now, but send a brief message when you can.

Ta tante Phyllis t'aime.

Subj: Sass
Date: 8/24 11:31:22 AM Pacific Daylight Time
From: AndrewTan@wol.com
To: etan@MIT.edu (Eric Tan)

Hi Eric,

Remember how Dad used to send us to our room if we sassed him? As I recall, his definition of sass was basically saying anything except "Yes, Father." Well, last night I sassed him, and he was the one who got sent to his room. In a manner of speaking. At dinner, he was needling Mom because she had served the wrong kind of sauce with a roast leg of lamb . . . it's always the cosmic issues that set him off. She apologized and got up from her chair to get what he wanted, and he almost shouted at her, "Sit down, Candace. That's what we have servants for," and rang the bell. So I said, very calmly, "Dad, I don't think you should shout at Mother like that. It isn't polite." His eyes were like saucers, but he didn't say anything. After about five minutes of everyone silently chewing and staring at their plates, he said, "Perhaps you're right, Andrew, I didn't express myself as politely as I ought to have done. Candace, I'm sorry that I raised my voice slightly, but. . . ." then he launched into Tirade No. 37B about how she doesn't pay enough attention to details in running the kitchen, but it was much more subdued than usual. I was *so* surprised that A. he told me I was right, and B. he apologized to Mom (though the "slightly" is vintage Raymond, isn't it?).

There's one more bit of news . . . don't laugh . . . I have a date! Isn't that hilarious? I met him at Brooks Brothers. We were both buying chinos. About my age, athletic looking, and the best part is . . . he's a doctor. Don't you love it? He seems nice. We're going to have dinner tomorrow. I'll give you a report in my next message.

Anyway, I have to run now. I'm having lunch with Nat MacDonald at the club. Remember him? He was a classmate of mine at Stanford, art history major; now he's working for the city landmarks commission. He called Dad, and I answered the phone.

Love to all Tans from your brother

Subj: Welcome to Bali
Date: 8/24 9:12:52 PM Eastern Daylight Time
From: jbreaux@denpasar.wasantara.net.id
To: RayjnKayjn@labell.net

Dear Dad,

I'm really glad you're coming to Bali. Of course you and Lu Ann are welcome to stay here, there's plenty of room, but I think we ought to consider putting you up at one of the nice, not-so-expensive hotels around here until the performances are over – I've been working long hours, and I'll hardly have time to eat dinner with you. Of course, after the last performance I'll have plenty of time to hang out.

There's another reason you might want to stay at a hotel. I guess if you're at the computer, you're already sitting down, but . . . this is going to be very difficult for both of us. This will be the hardest letter for me to write since I told you and Mama that I was gay.

Andrew and I have broken up. He went back to the States a couple of weeks ago. I am now living here with my new friend, a Balinese man named Wayan Renda. He's a brilliant dancer, and my partner in the new piece. Dad, he's 21 years old. I know that will be shocking to you, but we really care a lot for each other, and I have no doubt in my mind that I'm doing the right thing. I hope you won't be too upset. I thought about lying to you, and making him stay somewhere else, but that would be sneaky, and unfair to him. Anyway, you're too smart – you would've figured out that something was up.

I don't think I ought to go into an elaborate defense of my personal life – that's just what it is. You have always been open-minded and supportive, and I hope this won't change anything. However, I think it might be better if you didn't stay here – it would just be too strange for everyone. And if you reconsider your decision to come to Bali, I'll understand.

Dad, I love you. You and Chrissie are my only family, and even though we're separated now by geography, I still think of us as being together. I hope you won't be too upset by this.

Your son,

Joey

Subj: Re: I'm back!
Date: 8/24 9:13:11 PM Eastern Daylight Time
From: jbreaux@denpasar.wasantara.net.id
To: podonnell@sfchronicle.com

Hi Phil,

Welcome back, babee. Sorry, no time to write much more than that. Dad sent me a message a few days ago announcing that he and and Lu Ann were coming out for the premiere. I just sent him a message back, telling him about Wayan. I'm very nervous. A thousand problems with the piece, but it's basically coming together. I'm so glad you're back, Phil. There's so much I want to tell you, but at the moment I have a houseful of Balinese tailors making Dutch colonial policemen's uniforms, and a bored boyfriend who wants me to play with him.

Love ya,

Joey

P.S. Almost forgot, Chrissie's phone number is 408-550-8712. Tell her I'm sorry I haven't answered her letters. I guess you better tell her what happened.

Subj: The Big Talk
Date: 8/26 9:53:52 PM Pacific Daylight Time
From: AndrewTan@wol.com
To: etan@MIT.edu (Eric Tan)

Hi Eric,

Well, I finally screwed up my courage and had the Big Talk with Dad last night. Actually, he was great, very supportive. He said a few things that definitely let me know that he has been disappointed in me because I didn't go into a profession of some sort, the ol' "I respect your decision not to study medicine, but I wish you had done something else worthy of Raymond Tan's son." No, that's wrong. I'm making it sound more negative than it was. He did say some of the usual crap, but much less. The main thing he said was, Yeah, that's a good decision and a useful calling. He's going to set up interviews with some of the big Bay Area charities, not for jobs but for research, fact-gathering. Just being rich and "socially prominent" (barf) isn't enough. As Dad pointed out, in the beginning I might have to take a low-level

job to learn how they operate, maybe even enroll in some
courses.

I am beginning to realize that, to certain extent, I was spoiled. It
was the Chinese version of being spoiled, meaning that I was always a good little boy, but my life was guided by the principle
that if I did everything my father told me and made good grades,
I would get everything I wanted . . . and it would always be the
best (like in my story). One Toyota between the two of us would
have been fine for us at Stanford, but Raymond Tan's sons had
to drive new BMW's. I think Dad should have done with us
what most parents do: you're 21, you're on your own. It was
okay for you . . . with that brain of yours, it was always clear
that you would do postgrad work. (And don't think you're supposed to say something nice back to me, we both know you're
the brain.) But there was never any need for me to take charge
of my life . . . first Dad was in charge, they Joey took over.

I'm starting to think that getting dumped by Joey was the best
thing that ever happened to me. I feel so much stronger now. I
know he loved me . . . that part was equal . . . but I was basically
an accessory for Joey's Fabulous Life. How it would hurt his
feelings to hear that, but it's true. I'm starting to like making my
own choices. It's the little things, like controlling my diet. Joey
was always "surprising" me at breakfast with bacon and eggs
and hash browns, or pecan waffles and sausages, huge steaming
piles of heavy food first thing in the morning. It was easy for
him; he was dancing and working out all day. For me it was another half hour on the treadmill. This morning I had yogurt and
a slice of toast for breakfast.

Is the hour almost over, Doc? Sorry, Eric, but I've been thinking
a lot about these things. Also, I've been wondering, do you think
that maybe Dad was so nice to me when I told him about my
plan because I stood up for Mom the other night?

Love from your soul-searching kid brother

Subj: Re: The Big Talk
Date: 8/27 9:32:01 AM Eastern Daylight Time
From: etan@MIT.edu (Eric Tan)
To: AndrewTan@wol.com

---

hi,

maybe. i don't think dad's a bastard on purpose, he just gets impatient with people who don't keep up with him. maybe you're right – i think he likes to be challenged, and his needling mom is just a habit. i wish just once she would say, ray, shut up. he probably wishes he could stop doing it as much as we do. i think everything you said about joey makes a lot of sense. i always liked the guy, and he's a brilliant artist, but he was a little too intense for me, a little too bigger-than-life. a weekend in lenox with you and him was a lot more demanding than when you came up by yourself. he was always interesting and full of fun, but i guess i don't need to have that much fun. i'm glad you can come to these insights without a sense of regret. those were NOT wasted years. all the experiences and emotions you shared with joey were valid then, and they're valid now. i'm sure that in time, you'll be good friends again.

the house is filling up with baby stuff, why does it all have to be so whimsical? why is it assumed that babies have bad taste? hey, you didn't give me a report on your date. is he a nice guy?

the doctor's office is always open.

e

Subj: Dear Son
Date: 8/27 6:42:12 PM Central Daylight Time
From: RayjnKayjn@labell.net
To: jbreaux@denpasar.wasantara.net.id

Dear Son,

I'm sorry to say that I am shocked by your news. When your
mother and I received your letter telling us that you were gay,
we sat down and cried. We never told you that. Of course we
knew. You and Andrew had been "roommates" for a couple of
years by that point, without one word about girls. But seeing it
in black-and-white like that was a tough blow for us. That just
isn't the way it's supposed to be. I'm not talking about the doo-
doo the Church dishes out on this subject, you know how I feel
about that, but it's just not the natural order of things. Your
mother never had grandchildren, and Chrissie looks like she's
never going to get married. Hell, I suppose now she's going to
tell me she's a Lezbo. But your mother and I sat down that night
and decided that you were our son, no matter what, and so we
wrote you back and said what we said. It was somewhat easier
for us because we knew Andrew, who is such a nice young man,
so polite and well-bred. If you had come to us dressed in black
leather and told us you were prowling around in public parks, it
would have been a lot different.

I'm not disowning you or anything like that, Son, but I am
pretty heartsick to hear this. I'm sure it's not illegal or anything
like that, but 21 is just too darn close to child-molesting to suit
me. It's your life and you can live it however you please. It's not
for me to approve or disapprove. But Son, I'm just a retired
building contractor from Covington, Louisiana, and this is more
than I can handle.

I guess you've figured out that Lu Ann and I aren't coming, but
we both wish you success with your new composition. Joey, I do
love you. You're my son and I'm proud of your many

accomplishments, but I don't want to hear another word about this business.

Dad

Subj: The Big Date
Date: 8/28 11:53:52 AM Pacific Daylight Time
From: AndrewTan@wol.com
To: etan@MIT.edu (Eric Tan)

Hi Eric,

This morning I met with a friend of Dad's at the Kappan Foundation. It went pretty well. He suggested that if I was serious I should enroll in a summer seminar they have at Stanford, an intensive course in philanthropic administration. That would be weird, to be back in Palo Alto after all these years. He said if I had that, I should be able to find a good mid-level position, with my credentials and "background." I hate that, but I suppose, why not let it work for me? I guess the foundations might like the idea of having Raymond Tan show up at all their parties. Which he does anyway.

You asked about my date . . . what a disaster! Not a disaster, really, but definitely not a match. He was the one who invited me, so he chose Bacchus. Do you know it? New since we were in California (but so is practically everything). It's an ultra-romantic, generic continental restaurant in the financial district, very expensive but a bit tacky, with swags of red velvet everywhere, and fake Greek marble statues. Food was okay, if you like foie gras and lobster . . . and you know I do! He was actually a nice enough guy. He's a pediatrician . . . I guess they have to have nice personalities. Very smart, and knew about something besides medicine, so unusual for a doctor. But he lost any chance with me when the bottle of Dom Perignon was brought to the table as soon as we sat down. "I took the liberty. I hope you like champagne." It was so overpowering. I was very friendly throughout dinner, but I was a bit starchy when he asked me if I wanted to come back to his place for coffee. I said, "We just had coffee, and one cup is my limit. I enjoyed meeting you, Don, but I really ought to be heading home." He looked so disappointed.

Maybe it's mean of me, but it gave me a little thrill. It's been a long time since I've had that feeling of being chased after, of being completely in control of the situation. And he was quite handsome, too. During the dinner, he had talked about how hard it was to meet "quality single gay guys our age, all the good ones have been taken," etc. I think by quality, he meant well-off and decent-looking. I'm sure he's right, but even hinting at sex on the first date is a definite no-no. I may be out of practice, but I do remember that much.

Meanwhile, I'm starting to hang out some with Nat MacDonald. I really like him a lot. He's an architect, very smart. I would have guessed that he's gay, but he told me he was divorced. Of course, that's not exactly conclusive. Anyway, I'm not quite ready to start dating (though the look on that guy's face when I told him I didn't want to come home with him for "coffee" was a kick). Anyway, Nat's a good, interesting new/old friend. He's taking me to some sort of special performance at the Berkeley Rep next week. Also, I've played tennis with Marnie Steele twice a week since I got here. All in all, it's quite a buzzing social life for me. Poor Andrea Rudner has called me three times. I guess she doesn't have anyone she can take to the Inn for overdone roast beef and tell her opinions about Philip Roth to. Thank god she doesn't have E-mail.

I'm rambling. Send news about the pregnancy. Is there such a thing? I guess I mean, send Sophie my love.

Andy

Subj: Screech!
Date: 8/28 3:23:51 PM Eastern Daylight Time
From: jbreaux@denpasar.wasantara.net.id
To: podonnell@sfchronicle.com

Hi Phil,

I don't have time to write you, but I have to talk to someone – I
feel like I'm losing my mind. I almost picked up the phone to
call you, but you can't imagine how expensive it is here. Three
times what it is at home.

I feel like whoever it was who was trying to kill the Hydra –
every time I put out one fire, three more flare up. I won't go into
details: sound system at the Radisson sucks dead weenie, my
Barbara Hutton is hopeless, can't remember a goddamn thing. I
may have to cut my duet with her. Wayan's hanging in there, but
he's starting to get testy. If I say anything critical, he goes into a
pout. Everything is still basically fine between us, but it's just
such a strain. We haven't had time for anything resembling fun
in weeks. After the show, we're going to Jakarta for a week, do
some big city stuff. I booked a room at the Regent – no way I
can afford it, but I feel like I need to make it up to him
somehow.

It's all being exacerbated by . . . a little problem that seems to be
developing. I've been doing drugs in a smallish way. There's just
no other way I can stay up and get everything done that needs to
be done. The problem is, I'm the only one who knows the
answers to the questions, and I can't explain them to anyone
else, not really. In terms of movement, Wayan always knows exactly what I want, but he has no idea about the rest of it. How
can you explain what you want the set to look like to someone
who's never seen a set before? So I have to do almost everything
myself. I've conceived the piece on much too elaborate a scale
for the resources I have.

Don't lecture me, bitch – I'm not doing anything heavy, just a few choreographer's little helpers Angus got for me, and some pot at night to relax and get in the mood with Wayan. Better than a bottle of Scotch a day like Tim, right? But it's not good – sometimes in the morning I have these terrible panic attacks, a moment of not knowing where I am or who anyone else is. I'm going to be pure 24 hours before the performance. And of course stop completely after that.

And to top things off, Quentin arrived today. He dropped by the Radisson, "just to say hi, don't stop rehearsing just for me," but of course I had to be charming and talk to him, all the while feeling the time clicking away, like in a junky thriller movie. Will this dance piece reach the stage before the bomb explodes and destroys the planet? Stay tuned. . . .

Love ya,

Joey

Subj: Chit-chat
Date: 8/28 9:13:22 PM Pacific Daylight Time
From: podonnell@sfchronicle.com
To: jbreaux@denpasar.wasantara.net.id

Pal Joey,

One of the great shows, in my opinion Richard Rodgers' best score, and sadly neglected. Why don't they revive that instead of all the drippy stuff he did with Oscar Hammerstein II? And what the hell kind of a last name is II, anyway? I've been busy as a bee around here, playing interior decorator. I repainted the dining room – can you believe I have an actual dining room? I painted it pale mauve, almost lavender, and went out and bought a table for it. Walnut, round. Your sister was the first person to dine on it. She came up Saturday for lunch. She's such a sweetie-pie. I guess I was wrong about her, she told me that she's thinking of marrying that guy Allen. The biological-clock motive – she wants to have babies, but she's not sure Allen's the one. I said, dating someone for five years is a pretty good sign that you get along, at least. I didn't say it, but it's actually a long time to stay just dating, without at least trying moving in together. She said to tell you that she's mad at you for not answering her letters. She's going to write you about this marriage business, and if you don't answer her, she's going to cut you off without a dime. I tried to stick up for you, and told her how busy you were with the new piece. I did tell her about you and Andrew – she was pretty shocked.

What else can I tell you? I start work on Monday. My first big assignment is a gala premiere at the Berkeley Rep. Franklin Jones, the chief drama critic, was nice about letting me do it – it's a plum, and ordinarily he would get it, but I guess they want to trumpet my arrival. They're doing Medea, one of the fun Greeks. I love the poisonous cloak – oooh, that girl was nasty! The kid who drove my car out from Bahston finally arrived, over a week late. At least the car's in good shape, but now it smells like cigarette smoke, ugh. The rest is all boring homemaker's chit-chat, and I know you're not interested in that stuff. It's your latent heterosexuality peeking through.

Love from the mad interior decoratrix

P.S. Your premiere is in three days – I won't bug you again until then. Rip a leotard, baby! and send me a complete report IMMEDIATELY afterward. I mean 500 words, minimum, dated September 3.

Subj: Re: Screech!
Date: 8/28 10:31:52 PM Pacific Daylight Time
From: podonnell@sfchronicle.com
To: jbreaux@denpasar.wasantara.net.id

Joey,

Your message crossed mine in the cyberpost, so I got right back
on line. You sound terrible, lovebug. I'm not going to scold you,
but <<I get these terrible panic attacks, a moment of not knowing where I am or who anyone else is>> is worse than not good.
Just try to relax, and for heaven's sake, stop taking those pills.
Pot I'm not going to comment on except to remind you that it
was a problem for you fairly recently. But whatever they're calling it, speed is DANGEROUS. You don't want to have a psycho
attack while you're on stage. I just wish I could be there to help
you glue sequins to leotards or whatever it is that's keeping you
up so late. I'm sure Quentin will understand the challenges
you're up against there and take that into account. Don't forget,
he loves your work. His review of "Rodeo" was Blow Job City.

It was Hercules who slew the Hydra, and I can't think of a more apt
mythological parallel for what you're doing. Remember, Hercules
killed that Hydra, and you're going to knock 'em dead, too.

Love from Phil

Subj: Joseph Breaux review
Date: 9/2 11:57:04 AM Eastern Daylight Time
From: quentin.trent
To: christina.dellacasa

Tina,

My review of Joseph Breaux's new piece follows. As you will
see, I think it's an important work. I don't know what else

you've got kicking around, but please make every effort to give this the lead position. I would rather you held it until you can do so. (Mine will be the only review outside Indonesia, so no worry on that score.) The photographer, Alison Willis (awillis@indonet.net.id), promises to transmit what she has by the end of the day. Remember, I'm also writing a feature for A&L, so you have to share the good stuff with them. Thanks! I'll be here for another two days, if there's a problem.

Headline: Anything that doesn't include the phrase "Bali High"
Byline: Quentin Trent
Dateline: Denpasar, Bali

Bali has a dance tradition as elegant and sophisticated as any in the world, but Western dance is all but unknown here. When Joseph Breaux, one of the brightest rising stars in American dance, was awarded a Pullman-Oliphant Foundation grant to come to this tiny island in the middle of the Indonesian archipelago to study and perform, he was following in some distinguished footsteps: Ruth St. Denis and Martha Graham both raided the treasure-house of Southeast Asian dance for movement material.

Yet whereas St. Denis and Graham were appropriating gestural bites for a style very much their own, with his new work, "Elegy for Walter Spies," Mr. Breaux boldly tells his story with traditional Balinese and Western modern dance set side by side. What he has done, in effect, is to create a new genre. This piece is not yet another example of the dreaded fusion, but rather a dance mosaic, in which disparate styles tell the story formally as well as narratively.

And what a provocative story he has chosen! Walter Spies, the German artist, musician, and choreographer, came to Bali in 1927 and stayed for fourteen years, creating one of the most vibrant art colonies in the world. He had a profound impact on the arts here; among his many accomplishments, he choreographed the kecak, one of the most popular works in the Balinese repertoire. Spies was also a pedophilic homosexual. In 1938 a Dutch colonial court convicted him of committing sodomy with an underage boy, even though the lad's father had testified on Spies' behalf at the trial.

Using the music of Colin McPhee, a Canadian composer who was living in Bali at the same time as Spies, Mr. Breaux has choreographed what amounts to a defense of gay pedophilia, or at least a highly romanticized view of it – and he has audaciously cast in the lead roles himself as Walter Spies, and in the part of the Boy his own real-life lover, a 20-year-old Balinese dancer named Wayan Renda.

While many will find the subject matter offensive, taken on its own terms Mr. Breaux's "Elegy" is an astonishing technical accomplishment. He has recruited semiprofessional Western dancers living in Indonesia to perform the roles of the foreigners, and coaxed from them reasonable approximations of the exuberant movements that made Mr. Breaux's previous work, "Rodeo," such a joyous affair. The members of the Seka Kerobokan, the organization in Bali with which Mr. Breaux has been associated, dance the Balinese roles.

The result is a brilliant formal synthesis: the theme of "East meets West" is enacted literally on the stage. The music illustrates it, too: McPhee, a brilliant yet unjustly neglected composer, scored his music for traditional Western symphony orchestra based on Balinese principles, creating an evocative, at times bizarre sound world.

As Walter Spies, Mr. Breaux's performance is mercurial and eccentric, constantly threatening to wobble out of control yet never quite doing so, presumably portraying Spies' unstable mental condition. Every time the piece risks lurching into sentimentality (of questionable taste, at that) the choreographer's wit makes a correction. In a deliciously ironic set piece, Mr. Breaux,

who has been in Bali for four months, "teaches" the kecak to a
Balinese troupe famed locally for its exciting performances of
the work. The mostly Balinese audience was convulsed with
laughter.

Yet it was Wayan Renda's performance as the Boy that was the
dramatic linchpin of the evening. Mr. Renda may be only 20
years old, but he has an emotional maturity far beyond his
years. He is also an astonishingly talented dancer, who has taken
the enchanting movements of Balinese dance and used them to
create a character that plausibly inhabits a work of modern
dance. He is exhilarating to behold, moving with a sure-footed
grace that at times seems to defy gravity.

In the finale, the Boy comes to the jailhouse where Spies is being
held, and sings a song for him, accompanied by a gamelan, or
Balinese percussion orchestra. For this scene, McPhee's orchestral music is set aside in favor of a traditional Balinese composition, performed by the gamelan of the Seka Kerobokan. It was a
risky move for Mr. Breaux; it might easily have been a saccha-
rine rather than a moving moment. Yet Mr. Renda, who is possessed of a lovely high-tenor voice, makes a bittersweet, bravura
turn of it. One by one, the instruments of the gamelan drop out,
in the manner of the Haydn "Farewell" symphony, so that in the
end, the Boy croons plaintively, alone on the stage, standing
quite still.

Mr. Breaux's vision has been inhibited to some extent by the
quality of the Western dancers available to him here. In the role
of Barbara Hutton, the American heiress who came to Bali and
fell in love with Spies, Francesca d'Arco simply can't do what
Mr. Breaux had in mind for her in their comic duet. The quartet
of Margaret Mead, Gregory Bateson, Ruth Draper and Noel
Coward, all house guests of Spies' at various times (played by
Dawn Kennedy, Bart Dollar, Constance McKuen and Frederick
Pfitzer) succeed rather better because they are constantly moving
in a pack. The same dancers, with the women in male costume,

portray the grim-faced Dutch authorities with a heavy hand. The principal Balinese dancers, Komang Sukarta, as the Boy's Father, Kompyang Putri, as the Boy's Mother, and Rai Runtun, as Prince Gde Agung Sukawati, were, of course, completely persuasive in their roles, moving with the mesmerizing elegance distinctive of the island's ancient dance tradition.

Mr. Breaux has said that he hopes to bring "Elegy for Walter Spies" to the U.S.; one hopes that he will succeed in doing so. The theme of man-boy love will be repugnant to many Americans, though as Mr. Breaux's piece makes dramatically clear, the imposition of Western morals on tropical Asia can only have disastrous results. The two performances of the work here gave the impression that the preparation of the piece was rushed, and one would wish that in future performances Mr. Breaux will have the benefit of professional scenic, costume and lighting designers. Nonetheless, the piece is boldly original, and comprises more intelligence, wit and dramatic intensity – indeed, more ideas – than any new American dance work witnessed by this critic in years.

Subj: Omigod
Date: 9/4 8:53:25 AM Pacific Daylight Time
From: podonnell@sfchronicle.com
To: jbreaux@denpasar.wasantara.net.id

Omigod,

I'm sure you've already seen it but if not, go IMMEDIATELY to the Times website and read Quentin's review. It's beyond a blow job, it's every sex act in the Kama Sutra and Masters and Johnson combined. <<the piece is boldly original, and comprises more intelligence, wit and dramatic intensity – indeed, more ideas – than any new American dance work witnessed by this critic in years.>> Joey, you're FUCKING FAMOUS!!!! I'm a newspaper critic, and I can read between the lines: it's obvious that the Western dancers were a disaster, and the staging looked amateurish, but he understood what you were doing, and he was KNOCKED OUT. It's also clear that you haven't been exaggerating Wayan's talent. Petal, the Times publishes a review like that about once a year, and this is your year.

I have so much more I want to say, but my review of Medea must be finished and polished by 4 p.m. I'm afraid it rather left me yearning for Diana Rigg, but I've already been warned about saying that anything here isn't as good as New York. We're a cheerleading hometown paper. You'll never guess who I ran into at the theatre – Andrew! We had a nice little chat. He told me he might be moving back to San Francisco. We made a lunch date for next week. I hope you won't think I'm being wicked to tell you this, but he was with a very rugged-looking fellow named Nat MacSomething. Shoulders to sigh for.

Congratulations, Joey. I'm so proud of you.

Phil

Subj: Congratulations
Date: 9/4 4:14:53 PM Eastern Daylight Time
From: jahull@POF.org
To: jbreaux@denpasar.wasantara.net.id

Dear Joe,

Congratulations on the glowing review in today's New York Times. I know how important that is for a performer. Bob Blankenship has kept me apprised of your progress, and from what he tells me, all of those superlatives in Quentin's review were well deserved. Everyone here at the Pullman-Oliphant

Foundation is proud to be associated with you, and I personally couldn't be more pleased by your success.

The phone calls and E-mail are already starting to pour in: "How can I get in touch with Joseph Breaux?" I assume you have no objection to my giving out your E-mail address to serious impresarios and presenting institutions. Don't let them have it cheap! After that review, everyone in the dance world will be lining up to see it.
Again, hearty congratulations, Joe.

All the best,

Jerry Hull

Subj: Message from Sid Markowitz
Date: 9/5 9:42:21 AM Eastern Daylight Time
From: sidney_markowitz@nycitycenter.org
To: jbreaux@denpasar.wasantara.net.id

Dear Mr. Breaux,

I got your E-mail address from Jerry Hull at the Pullman-Oliphant Foundation. I hope you don't mind me getting in touch with you this way. First, I want to congratulate you on the marvelous review of "Elegy for Walter Spies," by Quentin Trent, in the New York Times. I believe that Quentin is a straight shooter and the best dance critic in America. After that review, I'm sure you agree with me!

Of course, my main reason in writing you is to open a line of communication to explore the possibility of you performing the piece at City Center at some point in the future. I'm afraid the fall and spring seasons are pretty firmly booked, but by next June we have some open dates. I hope you'll keep us in mind; we would be delighted to present the American premiere of this work.

Again, congratulations. I'm looking forward to hearing from you.

Sid Markowitz, President
New York City Center Foundation for the Performing Arts

Subj: Congratulations
Date: 9/5 12:02:14 PM Eastern Daylight Time
From: norman@joyce.org (Margo Norman)
To: jbreaux@denpasar.wasantara.net.id

Dear Joe,

Congratulations on that stunning review in the Times. I always knew you would be a great choreographer, and I'm not just saying that to suck up to you. It's true. I said those exact words to Tim Winner the day they announced the POF grant last spring. Tim called me up this morning; he asked me to tell you how proud he is of you.

Joe, we here at the Joyce would be thrilled to present the American premiere of "Elegy for Walter Spies." I'm afraid we can't think about anything before next summer, unless somebody drops out, in which case you would be the first person I would call. I assume it will take you a while to prepare the piece here, anyway. After reading Quentin's review, I'm dying to see Wayan Renda dance. I don't always agree with Quentin, but he never exaggerates about dancers.

Let me know when you're back in New York, and we'll have lunch someplace swanky, on the Joyce.

Cheers,

Margo

Subj: I'm pissed!
Date: 9/5 12:40:26 PM Pacific Daylight Time
From: AndrewTan@wol.com
To: etan@MIT.edu (Eric Tan)

Hi Eric,

I am *so* goddamn pissed off. Why the hell did Quentin Trent
have to say that that guy is Joey's "real-life lover"? It has
absolutely nothing to do with the artistic merits of the piece.
Now everybody who knows us has read it in the goddamn
newspaper of record: Joe Breaux dumped Andrew Tan for a 20-
year-old kid. If that's how old he really is. Every time I hear
about that guy, he's a different age. Joey told me he was 21, then
Phil O'Donnell said he was 19, and now in the New York Times
he's 20. Oh, what difference does it make? It's so humiliating!
When I read Quentin's review, all I could think about were those
blissful days we spent together in Walter Spies's bungalow when
we first got to Bali. I'm starting to feel angry again; I thought I
was over all that. Of course I know it's not Joey's fault . . . it's
not such a great thing for him, either. He told me what the piece
was going to be about, and I told him I thought it sounded
great, but that was before I found out he was screwing his how-
ever-old-he-is partner. Eric, I'm Barbara Hutton! It's too close,
the dumb heiress chasing after the fag, who can't get away fast
enough.

What am I going to say to him? I have to write him, as we need
to decide what to do with the apartment. I hope he will agree to
sell it, otherwise it will be too complicated. I'm not going to just
give him half an apartment in Greenwich Village.

Grrrr.

Me

Subj: Re: I'm pissed!
Date: 9/5 6:21:09 PM Eastern Daylight Time
From: etan@MIT.edu (Eric Tan)
To: AndrewTan@wol.com

---

hi,

i have three things to say:

1. don't write joey for at least three days, until you are feeling
calmer. and you don't have to be that nice about it when you do
write him.

2. don't waste your emotional energy being angry. you're starting to get over this just fine, this was just a little bump in the
road.

3. quentin trent is a highfalutin gossip monger. i hate the new
york times – they set themselves up as this great institution with
such high aesthetic and literary values, but they so desperately
want everyone to think they're hip. i was SO pissed off for you
when i read that. but you know what? your friends will also be
pissed off about it, and to the other people who read it, it will
just make joe look like the asshole he is.

is that any consolation? in a few weeks, it will be completely for-
gotten by everyone, including you. i better run – sophie and i are
going to the theatre tonight – coriolanus, i don't remember that
one. classes start next week, it's starting to get crazy here.

double grrrr

e

Subj: Joseph Breaux review
Date: 9/6 12:15:40 PM Eastern Daylight Time
From: jorge.ortiz
To: christopher.o'malley
CC: christina.dellacasa, quentin.trent

Chris,

We've already received about thirty faxes and E-mails about
Quentin's review of the Joseph Breaux dance piece in Bali, most
of them from irate religious types. I culled three of them, and cut
them down to size. I chose two angry ones with titles, and one
that makes no comment on the piece but at least doesn't want to
lynch the guy. Here goes:

To the Editor:
I was sickened and saddened to read Quentin Trent's glowing
account of Joseph Breaux's obscene ballet in Bali ["Joseph
Breaux Hits a Bali High," Sept. 4]. It is inconceivable to me that
a newspaper with the prestige of the New York Times would
give its seal of approval to a work of "art" that glorifies child
molestation. That sort of filth may be acceptable in a place like
Bali, but in America, we are growing increasingly impatient with
the eagerness of the powers that be to coddle and abet behavior
that violates the law of God and, in many states, that of man. I
will take issue with your reviewer and say that I will do everything in my power to oppose the importation of this highly offensive muck. We have too much of it here already.

Clifford G. Grimm, President
Save the Family Foundation
Arlington, Va.

To the Editor:
As a former member of the Pullman-Oliphant Foundation executive board, I was dismayed to see the foundation mentioned in

Quentin Trent's review of Joseph Breaux's dance performance in Bali. Public health experts tell us that the sexual molestation of children is on the rise everywhere in this country; I would think that the last thing our charitable foundations should be funding, and our leading newspapers praising, is a tasteless work that glorifies such criminal and immoral behavior. I retired from the foundation nine years ago, but I can assure you that if a proposal for such a project had come to the board when I was a member, it would have gone straight into the rubbish bin, where it belongs.

Millicent Lovelace
Short Hills, N.J.

To the Editor:

As a retired art dealer who once represented the Walter Spies estate, I took a special interest in Quentin Trent's review of Joseph Breaux's new ballet based on the artist's life. Mr. Breaux seems to have gotten most of his facts straight, but I thought it was worth pointing out that Spies was, to a certain extent, a victim of the mores of his time. The boy in question was sixteen years old, and the Dutch law under which Spies was tried and convicted set the age of consent at eighteen. In the Netherlands today, the age of consent is fourteen.

Hubert Poon
Huntington Beach, Calif.

Subj: Hot copy
Date: 9/7 4:20:51 PM Eastern Daylight Time
From: Erica_Golden@IDS.org
To: thumbelina@indonet.net.id

Dear Pam,

I ran into Jerry Hull at the Joyce, and he bit my head off for gossiping about Joe Breaux. It does seem that your prognostications about the demise of "Elegy for Walter Spies" were a bit premature, after reading Quentin's ecstatic review. Joe's reputation is made. All he has to do now is live up to it, which is the hard part. However, it was obvious from the review that your basic point about the Western dancers was valid. I apologized, and then Jerry did a little bit of gossiping of his own. He made me promise not to tell you, since you now have the reputation of being the world's biggest blabbermouth. I'll tell you, but you must *promise* not to tell anybody there, especially Bob Blankenship. (This is starting to sound too much like high school, isn't it?)

Well, of course everybody in New York is talking about the scandalous Joseph Breaux and his 20-year-old Balinese genius. The question is, Who's going to get the premiere? The season's just beginning, and everybody's booked solid . . . or are they? It seems that the Berliner Neu Tanzteater, which was supposed to be performing at BAM in December, is canceling. In fact, I think the group is dissolving. Rudolf Kraus and Hans Buchermann have left to form their own company, which means that it's now a bunch of nobodies except for Eva Roeder. Maybe BAM gave them the heave-ho, it comes to the same thing. So Jerry has been lobbying Bernard Kuykendahl like mad to give the slot to Joe. Isn't that perfect? BAM's the right place, I think. They've got the money to help him restage it; the Joyce and City Center could only give him the stage. And it's way too hot for the Lincoln Center Festival to handle. Plus it's a big hall

– this will be a hot ticket. All the dance people in the country
will come, and the gays in New York will come for a gander at
this Renda kid. The picture of him in the Times made him look
so dishy.

There's more: it just so happens that the Brooklyn Philharmonic
was planning to do some Colin McPhee thing next year, so
there's the possibility that Joe could have a real orchestra! If the
new conductor, that Danish guy, will go along with it. He's
pretty stern, I understand. So, talk about a meteoric rise! There
are still a lot of ifs. No one will come out and say it, but some
people are actually kind of scandalized. Alice Sloane called me
this morning, and she said that she had heard that the boy is
actually sixteen, and might not be allowed to come into the
country. I know it's not true – if you say he's nineteen, he's nineteen (where did Quentin get twenty?) – but the point is, people
are talking. She said exactly what you said, we're all supposed
to say that there's nothing wrong with it, live and let live, but it
really is a bit gross to act out your own sex life on stage.
Everyone knows that there's practically no such thing as a
straight choreographer, and so many people in the dance world
have, shall we say, unorthodox preferences, whips and chains
and all that scary stuff. But the point is, Joe's rubbing our noses
in it. There's also been a sort of backlash, on the part of the
pro-Joe faction, against Quentin for letting the cat out of the
bag about Wayan Renda being his lover. That really was
naughty of him. Think of the poor boyfriend! He was very well
liked in that Mark-Mikell-Tim crowd. Tina Della Casa told me
that there was even some discussion at the Times of publishing
a correction, but after all it was true – and talk about closing
the barn door after the horse got away. Where are all these
cliches coming from?

Maybe I better get back to pretending that I have work to do.
Remember, not a *word* of any of this, you understand? Did
you agree with Quentin's assessment of the piece? How was it

received over there – I know they're supposed to be tolerant, but I'm surprised the Balinese P.T.A. didn't tar and feather Joe!

Let me hear,

Rica

Subj: Message from Andrew
Date: 9/8 10:23:39 AM Pacific Daylight Time
From: AndrewTan@wol.com
To: jbreaux@denpasar.wasantara.net.id

Dear Joey,

I think the time has come for us to be in communication again. The famous two months were over a few weeks ago, but I think we both knew that was just something you came up with to make what you were doing seem more civilized. Joey, I don't think I really need to say this, but, for the record, it's over. I'm starting to get over it, but please don't think that this message means that all's forgiven and I'm ready for us to be buddies again. I do forgive you, but the wound is deep, and it will take a long time to heal. You were the most important person in my life, and losing you was like having a limb ripped out. I hope that one day we'll be friends again, but it's not going to happen this year.

I keep revising this message, seesawing between nice and pissy . . . I don't know where it's going to end up. You know me, I hate to make a scene, even in cyberspace. But goddamn it, I gave you everything, I devoted my whole adult life to that relationship, and I never once cheated on you. Don't think I didn't have plenty of chances . . . cute waiters who wrote their phone numbers on the check, gym bunnies saying "hi" to me in the produce section at Jefferson Market. If I had wanted a little on the side it

would have been *no problem*. But I didn't want it . . . know
why? Because I LOVED YOU, MAN. I knew you occasionally
had a little fling now and then, but I didn't care; you were discreet
enough not to tell me (though not clever enough to check your
pockets for matchbook covers and receipts from that sauna downtown before you dumped your clothes in the laundry basket). No,
it isn't the sex . . . I never thought I owned your dick. It isn't the
sex, it's the humiliation, the most embarrassing emotion of all.

I hardly know what to say about your piece. On the one hand, I
rejoice in your success (at least in theory), and recognize that
Quentin's review solidly establishes your reputation as a leading
choreographer. But why did he find it necessary to say that that
guy is your "real-life lover"? It has absolutely nothing to do
with the artistic merits of the piece. Now, for everybody who
knows us, it's official, proclaimed to the whole damn world in
the newspaper of record: Joe Breaux dumped Andrew Tan for a
. . . how old is that kid, anyway, Joey? Every time I hear about
him, he's a different age. I realize it was a work of art, and that
you were working with the materials you found in Bali, and I
know it wasn't your intention to hurt me. It's all too obvious
you weren't thinking of me at all when you created that piece.

Now, about the apartment. I'm tentatively planning to return to
the Bay Area to live, but in any case I would never want to live
at 12 Horatio Street again. We bought that place nine years ago
for $106,000, going fifty-fifty, and today I would estimate its
value at something like $400,000. I would like to sell it. If you
agree, then obviously we simply split the money. If you want to
stay there, then I propose that we have a certified appraisal
done, to find out the real value of the place, and you ought to
pay me half of that. I don't care what sort of payment plan you
want, you can send me $200 a month for the rest of your life.
But it wouldn't be right for you not buy me out. I hope you'll
agree that selling is the better idea; you're not the Joey Breaux I
knew if you could really bring that guy back to sleep in our bed.

Joey, I still love you, man. But it's going to be a long time before I will want to talk to you or see you. Please don't be your usual overpowering self, and try to make everything all right, because it won't work. I'll let you know when I want to talk. I'm going back to New York on Tuesday to get all my personal stuff and ship the furniture and pictures that came from Jones Street back to San Francisco. That's going to leave the apartment sort of semifurnished for the girls, but this was a sweetheart deal for them, anyway.

I hope you're well.

Andrew

Subj: Re: Hot copy
Date: 9/8 11:20:15 PM Eastern Daylight Time
From: thumbelina@indonet.net.id
To: Erica_Golden@IDS.org

Dear Rica,

Yeah, yeah. But when I sent you that message, he had just had a rehearsal in which two of them quit and another didn't show up! And Bob had just told me that the Barbara Hutton couldn't remember her part from one rehearsal to the next. I will say, though, that if anyone was indiscreet, it was you. Darling. Telling Jerry Hull what I said – not that I give a damn what he thinks of me. I don't know the man. But enough about all that – who cares?

That certainly was a hot little scoop about BAM. That Joseph Breaux is one lucky fellow, isn't he? Of course it was brilliant of him to get the piece on the stage in time for Quentin Trent – that's called making your own luck. And yes, I basically agreed with what Quentin wrote. He certainly could have been harder

on the dancers, the Western ones, I mean. And he said next to
nothing about the Balinese, except for Wayan Renda. The Prince
is a big part. I'm sure he was afraid of saying something stupid
about a style of dance he knows nothing about. But Quentin's
always more interested in the piece than the dancers, and so am
I. His midget colleague at the Times thinks that it's criticism to
say that So-and-so's Ondine wasn't as good as Fonteyn – well,
so what? That's like saying, Don't go see the new Tom Stoppard
because it's not as good as "King Lear." I hate that.

I'm meandering. Quentin's main point was absolutely right on
target: I can't think of another new piece with a radical concept
– in this case, the two completely different dance worlds on
stage at the same time – where the concept didn't hijack the
piece. It worked so well here. The phrase "brilliant formal synthesis" doesn't exactly make me tingle all over, but I suppose
that's what it was. The piece was so much fun to watch, and Joe
has a marvelous sense of humor. The kecak scene was just one
example; I think with real dancers, the Margaret Mead etc. business will be hilarious. Most so-called humor in modern dance is
so prissy. This piece had a fart joke.

What else. I personally thought the designs were fine. He could
have covered Wayan up a little bit more – his sarong was practically falling off of him – but I suppose that will go down well in
New York. The sound system was horrible, but that's Indonesia
– nothing ever works right here. You asked about the reaction of
the local people – I honestly don't think most of them got it.
They're not like Americans, who are always on the lookout for
something to be scandalized about. And I say, Who cares if
Quentin wrote that Joe and Wayan are lovers? I disagree that it
has nothing to do with the piece. Don't you think "Who's Afraid
of Virginia Woolf" gained a little something because everyone
knew about Elizabeth Taylor and Richard Burton's quarrels?
Dance is show business, too, no matter how pompous some of
its practitioners are.

Let me know the minute the embargo is lifted on the news about BAM. I'm dying to swank around and be the first one to tell everybody.

Hugs,

Pam

Subj: So goddamn sorry
Date: 9/10 1:22:53 AM Eastern Daylight Time
From: jbreaux@denpasar.wasantara.net.id
To: AndrewTan@wol.com

Dear Andrew,

I'm so goddamn sorry I can't even tell you. Your letter made me cry – you know I never do that, I'm a macho Cajun dude from Louisiana. I realize that saying I'm sorry doesn't do any good. But it's true. I keep racking my brain: what can I do, how can I make it up to him? And of course, I can't. You're too good and kind and decent a person to have had something like this happen to you. I failed you, and I'm so goddamn sorry.

I was so happy to hear from you. And of course I'll respect your wishes and not pester you – you know me so well! That's always my first instinct, to try and find some way to MAKE everything be all right.

About Quentin's review: I am really heartsick about that. It was irresponsible journalism, and abominably cruel to you. It's not exactly a great help to my career, either, but I won't complain to you about something that is entirely the result of my own actions. I asked him not to say that, but he started laying on this bullshit about how his duty was to the readers – as if they need to know about my personal affairs! (Wayan is twenty. He had a birthday two weeks before the premiere. It was PATHETIC of me to lie to you about his age, as if that made any difference.)

Yeah, let's sell it. I can't live there. It's going to be so sad to see it again with all your stuff gone. When you talked about our bed, that was what made me cry. I'm crying now. Our bed. Fourteen years. O God, why couldn't I have been born with a constant heart?

I won't tell you any news, you don't want to hear it. I would LOVE to hear what's going on with you, but I respect your desire for us to be apart. Phil told me he saw you at the theatre with Nat MacDonald. God, that's a blast from the past. Please give him my regards. Actually, I suppose you probably don't want to do that. Remember, man, the day you feel like you can pick up the phone and call me and say anything, just say, "Hi, it's me, I had bacon and eggs for breakfast, gotta run," that will be the happiest day of my life since this whole miserable episode began.

You have carte blanche to handle the sale of the apartment. I think it's better if one of us manages it, and you'll do a better job than I would. You don't have to tell me the price, pay yourself a fee for doing it, and send anything for me to sign through Dan Greenberg. I don't think I could bear to talk to you on the phone about something as trivial as the price of real estate. Whatever you decide will be all right. I'll be back in New York in a couple of weeks. Sort of winding down here. God knows where I'll stay in New York. I may send you an E-mail with my contact information, nothing more.

That's it. I love you, man.

Your Joey

Subj: Re: Omigod
Date: 9/10 1:22:59 AM Eastern Daylight Time
From: jbreaux@denpasar.wasantara.net.id
To: podonnell@sfchronicle.com

Hey there,

Sorry to be so slow in responding to your great message, but
Way and I just got back from Jakarta, where I basically blew
every cent I have showing him a nice time. So yeah, I guess I am
fucking famous. I can't believe it, really. That was some review. I
am SO happy he was so glowing about Way, and SO pissed that
he said he was my lover. That's probably the last straw as far as
my father is concerned, if he saw it, and it was so cruel to poor
Andrew. I finally got a message from him; it was incredibly sad.
It made me cry. I just answered him. We're selling the place on
Horatio Street. I don't really want to talk about it.

City Center and the Joyce have already made offers to present the
piece – can you believe it? I need to come up with a name for the
group – I guess just plain ol' Joseph Breaux Dance Group. Stuff
like "Dance Theater" and "Dance Project" sound so pretentious.
I also need to find a business manager. Actually, I don't feel like
talking about that, either. I'm kind of sick of thinking about
dance.

We had a fabulous time in Jakarta. They asked to see Wayan's
ID when we checked in at the Regent, which was kind of embarrassing. During the day we went shopping and relaxed by the
pool, and at night we boogied. Way has a much greater capacity
for hanging around in smoky clubs with loud music than I do.
Skip the lecture – I know, what did I expect from a kid his age?
Funny thing, he didn't want to dance at those places, which was
fine by me. My ruination was a place called Plaza Senayan, a
shopping mall that is basically Trump Tower in Indonesia. I
spent a fortune on clothes for Way. He's going to cut such a
dashing figure in New York, in his chic new outfits from Prada

and Gucci and Dolce & Gabbana – those clothes are designed
for a tall, slender frame like his. Meanwhile, I'll be in rags – I'm
completely broke! I don't want you to get the wrong idea, it was
all my own folly. He didn't ask me to buy him one thing, and
made me put a couple of the really expensive things back on the
rack (not all of them, I admit). You know how I feel about shopping, but it's fun buying for him – he was so happy every time I
bought something for him, and he looks so stunning in them.

I think I might break down and tell you a few of the gory
details. I mentioned that we were going through some semi-
rocky times before the performance? Well, I knew it was just because of the stress of preparing the piece, and the other little
problem I mentioned (which I have completely stopped, by the
way). Once we got to Jakarta and finally had a good night's
sleep, it was like unleashing a force of nature. The sex has
always been good, but now it's spectacular. And don't tell me
how innocent I am after fourteen years of marriage – I'm talking
four, five times a day. I'm not bragging, Phil, believe me, it's him.
He has incredible endurance, I don't know how he does it. He
looks so delicate, but he's as strong as I am, like some magnifi-
cent, healthy animal. On Friday, our last full day in Jakarta, we
were at it all morning long. Then around noon we went down to
relax by the pool – I was worn out, actually. I had just started to
unwind, and then Way caught my eye and nodded up in the direction of the room – and we went upstairs and did it again!
When he gets going he's literally insatiable, and no matter how
exhausted I am, he can always get me aroused. It's kinda spooky,
actually, like he's got some kind of magic power.

I hope I'm not making a mistake by telling you all this. I'm not
worried about offending YOU, god knows. You love to hear me
talk dirty. But I'm not sure it's nice to Wayan – you'll be meeting
him soon, and I don't want you to look at him and think about
what we're up to. Hmmm, I'll have to think twice before I send
this. But it's just so phenomenal – I've never experienced
anything like this. If I don't tell someone, it's like having a stolen

Rembrandt that you can't show anybody. Still, it really isn't just sex. It's a lot more than that. I guess I'll send this. But don't mock it, Phil. I'm desperately in love with him.

OK, here's my plan, if you can call it that: in a couple of weeks, I'll close down the house in Kerobokan, and Wayan and I will fly to San Francisco, where you will put us up – so kind of you to invite us. Really, is that OK? Just for a few days? I haven't seen you in SO long, I really want you to meet Wayan, and it will postpone at least for a while the problem of where to stay in New York. I could kick the girls out, of course, but now the place is for sale. Also, Andrew said something in his message about how if I was the Joey Breaux he knew I would never bring Wayan back to Horatio Street to sleep in our bed. That really got to me, and of course he's right. But where can I stay? I'll have to find a decent, cheap hotel until I find a place to rent. Way is going to be so disappointed, after my villa here and the Regent in Jakarta – I've tried to explain it to him, but I don't think he believes me. He thinks that because I'm American, I can pay for anything. Anyway, it will be so much easier to work that out in California than here. I have to somehow try not to bump into Andrew; that would be terribly awkward.

God this is a long message! Sorry about all the sexy stuff, but I wanted to tell someone, and who but you? But BE NICE. Let me know what you think about my so-called plan.

Love ya,

Joey

Subj: Re: Congratulations
Date: 9/10 1:23:08 AM Eastern Daylight Time
From: jbreaux@denpasar.wasantara.net.id
To: jahull@POF.org

Dear Jerry,

Thanks for all the kind words. Sorry it has taken me a while to respond, but I was in Jakarta for a week, for a bit of R&R. I was bowled over by Quentin's review, though quite annoyed that he felt it necessary to go into my personal life. His story in Arts & Leisure comes out tomorrow; I hope he's more discreet. I hope this hasn't been a problem for you and the foundation. I saw the letter in the Times from that lady who used to be on the board. If I've caused you any embarrassment, I sincerely apologize.

You were right, I've already heard from Sid Markowitz and Margo Norman, offering me premieres. The problem is – you guessed it. Your generous grant was enough to cover the premiere of the piece here, but to do it properly in New York will cost a lot of money (obviously). City Center and the Joyce are great places to do it, of course, but how much money will they be able to give me up front?

Please don't think I'm hinting – I fully realize that the POF doesn't fund something like that, and even my little production in Bali was me being grandiose, as usual. I hope you don't mind me asking you about this, but you're one of the few people I know in New York who understands the performing arts business who is actually a real human being. I desperately need to hire a business manager. Any advice will be welcomed. I plan to come back in a couple of weeks, first to San Francisco, then to New York a week after that. I'll call you as soon as I get back to the States.

Thank you so much for all your support, Jerry.

Best wishes,

Joe

Subj: Re: Message from Sid Markowitz
Date: 9/10 1:23:13 AM Eastern Daylight Time
From: jbreaux@denpasar.wasantara.net.id
To: sidney_markowitz@nycitycenter.org

Dear Mr. Markowitz,

Thank you for your kind words and your generous offer to present the American premiere of "Elegy for Walter Spies." I apologize for being slow to respond, but I have just returned from Jakarta, where I went for a short holiday.

I'm planning to take a few weeks off before I begin considering what to do with the piece next. I am deeply honored that such a great hall as City Center has offered to present it, and of course I will, as you say, keep you in mind. I plan to be in New York by the first of October, and I'll be in touch with you again at that time.

Sincerely yours,

Joseph Breaux

Subj: Re: Congratulations
Date: 9/10 1:23:18 AM Eastern Daylight Time
From: jbreaux@denpasar.wasantara.net.id
To: norman@joyce.org (Margo Norman)

Dear Margo,

Thanks for the great message. Sorry it has taken me a while to respond, but I was in Jakarta for a week for a bit of R&R. Yeah, I was bowled over by that review, though quite annoyed that he felt it necessary to go into my personal life. His story in Arts & Leisure comes out tomorrow; I hope he's more discreet. Of course, there's nothing I can do – it's the New York Times, more powerful than God. Yes sir, please kick me again.

I don't know what I'm going to do next. I'm starting to get in over my head – I need somebody like Victor Winters was for Tim, who can run the business end of things. I need money to do this piece – I know I can get it, but I just don't know how. You know how much I love the Joyce, but I'm not making any decisions until I've had a chance to sit down and have a good think.

Yes, definitely lunch, but not swanky. After seven months in Indonesia, I'm dying for some good delicatessen. French fries. Pizza! I promise I'll call you as soon as I get back to New York.

See you soon,

Joe

Subj: Message from Andrew
Date: 9/11 7:39:28 PM Pacific Daylight Time
From: AndrewTan@wol.com
To: jbreaux@denpasar.wasantara.net.id

Dear Joey,

What you propose about the sale of the apartment is agreeable to me, though of course I won't take a fee . . . it's my home. It was considerate of you to suggest channeling everything through Dan.

Be well,

Andrew

Subj: Ya big tease
Date: 9/12 9:12:34 AM Pacific Daylight Time
From: podonnell@sfchronicle.com
To: jbreaux@denpasar.wasantara.net.id

Ya big tease,

You give me the best material I've had in months, and then you
snatch it away from me. Joey, how I can I mock that? I would be
afraid of being struck by lightning for blaspheming the sacred
rites of Aphrodite. Actually, I was moved that you shared something so intimate with me. I'm afraid that throughout most of
my life, sex really was just sex. The two years I was with Steve
were more like, "Y'in the mood? Nah, me neither. Let's go see
what's new at World of Video."

So, now I will discreetly draw a veil across your Rhapsody in
Paradise, and move on to earthly matters. Have you seen the
Arts & Leisure piece? It's spectacular – page one, with a cute
picture of you. You're below the fold, they gave the top of the
page to some has-been named Gustav Mahler. You've probably
picked it up on the internet, but it's not quite the same as having
the actual newspaper in your hand, reading about the glorious
talents of your old roomie while having your mid-morning crap.
Congratulations, darling (this is getting a little monotonous).
Quentin was considerably more restrained than he was in the
review. Thank god he laid off that business about your "true-life
lover."

My main news is my lunch with Andrew. We went to a fancy
Italian restaurant downtown, just off Union Square. It was odd,
a tiny bit as though I was meeting him for the first time. It's not
that he's changed, but . . . maybe it was seeing him in a setting of
his own. I guess what I want to say is that I really like Andrew,
but we would never have become friends if it weren't for you.
He's one of the perfect homosexuals, if you know what I mean. I

don't mean that to sound bitchy, honestly, but he's the kind of
homosexual my mother wanted me to be, once she realized it
was a lost cause. Maybe it's just a class thing – he looks stunning
in an Armani blazer, but the same coat on me looks like J.C.
Penney.

We spent half the lunch talking about Medea and my review,
which he had read carefully, polite lad that he is. He had some
interesting thoughts about the play, actually. He told me that he
had received your E-mail, that you're selling the apartment on
Horatio Street, and then he seamlessly diverted the conversation
to the subject of real estate. He wasn't very forthcoming about
himself, except to say that he was thinking of becoming a philanthropic administrator. He would be quite good at that – he's
smart, has a nice sunny personality, and of course that's his
crowd. I tried to find out about Nat MacShoulders, but he stuck
to the facts. I gather you knew him at Stanford. He's an architect
at the landmarks commission now, one of those people who tells
you what color you have to paint your house. Dr. Tan is on the
war path against them – Andrew was very funny about that. I
must say, he seemed relaxed and confident and happy.

Of course you're invited, presh! You don't even have to ask. I
am a little concerned about your privacy, though. Your bedroom
is right next to mine. Does she do a lot of squealing while you
two are unleashing the forces of nature? You'll have the place to
yourselves during the day, but it sounds as though you've got a
round-the-clock operation going. I'm only pulling your leg,
petal, of course it will be fine. I told Andrew that you were coming to San Francisco and were concerned about bumping into
him, and he just nodded and smiled.

I'm afraid I don't have much else that will interest you, it's all
interior decorating and work gossip. Everyone was very compli-
mentary about my Medea piece. I'm only on week two, so everyone still has to be nice to me, but I can already see a few evil

bitches lurking in the shadows, waiting for a chance to waylay me with editorial stilettos.

Can't wait to see you, fella!

Your doting innkeeperess

Subj: Everybody loves me!!!
Date: 9/14 7:23:09 AM Eastern Daylight Time
From: jbreaux@denpasar.wasantara.net.id
To: podonnell@sfchronicle.com

Ya not fuckingonna believe this, Phil – BAM wants me to do the piece in DECEMBER, the main stage, TEN performances with the goddamn Brooklyn Philharmonic! A real orchestra! Can you believe it? In DECEMBER, when you can sell out midgets reading the phone book. I can't believe it. I just got an E-mail from Bernie Kuykendahl. I will forward it to you. He was incredibly nice – what an honor it would be for them, "Rodeo" was the most brilliantly original new piece to come along in ten thousand years, etc. etc. What happened was that the Berliner Neu Tanzteater, which was going to do some caca doo-doo postindustrial wasteland "Nutcracker" that everyone would have hated, canceled on them, and they needed a replacement fast. Obviously, there were lots of other people he could have called, but, as you would put it, he called fabulous tiny moi.

It seems that the Brooklyn Phil was already planning some kind of Colin McPhee event, so they actually have the scores already. It's amazing how lucky I've been with this piece. Bernie suggested that the terms be worked out with my business manager, which I don't have yet, and he knows it, but he was being nice and at this point I obviously have to find one – but he offered a $20,000 advance. So now I can stay at the goddamn St. Regis if I want to. I don't know how much this will end up paying, but it's a big house, and ten nights adds up to a PILE. With the orchestra, they're going to charge a fortune for the tickets. But business-wise, I am getting in WAY over my head. I've gotta find somebody good, fast.

Phil, I'm starting to get nervous. I don't think I deserve all this good fortune. The world's cutest boyfriend, the world's most fabulous career, and wads of money. Naturally, I'm floating on air, but I gotta say, it doesn't seem fair to Andrew. He stood by me all those years, and now he finds out my news from the New York Times.

I need to get back to the States as soon as possible. I still want to come visit you, but it may be for only two or three days. Shit, just when I thought I was going to be able to loaf and play around with Wayan for a while, it's another marathon – do in three months what should take twice that time. Bitch and moan. I booked a flight arriving the 20th?

Love ya,

Joey   •

Subj: Venting
Date: 9/14 1:17:59 Pacific Daylight Time
From: AndrewTan@wol.com
To: etan@MIT.edu (Eric Tan)

Hi Eric,

I have to admit, I'm getting a little bored with seeing pictures of the Great Genius of Dance everywhere. He was in the paper again today, did you see? They're putting his piece on at BAM, ten performances. Maybe it's petty of me, but I'm finding it damned hard to keep being a good sport. When I think of all the dreary dinner parties I went to so Joey could suck up to some big shot, all the boring performances he dragged me to in freez-

ing lofts and church auditoriums, all the business letters I wrote
for him . . . it pisses me off! It's a good thing for him I don't need
money: I would sue his butt for palimony in a second.

That's all. It's called venting. I'm fine. Nat MacDonald made a
nice little pass at me the other day. I was expecting it; he had
made it pretty clear. He's just now coming out. I told him,
maybe it's not such a good idea for a guy who's just coming out
to date a guy on the rebound, but I didn't say no. He's a catch.
He's big and dark, like Joey, sort of rugged-looking more than
handsome, I guess. You would like him. He's really smart and
well read but not pompous, and he's nice and *calm*. I'll keep
you posted.

I'm flying out to New York on Wednesday to pack up all my
stuff, and was thinking maybe I'd spend the weekend with you
and Soph. Where are you going to be, Boston or Lenox?

Love from your brother

Subj: Urgent message
Date: 9/14 5:01:37 PM Eastern Daylight Time
From: Clifford_Grimm@stff.org
To: kuykendahl@BAM.org

Dear Mr. Kuykendahl:

It has come to my attention that the Brooklyn Academy of
Music intends to present a pornographic "ballet" entitled "Elegy
for Walter Spies," by the homosexual "choreographer" Joseph
Breaux. On behalf of the more than 3 million members of Save
the Family Foundation, I urge you to reconsider this decision.
This glorification of sodomy and pedophilia is deeply offensive
to all people who believe in the law of God. The American family is in a state of crisis, and your institution will be contributing
to its continuing peril if you present this filthy muck.

If you persist in presenting this "ballet," I shall coordinate with other institutions and foundations dedicated to the preservation of the American family, to organize protests. I fervently hope this will not be necessary.

Yours truly,
Clifford Grimm, President
Save the Family Foundation

Subj: Yes, we do
Date: 9/15 9:51:00 AM Pacific Daylight Time
From: podonnell@sfchronicle.com
To: jbreaux@denpasar.wasantara.net.id

Angel,

You deserve it all – you're a fabulous thing! But you are a wise niece to be fearful of the wrath of the gods. Everything was hunky-dory for Oedipus until that darn plague came along, and the nosy oracle started asking a lot of questions. But I don't think you can be accused of hubris: you're ambitious and self-confident, but that's quite another thing.

You're not the only one with romantic news, babycakes. I actually have a date, with an actual man. Don't laugh – he's an actor. But he's not arty, not actory. He's like a plumber when you need a plumber . . . he's satisfactory. That's Sondheim, peasant. Nobody double-entendres the way he does. I met him (the fella, not Sondheim) at a party at Franklin's house on Saturday night. He invited me to the movies this weekend – isn't that camp! I said, only if you take me out for a hot-fudge sundae afterwards. He's cute, in a nerdy sort of way. Definitely not the leading man. Think Roddy McDowall before he got into the ape thing. He's younger than me, about your age, I think. Nothing will come of it, of course. Sometimes I wonder if I'll ever have another serious relationship. I'm too camp for myself most of the time – who else would put up with it? But it will be fun to have a new friend to drag to the theatre.

I think they actually want me to do some work now. A forecast of the fall Broadway season in a thousand words – in other words, a little press-release anthology.

The 20th is simply elegant. Give me the flight details, and I'll meet you at the airport.

Phil

Subj: Bernard Kuykendahl replies
Date: 9/15 2:51:07 PM Eastern Daylight Time
From: kuykendahl@BAM.org
To: Clifford_Grimm@stff.org

Dear Mr. Grimm:

I am writing to acknowledge receipt of your message. I don't believe you have anything close to three million members, and I'm certain that none of them are subscribers of the Brooklyn Academy of Music. Therefore, I can't imagine what possible business it is of yours what we present here. If you send me any more messages, I will delete them unread.

Sincerely yours,

Bernard Kuykendahl, President
Brooklyn Academy of Music

Subj: Re: Venting
Date: 9/15 7:21:12 PM Eastern Daylight Time
From: etan@MIT.edu (Eric Tan)
To: AndrewTan@wol.com

---

hi

i don't blame you, it's just human nature. i'm sure joe has
thought of all those things, too.

it will be great to see you again so soon. we'll be in boston – no
time for lenox. everything is getting a little hectic here, with
classes starting. i'm teaching the freshman course this year,
which is a lot of fun, but so much preparation. i actually have to
do stuff like give exams.

also, we're interviewing girls to be our au pair. pretty soon sophie will be too preggers to do much around the house, and
we'll definitely need someone here full-time after the baby, so
there may be a bit of coming and going of teenage irish girls.
sorry about that.

gotta run now. glad to hear about nat.

e

Subj: Back to the U.S.A.
Date: 9/16 10:15:52 AM Eastern Daylight Time
From: jbreaux@denpasar.wasantara.net.id
To: podonnell@sfchronicle.com

Hi Phil,

We're getting packed up and ready to blast out of here on
Friday. The landlord found some Japanese kids to take over the
house, so I'm getting a nice little bundle of cash back. I sold the

Beemer for almost what I paid, which was very satisfying. I used part of the money to buy Way's parents a big new Sony TV and a DVD player. I also gave them the nice leather sofa and brass lamps that Andrew bought. They were so thrilled – I've never been to their house, but I think it's basically a hovel. I felt a little bit like the white slaver bartering for the chief's daughter, but it certainly went over well. His mother brought over a big plate of horrible little green cakes this morning. Way's already eaten half of them. How does he stay so lean?

We went to the American consulate in Denpasar today to get his visa. It was very unpleasant. You know me, I totally don't care what people think, but the guy who interviewed us really treated me like the evil child molester. In fact, Way's father is only four years older than me, which is kinda scary. He was exactly Wayan's age now when Wayan was born. I would say he looks ten years younger than me – not that I look old, but Mr. Renda is just so boyish, not a line in his face, the same big eyes as Way. Also, he's almost a foot shorter than him (how did that happen?). So I suppose we did make a rather odd-looking trio. The consulate guy pretty much had to say yes – we had faxes from Bernie Kuykendahl and both of the senators from New York. That was all Jerry Hull's doing. Also, I had to transfer some assets into an Indonesian bank account in Way's name, so it would look like he wasn't so poor.

The guy may have had to say yes, but I guess he didn't have to be nice about it: "May I ask where Mr. Renda got the money in this account?" he said. So I said, "He earned it. It's his salary." He looked me straight in the eye with a disgusted little sneer and said, "You pay him a salary for his services?" I smiled my gayest, sunniest smile and said, "Yep! I sure do, and he earns it." I thought the guy was gonna puke, but I went on, "He receives a salary as a leading soloist in my dance group. I think if you look at the review of Mr. Renda's performance in the New York Times, you'll see that he is an internationally recognized performer." The guy nodded his head and said, "Oh, yes, I have read that review," with a prissy little smirk. It was never exactly confrontational, but it was pretty obvious he hated giving us the visa.

Jerry Hull has been doing a lot of advance legwork for me. Apparently there's no problem for the other Balinese soloists, they're older and have families, so they don't pose a risk of becoming global wetbacks. He tells me that I can find a good gamelan and corps of Balinese dancers for the kecak in the States. How would he know if they're any good? But then, how would I know?

Angus is giving a going-away bash for us, a beach party. Way just stuck his head in the door and reminded me for the third time that I promised to watch some stupid kung-fu video with him, so I gotta run. Not much more to tell, anyway. I may not have time to check in with you again before I leave. See you soon!

Love ya,

Joey

P.S. Oh yeah, the flight. NW006, arriving SFO 9:00 p.m., Sept. 20. It would be so great if you could meet us. Be prepared – I've put on a little weight.

Subj: Thanks
Date: 9/24 4:52:10 PM Eastern Daylight Time
From: Danzguy@NYAN.net (Joseph Breaux)
To: podonnell@sfchronicle.com

Hi Phil,

As you can see, I got my old E-mail address back. I suppose I should use something more dignified now that I'm a famous choreographer.

Thanks so much for showing us such a good time. It was a great
few days, just not long enough. I wish we'd had time to cruise
down to Palo Alto, maybe go to Monterey to see the aquarium,
etc. I hope Way wasn't too much of a handful – he's always
lively, but he was SO excited to be in America. So was I! It's
great to be home.

I really liked Fritz. Is that his real name? He's a super-nice guy,
very funny. He was so sweet to Way, who also really liked him.
You're right, he's not actory, he doesn't have that "ya gotta love
me" thing happening the way actors usually do. He let you be
the star of the evening, which is VERY un-actory. I think you're
right to take your time and see what happens. It's always bad if
you get your hopes up after four or five dates – not that I know
anything about dating.

Our room here at the St. Regis is nice but it ain't that nice, considering what I'm paying for it. Way just seems to take it for
granted that we stay in the best hotel in town everywhere we go,
and have room service whenever we want. I explained to him,
when we find our own place, he has to pick up his own socks
and underwear, and wash the dishes after we eat the simple little
dinner that I cooked (or, let's face it, the take-out whatever). He
just laughed and pinched my tit. Anyway, it's only for two more
nights – Jerry found me a furnished place across from Lincoln
Center, some opera singer's apartment. $3500 a month for a tiny
one-bedroom, which is outrageous, but what can I do?

We didn't have a chance to be alone together much in San
Francisco – you told me in Golden Gate Park that you liked
Wayan. Do you really? Tell the truth – did you really like him?
He was acting a little goofy, a combination of exhilaration about
being in America and showing off for your benefit. Be brutally
honest and tell me that you truly believe that I have the cutest
little honey in the world. We had dinner last night at Le Cirque.
He didn't touch his food, he just won't eat anything that's not

fish and rice. He looked so adorable in his skimpy little see-through number from Gucci – outrageously pink and femme! – and when they brought the desert, I gave him a beautiful Piaget watch I had bought in the afternoon while he was napping. You should have seen him – his face lit up with joy, and he jumped up from his chair and ran around the table and kissed me. It was so sweet. Everyone stared at us, but who cares. Half the people in the restaurant were queens, anyway. And then when we got back to the St. Regis. . . .

I know what you're thinking – you didn't say anything when we were in San Francisco, but you didn't have to. I know you. Do you really think I'm spoiling him? Maybe I am, but honestly, he doesn't ever ask for a thing, and why not, if it gives us both so much pleasure, ya dig? I did tell him, no more shopping for clothes. He has so many already, and at home he never wears anything but his sarong. Tomorrow the top of the Empire State Building, Sunday the Statue of Liberty. I haven't done either of those since I first moved to New York.

Tonight I have to go over to the apartment on Horatio Street for the first time. I'm dreading that. The "dancing dairymaids," as you call them, have moved out, so there will be no one there but the ghosts. On the flight to New York, it occurred to me, if I ever choreograph a piece that doesn't include Wayan, I'm going to dedicate it to Andrew.

Love ya,

Joey

Subj: Pere-de-Sucre
Date: 9/25 11:14:20 AM Pacific Daylight Time
From: podonnell@sfchronicle.com
To: Danzguy@NYAN.net (Joseph Breaux)

Mon cher Pere-de-Sucre,

. . . and when you got back to the St. Regis, he curled up with
his teddy bear and fell fast asleep. I've had it with your smirking
in-your-windows. Joey, he's beyond adorable, he's totally wor-
shipable. Now I understand, sort of. He really is exquisite. Such
lovely skin, I kept wanting to reach out and touch it. He's so
perfectly smooth, I've never seen a male person who was technically a grown-up who didn't have one hair on his body. (Does he
have any Down There?) It was so provoking, the way she was
always sashaying around the house with nothing on but that
sarong draped around her non-existent hips. Darling chi-chi's,
like tiny chocolate kisses. I have to say, he IS a frisky little fella,
but always perfectly polite. When I could understand what he
was saying. His English is pretty basic – isn't that going to be a
problem for him in New York? You can't always be shepherding
him around. I don't think he could even manage to get
somewhere in a taxi, could he? Of course, the drivers there don't
speak English, either.

And yes, Joey, you are spoiling him rotten. OF COURSE he
doesn't ever ask you for anything – he's too busy opening up the
latest little prezzy you've bought him. When did you get into this
fashion thing? Gucci? PINK? All that designer stuff used to
make you puke. It's like Wayan is your Barbie doll or something,
the way you keep dressing her up. (I meant that in a caring way.)
It's your business, m'dear, but aren't you spending money you
don't have yet? I feel weird giving you advice about money, so I
should shut up. But Piaget? What's wrong with a dinky little
Movado? Personally, I consider Swatch high class. In my vast
experience with child-rearing, I've found that the problems with

spoiled babies don't make themselves known until the candy supply stops, when Daddy says no. Joey, he's obviously NOT a tart, but it's also clear that he's heavily into this notion of himself as the glamorous plaything of an American millionaire, which you are not. I'm going to shut up. One last thing: what's going to happen when he gets bored and homesick, as he inevitably will? Remember, you asked.

Yeah, I'm having fun with Fritz. His real name is Hugh, not so great for the playbill. He's playing Snout in a new production of "Midsummer Night's Dream" at the Castro Playhouse. I'm almost to the point of having to tell Franklin that we're dating – how can I review him? "Fritz Fellowes, in the role of Snout, has the cutest little mole on his left hip, and is a Maria Callas fanatic." I would really rather not get into that at the Chron, but what if he becomes a star? I'm trying not to get carried away, but Joey, he LIKES me. It's been so long since I've made snugglies with somebody who actually liked me back. We're going to do the Napa weekend thing, I'm taking Friday off work. That seems like a big step, somehow.

Nervous Nelly

P.S. You didn't tell me about Wayan's tattoos – they're so sexy! They're obviously real, the magic kind, not like the boys on Eighth Avenue who are trying to look like trade. They make him look so savage, like whatsisname's sidekick in "Moby Dick."

Subj: Fwd: Horatio Street Apartment
Date: 9/28 7:25:46 PM Eastern Daylight Time
From: dgreenberg@gdts.com
To: AndrewTan@wol.com

Dear Andrew,

I have received the following message from Joe. I thought it best
to simply forward it, rather than retyping everything. Please tell
me what you want to do.

Best,

Dan

>Date: 9/28 13:10:10 -0400
>To: dgreenberg@gdts.com
>From: Danzguy@NYAN.net <Joseph Breaux>
>Subject: Horatio Street Apartment

>Dear Dan,

>Here's my new contact information. I am now living
>at 22 West 65th Street, apt. 14G,
>New York, NY 10023. Tel.
>799 3111. As you can see, I have my old E-mail address
>again.
>
>I have a proposal, or rather a request I would like you to con-
vey to
>Andrew for me. As you may know, I'm performing a piece at
>BAM later in the year. I have three Balinese dancers coming to
town in a
>few days. They will need a
>place to stay until the end of the run, December
>19. Rather than pay a fortune for them to stay at a hotel,

>I thought perhaps we
>could put them up at the Horatio Street apartment. The place
is almost empty now,
>but if I buy a new bed and perhaps
>rent some furniture, it will be adequate for them.
>I propose that the Joseph Breaux Dance Company pay Andrew
and me
>$3000 a month rent – I've looked around, and that seems at or
>above the going rate. Of course I won't pay myself,
>but I now have a business manager, Lauren McIntyre,
>who will send Andrew a check for $1500, drawn
>on the company's account, on the first
>of October, November, and December. Then
>we will proceed with the sale of the apartment in the new year.
>
>Please tell Andrew he's under no obligation to agree to this.
>
>I hope all's well with you. If you and Heather would like to
>come to see the piece, just let me know, and I'll send you
tickets.
>
>I hope all's well with you.
>
>Joe

Subj: Chateau de Sade
Date: 9/28 7:25:51 PM Eastern Daylight Time
From: Danzguy@NYAN.net (Joseph Breaux)
To: podonnell@sfchronicle.com

Hi Phil,

Greetings from Chateau de Sade. This apartment is the grimmest
little dungeon I've ever seen. It belongs to an Austrian mezzo
named Gabriele Reinhardt, who obviously read "Venus in Furs"
when she was a teenager and never got over it. The walls of the

bedroom are black! and the chairs in the living room are black leather, and a dining room table that looks like a relic of the Spanish Inquisition. When Way first walked into the place, he looked around and said, "Why so dark?" And it's true – at night, even if you turn on all the lamps, it has this Gothic gloom. And it seems so tiny, after the splendor of the garden suite on Larkin Street. Wayan and I keep bumping into each other. He's already busy trying to propitiate all the gods lurking around the place. He's in such a tiz because he can't find the right ingredients for the offerings. He leaves these little folded-up pieces of paper with rice everywhere. It is the MOST ridiculous religion.

Well, I'm starting to pull the piece together – I've got a rehearsal space in Chinatown, the Balinese soloists are on their way here, and I've begun casting the Western roles. The bit parts will be easy. I know who I want, but I want someone really great for Barbara Hutton. I'm hoping that Tim will let me use Angelina Monceau. In a way I wish I could recast Walter. You were nice about it, Phil, but I really think I'm almost too heavy to still be dancing. OK, it's only ten pounds, and you can tell me how fabulous I look all day long, but ten pounds is a lot for a dancer. I really feel it. But I know I have to do it – everyone will want to see me and Wayan together. I shouldn't admit it, but I know that part of the reason it's selling so well is curiosity about scandalous Joseph Breaux and his boy wonder. But this is the last time I'm dancing on the stage. I'm thinking of making an announcement, then the tickets will disappear.

That's so great about you and Fritz. I wanna hear all about the Napa weekend. Even gory details, if you feel like it. This place does have a sofa-bed, so I can put you up. I'm sure you can wangle a Broadway trip out of the Chronicle – or is that Franklin's prerogative? Bring Fritz.

Love ya,

Joey

Subj: Chateau de Masoch, dummy
Date: 9/29 2:15:23 PM Pacific Daylight Time
From: podonnell@sfchronicle.com
To: Danzguy@NYAN.net (Joseph Breaux)

Angel,

You're the queen of the gory details – I can't compete with the
magic tropical booty unleashing the forces of nature. Fritz and I
just do the normal fooling around. Actually, believe it or not, I
like him for his personality. He peddles a very amusing line of
chat, and he's NICE. He likes me. In Napa he told me I was
sexy! How I howled. I couldn't help it – I'm as sexy as Helen
Hayes. Napa was fun, a little too tidy and perfect for my tastes.
Sort of like Switzerland in California (not that I've ever been to
Switzerland). We stayed at a reel purty little inn, and the food
and wine were delicious, I must admit.

I'm sorry about your apartment, but welcome back to the big
city. I think I've heard of that singer. Doesn't she do the evil
bitches in Wagner? I might have seen her as the evil bitch in
"Lohengrin" at the Met a few years ago.

I still think you're making too big a deal about your weight.
Why don't you just go on a diet like everybody else? If you do
stop performing on the stage, that's not the reason, it's because
you now belong to the No Longer Young Club. Just relax, honeybun. The older you get, the less you care about getting old.

I seem to be hopelessly banal this morning, so I'll get back to my
polite dismissal of a really rotten "Mikado." Why do they still
bother with that shit? They try to make it contemporary, and
that just makes it worse. But I'm not allowed to say, "It sucks,"
we're supposed to accentuate the positive here. "Although the
ushers were remarkably attractive young people, well-groomed
and nicely dressed, and the jug wine served at intermission was
reasonably priced, the direction, acting, sets, costumes, and

lighting were less than entirely successful." I wish the editors here would realize that the readers love nasty pans. If I had wanted to be nice to everyone, I would have been an airline stewardess.

Give Junior a chuck under the chin from

Great Aunt Phyllis

Subj: Re: Fwd: Horatio Street Apartment
Date: 9/29 6:53:05 PM Pacific Daylight Time
From: AndrewTan@wol.com
To: dgreenberg@gdts.com

Dear Dan,

That sounds fine. The real estate market in New York seems to be stable, so we might as well sell in January as now. I hope all's well with you and Heather.

Thanks,

Andrew

Subj: News
Date: 9/29 6:53:08 PM Pacific Daylight Time
From: AndrewTan@wol.com
To: etan@MIT.edu (Eric Tan)

Hi Eric,

Your new videocam is totally cool, dude. How much was it? I'll get one, too. How does that work? You're sending me your picture, while I'm sending you mine? It seems so futuristic.

Well, guess what? I think the Kappan Foundation might be offering me a job. You remember I met that friend of Dad's there
back in August? Well, it turns out that Mattie Kappan, who runs
the foundation for the family, was a St. Kit's boy, a couple of
years behind me. I ran into him at the club last Friday, when I
had my weekly tennis date with Marnie Steele. He remembers
me much better than I remember him . . . that's always the way
it is, I guess . . . when you're fourteen, the seventeen-year-old
guys seem so cool, applying to college and Going All The Way
(or telling everyone they are). Apparently, I published a poem of
his in Golden Hours when I was the editor. I pretended to
remember.

Anyway, I met him for lunch today, the grill at the club. The pay
is token, but there are a lot of great perks. A nice office and a
car, which I need now. I would be in charge of winnowing
through applications from performing artists, writers, painters,
etc., or rather organizing committees to do so. He said that the
guy who has been in charge of the arts is getting ready to retire,
and although he didn't say so, I had the impression he was hinting that I was being checked out as a possible successor. It all
seems so improbable . . . he thinks I'm a literary expert because I
published his poem in a schoolboy magazine! To tell you the
truth, Mattie's not the brightest guy in the world. But I think
being Raymond Tan's son and playing tennis with Ernest Steele's
daughter at the Pacific Club are more important qualifications
for the job than a great resume, which I certainly don't have. It's
barfy, but what am I supposed to do about it? And here's the
hilarious part . . . at the end, he quietly added that the foundation has been looking for ethnic diversity for a long time. I
laughed and told him I was Chinese only in theory. Once more,
the slitty eyes come to the rescue.

Anyway it sounds like fascinating work, and it's doing
something important, something that matters. And I'm sure I
can do a good job . . . it's really just a matter of taste, which

playwrights, composers etc. do you want to support. I've been involved in the arts scene for fifteen years, and what I don't know I can learn. The best part is, Dad was so pleased. I think it's more or less the sort of thing he has wanted for me for a long time . . . you're the scientist son, and I'm the artistic son, but now I'm actually doing something. I think he wants to give me some money. He said one of his trademark enigmatic sentences, that he "realized that the emoluments of a career in the philanthropic field are usually inadequate to provide for the independence and style of living that such a position requires," something like that. I think that means I'll be getting a call from Norman Chin like the one you got when Sophie got pregnant. I have to admit, I wouldn't mind kicking half a mil into my account at Morgan. And of course it's great for everybody, taxwise.

I've got to get out of the house, though. Dad and I are getting along better than ever, but Mom's making me batty, always wandering in to ask if I'm hot, or cold, do I want coffee, do I want tea, closing windows I just opened. I know she just wants to baby me, but it's maddening. Nat's coming for dinner tonight. Mother and Dad seem to have just assumed that he's their new son-in-law. He's just the right type for Dad, I know . . . white and rich. He almost said it; he's such a snob it makes me sick sometimes. More to the point, Nat's the right type for me. But . . . I'm not ready. I know he thinks it's weird that we haven't gotten physical, but I can't help it. I tried to explain to him: I *really* want to, I like him a lot and everything, but I've only had sex with one person in my adult life, and when it gets to the unbuttoning stage, I just sort of panic. He's been really nice about it, no pressure. Actually, when I said that, he was very funny. He said, "I can top that. I've had sex with two people in my life . . . and one of them was my wife." But I'm starting to feel a little bit like the class tease. He's not going to hang around forever.

You see! E-mail is still the best for some things. You wouldn't have caught me saying *that* into a videocam. This was a long letter, but there was a lot to tell.

Love to you and Sophie from your kid brother

Subj: Re: News
Date: 10/1 9:29:00 AM Eastern Daylight Time
From: etan@MIT.edu (Eric Tan)
To: AndrewTan@wol.com

---

hi,

that's great news! i really don't have time to chat, i promise i'll call you this weekend. i'm forwarding the info about the video-cam. you really ought to get one – it's much more fun if both parties have it. mattie's older brother, sid, was in my class at st. kit's. he was the dumbest kid in the class. they gave him c's as a gift, because his old man was so rich. i guess they were hoping for a new chem lab or something.

talk to you soon,

e

Subj: Good to hear
Date: 10/6 9:14:05 AM Pacific Daylight Time
From: podonnell@sfchronicle.com
To: Danzguy@NYAN.net (Joseph Breaux)

Hi Joey,

Thanks for calling – I've been itching to scold you, but I know you're busy. No, it's not boring that you're always talking about the piece – of course, it's the most important thing going on in your life. But when I was a child, my mother always told me, "Phyllis, when you're having a conversation with someone, always remember to say, 'And how are you?'" You did ask, "How's Fritz?" and when I said "He's fine," you returned to the fascinating subject of the negotiations with Tim Winner over that French girl you want for your piece. It's OK, I know how distracted you are.

What I would have told you is that Fritz and I seem to be sort of slowly drifting in the direction of boyfriendom, which worries me. That's always when things start to go wrong. But we really are having such a nice time together. The other day, he said, "Maybe someday it would be nice if we lived together." I didn't say no, I said maybe it would – someday. I think it's way too soon even to be in the hint-dropping stage.

Keep me posted about the piece, about you and Wayan, but you can skip the shopping updates. To me, Dolce Gabbana sounds like a syrupy Italian dessert.

Mistress Manners

Subj: It's official
Date: 10/9 4:25:13 PM Pacific Daylight Time
From: AndrewTan@wol.com
To: etan@MIT.edu (Eric Tan)

Hi Eric,

Well, it's official. I am now the Coordinator for Grant Evaluations, Arts Division, at the Kappan Foundation. Isn't it a bogus title? "Coordinator" is one of those words that seems to mean, we don't know what to call it. We agreed on a six-month trial period. I'm starting to like Mattie. It's true that he's not all that bright . . . sometimes I have to explain fairly obvious things to him twice . . . but he's always cheerful, and so easy-going. Everyone at the foundation adores him; I think he's probably the world's nicest boss. To tell you the truth, the place seems way overstaffed to me. They have so many committees, and everyone knows that all the time spent at committee meetings is time not spent doing real work. Lunch for everyone seems to be 12:30 till after two. Yesterday we went to a beautiful new Chinese restaurant on Powell, and he didn't ask for the check till almost three o'clock. We've also had a few tennis dates . . . I think that's the real reason he hired me, for lunch and tennis.

The other big news is, Nat and I have Done It. This is another "not suitable for videocam" type message. I feel a little bit weird talking to you about this . . . aside from the fact that you're my brother, you're one of the coolest people I know about the gay issue. But it's one thing to talk about romance, and another thing to talk about the moving parts. Let's just say, it was really different than it was with Joey. More controlled, I guess . . . I'm not sure what the right word is. Obviously it was passionate, but with Joey it was always a bit athletic, almost rowdy. Nat's more mellow, very tender. Of course, Joey was tender too . . . hmmm, that's enough of that. He gave me a nice little ultimatum: I'm crazy about you, but either a romantic relationship becomes physical or it starts to hurt. You tell me you really like me, sooo . . . put out or shut up, I guess you might say. Once we got started, I couldn't figure out why I was so hung up about it. I have to admit, just on the physical level it was *great* to get laid again. On paper he's perfect . . . he's exactly my type, very smart, super-nice, and I can see that he really has a crush on me. It feels wonderful to be wanted, but I'm still not sure if it's the real thing.

He wants us to go on a trip together. He's right; that's the best way to find out how you feel about someone. It was on that first trip to Italy after Stanford that I really fell in love with Joey.

That was the one time I was in charge. He had never been outside of the country before, and even though I had never been to
Italy, we had been to France two years before with Mom and
Dad, so I had had the experience of being in a place where
everything was different. My French was pretty decent, which at
that time was still more useful there than English, so I was the
one who did all the talking (which drove him crazy . . . "What
did he say? What did he say? You gotta tell me what they say!").

I can pinpoint the exact moment we plighted our troth, or whatever it is . . . it was in Tivoli, we had gone to see Hadrian's villa
and the fabulous gardens at the Villa d'Este, then to a little trat-
toria on a hill, where we sat outside and ate a huge steak and
got so bombed on cheap chianti that we missed the last bus back
to the city. The owner seemed to know what was up, and he told
us we could stay there, in a little room in the attic with a view
across the gardens. It was . . . well, it was one of those times of
your life that you can't really explain except with cliches, so you
don't even talk about it. Joey and I had a lot of great times together . . . the week we stayed at that castle in Wiltshire, the time
we got snowed in in Nantucket, the *first* visit to Bali . . . but
that night in Tivoli was a watershed (see what I mean about the
cliches?). After that, there were no doubts, we were as close as
two people can be. Even Joey and I never really talked about it
. . . if we were feeling sentimental, one of us would just say,
Remember that night in Tivoli?, and we would get all misty and
melty.

Like now. Why did I bring that up? That's what Nat's up against
. . . definitely a stacked deck. OK, that's my news. I've been
looking for apartments. I don't want to be too close to Jones
Street. I'm hoping to find something I can afford in Pacific
Heights. Love to you and Sophie.

Andy

Subj: Breaux saga continues
Date: 10/10 3:12:59 PM Eastern Daylight Time
From: Erica_Golden@IDS.org
To: thumbelina@indonet.net.id

Dear Pam,

The Joe Breaux saga continues. Of course you know he's here to
do his piece at BAM. It's already pretty much sold out. I'm going
opening night – Dancezine asked me to write about it. Last night
Jerry and Alexandra Hull threw a little Welcome Home, Joe
bash, and everyone had their first look at the famous Wayan
Renda. He's different from what I imagined, a little more . . .
manly, I guess. He's adorably cute, but there's nothing little-boy
about him. I think I was expecting one of those swishy Asian
twinkies, but there's something very fresh and unspoiled about
him. You never mentioned the tattoos, they're so exotic-looking.
Joe's put on a bit of weight.

But my dear, talk about "You can take the boy out of Bali . . ."
He was like a little savage. It was a buffet, but you know the
Hulls' place on Central Park West, you could play softball in
their living room. There were plenty of places to sit, but the boy
sat on the floor in front of Joe, like a faithful doggie, and ate
with his hands! You should have seen Alexandra – I'm sure it
was some priceless Persian antique rug he was sitting on, she
came running over with a napkin and made him a little place
mat. I tried to talk to him, but he doesn't seem to speak a word
of English.

It was a weird evening, very subdued. Of course, everyone was
very welcoming to Joe, *everybody* loves Joe, but it was so
strange, him being with this young guy. Most of the people in
the room have children older than Wayan. And most of them
know Andrew. I heard a couple of people whispering "Are we
supposed to ask about Andrew?" After dinner, little Wayan went
into the Hulls' bedroom and watched cartoons on TV. Tim

Winner was bombed, as usual, and made a nasty remark. I stuck up for the kid – I watch cartoons. Bugs Bunny is one of the great philosophers of our time, in my opinion.

That's all, just thought you'd get a kick out of that.

Big kiss,

Rica

P.S. A friend of mine over at BAM told me that she had heard that Jens Munk hates the piece, thinks it's immoral, and may pull out. He's just arrived at his post, and it would make him look a little bit temperamental. Maybe he is.

Subj: Re: It's official
Date: 10/10 7:02:19 PM Eastern Daylight Time
From: etan@MIT.edu (Eric Tan)
To: AndrewTan@wol.com

---

hi,

that's great news, on both counts. i think we knew the kappan offer was coming. kid, you shouldn't feel weird talking to me about sex – if anything, you're shyer about it than i am. the first five or so years you were settled down with joe, before i met soph, i was fairly promiscuous, especially in england. you met the ones i actually dated, but i didn't tell you about some of the others. i don't mean that i had a one-night stand every saturday night or anything like that, but there were a lot of mornings when we both knew, as we went through the ritual of the telephone-number exchange, that there weren't going to be any calls. feeling desired is an important part of a happy life, and i'm no biologist, but i would assume that getting laid from time to time is good for your health. i always found it pretty easy – i think horny women are slightly more likely to go home with a

chinese guy, because they think we're nicer. i guess there aren't
any chinese serial killers. of course, we have a bad reputation in
another department. . . . andy, you should never worry about the
gay thing with me. i know you don't, really. i've thought about it
myself a couple of times. not seriously, but if it had been the
right guy, at the right moment, the wine, the music. . . .

love, that's different, nobody understands that. i guess i have
picked up more experience about this stuff than you have. i always thought it was a little strange the way you and joey settled
down at such a young age. i wouldn't presume to tell you what
to do with nat, i don't know the guy – but enjoy yourself! he
sounds like a good guy, just see what happens. you're definitely
a catch, so you can afford to be choosy. if it doesn't work with
nat, the right guy will eventually find you.

how's that for a pompous advice marathon, not that you asked
for it. talk to you soon, kid. we love you

e

Subj: Silent as. . .
Date: 10/16 9:00:08 PM Pacific Daylight Time
From: podonnell@sfchronicle.com
To: Danzguy@NYAN.net (Joseph Breaux)

O sepulchral one,

I know how busy you are, but this tomblike silence is starting to
take on an eternal aspect. I'm not chastizing, but surely you can
squeeze in a five-minute news briefing every week or so. Just tell
me you're fine.

I'm not. Fritz and I had a big fight, so that's the end of that. I
knew it, it always happens when they want to be my boyfriend. I
won't even tell you what the fight was about, it was too stupid.

Of course I will – it was actually over music. I was making him listen to one of my scratchy old Ella Fitzgerald LP's, and then out of the blue he said, "Phil, you know you don't have to be such a campy queen." He told me I'm always talking about how old I am, I'm not that old, I deliberately make myself look frumpy, why can't I wear some contemporary-looking clothes, listen to some new music once in a while. Of course most of what she said was perfectly true, but it really pissed me off. If it had been Judy or Ethel Merman, I might have let it go, but Ella Fitzgerald was a great artist. Not that Judy and Ethel weren't great artists, but . . . oh, skip it. I gave him quite a tongue-lashing. I told him he needed to see the opening number in "La Cage" again: I am what I am. The day I was born, when the nurse tried to put that diaper on me, I said, "White's not my color, dear – do you have anything in beige?" Men are like streetcars, they come and they go, but camp is eternal. Nothing has ever happened to me in my life that was so awful that I couldn't cheer myself up with "The Women" or "Baby Jane" or "Imitation of Life" (the Lana Turner version). Tonight I think it will be "Valley of the Dolls." When Barbara Parkins goes back to that little town in New England and they reprise Dionne's theme song, I simply melt. My father believes that homosexuality is just arrested adolescence, that we don't want to grow up and act like men. Sometimes I think he's right.

Mister, that's me singing on the jukebox.

Baby Blue

Subj: Problems
Date: 10/19 5:21:11 PM Eastern Daylight Time
From: Danzguy@NYAN.net (Joseph Breaux)
To: podonnell@sfchronicle.com

Hi Phil,

First of all, I'm SO GLAD you and Fritz patched things up.
Andrew and I broke up five or six times the first year. It's all part
of the process – I hope that doesn't sound callous, but it's true.
I'll call you over the weekend, promise. Now, on to the fascinating subject of ME. It's hard for a Cajun to come out and say,
You were right and I was wrong. But Phil, it's just the way you
said. He's getting bored, and he's starting to have these sullen
moods, doing nothing, saying nothing for hours. And at night he
drags me to horrible places like Splash and the Monster, where
he gets cruised like mad (of course), which doesn't make me jealous, exactly, but it ain't much fun. I have to tip the bouncers $20
because he's underage! He won't come with me to decent restaurants any more, and he won't eat any Western food at all.
There's a crummy, overpriced Malaysian restaurant on
Columbus, that's the ONLY place he'll go. I'm so sick of it, and
we have take-out from there literally every night we don't go
there. He's made friends with one of the busboys at this place, a
twinkie named Amir. It's so frustrating, Way lies around the
house, staring off into space for hours, doesn't answer if I ask
him a question, and then little Amir comes over, and suddenly
they're yammering away and shrieking with laughter. Amir's a
nice boy, but he's practically moved in. Twice this week, when I
went to bed I left the two of them in the living room watching
their fourth video of the evening, and I woke up alone, to find
them sleeping on the floor, the TV screen blue. We have these
kung-fu marathons, and those movies with the American body-
builders blowing away the gooks – it's so weird, they seem to
love movies where the big blond guy is killing people who look
just like them. And now he's discovered porn. Andrew and I had
a few videos, and Wayan and Amir watch them over and over.

He doesn't watch them with me, only with Amir. I try to explain to him, it's more fun to DO than to watch. I'm afraid things are cooling off in that department. I knew it would cool off a bit – it had to. If it had gone on the way it was in Jakarta, it would have killed me. We still do it a lot, but . . . now it's like a job for him, if you know what I mean. When I try to talk to him about any of this, he just says, "Whatever you want make you haffy, babee." And you were right, I've spoiled him rotten. It's not that he's greedy, but shopping is the only thing he knows how to do here besides stand around at Splash and get cruised. He has no idea about the value of money. We were at Barney's (what the hell am I doing at Barney's? I've got a show to put on!) and he found this fluffy little white sweater about the size of a gym sock, some Japanese designer. He tried it on and of course he looked totally adorable in it – Phil, it was $2,000! When I made him put it back, he tried to make a scene, but I didn't fall for it, I just dragged him outside. He was actually whining. You know I don't care what people think, but it was pretty embarrassing. It really looked like the dirty old man and his rent-a-twink. I tried to explain that the sweater cost more than his father earns in a year, but he just didn't get it. Jerry Hull gave me a welcome-home party. Half the New York dance world was there – everybody was really nice, but I could see some of them were pretty scandalized. Most of the people there knew Andrew, and here I was with Wayan. He sat on the floor and ate with his hands – I'm used to it, but people like Jerry and Alexandra Hull definitely aren't. And now, to top it all off, Jens Munk, the pompous asshole, has decided not to conduct. Did Quentin's evil little item about him getting out because of "moral objections" show up in the national edition? It's not really a big deal, the assistant conductor, Eric Small, who's going to do it, is excellent, nice guy, knows the scores, etc. Nobody was booking this because of Munk, but still, it's a slight drop in starpower.

So that's what's happening in my life. This has been going on for a while – I didn't want to tell you, I kept hoping it would get better. But it's getting worse. I know you can't tell me what to

do. Sometimes I just want to snatch him up and run back to
Bali. After BAM, I might do just that. We have the first complete
run-through next week.

Love ya,

Joey

Subj: Re: Problems
Date: 10/20 8:53:12 AM Pacific Daylight Time
From: podonnell@sfchronicle.com
To: Danzguy@NYAN.net (Joseph Breaux)

Dear Joey,

You know me, I'm always right about everything that has to do
with other people's lives – and wrong about everything in my
own. But do you ever hear me say, "Toljaso"? Oh Joey, I'm so
sorry! I wish I could think of something useful to tell you, but I
keep coming back to variations on that thing I don't say. It was
inevitable, uprooting a kid his age from his tropical island and
transporting him to the most frantic place on earth. I guess what
I would tell you is, try not to blame him. Just as I'm sure you
unwittingly committed a hundred faux pas in Bali, he can't possibly understand the bizarre way New Yorkers live. Do you remember your Whitmanesque paean to the wondefulness of
everything Balinese, the famous "twinkling kites" message?
Well, that's how he feels at Barney's. I'm sure when he was a little boy he wanted to play with dolls, or whatever it is little girls
do in Bali, and dreamed of growing up to be the most fabulous
queen in the tropics – and then he met you, and you bought him
all those davoon frocks, just like the ones in the magazines, and
made his dream come true. As for what's happening in the cruise
bars, that's just the way it is. Cute young fellas NEED to be noticed; he can't help that. So try not to blame him too much for
acting the only way he knows how, and try to hold on to all the

stuff that made you so happy in Bali. I just spent a few days with him, but I can see he's not a bad kid. I'm sure he does want to make you haffy. Who knows, maybe you can cook up a biconti-nental arrangement, build him a house in Bali and spend half the year there, something like that.

You were real sweet on the phone – sorry about the drama-queen message a few days ago. Sounds like you're the one with the drama now. I think it's time for an intermission – try to calm down. The most important thing now is the piece. As Auntie Tru used to say, keep your chins up. We love you.

Phil

Subj: Disaster!
Date: 10/26 8:12:51 PM Eastern Daylight Time
From: Danzguy@NYAN.net (Joseph Breaux)
To: podonnell@sfchronicle.com

Hi Phil,

Oh god, now it's a disaster. I don't know what I'm going to do – he didn't show up for the first run-through. I didn't tell you before, he's been refusing to come to rehearsals. Well, not REFUSING, just not doing it, "I don't need, already know." Which is true, actually, there's no way he won't do his part per-fectly. But today was the first run-through with everybody there, and he just didn't show up. I knew it was a mistake not to come fetch him, but I was there all day with individual rehearsals, doing some interviews the BAM press office set up, blah blah blah, and the run-through wasn't until four. It was so easy, all he had to do was tell the driver "Canal Street and East Broadway," he knows exactly where it is. It was so embarrassing, with every-one else there five minutes early, and then at a quarter past I called, and it was just as I feared – the line was busy. He's dis-covered the Internet. My password on NYAN is stored, and I haven't been brave enough to change it so he can't use it – that would really provoke a showdown. Fucking little Amir showed him how. They sit there for hours, looking at porn. They make it so easy for you now, if you go to one FOOT-LONG BLACK DICK NON-STOP PUMPING DUDES, ten more find their way to you instantly, with the watermelon-tit girls right behind. I hate that shit.

I hopped in a cab, and sure enough, there he was, watching some Australian college kid masturbating on a live videocam site. I really freaked out, started screaming at him. I sort of hit him, not really hit, but shoved him out of the chair so he fell down. He gave me the most terrified look with those big brown eyes, and my heart just sank. He ran into the bathroom and locked it, and wouldn't come out. It's the kind that's easy to pick – stick a pin in the little hole and it opens – so I came in, and he was sitting on the floor, crying. "I sorry, I forgot, now you angry for me." When I moved toward him, he cringed – that just killed me. I took him in my arms and hugged him, but he was as tense as a board.

I tried to explain to him that I had just paid out more than $1,000 for all those people to come rehearse, and then they couldn't do it. There was no way I could bring him back after that, so I called and told them he was sick. It's so frustrating trying to talk to him about anything important. His English is so basic, and he just says, "I sorry, my mistake, please not be angry for me." I can't believe I knocked him down, but I was just livid at the sight of him watching that guy masturbate while I'm working ten hours a day to create a production that will make him a star. I just lost it. In all the years I was with Andrew, I never once did anything like that, never. Of course, Andrew never screwed up. He was the perfect wife, I see that now.

So now what? I asked him if he wanted to go to Barney's, of course he said no. It was kind of a stupid thing to say, I just wanted to try to make it up to him somehow. I ordered some take-out from Jalan-Jalan, and he wouldn't touch it. He's spent the past two hours just lying in bed, doing nothing, his eyes half-open, like he's in a catatonic state. If I ask, he says, "I am fine, resting only."

Love ya and MISS ya,

Joey

Subj: Tsk-tsk
Date: 10/26 8:56:12 PM Pacific Daylight Time
From: podnnell@sfchronicle.com
To: Danzguy@NYAN.net (Joseph Breaux)

Dear Mr. Kowalski,

Perhaps you were right the first time: maybe it is the Chateau de Sade. I'm not sure I should joke about it. It sounds so dreadful, I almost can't say what I really think. You were always hot-blooded – the most terrifying moment of my life was when you almost got into a fistfight with that Nigerian cab driver on Eighth Avenue. But little Wayan, he's your baby! Not to mention your partner. And you're so much bigger than he is! I won't be severe with you, as I'm sure you're already racked with guilt, but that's not the homosexual way, darling.

Please write again soon and tell me that you've worked it out. The problem, as you say, is that you can't really talk about things with him. "I'm sorry" lacks nuance.

Tsk-tsk, naughtykins.

Blanche

Subj: He laughed
Date: 10/28 10:14:51 PM Eastern Standard Time
From: Danzguy@NYAN.net (Joseph Breaux)
To: podonnell@sfchronicle.com

Hi Phil,

I know, I know, I've been in a state of torment. We made it up
last night – I was on my knees with my little English-Indonesian
dictionary, trying to find some way of begging for forgiveness,
and finally he laughed – I probably said "My mother sells chick-
ens on the moon" or something like that. He just started
giggling and jumped down on the floor and kissed me, and we
had a grand ol' time making up. It was like Bali again. I reread
my original message, and I can understand why you were
shocked. I exaggerated what happened, it was more like a manly
whack on the shoulders – "Hey, man, what the hell are you
doing!" – and it caught him off guard and he fell. I didn't hit
him. I could never do that. I'm so relieved – you can't imagine
how happy I felt when he laughed.

Today we finally did the first run-through of the piece. I let him
stay home in the morning, to give him a chance to show he's reliable. He was almost an hour early. His "parents" were already
there, so they had a good jabber in Balinese. Tomorrow
afternoon, the four of us are going to the top of the Empire State
Building. Again. Should really be fun – a perfect fall weekend
afternoon, half of Europe in town, the wait shouldn't be more
than a few hours, listening to people speaking Balinese. I'm
going to try and get out of it, let him go with "ma and pa." The
other guy, the one playing the prince, is being very standoffish. I
think he has a son around Way's age.

And the piece looks GOOD. There are still a million kinks to get
out, but the piece is getting there. Today was already better than
the premiere – the dancers are so much better, there's no com-
parison. Everyone was really knocked out by Wayan, but he

seemed strangely embarrassed when everyone fussed over him. In Bali he used to love that. At this point, I feel at least a couple of weeks ahead of schedule. Do you know what that feels like?

Yippee!

Love ya,

Joey

Subj: Yippee?
Date: 10/30 3:15:02 PM Pacific Standard Time
From: podonnell@sfchronicle.com
To: Danzguy@NYAN.net (Joseph Breaux)

Dear Mickey,

We boys and girls know what a cheerful, enthusiastic little mouse you are, but aren't these mood swings getting to be a little extreme? Ta tante will grudgingly accept your latest ecstatic upturn, though when I compare the two messages, we go from <<I can't believe I knocked him down>> to <<I didn't hit him. I could never do that,>> it was just a <<manly whack>>. That could be construed as sugar-coating, but I hate semantic niggling, and I accept that knocks and whacks and so forth are subject to varying interpretations. I wouldn't really know, having never knocked or whacked myself.

I'm glad to hear that you two have kissed and made up, even more happy to hear that the piece is coming along. Gotta run, presh, gotta get a review done.

Daisy Duck

(so much more chic than Minnie Mouse, who had to be either diesel or a fag hag to hang out with a fairy like Mickey)

Subj: P.O.'ed
Date: 11/3 11:41:31 PM Eastern Standard Time
From: Danzguy@NYAN.net (Joseph Breaux)
To: podonnell@sfchronicle.com

Hi Phil,

I'm beginning to feel a little bit hysterical: Wayan is ruining the
piece. He was an hour late today, the second time it's happened,
so we had to completely rearrange the schedule. If I speak to
him sweetly, he pays no attention; if I yell at him, he gets all
downcast and dejected and says "I sorry, you are right, my mistake." But today was the second time. He just doesn't seem to
have any interest in doing it. In Bali, everybody knows every single part by heart, so when the festival comes, they just do it. All
that rehearsing when I was there was for my benefit. He doesn't
understand that it's not enough that he know his part, everyone
else has to know it, too – they've got to be able to play off it.
The other dancers are being nice about it – what choice do they
have? – but it's just SO unprofessional. It's always weird when
one of the soloists is the choreographer's boyfriend. I try not to
give him special treatment, but in a way his age makes it easier.
Everybody realizes he's just a kid. It's so absurd – he's my second
lead, he's living with me, and I can't get him to turn up on time.
I feel like I need to hire a nanny. Seriously.

Don't say a word, bitch – of course you're right about these extreme swings. Of course I know, how can I expect professional
behavior from a nonprofessional. I haven't even told you the
worst part. My Visa bill came in today, and there were more
than $600 in charges to porn sites. It took me a while to figure it
out, because they have these dummy names like Laguna Holiday
Shop and Santa Monica Ranch, its always California. At first I
thought it was a mistake, or fraud, but when I called Visa, the
lady said, "Sir, they are fees for limited-access websites." Then
the penny dropped. It really is like dealing with a little boy: "I
didn't do it, Amir did it." As if that makes any difference. He

claims he didn't know it cost anything, "I tinking only for securitas, not for pay." That is possible, given his complete cluelessness about money, but he always lies when he thinks he's going to get into trouble. That came a week after the phone bill with $180 in calls to Bali (though that wasn't so bad, they were all to his parents). So now Amir is banished, and the NYAN account has a new password, NOT saved. I also cracked down on the offerings – actually, it was a compromise. I let him leave the little trays, but no more incense. The place was reeking. That stuff is supposed to be burned outside. And I'm sorry, but when the rice starts attracting ants, I throw them out. So now we have the big-time pout going on.

I feel like I'm the one entitled to pout. In fact, I'm getting P.O.'ed to the max. I gotta just hold on until 10:30 p.m., December 19. Then I'm taking him back to Bali, and see what's up. How's that for a vague plan? If you answer, just send news – no advice, no lectures, no bucking up.

Love ya,

Joey

Subj: Gee
Date: 11/5 6:25:20 PM Pacific Standard Time
From: podonnell@sfchronicle.com
To: Danzguy@NYAN.net (Joseph Breaux)

Gee,

It's so much fun to write a letter to someone who tells you what to write about. Only news . . . let's see. I made the terrible mistake of buying a different brand of dog food, and poor Fifi has had the worst case of the goopy-poops. My nephew Jason scored two goals in his soccer game on Saturday, and let me tell you, I was one proud Uncle Phil! Today I went to the market to buy groceries, a chicken, vegetables, and a few household items that were running low. I intended to buy some grapefruits – you know how I LUV my grapefruit – but they were so expensive I got oranges instead. Speaking of citrus fruit, while I was at the store, I impulsively decided to make a lemon chiffon pie, so I bought a lemon zester. It cost a bit more than I would have expected to pay for such a simple tool, but it seems to be a sturdy model, so I look upon it as an investment. The ol' gas tank was getting low, so on the way home I stopped at the Arco station and got another stamp for my Collect Noah's Ark Animal series. One more full tank and I'll be able to send the card in for a pair of camels. The Ark itself costs extra. A perfect Christmas gift for Jason, don't you think? San Francisco has been even chillier than usual for this time of year, and foggy all the time. Oh dear, I had so much more to tell you about the weather, but the microwave timer just beeped, so I better take that Stove Top stuffing out before it gets all gluey. I've gotten to the point where I prefer it over mashed potatoes with my baked chicken. What's your preference, Joey?

Twinkle and shine,

Phil

Subj: Hardy-har-har
Date: 11/8 9:23:18 AM Eastern Standard Time
From: Danzguy@NYAN.net (Joseph Breaux)
To: podonnell@sfchronicle.com

Hi Phil,

Hardy-har-har, very funny. I just wanted to let you know that I'm going to be on Charlie Rose next week. Isn't that cool? Me, Mark, and Tim – I think the program is basically, "Why are all choreographers such big fags?" I must say, though, it's kind of great to be on an equal footing with Tim and especially with Mark, who is really the Mother of Us All.

The piece is getting into great shape. At this point, Wayan is basically no longer a part of the creative process. It was easier just to tell him to forget about rehearsals than to schedule them and have him not show up, or arrive so late as to make it pointless. I thought about having a car service arrive at the apartment and pick him up, but I decided I can't make him do it if he doesn't want to. One of the boys in the corps just walks through his part. It's very embarrassing with the other dancers, but . . . a weird personal life isn't so weird in dance. I'm still confident that he'll be brilliant in the performances. It's me I'm worried about. I've gained more weight. Phil, I'm now fifteen pounds heavier than when I left for Bali. That's a lot. I can't seem to control my appetite, and the two or three glasses of cheap wine every night have become a bottle.

Things are going OK with Way, I guess. I don't know what's going on in his life, really. I don't see very much of him, I'm working so hard. Whenever I ask him if he's bored, he kisses me and says, "No, I always haffy with my Joe," but it's like he's saying a mantra. Sometimes he and Amir go out together – I don't care where they go, as long as Way gets home before midnight and Amir's not with him. And you know what I'm thinking, when I'm sitting there alone, drinking cheap wine and watching some piece of shit on TV or pretending to read? I'm thinking that if I were back at Horatio Street with Andrew, he would let me talk about the piece all I wanted, and he would have smart solutions for some of the boring little problems.

I've been feeling so run-down, I went to see the doctor last week. It had been a couple of years. He did some tests, basically told me I was strong as an ox, to slow down, get enough sleep, eat three squares a day ($250 for that?). He also did an HIV test –

negative. I knew that, but I had never had the test. Anyway, I'm
fine. So much to do!

Love ya,

Joey

Subj: Boob tube
Date: 11/14 9:31:52 AM Pacific Standard Time
From: AndrewTan@wol.com
To: etan@MIT.edu (Eric Tan)

Hi Eric,

I've just signed a one-year lease on a nice little house in Pacific
Heights, with an option to buy. It's a two-bedroom brick bungalow from about 1920, Art Decoid, on half an acre of land. I
won't go into an elaborate description, because you'll get a
complete video tour as soon as I take over the place, in three
days.

Did you see Joey on the Charlie Rose show last night? I saw it in
the paper, and I kept telling myself I wasn't going to watch it,
but of course when eleven o'clock rolled around, I couldn't resist. He looked great, sounded smart. You know what? I miss
him. I had that hot little flash in my chest, not that I wanted to
cry, but the disbelief . . . I can't believe he's gone. It was a mistake. I really shouldn't have watched, just as I was beginning to
feel comfortable with Nat. He and I are going to London for a
week, before I start work at the Kappan. Probably leaving next
week. Northwest flies out of Boston, so maybe we can stop off
for a day or two on the way back. "Meeting the family" is such
a big step, but he's already met Mom and Dad. It will be fun to
be back in London, and it will certainly tell me a lot about
where Nat and I are headed.

Say hi to the Soph; that was so cool to see the sonogram of my nephew. Name? I bet you want to name him after Dad, but don't make him a "II." That's so rich-kid pretentious.

Love from your conflicted brother

Subj: Here I come
Date: 11/14 11:12:00 PM Pacific Standard Time
From: podonnell@sfchronicle.com
To: Danzguy@NYAN.net (Joseph Breaux)

Joey,

We hung up less than an hour ago, but I've been thinking – are you sure you don't want me to come out? New York is definitely Franklin's prerogative, but if I explain the situation, he might okay a cheap flight and let me do some of the things he didn't cover when he was there in September. He puts on that Sheridan Whiteside act, but he's actually a soft-hearted old geezer, I think he'll do it. I don't want you there alone. The problem is, I haven't been here long enough to get any vacation time. Actually, I'm not asking, I'm telling: if Franklin says yes, I'm coming as soon as I can.

No more crazy talk about canceling the piece. You may have created it for him, but the piece is entirely your brainchild, and you CAN perform it without him. Change the linens on that sofa bed.

Phil

Subj: Urgent message from Joe Breaux
Date: 11/15 5:38:58 PM Eastern Standard Time
From: Danzguy@NYAN.net (Joseph Breaux)
To: BBlankenship@indonet.net.id

Dear Bob,

A terrible problem has come up in my production of "Elegy for
Walter Spies" at the Brooklyn Academy of Music. Wayan Renda
has returned to Bali. I believe his flight arrived November 14 at
11:10 a.m., Bali time. He left without giving me any advance
warning – he just up and went.

Bob, I realize that you didn't approve of my relationship with
Wayan, and I respect your views. If someone had told me before
I left for Bali that I would ever do such a thing, I would have
told them they were crazy. But I did do it, and it resulted in the
best piece of work I've done so far in my career. I won't go into
the particulars of my relationship with Wayan; that's not
relevant. I will only say I had no idea he was so unhappy here,
and was completely shocked when I found his note, saying he
had left.

The point now is to get him to come back and do the
performances. It has nothing to do with our personal relationship: at this point a major undertaking by the Brooklyn
Academy of Music, with the participation of the Brooklyn
Philharmonic, 23 dancers, and a gamelan from Berkeley is about
to collapse. Ordinarily in a case like this you simply replace the
dancer. But you saw the piece: How can I replace him? I don't
mean because of his great talent but because of his unique combination of mastery of Balinese movement and the modern
dance I taught him.

I was hoping you might talk to him and his father. Please explain
the gravity of the situation, that he is harming many people by
this action. You can tell him that he doesn't have to stay with

me; we'll put him up at a hotel. I can't pay him more than we originally agreed on; that would really be unfair to the other performers. But surely the Rendas can use $10,000? Maybe you can reason with the father.

I hope you will forgive me for asking for your help in such a disagreeable matter, but frankly, I'm desperate. I didn't know who else to turn to. You certainly don't have to say yes, but I would be so grateful if you could try to persuade him to come back.

I hope this message finds all well with you.

Best wishes,

Joe

Subj: The Breaux Disaster
Date: 11/15 6:01:35 PM Eastern Standard Time
From: Erica_Golden@IDS.org
To: thumbelina@indonet.net.id

Dear Pam,

That Joe Breaux certainly gives people a lot to talk about! First there was Jens Munk pulling out, though that was really nothing, or would have been nothing except Quentin Trent wrote a poisonous little item for the Times.

And now the big disaster: Wayan Renda ran away from home! or rather, ran back home. Two days ago. Of course Joe had bought him a round-trip ticket, and apparently the kid found it and booked himself on the next flight out. Lauren McIntyre, Joe's new business manager, is an old buddy from Dancespace days, she told me all about it. He left a note, but Joe won't talk about it. He's pulling his hair out, of course – who can blame him! In three weeks he starts a sold-out ten-performance run, and he just lost his co-star. He keeps telling everyone that he's irreplaceable – well, romance aside, he has a point. It's really not quite the same thing as finding a new Giselle at the last minute. Joe created a whole new style of dance for him. Joe has a meeting with Bernie Kuykendahl tomorrow morning, and I think Bernie will teach him the meaning of "replaceable." As in, find a new dancer, or you replace the however many thousands of dollars I've advanced you. Bernie's a tough old bird.

Joe's P.R. rep put out an announcement last week saying that the BAM performances will be his final appearances as a solo dancer on the stage. From what I've been hearing it's a good decision. He can still make it look right, but so much better to retire before everyone is laughing at you behind your back, as it was with Twyla and so many others.

That's all I know, hon'. My life seems to be brightening up – IDS has *finally* approved my request for an assistant. I've found a really bright young guy, 25, getting his Ph.D. in dance history. I really wanted it to be a scholar, not a dancer.

Otherwise it's the same ol' same ol'.

Miss you, sweetie

Rica

Subj: Reply from Bob Blankenship
Date: 11/16 6:28:19 AM Eastern Standard Time
From: BBlankenship@indonet.net.id
To: Danzguy@NYAN.net (Joseph Breaux)

Dear Joe,

I did as you requested, and dropped by the Renda home this morning. The father came out to see me, and didn't invite me in, which was most unusual. He was very polite and affable, but completely evasive. When I tried to address the point of Wayan's leaving New York, and abandoning your production, he began chuckling, and saying, "Yes, yes, we're so happy to have him home again, Wayan had such an interesting visit to New York," and so forth in that vein.

Joe, the longer I live here, the less I understand the Balinese. But it was very plain to me that Wayan will not return to New York. It would have been most inappropriate for me to press the issue; Pak Renda's complete evasion and the way he was laughing meant, "Please don't ask me to discuss this, because I won't." I don't think the money would have made any difference; the Balinese can be incredibly greedy, but at the same time their lives are controlled by other influences which are just as powerful and utterly inscrutable, having to do with their religion.

I am sorry I can't be more helpful. I know this is a blow to your production, but best of luck in finding a good replacement. New York must have any number of talented young Asian dancers. Remember, "The show must go on!"

Best wishes,

Bob

Subj: Thanks, but really...
Date: 11/17 4:52:51 PM Eastern Standard Time
From: Danzguy@NYAN.net (Joseph Breaux)
To: podonnell@sfchronicle.com

Hi Phil,

Thanks for your nice offer – I really do appreciate it, but it's not necessary. I've postponed my nervous breakdown until after the performances. I had a meeting with Bernie Kuykendahl this morning, who basically told me I had a choice between finding a new dancer for the Boy and making the best of it, or bringing my professional career in the field of dance to an end forever. He was blunt and persuasive. He had the BAM accountant there, who showed me what would happen if I canceled. Not only would I have to pay back all the money I've been advanced, there's also the return of all those thousands of tickets, the cost of booking another act for the most profitable time of the year, and on and on. They never used the S word, but they didn't have to (not that they would get much out of me if they did sue). Of course they were right – all that stuff about canceling the show was just hysterics. Once he saw that I was going ahead with the piece, he was incredibly nice: no apologies necessary, just tell me how I can help, like that. He's a very impressive guy. I can't imagine him not getting his way.

He made the point, which is true, that there are a lot of talented young Asian dancers at the moment, though none of them are Balinese. Bernie said, how many New Yorkers can tell the difference between Balinese and Chinese and Filipino? I reminded him that I have three other Balinese soloists, plus the gamelan. The kid has to look like his parents. As for the Balinese gestures that Wayan used so beautifully, they'll probably have to go. Maybe the Balinese soloists will be able to teach the new Boy, but I doubt it – they start training the kids there when they're still toddlers, practically. It'll have to be just an approximation. It's a real blow, but I don't have a choice. Realistically, it was ten per cent of the piece at most. I was thinking of going back to Bali, A. to try and convince Wayan to come back to do it, or B. recruit someone else, but I've given that idea up. Bob Blankenship tells me that for whatever reason, Wayan will never come back, and I can't imagine that I would get much cooperation from the Balinese in recruiting someone new. I think I have a BAD reputation there now.

I'm fine, basically. I'm too busy trying to save the piece to have much time for feeling blue about Wayan. Word is out – Wanted:

Cute Asian dancer who can pass for sixteen, familiarity with traditional Balinese dance a plus. Bernie has people at the BAM office working with the companies and dance academies in Chicago and California, so it's possible that you may see me soon, after all.

Love ya,

Joey

Subj: Attaboy
Date: 11/19 11:58:35 AM Pacific Standard Time
From: podonnell@sfchronicle.com
To: Danzguy@NYAN.net (Joseph Breaux)

Attaboy, Joey,

now you're talking. You've got a lot to offer with this role, so you should have a big pool of talent to choose from. I do hope you can come out here. The biggest rice bar in town is just a few blocks away, on Polk – you should have some fun recruiting there. On Saturday night, every Asian twinkie in town is turned out in her fabbiest frou-frou, waiting to get pounced on by the evil rice queens.

I never had any ricely tendencies before, but living out here, I'm starting to understand it. If you do come visit, I'll have to hide the gardener from you. He's the landlord's son, just graduated from college. The landlord is Chinese, his wife's Italian, and their son is a total dreamboat, the perfect white teeth and lustrous black eyes of a Chinese boy, and the strapping build of an Italian. His name is Tony Wang, but we call him Rice-a-Roni, the San Francisco treat. When I saw him out there this morning, wearing nothing but a very snug pair of Levis, I had to reach for my smelling salts. Then he said, "Good morning, Mr. O'Donnell," and ruined everything. But remember, I have dibs.

Why am I telling you about my gardener? Actually, it's his father's garden, but if Raymond Tan can have a gardener, why not me? You sound SO much better, Joey. You have a decent amount of time, and you said yourself that you were a couple of weeks ahead of schedule – so, full steam ahead! You seem remarkably composed. I'm not sure whether I should say this . . . but I think you're better off without Wayan. His timing was disastrous, of course, but it was obvious that the two of you were much too volatile together – all that agony and ecstasy, sturm und drang. It's no good when both halves of the couple are so hot-blooded. Are you ever going to tell me what happened?

Luv 'n' kisses,

Phyllis

Subj: Jungle drums
Date: 11/19 10:29:09 PM Eastern Standard Time
From: thumbelina@indonet.net.id
To: Erica_Golden@IDS.org

Dear Rica,

The jungle drums are beating again – I've got more gossip from my maid's brother's friend in Seka Kerobokan. Well, as you know little Wayan ran away from Joe Breaux and came back to Bali. It turns out that the reason is because the dukun, the same one who put the love spell on Joe in the first place, determined that Joe was making bad luck for Wayan! Isn't that hysterical? Apparently Joe was messing with his offerings, which are an essential part of their religion. Joe was throwing them out. Wayan called his parents and told them, and they brought the dukun over and he asked Wayan a lot of questions over the phone, and he decided that if Wayan didn't leave quick, something terrible was going to happen to him.

So now Wayan's back at the antique store. I was walking by the other day, and I stopped to say hello. He was as bright and cheerful as could be. I don't know him very well, so I just asked him how his trip to New York was, and he said, "Oh, great, I saw so many interesting things. Mr. Joe was so nice to me," and that was it. I don't think he has a clue as to how much trouble he caused. I saw Bob last night at our reading group, and he agreed with me, life has been dull around here since Joe left. He's one of those people who just generates excitement everywhere he goes. Bob said that all the people in the seka really miss him. Once they realized that Joe's intentions to Wayan were honorable, even though they disapproved, they just blew it off. One thing I'll say about the Balinese, unlike most Christians I know, they're very forgiving.

The book our group is reading is "This Earth of Mankind," by an Indonesian writer named Pramoedya. It's fabulous – have you ever heard of him? He made the whole thing up while he was in prison in the early Suharto days. He didn't have any paper, so he told the story to the other prisoners, and they memorized it, sort of like "Fahrenheit 451," if you remember that. You should check it out – it's sort of like if Tolstoy had written "Gone with the Wind" about Indonesia.

My main news is that Nyoman is having her baby, so she has to go back to her village for the 927 rituals required for a baby, and will be gone for a few months. Then we'll have the baby around the house, which I'm not so sure about. We've found a Javanese girl to fill in, but it takes so long to teach them how you like everything to be done. I know I'm breaking your heart with my servant problems, so I'll let you go. Let me hear.

Big kiss,

Pam

Subj: The new Boy
Date: 11/20 10:12:51 AM Eastern Standard Time
From: Danzguy@NYAN.net (Joseph Breaux)
To: podonnell@sfchronicle.com

Hi Phil,

We've narrowed it down to five, three in New York (one is actually Providence, Rhode Island), and two in California. One kid's in L.A., the other in Oakland, so I'm making the L.A. kid shuttle up. Sooo – I'm on my way! I'll arrive Friday afternoon and leave Sunday. I'm sorry it's such a short trip, but as you can imagine, I don't exactly have time to sit around sipping cappuccino with you in North Beach. But we'll have a nice dinner, maybe do a little gardening. . . .

I think the L.A. boy might be the best. It's so hard to tell from a video. The choice is basically between taking a chance on a young dancer who will make the story credible, and somebody with some experience on the stage. I can't tell you how many excellent Japanese and Chinese dancers in their twenties I've auditioned, but they all look too old. This isn't just a romance with a young guy, I'm supposed to be on trial for having sex with an underage boy. The L.A. boy is Malaysian, so he looks exactly right, and he's eighteen. He's very pretty, actually more boyish than Wayan. He's obviously talented, but his stage experience is limited. It's a big part, with a lot of pressure. That's why Wayan was so perfect – he had been a soloist virtually all his life, but there's no use going into that. One of the New York dancers has performed a lot, and he's had a few solo parts with Owen Adam's group – but even though he's only 22, he just looks too old. He's Chinese, and about a foot taller than Komang, the Boy's Father. The Oakland guy is a possibility, a good dancer, but I have high hopes for little Andrew Othman (why did his name have to be Andrew!). It would be so great to have a Malay boy the right age.

I shouldn't take the time to write a long message, but I've been wanting to talk to you about this, and I would rather do it this way – when I'm in San Francisco, I want us to have some FUN. You asked what happened. It was very simple: I came home and found a note on the dining-room table which said, "Joe you nice friend and love me, but me doomed here. Dangerous to stay in this place. I sorry my mistake. I hope not to damage you. Now I go to Bali. Please to love and pardon me. Your baby Wayan." He obviously sat down with the dictionary and tried to translate his thoughts word by word. He knew where his ticket was, so he just called up Northwest and got on the next plane to Singapore.

The first night, I cried my eyes out. I was overwhelmed by incredulity. It was the first time in my life I've ever been dumped. I don't think the pre-Andrew era counts, but even then, I was always the one who broke it off. I was so mystified by his note; I think it has something to do with their ridiculous religion. It seems preposterous that he would have run off like that because I wouldn't let him burn incense, but who knows – maybe the little trays of rice don't work without incense. My next reaction was hysteria about the piece, which you know all about, and feeling lonely – I missed seeing his cute little butt and sweet little smile around the house. But by the fourth or fifth day, I had really stopped thinking about him much. This is going to sound terrible, but it was like when Nijinsky died. Remember how much I loved him? I was inconsolable when he died, sobbed like a little kid, but I got over it in a few days. It's because the relationship with an animal is purely physical – it's not like when a person dies, and you think time after time, for months and even years, "Gee, ol' So-and-so would've gotten a kick out of that."

Phil, this is the ultimate "Toljaso." My relationship with Wayan WAS purely physical. I don't mean purely sexual – there was much more to it than that, but once we stopped dancing together, the only thing I could connect with was the cute butt and the sweet smile. It really was like Nijinsky – I liked having him around because he was fun to play with.

And do you know who I miss so much it crushes my guts? Of course you do. A hundred times a day, I think, "God, how I wish I could talk to Andrew about that." You were exactly right: I dumped the perfect partner for a kid I couldn't talk to. The dance communication was incredible, but that's my art, not my life. Wayan and I never had the slightest understanding of each other. And now I'm alone. You're right: it's no good when both guys are so hot-blooded. Andrew was the perfect yin to my yang. He was my anchor, he kept my feet on the ground when my brainstorms threatened to fling me into the sky. Have I mixed enough metaphors yet?

I know all too well that there's nothing I can do about it. I want Andrew back so much it kills me, but I can't call him or send a message until I hear from him. Remember what that was like, when you first came out (I forgot, you were out at birth) and started dating, waiting for the phone to ring, for the voice on the line to be Him, saying what you wanted to hear? That's what the rest of my life looks like. I'll get over it. As you say, I'll cope. But somehow, some way, I'm going to get Andrew back. Maybe it'll take ten years, but I'm gonna get him back.

So, that's my story and I'm sticking with it. Don't worry about picking me up at the airport, I'll shuttle in. I should be there by around six. And remember, despite this grim message, we're gonna have some FUN.

Love ya forever,

Joey

Subj: FUN GUY
Date: 11/20 8:32:55 PM Pacific Standard Time
From: podonnell@sfchronicle.com
To: Danzguy@NYAN.net (Joseph Breaux)

Ya lucky duck,

Any person who can live to the age of 36 years (right?) and say he's
never been dumped deserves not one morsel of pity. But I'll give
you all you want, anyway. Oh Joey, this has been so painful for me
to watch. You and Andrew were so good together. You know I always thought he was a bit square – I never once heard him say a
single curse word – but in a wife that's GOOD. He was really the
partner you needed and deserved. But honeybun, he's gone. I feel a
cliche coming on, something about spilt milk – remember that one?
Or I could get Bardic on you and tell you that all the world's a
stage, and we're just players who do our numbers and then exit
stage left. Unfortunately, by the time the reviews come in, the show
has closed. Remember, you're an artist, and every experience,
whether joyous or painful, is raw material for your work. I'm not
being a Pollyanna, it's true. That's Mimesis 101.

You're right – when you're here we shouldn't be a pair of
gloomy Guses, talking about your problems. We should talk
about MY problems. Just kidding. You sound like you need
some FUN. (Are you aware that you always write FUN in full
caps? You're just a FUN GUY.) So I will continue briefly in the
unasked-for-advice mode, and tell you that I think that you must
try to forget about getting Andrew back. Remember the chagrin
you felt when you saw that note from Wayan? Does the phrase
<<overwhelmed by incredulity>> ring a bell? Multiply that by a
factor of, oh, a thousand, and you'll have a glimmer of how
Andrew felt when you told him that after fourteen years of marriage you were dumping him for a Balinese teenager. That was
the dumping of a lifetime.

I don't want to rehash all that, and I'm not trying to make you feel remorseful – I know you already do. But as a veteran dumpee, let me tell ya, even if he wanted to come back to you, he couldn't. He's a soft-spoken, passive sort of guy, but he has character and class – his pride wouldn't let him take you back. I'm not saying you two will never get back together again, but if it ever happens, there's a rock-solid one-year waiting period, more likely two or three, and it will have to be his idea.

OK, I've been wise enough for one wee message. See you soon.

Phil

Subj: Thanks and apologies
Date: 11/24 11:01:01 PM Eastern Standard Time
From: Danzguy@NYAN.net (Joseph Breaux)
To: podonnell@sfchronicle.com

Hi Phil,

I just got in, wanted to quickly post off some electronic bread and butter. It was great to see you – sorry it was so quick. Fritz and you really seem comfortable with each other now – that's so great. I don't know where he ever got off saying that you were campy – anybody who does a Bette Davis imitation as good as that is a little camp herself. It's clear he really adores you. And why not? You're adorable!

I feel like I sort of owe you an apology for bringing that kid home. You were nice about saying it was all right, but still, it was a little bit trashy. But he made it so clear that he wanted to come home with me. I'm just a fella who can't say no. I haven't done anything like that in so many years, and it was FUN. (I guess you're right, I DO do that.) Don't forget, it was your idea that we go to that place.

Andrew Othman arrives tomorrow. Keep your fingers crossed
for me. I may not be the best correspondent until opening night.

Love ya,

Joey

P.S. Happy Thanksgiving

Subj: Message from Andrew
Date: 11/25 7:25:53 PM Greenwich Mean Time
From: goodgestreetcaf@bix.co.uk
To: etan@MIT.edu (Eric Tan)

Hi Eric,

Greetings from London. I was walking by a little cybercafe and
thought I would step in and say hi. Nat and I are having a ball.
It's been so long since I've gone somewhere as a regular tourist.
We went to Hampton Court yesterday . . . it was fantastic! Every
time I was in London before it was with Joey, and he always set
the agenda. We would go to the Tate and the National Gallery
and that sort of thing, but it was always dance over theatre, and
he would never have dreamed of going somewhere as touristy as
Hampton Court . . . well, the reason the tourists go there is
because it's fascinating. The Mantegnas were spectacular, the gardens unbelievably beautiful, etc. I told Nat, I want to go to the
Tower of London and see the crown jewels. We've gone to the
theatre almost every night, saw Sir Thomas Wiggins in Merry
Wives of Windsor. He was wonderful, but it's not such a great
play. Tomorrow we have tickets to the Royal Opera, Madame
Butterfly. Not one of my favorites, but it was either that or
Wagner. It's a young Italian soprano who's supposed to be great,
so at least it will sound right. I spent a fortune yesterday at Paul
Smith . . . you know how I love his stuff. I'm having a real
London holiday.

For Thankers we went to the grill at the Savoy. I had the *best* Dover sole. Nat ordered the turkey dinner, the coward. He's sitting right next to me, writing a message to his parents . . . even though he can't see my screen I feel a little weird talking about him. It's going fine, I'm having a nice time with him. It's funny how we say "talk" and "chat" in E-mail, when what we're really doing is typing. Anyway, we'll see you on the first. I already gave you the flight details, I forget, around four in the afternoon.

Love to all present and future Tans from your brother

Subj: Reine de poulet-riz
Date: 11/26 3:51:01 PM Pacific Standard Time
From: podonnell@sfchronicle.com
To: Danzguy@NYAN.net (Joseph Breaux)

Ma chere reine de poulet-riz,

It wasn't that it was trashy – a single gentleman has to have the occasional boink, so important for the complexion – but he was such a bitty little thing, his waist hardly as big around as one of your thighs. If I looked hesitant when you asked, it was because I was afraid you would break him. He was a cute little bug, I gotta admit. Fritz was very amused. He and I never go to places like that. I didn't get a nibble, but I suppose Fritz and I looked very coupley. But they were certainly swarming all over you – is there some sort of chicken-and-rice hoodoo vibe? "Come and get it, kiddies, Daddy has the magic wand"? And where's the grown-up rice? Does rice ever date rice, or is it always white on rice? (C'mon, that was good.) It seems very weird to me – is it always this white daddy thing? It really seemed like the creepy old child-molester types were luckier than the cute young white guys. I know you're too busy to explain the mysteries of rice, but I do find it fascinating.

Joey, you're not turning into a chicken hawk, are you? It's a loser's game – you'll be amazed how quickly middle age comes galloping along, and while you keep getting older, the babies are always babies. I'm not lecturing, I know it was different with Wayan, and Miss Saigon was just a flingette. But it IS two in a row. Give a grown-up a chance.

Welcome home, and congratulations on finding your Boy. And you're right, thank god he's a baby het. It was great to see you, Joey. Now buckle down and get to work.

Me

Subj: Re: Reine de poulet-riz
Date: 11/27 9:20:49 PM Eastern Standard Time
From: Danzguy@NYAN.net (Joseph Breaux)
To: podonnell@sfchronicle.com

Hi Phil,

I don't get it either. Saturday night was like my third or fourth visit to a cruise bar over the past ten years. I know they're attracted to me because of my body, which let's face it, is my main marketing tool. I think they're also turned on by the hairy chest, maybe because they don't have any themselves.

The age thing is completely mysterious to me. How can old be good? But that's definitely the way it seems to be. I don't think I'm turning into a chicken hawk – both Wayan and little Justin chose me. It's a matter of saying no to compliant, horny youth and beauty. My motto is, when in doubt, say YES! But you're right, I need to get the age differential into single digits. As if I have time to date right now. "Date" – what a terrifying word.

Forget I mentioned it. I hate sex. I'm running to JFK now to meet Andrew O. and his mother.

Love ya,

Joey

Subj: Heaven
Date: 11/28 11:55:41 PM Pacific Standard Time
From: Justin 777@wol.com
To: Danzguy@NYAN.net (Joseph Breaux)

Dear Joe,

This is Justin, from Saturday night at Celadon. I can't stop thinking about you. I believe something very special happened Saturday night, I hope you feel the same. Joe, I have a confession to make – I lied to you when I said I had done that before. Saturday was my first time. I had done some of the other stuff, but it was my first time for that. That's why I was so nervous in the beginning. I lied because I was afraid you might not go through with it, you were being so kind and considerate. I never thought I could feel such extacy. It was like I died and went to heaven. I never knew a man could be so strong like you. I know a handsome, successful man like you probably has so many boys anytime he wants, but what I feel for you is so deep and so special. Now when I lie in bed at night, I can't sleep, I keep remembering every precious moment we spent together, and it makes me ache with desire. Thank you for being so gentle and tender with me, and I'm sorry if I did something wrong. Joe, I hope you will remember me, and call me or send me E-mail sometime.

With all my love,

Justin Thieu

Subj: honored
Date: 11/29 9:23:15 PM Eastern Standard Time
From: Danzguy@NYAN.net (Joseph Breaux)
To: Justin777@wol.com

Dear Justin,

Of course I feel the same. Remember you? – I'll never forget
you. Justin, I knew it was your first time. You've given me the
most precious gift one guy can give another – I am so honored
that you chose me. The reason I was so strong is because your
beauty and passion filled me with desire. Everything you did was
perfect. I wish I could make love to you tonight, Justin. I want
to look deep into your beautiful eyes again, to hold your exquisite body, so delicate and pure. Why do we have to be so far
apart?

I will call you this weekend. You are my beautiful boy.

Your lover,

Joe

Subj: Coming up for air
Date: 12/2 9:12:09 PM Eastern Standard Time
From: Danzguy@NYAN.net (Joseph Breaux)
To: podonnell@sfchronicle.com

Hi Phil,

Thanks for calling last night, sorry I've been out of touch. I did
check out your piece about the O'Neill festival, it was great. I
have to confess, I never really got it. "Long Day's Journey into
Night" may be the greatest American play, but the others are
just TOO LONG.

You can't imagine how frantic it is here. I hope I haven't made a mistake with this kid. He's very talented and well trained, but he's so timid, so afraid of making mistakes. The Boy has to be bold – he seduces Walter, not the other way around. It's really tough for me; I keep seeing Wayan in the part and finding the kid disappointing. The main problem is, whenever I stop him and say, No, do it like this, he tenses up and looks at me like a deer caught in the headlights. His mother is coming to the rehearsals now, I hope that will help. The Balinese are trying to teach him a few rudimentary movements, but it just ain't happenin'.

I'm doing fine – just coming up for air.

Love ya,

Joey

Subj: Home again
Date: 12/2 8:41:00 PM Pacific Standard Time
From: AndrewTan@wol.com
To: etan@MIT.edu (Eric Tan)

Hi Eric,

It was so great to see you and Soph. It's really true what they say: she does look radiant. You do too, actually. I have to admit, it made me feel a tiny bit . . . not envious, but a little down that I'll never have kids. When I said that to Nat, he said, Yes, we can have kids. Gay men can adopt, it happens all the time in San Francisco. That's when I realized, he is *way* more serious than I am. I like him, but if I were going to adopt a child, it wouldn't be with him. I was nice about it, but that's what I told him. He was pretty dejected. I'm not sure where we go from here. I can't quite figure it out . . . I do like him, I like him a lot, but it hasn't gone beyond that. I just don't think he's The One. We'll see. . . .

Actually, what I feel is that I found the right guy, and he turned out to be the wrong guy. If Joey had suggested adopting a kid, I would have said yes immediately. I keep itching to call him up, but I just can't. And I found out that his little playmate ran back to Bali. I bumped into Phil O'Donnell at City Lights, of all places. I hadn't been there in years. He was with a guy who had every appearance of being a new boyfriend, an actor, who claimed he was just about to head off for a rehearsal. He seemed very nice. So Phil and I went for a coffee at the Tivoli. I couldn't resist . . . I asked about Joey. He was nice about it. He kept saying, "Tell me when you've heard enough." He told me that Joey was miserable and wanted us to get back together. I told him that I wasn't miserable, and I didn't think I would ever take him back . . . almost the truth. I'm not really miserable, but there's not a day goes by I don't think about him, and wish my fairy godmother could wave her magic wand and make the past year disappear. I miss him a lot. I miss his restless energy, his raucous, goofy laughter. I miss the way he would secretly dart those black eyes at me, to see my reaction whenever someone said something pompous or silly. The worst part is . . . I don't feel young anymore. But he insulted me in a way I can never forgive, not really, not deep down. He's only miserable because he's alone now. If his little Balinese buddy came back, he'd get over it pretty quick. I made Phil promise not to say anything to him. I'm sure he won't . . . he puts on that camp facade, but he's an honorable guy.

Monday is my first day at the Kappan. Stand by. . . .

Love from your brother

Subj: Call to arms!
Date: 12/3 12:12:24 PM Eastern Standard Time
From: Clifford_Grimm@stff.org
To: aaronvoss@wol.com

Dear Aaron Voss,

First of all, thank you for your continuing support for Save the
Family. In the past, you have helped us not only with your
prayers and your generous financial contributions, but by
marching with us in our fight against pornography, homosexuality, pedophilia, and other threats to the American family. I write
you today to invite you to join battle with the forces of evil yet
again. On December 8, the Brooklyn Academy of Music in New
York City will present a pornographic "ballet" entitled "Elegy
for Walter Spies," by a notorious homosexual "choreographer"
named Joseph Breaux.

The subject matter is too obscene for me to go into any detail,
but it is essentially a "celebration" of homosexual pedophilia.
Walter Spies was an "artist" who lived in the tropical island of
Bali, where he preyed on young boys and converted them to the
sodomitic lifestyle. In 1939 the Dutch colonial authorities
arrested this depraved pervert and convicted him of child
molestation. Mr. Breaux's "ballet" portrays this predator as a
hero, and advocates the view that sodomizing children is an acceptable alternative to the institution of the family. Furthermore,
he is performing this "ballet" with a boy he himself seduced in
Bali and made his personal catamite! The newspapers incorrectly
state this unfortunate lad's age as 20, but my own investigations
have revealed that he is actually 16. How bitterly ironic that a
person (I won't say "man") bearing the name of the earthly father of Jesus, the epitome of the wise and caring patriarch,
should be waging war against the institution of the family.

Sixteen is the age of consent in New York City, so the legal arm
of STFF can't take any action. But we can and we will fight this

abomination. You've marched with us before, Aaron Voss, and we would be honored if you joined us once again. I am writing to you and all the other STFF family members who have previously answered our calls to arms, to invite you to come with us to New York City on December 8 to protest the presentation of this pornographic filth. Buses will leave STFF headquarters in Arlington, the staging area nearest you, at 9:00 a.m., December 8. If you need transport from your home, we'll find a volunteer to drive you. Overnight accommodations in New York City will be provided by our local members—it may be a cot in a church auditorium, but it will be clean and safe, and as comfortable as we can make it. (Yes, there ARE god-fearing folks in New York City!)

As usual, we expect members of the STFF family from all over the nation to join us in our battle to Save the Family. I hope you will be one of them. If you're unable to come, I know your prayers are with us.

God bless you, Aaron Voss.

Clifford Grimm, President
Save the Family Foundation
Arlington, Va.

Subj: Re: Home again
Date: 12/3 3:24:51 PM Eastern Standard Time
From: etan@MIT.edu (Eric Tan)
To: AndrewTan@wol.com

---

hi

trust your instincts – you're being honest with him, so whatever you decide to do will be right. does that sound like dear abby, or what? finals start next week, so i can't really chat. i called dad last night, and asked if he and mom wanted to come to lenox for christmas this year, like we did a few years ago. what do you think? soph will be too preggers for flying, and lenox is the most christmassy place in the world. it's been a white one four years in a row.

hang in there, kid

e

Subj: First day
Date: 12/4 6:24:51 PM Pacific Standard Time
From: AndrewTan@wol.com
To: etan@MIT.edu (Eric Tan)

Hi Eric,

Well, today was my first day at the Kappan. It went fine, every-body was really nice to me. Mattie had a special meeting to in-troduce me, and said all these ridiculous things about me, how I was a noted short-story author, a well-known figure in the mod-ern dance world, etc. It was absurd . . . I almost got the feeling he was trying to justify hiring someone with no experience. But once Clayton Ashcroft, the head arts guy, explained what my duties were, I didn't have any doubt that I could handle it. It's mostly administrative, organizing grant requests, making sure all our criteria are met, recommending people for the review com-mittees, etc. Actually, I think it's going to be great.

The "research" will mean going to all the theatre, dance, and music events I can, reading books by new authors . . . sounds tough, hunh? There will be a certain amount of travel, though it's sort of up to me how much. Clayton subtly let me know that money's never a problem there . . . it's strictly fly business class and book the Ritz-Carlton. I've already got a burgeoning lunch schedule lined up, to meet our contacts at the major local arts institutions. Mattie went through his rolodex and tagged the people I need to meet, and told me to call them up, turn on the charm, and make a lunch date . . . the best restaurants in town, Kappan pays, of course. Everyone I called was very glad to hear from someone at the Kappan Foundation . . . it's like being given Instant Clout.

Eric, I'm afraid I've bungled Christmas. I forgot about Sophie and flying, and I guess I just sort of assumed you guys were coming out here again. Nat invited me to his family's home for Christmas Day dinner, and since the Tans always do dinner on Christmas Eve, I said yes. Regardless of what's happening (or not happening) between him and me romantically, I think it would be rude of me to cancel. Sorry! What if I fly out after Christmas? We can do New Year's together. I know you understand . . . ordinarily Dad would go into one of his sulks over something like this, but since it's his beloved future son-in-law, I don't think he'll make a big fuss. I have to admit, the way Dad sort of campaigns for Nat doesn't really help him (Nat) that much. Sorry about that!

Andy

Subj: Those pesky Christians
Date: 12/4 11:01:09 PM Eastern Standard Time
From: Danzguy@NYAN.net (Joseph Breaux)
To: podonnell@sfchronicle.com

Hi Phil,

Those pesky Christians are after me. Bernie called me into his office this morning to tell me that some right-wing Christian goon squad from Virginia is coming to stop me from turning all the little boys of Brooklyn into queers. Of course he was totally cool – he's having a press conference tomorrow to state his unequivocal support of the piece, and to denounce this group as a bunch of bigots who know nothing about my work. The group is called Save the Family. The president, a sick fuck aptly named Clifford Grimm, still thinks that Wayan is performing. He told all his followers that Wayan was sixteen, and calls him my "personal catamite." I had to look it up. These puritanical people LOVE to toss around the terminology of wickedness. I bet half the men who belong to his group got wood when they read about me and my personal catamite. (Actually, these catamites sound great! – where can I get one?) He's the one who wrote that nasty letter to the Times, if you remember.

Bernie's doing all he can, but there will definitely be a demonstration at BAM on opening night, which means it will be a big circus, with the TV news and so forth, and it's spooking the orchestra and the dancers. The kid was already a nervous wreck, but now he's in a state of total panic. Phil, I have to tell ya, the piece is not looking good. I don't know what it is, but the funny parts aren't funny and the romantic parts aren't romantic. The kid looks perfect, he dances well, but it's just not working. He won't look me in the eye when we dance. If I were watching it, I wouldn't believe it for a second. I've had to scrap all the Balinese gestures – the poor little dickens tried, but he just couldn't do it. I think you really have to be Balinese. The Balinese dancers are completely mechanical – I know they're bored to death. If it weren't for the hundred-dollar bills I keep handing out, they would have run back to Bali just like Wayan did a long time ago.

DON'T write me back and tell me it's just the usual opening-night jitters. I don't look good, my co-star is having a nervous breakdown, the orchestra is bored, the projections look like shit, and I'm being attacked by the god squad.

Tell me how well I'm handling this.
SCREEEEEEEEEEEEEEEEEEEEEEECH!!!!!!!!!!!!

Love ya,

Joey

Subj: Fingers crossed
Date: 12/5 11:32:15 AM Pacific Standard Time
From: podonnell@sfchronicle.com
To: Danzguy@NYAN.net (Joseph Breaux)

Dear Joe,

OK, you're allowed to screech as much as you like. I will say just two things:

It's sold out. Even if you don't get great reviews, you'll still have quite a handsome pile of shekels for yourself at the end of it all. I realize that's not why you're doing it, but no matter what happens, you're going to be richer than you've ever been in your life.

These bible-thumpers are the best thing that could have happened to you. If the piece is as much of a disappointment as you fear (which it won't be), they will distract a lot of the attention.

Have a good screech and get back to work. I've got my fingers crossed. Sorry, hon', I gotta get a review in by three o'clock. Let's do a phoner tonight.

Your loving Phyllis

P.S. Lucian Poole here at the Chron did a little news story about you and the thumpers today, with a head shot of you that looks at least five years old. Not to imply that you've changed one molecule in the past five years, petal. I'll snail-mail it.

Subj: Sighs
Date: 12/6 12:04:3 AM Pacific Standard Time
From: Justin777@wol.com
To: Danzguy@NYAN.net (Joseph Breaux)

My darling Joe,

When I hung up the phone, I was so happy I cried. When I saw
your picture in the paper today, I was so surprised. You told me
you were a dancer, but you were so modest about it. I didn't
know you were FAMOUS! Just to think that an important man
like you would call me and say all those sweet and lovely things
makes me so proud I could DIE. I think I am the luckiest guy in
the whole world. I love you, Joe, I love you with all my heart
and soul. Tonight I am going to sleep with your picture from the
paper next to my heart.

Yours FOREVER,

Justin

Subj: The battle of BAM
Date: 12/9 11:32:10 AM Eastern Standard Time
From: Erica_Golden@IDS.org
To: thumbelina@indonet.net.id

Dear Pam,

Last night Joe Breaux's piece opened at BAM – what a *disaster*! Actually, the piece itself came off pretty well, considering
the circumstances. Some right-wing religious group from
Virginia was there to protest – save the kiddies from the evil
homos. There were about fifty of them. It was actually a little bit
scary. They were waiting at the artists' entrance – Joe was
already inside, but when the boy who's playing Wayan Renda's
part arrived, they attacked him. I don't mean they hit him, but

they surrounded him, praying and singing hymns. An old man got down on his knees, and hugged the kid, saying, "Renounce this abomination. Let the healing love of Lord Jesus cleanse you," that kind of crap. He probably copped a feel while he was at it. The police rescued the boy, who was sobbing by this point. This was all on the local news. Apparently, the protester thought he was Wayan Renda. The cops made them stand across the street, but they made a big racket, singing hymns and chanting their stupid slogans. My favorite is "Adam and Eve, not Adam and Steve" – those people really need some fresh material.

The performance got off to a very rocky start, but steadily improved. Joe made a curtain speech before it began, explaining that the boy had been harassed by the protesters and was suffering acute nervous anxiety, something like that, but had agreed to go on with the performance, asking the audience's indulgence, etc. When the curtain went up, and the orchestra began to play, the protesters outside started singing "Onward, Christian Soldiers" as loud as they could. You know how bad the street noise at BAM is, it sounds like the traffic is running right through the hall. Well, the singing was almost as loud as the orchestra. The police finally moved them all the way over to Flatbush Avenue, but it took a while. The first ten minutes of the piece were essentially obliterated.

In the beginning, the boy walked through it like a zombie, but by the end of the first half, he had gained some confidence and actually danced quite beautifully. Joe danced well enough, but for anyone who remembered those spectacular Endymions, it was clear that he has definitely done the right thing by retiring from the stage. I loved the music – it was so strange, I've never heard anything like it. It was an interesting piece, Pammy, but I must say, I didn't love it as much as you did. You know I'm no prude, and I despise these self-appointed guardians of public morality as much as anyone, but . . . don't they have a point? It really is a glorification of child abuse, isn't it? So the boy was sixteen, so the father approved – I say it's spinach and I say the hell with it. I'm not sure what I'll say in Dancezine – I don't want to be ostracized by the gay mafia (which we're not allowed to say exists). I did think the bits with the house guests were hilarious, and Angelina Monceau was delightful as the fag-hag heiress. But as a whole, I found it rather tasteless.

You wanted my report – I bet you weren't expecting anything quite as juicy as this!

Big hug,
Rica

WOL INSTANT MESSAGE
From: Justin777
To: Woofus, GuySimon

Justin777: guys turn on TV NOW – joe is on CNN!!!!!!!!!

Woofus: oh god he's totally GORGE

GuySimon: i just caught end but i saw ballet part. justin i cant believe yr having affair with somebody FAMOUS.

Justin777: Im in total SHOCK

Woofus: i hate those protesters

GuySimon: his body is inCRED

Woofus: jus u r SO lucky, hes SO cute

Justin777: sorry guys gotta get offline. maybe hes trying to call me

Woofus: GOD u r so lucky

GuySimon: bye

Subj: Toljaso
Date: 12/9 11:43:22 AM Pacific Standard Time
From: podonnell@sfchronicle.com
To: Danzguy@NYAN.net (Joseph Breaux)

Dear Joe,

Toljaso, toljaso. You knew the review wasn't going to be as
glowing as the first one – that one was engraved in plutonium –
but it was pretty good. Oh, I love being right when I predict
something good – the thumpers gave you all the cover you
needed for the boy. "It is impossible for this critic to offer an assessment of Andrew Othman in the role of the Boy; one wishes
rather to congratulate this youngster for consenting to perform
at all after having been manhandled by a group of protesters
two hours before curtaintime." You see what a wise auntie you
have? And although he wasn't very nice about you, it was in the
context of praising your decision to retire from the stage as a
soloist, and a generally favorable review of the piece. Reading
between the lines, I think he was probably more disappointed
than he let on, but he had such hot copy with the thumpers, he
had to take your side.

CNN is running a little story about you today – have you seen it
yet? You must have known it was in the works, because there's a
tiny snippet of video from the piece, you and the boy. Of course
they had to go for the most titillating bit.

Fritz is already dropping hints about Christmas, do I want to go
to Sacramento with him to meet his folks. No, I don't want to
go to Sacramento with him to meet his folks – the very thought
of it fills my soul with terror. Christmas has become nothing but
a source of anxiety for me. Gotta get to work, angel. What are
you doing for this holy season of peace and joy?

Sibyl

Subj: CNN
Date: 12/11 10:30:19 AM Eastern Standard Time
From: Danzguy@NYAN.net (Joseph Breaux)
To: podonnell@sfchronicle.com

Hi Phil,

Yes, I've seen it. So has my father. After the premiere, I sent him
the first message since he canceled his trip to Bali, a nice, newsy
note – a premiere at BAM with a sold-out run qualifies as news,
I would say – and inquiring in a very general way about
Christmas, but he hasn't answered. He was always an overnight
replier. So I called Chrissie, and she said that he had seen the
CNN story and was upset about it. It's definitely not the kind of
thing that goes over well in Covington. She sort of soft-pedaled
it, I think – "upset" probably means I'm disowned. It was OK to
have a gay son as long as he was in New York, in the obscure
world of modern dance, which is unheard of in Covington, but
when it's "My son, the homo" on TV, glorifying a German child
molester, forget it. Everyone down there who saw it would be on
the side of the Grimmlins. I guess Chrissie's really getting married. They're spending Christmas in Oregon with Allen's family.

The story just won't die. Now the goddamn cardinal is coming
down to protest with them, the radio talk shows are full of it.
Bernie Kuykendahl said BAM has been getting some really nasty
phone calls, so now the NYPD is tapping in. I met with one of
the detectives yesterday, who told me there had been some death
threats against me, but he said they weren't the kind that they
take seriously. How can they tell when a death threat is OK? He
was really nice, I'm pretty sure he was a church member. Totally
professional, but . . . simpatico, if you know what I mean. Being
famous is so much FUN!

At least the piece is in good shape now. The kid is improving
with every performance. Nothing like what it would have been
with Wayan, but he's getting bolder and more poised. Quentin

came back last night, and I think tomorrow there will be a little postscript review, reassessing the piece now that it's being performed in a reasonably calm atmosphere. There has been complete, global silence about any possibility of staging it somewhere else – big surprise. Everything's going fine now, but I can't wait till it's over. I guess I'll spend Christmas eating pizza and watching Jimmy Stewart standing out on that bridge, for the fortieth time. Obvious enough hint?

Love ya,

Joey

Subj: Apologies?
Date: 12/12 11:02:14 AM Eastern Standard Time
From: jahull@POF.org
To: kuykendahl@BAM.org

Dear Bernie,

I'm so sorry about what's going on over there – what a disaster for you. There's no way you can win. You're obliged to support your artist, but in doing so you alienate a few million people. To the extent that the Pullman-Oliphant grant to Joe is in any way responsible for this debacle, I sincerely apologize.

It hasn't done me much good either, I can tell you. Some of the more conservative members of the board were talking behind my back about asking me to resign, so I got out Joe's proposal and sent them all a copy of it. Of course, they had seen it before. It was a great proposal, and mentioned nothing that could have even remotely suggested that a furor like this was in the offing.

If there's anything I can do to help out, just let me know.

Best,

Jerry

Subj: Bah, humbug
Date: 12/12 11:34:49 AM Pacific Standard Time
From: podonnell@sfchronicle.com
To: Danzguy@NYAN.net (Joseph Breaux)

Dear Tiny Tim,

I always wanted to do a short called "It's a Crummy Life": a
tall, skinny guy is standing on a bridge, and an angel comes
along and says, "Go ahead, jump. If I were married to Donna
Reed, that's what I'd do," and then the guy jumps into the river.
THE END. I love Jimmy Stewart, but I loathe the sugary junk he
did with Frank Capra. I think Mr. Smith should've minded his
own goddamn business and stayed the hell away from
Washington – I'm sure Claude Rains had some very good reasons to build that dam.

Am I getting you into a Christmassy mood? Of course you're
invited, petal, it will be swellegant. You can go trawling at
Celadon every night, and pave Polk Street with broken hearts.
Best of all, now I have an excuse not to go to Sacramento to
make my debut as the daughter-in-law. For Christmas dinner, do
you want to cook, like the old days? Or go to a restaurant. If the
latter, I'd better book now.

I'm sorry about your father, Joey. I'm sure he'll get over it – he's
a good man. Just give him time. That's great about Chrissie, I
guess. I have to admit, Allen struck me as a big baboon, but I'm
sure most people think Fritz is a total nebbish.

Raindrops on roses and whiskers on kittens,

Scroogina

Subj: Extacy
Date: 12/12 11:49:23 PM Pacific Standard Time
From: Justin777@wol.com
To: Danzguy@NYAN.net (Joseph Breaux)

My darling Joe,

I am in complete extacy to think that I will soon be in your arms
again, my darling. Your calls mean so much to me. Rufus and
Simon invited me to go to Celadon with them tonight, but I said
no, because I had a feeling you would call! I have to pinch myself, to be sure I'm not dreaming–my lover is a world-famous
dancer, his handsome face on television all around the world.
Your dance composition looks so beautiful, so romantic–when I
saw it, I imagined myself in the role of the boy, and I felt so
happy I nearly burst. I hate those so-called "Christians" who are
persecuting you. I thought Christians were supposed to believe
in love, and those people are just full of hate, in my opinion.

You make me so happy when you call me, my darling. I know
how busy you are, so I don't call you, but I hope you don't mind
me sending you these E-mail messages. I try to keep them short,
but I could write all night, and never tell you how much I love
you. When I think that in eight days I will be back in your arms
again, my body aches with desire until it feels like it will catch
on fire. I'm the luckiest guy in the world. We belong together
FOREVER.

Your baby Justin

Subj: Detail
Date: 12/13 10:50:43 PM Eastern Standard Time
From: Danzguy@NYAN.net (Joseph Breaux)
To: podonnell@sfchronicle.com

Hi Phil,

There's one little detail I neglected to mention on the phone.
That's because I'm embarrassed about it, and I don't think you'll
approve. Phil, I'm coming to San Francisco to spend Christmas
with you, but I'm also coming out to see Justin, the Vietnamese
boy I met at Celadon. Of course he won't come to Christmas
dinner, and I will make sure that you and I have two or three
evenings alone together, but I do want to spend the nights with
him. I feel incredibly awkward asking you to let him stay there.
Is there any way I can offer to stay a few nights with you, and
then a few nights at a hotel with him? Of course you realize that
the ONLY reason I am proposing this is out of a desire not to be
a pain in the butt to you. I do think that might be best.
Remember, I've got piles of money now. He really did like you
and Fritz a lot, you know. He howled at Fritz's imitations
(although I'm not sure he was always familiar with the
originals).

Please don't scold me, Phil. He's such a sweet kid, and he's blissfully happy that he's going to see me again. Do you know what
it's like, to make someone blissfully happy?

Love ya,

Joey

Subj: Almost over
Date: 12/14 11:25:43 AM Eastern Standard Time
From: kuykendahl@BAM.org
To: jahull@POF.org

Jer,

Thank god this nightmare is almost over. Three more
performances, and then those hillbillies will go back to
Dogpatch and we can all get back to business. Actually, the police tell me that a lot of the people out there have no affiliation
with any church or organization, they're just freelance loonies
with nothing better to do.

I appreciated your note, and of course it was completely unnec-
essary to apologize; I don't blame Pullman-Oliphant for this in
any way. To a certain extent I blame Quentin Trent, for vastly
overpraising an experimental piece that was interesting, at best.
But I knew what I was letting myself in for, so I really have no
one to blame but myself. I have to admit, the morning I read
Quentin's review from Bali, I said to Donna, "That's a piece that
will sell out." Well, I sold the house out, and now my office has
been turned into a P.R. wasteland. Joe handled himself well, but
he overreached.

Thanks for taking the time to commiserate.

Bernie

Subj: Worried
Date: 12/14 10:43:22 AM Pacific Standard Time
From: podonnell@sfchronicle.com
To: Danzguy@NYAN.net (Joseph Breaux)

Joey,

Don't you dare mention the word hotel to me again, you heartless
brute. Of course you can bring Justine Jailbait with you. She's a
sweet lassie, very polite. But darling, I'm worried about you. OK,
I won't lecture, but cherry-picking is a perilous sport. If he's a
freshman at USF, then he must be eighteen, not that he looks even
that . . . but aren't you worried about fathers and big brothers
coming after you with shotguns? I'm making light of this because
I don't know how else to deal with it. How do you expect this relationship to progress? You and Wayan had something
enormously important in common – Justin told me he wants to
design ladies' shoes. That's a noble calling, but I don't see you two
getting into a big gabfest about heel heights, if you know what I
mean. He speaks English, that's a step in the right direction, but
what are you going to talk about? You know, he actually thought
that my autographed portrait of Miss Loretta Young, personally
inscribed to me etc. etc., was a picture of a drag queen. Darling,
he probably thinks that Richard Nixon fought at Valley Forge.

I think I will lecture you, Joey. The reason you're making him
blissfully happy is because you busted his cherry (I'm assuming,
but I'm always right about these things). I'm sure you were very
sweet to him, but he's falling in love with love, with sex, with
becoming a man, not with you. Look, you know what I think:
those nerve endings are there for a reason. I have no problem
with you bringing little Justin over here and boinkin' her till she
limps. But let's make sure we're straight about how this is going
to play out – this time you're going to get bored long before he
does, and then you're going to have a brokenhearted teenager on
your hands. In my church, all sex is moral so long as both sides
know what they're getting into. Even though Wayan was almost

as young as this child, you and he were more of an even match –
there, it was a case of duelling cultural cluelessness. But this is
different – Justin hasn't had a peek at the rulebook yet.

Joey, aren't you devoting an awful lot of energy to keeping your
dick happy these days? I know I'm being stern with you, but
shouldn't you be thinking about trifling matters like where
you're going to live and what you're going to do after the piece
closes, five days from now? I love you like the kid brother I
never had, you know that. You're the only person in the world I
would ever speak to in this way. But I'm afraid you're getting
lost. I don't really care about what happens with this boy – she
might as well have her first broken heart over you as anyone
else. But then what? – for you I mean. Back to Celadon, to pick
another cherry? Make another naive child blissfully happy for a
month or two? You don't HAVE to have sex, you know (god
knows I can testify to that).

OK, I've had my say. I know you'll realize that I've said all this
out of love. You will always have me on your side. You are a
GREAT artist, poised to become one of the nation's leading
choreographers, and I want you to treat yourself with respect.
That's all.

Phil

Subj: Maybe you're right
Date: 12/16 12:09:38 AM Eastern Standard Time
From: Danzguy@NYAN.net (Joseph Breaux)
To: podonnell@sfchronicle.com

_____

Hi Phil,

You asked me before if I was turning into a chicken hawk – now
you talk about cherry-picking. They're such disgusting expres-
sions, as though I'm hanging around the schoolyard with a bag

of candy. It's not like that at all. In both cases they chose me. Justin was the one who said "hi" at Celadon that night. And it's not just <<keeping my dick happy>>. There's something so inexpressibly touching about giving a boy his first time, to see the expression of nervous fear on his face melt into pure, intense joy. The passion that gets loosed is so overwhelming. I've always had a thing about stuff like joy and passion.

I wish I could show you the messages he sends me, they're so sweet and innocent. But . . . maybe you're right. Maybe the problem is the message I'm sending him, trying to make his fantasy come true when I know it won't. Also, Phil . . . part of it is that I've finally realized that I've lost Andrew. I've been waiting all these months to hear from him – I thought maybe when the piece opened at BAM, I would get a little note of congratulations, or a word of sympathy about the Grimmlins. I've thought so many times about calling him myself or sending an E-mail. I promised I wouldn't, but at this point I don't think he would really mind. But now I realize, even if one of us did call or send a message, and we got together when I'm out there next week – what would be the point, really? It would just make us both feel sad. It's over, I know it. And I know I'll never find someone like him again. But when I was with Justin, it almost felt like when Andrew and I first met. I shouldn't quote from Justin's messages, but he always says exactly the same thing that Andrew used to say, "I feel like the luckiest guy in the world." I'm not sure I can give that up.

Phil, you're wrong about me being <<poised to become one of the nation's leading choreographers>>. The goddamn "Christians" have made me a pariah. Of course everyone tells me that they support me, and how much they despise the Grimmlins and everything they stand for – but I have not received one phone call, not one nibble from any arts institution in the country. They look at me and think, "If he comes to my hall, he's going to bring the religious fanatics with him. No thanks." I'm not saying I'll never work again, but one thing's for sure; it'll be a

long time before I'm invited back to BAM. As in never. I'll probably have to go to Europe. Maybe I'll go back to Bali.

I'm the lucky guy, to have a friend like you. See ya Monday
night.

Love ya,

Joey

Subj: Re: Maybe you're right
Date: 12/16 10:21:10 AM Eastern Standard Time
From: podonnell@sfchronicle.com
To: Danzguy@NYAN.net (Joseph Breaux)

Dear Joe,

I've GOT to get a big holiday preview ready by the end of the day,
but I had to get back to you quickly. Hon', that was the saddest
li'l ol' message your Aunt Phyllis ever read. You're doing right not
to call Andrew. I can't explain, but you're right not to do it. (Of
course, now you can figure it out.) I know you're mourning him,
but you are WRONG to say you'll <<never find someone like him
again.>> Well, of course there's no one else EXACTLY like him.
But trust me, you are a prime steer, and you won't be on the hoof
for long. I keep forgetting, you're a beginner at this. You're at the
worst point, the Sinking In period. But from now on, every day
will be a little better, and before you know it, you'll say to yourself, Jeez, I haven't thought about him in DAYS. Then weeks.
Then one day some really gorgeous guy will smile at you and say
"hi." No, that's me, and they were never gorgeous – in your case,
he WILL be gorgeous, and you'll be the one who says "hi."

Gotta run – 1,200 words by four o'clock. Trust ta tante, you'll
feel better sooner than you think and find yourself a GROWN-
UP with a BRAIN.

Me

Subj: Private stuff
Date: 12/22 11:58:20 AM Pacific Standard Time
From: Justin777
To: Woofus

Dear Rufus,

I've never been so happy in all my life. The second night was
even better than the first – he's such an amazing lover. You
asked me to send you a message to tell you all the private stuff
I was too embarrassed to say on the phone. I'm too
embarrassed to write most of it too. All I can tell you is, inter-
course is so much better than . . . BJ's, you won't believe it.
You shouldn't be so afraid to try it. If you really love Jason, the
next time he asks you, you gotta say yes. The first time, I was
so scared, but he was so gentle with me. He said we didn't
have to do it on our first date–I was the one who said, let's do
it. It's hard to explain, Ruf, but the first few seconds it hurt so
bad I thought I was going to scream–then it turned into extacy
like I never felt before. Now it doesn't hurt at all, sometimes
just a tiny bit at the beginning. I am so incredibly lucky to have
such a kind, gentle, and GORGEOUS man to show me how.
Also–Ruf, this is TOTALLY SECRET–I did something this
morning I thought I would never do. I swallowed . . . it. He
didn't ask me to–it was my decision. I know you're not
supposed to do that, but it made him so happy. I wanted to
prove to him that I really love him. I would do ANYTHING
for him. I would DIE for him.

I'm so PROUD I can satisfy a strong man like Joe. He's so sweet,
he said maybe for my birthday in January we'll go to a gay inn
in Monterey for the weekend. Isn't that romantic? He thinks I'm
going to be nineteen. Do you think I should tell him I'm really
only seventeen? It's almost the same.

I can't believe I'm telling all this private stuff, even to you.
There's some stuff I'll never tell. It's really better not to talk
about it. If I send this, pretend you didn't get it. And if you say

one word to Simon, if you even tell him that this message exists, I'll KILL you.

Justin

Subj: I love you
Date: 12/23 5:22:31 AM Pacific Standard Time
From: Justin777@wol.com
To: Danzguy@NYAN.net (Joseph Breaux)

My darling Joe,

You're asleep in our bed, our little corner of heaven, but I was too happy to fall sleep. I hope you won't think this is wierd, but I snuck into the living room to send you a message, to say some things that might be too embarassing in person. Joe, I love you with all my heart and soul. When you are making love to me, I feel such extacy throughout my entire body I wish it would never end. I am praying, let this moment last for all eternity. You are so strong, sometimes I think you can't be a man, you must be a god. That's how you seem to me.

I think we made the right decision, to stop using condoms. It's so much more romantic, a symbol that nothing can come between us, that I belong to you COMPLETELY. I am sure you are the healthiest man alive, and I am the luckiest one.

I love you, my darling.

Justin

P.S. Can I ask one favor—can you shave closer tonight? I'm starting to get a little red in a couple of places. I'm sorry to ruin the romantic message, but I was too embarassed to say anything in bed. You look so sexy with a stuble, but it's my fault, my skin is too soft.

Subj: Our secret correspondence
Date: 12/24 12:22:10 PM Pacific Standard Time
From: Danzguy@NYAN.net (Joseph Breaux)
To: Justin777@wol.com

Baby Justin,

This will be our secret correspondence, where we can tell each
other our deepest, most intimate thoughts. Justin, I love you too.
But I want you to remember some of the things I told you the
night I arrived – I can't live in San Francisco, and you have to
continue your studies. It's going to be tough for both of us, but
we must accept that we will not be able to stay together. Our
love will be like a flame that burns brightly but only for a short
time. After New Year's, I must go back to New York, and then I
will return to Bali, to resume my work there. I promise I will
come to San Francisco to visit you as soon as I can, and maybe
when you have vacation time, you can come visit me. But while
we're apart, I want you to make new friends, to date other men.

You're sweet to talk about coming to Bali with me, but you're
much too young to settle down, especially with someone my age.
It's much more important for you to get your degree. Think of
me as your mentor – do you know what that means? Someone
older who loves you and tries to give you good advice. I want
you to live life to the fullest, to have many lovers while you are
young, and then to settle down with a good man. I will always
be so proud that the most beautiful boy in San Francisco chose a
hairy old man like me for his first lover. I will cherish our mo-
ments and hours and days together for the rest of my life.

Your loving mentor,

Joe

P.S. I'm sorry about the beard, baby! I'll never be smooth – I'm
just a rough, scratchy ol' guy. But I will make it as smooth as I
can before tonight.

Subj: The big run-in
Date: 12/26 6:52:12 PM Pacific Standard Time
From: AndrewTan@wol.com
To: etan@MIT.edu (Eric Tan)

Hi Eric,

Well, it had to happen. I ran into Joey today. Nat and I went to
the Asian Art Museum to see that big Shang bronze exhibit from
Taiwan. It was the day after Christmas, so of course it was
jammed. We wandered into a small side gallery, and four people
were there: Phil O'Donnell, his new boyfriend Fritz, Joey, and a
cute little Vietnamese boy who looked about sixteen years old.
Nat saved the day, boomed out, "Joe Breaux! How the hell are
you doing?", and clapped him on the back. Phil took my arm
and started asking me how was my new job, how was my new
house, thank you for the Christmas card. Fritz knew what was
going on, and started talking to the kid, and dragged him over
to look at a display case at the far end of the gallery.

It didn't work, of course. Joey looked at me, and I looked at
him, and we went into a full, strong hug. I could feel his heart
pounding. We hugged for a long time, then we pulled back and
looked at each other: he had tears in his eyes, I had tears in
mine. He couldn't talk, I couldn't talk. Phil and Nat walked
away, Fritz and the Vietnamese boy left the gallery, some other
people came in. Finally, I said, "We can't do this. Nat and I will
leave." I was choking up so badly, I was almost croaking. He
opened his mouth to say something like, "Oh no, I'll go," but I
put my index finger to my lips, the way we always used to do to
avoid a pointless argument. We stood there for a few seconds,
both of us wondering if the other one would say it, but by then I
was starting to really cry, so I just said, "Bye, Joey," and he said,
"Goodbye," and I walked away. At the door I turned around,
and he was still looking at me. I could see he was crying, too, his
lips were pressed together so tightly. Then I left.

Nat couldn't have been sweeter, he even offered to take a taxi
home, but of course I drove him. We talked about it a little bit. I
told him that this had nothing to do with him and me, but I'm not
sure that's true. I managed not to really cry, and even after I
dropped him off, I felt calm. Today was one of those brisk, breezy,
perfect San Francisco days. I drove home, parked the car, went in
and hung up my coat, and sat down at the kitchen table and cried
for half an hour. It was like someone had died, but it wasn't someone, it was something. It was the love of my life . . . the apt cliche.

I had no idea I would take it so hard. Of course, the surprise ele-
ment made it much worse. I'm writing all this in E-mail, because
if I called you I'd start crying again. I'm crying a little bit now,
but at least I don't have to talk. Joey didn't look well . . . he
looked pale and tired, as though he hadn't been getting enough
sleep. The most awful part was seeing him with that little boy
. . . that's what he was, a little boy. I felt so sad for Joey. I was
grateful to the other guys, making sure there were no introduc-
tions, that would have killed me, to shake hands with his latest
plaything. He was so small, wearing tight black pants and a tiny
stretch tee shirt that made him look like a child. The one bit of
advice Nat offered in the car, which was sweet of him, was that I
should assume nothing about Joey and the boy. But that boy
was *cute,* as cute as the other one. I assume everything.

I don't know whether I was hoping or dreading that Joey would
say, "Call me." And I was dead sure that he felt exactly the
same. The first thought that popped into my head when I finally
turned around and left him was, "I'll never see him again." It
was a strange thing to think, since I had just bumped into him
accidentally. But it was vivid, as though someone had whispered
it in my ear.

Well, that's enough of that. I'll be seeing you in a couple of days . . .
thank god, I need some Lenox time.

Andy

Subj: ALONE
Date: 12/26 6:58:49 PM Pacific Standard Time
From: Justin777
To: Woofus

Oh Ruf,

I'm SO depressed I wish I were dead. I am at home, ALONE,
and I can't even call you on the phone, in case he calls. Joe and I
and his friends went to the Asian art museum today to see the
Chinese exhibit, and Joe bumped into his ex. He's a really handsome, distinquished Chinese man. They hugged right there in the
middle of the museum, and started crying a little bit, but they
were both discrete. I knew right away that's who he was, so I
got away from them, so they could be more private. They were
together for ten years, Joe said, and it was the first time they had
seen each other since they broke up, so I knew Joe would be
upset. We left the exhibit right away, and went walking in the
park. I tried to comfort him, but he wouldn't talk to me. Finally
he said, "Please, I can't talk to you right now. I really need to be
alone." And then he just ran away and left us there.

I didn't know what to do so I came home. Ruf when I got home
there was a message from him on my answering machine telling
me not to come to him tonight, he had to be alone. He sounded
nice and he called me baby, but I just couldn't believe it. I STILL
can't believe it. Just like that, "I'm sorry baby, but I have to be
alone tonight." I know he's upset, but why won't he let me come
to him, so I can comfort him?

What makes it so hard to bear is that last night was by far the
most perfect night of our whole relationship. I came to him at
11:00–of course I had to go home for Christmas dinner, and he
and his friends cooked their own. Phil and his boyfriend had already gone over to the boyfriend's house so Joe and I could have
our own private Christmas. There was a fire in the fireplace, and
he gave me the most exquisite gift, a gold ring from CARTIER!

It's three little rings together, one white, one yellow, one red, but all gold. It must have cost thousands of dollars. He said it was a token of our love. All I had for him was the drawing I made of him, the one I showed you–him lying in bed asleep. I was embarassed I didn't have something better, but he knows I'm just a poor student, and what can you give a wealthy man like him, anyway? He must have everything he wants. At least the frame looked nice. He was so sweet about it–he said it was the most thoughtful gift any lover ever gave him, and I was so talented I was sure to be a successful designer.

And then we made love, right there on the carpet, in front of the fireplace. It was the most romantic night of my entire life. It was a night of incredible extacy. We did all the positions, and we didn't stop until the sun started to come up, when we collapsed in each other's arms. I would do ANYTHING to make Joe happy. I would DIE for him. And now, after six nights of extacy in Phil's lovely apartment on Larkin Street, here I am, ALL ALONE, in my cold, ugly little room with hardly any furniture. Thank god my roommates are all gone, so I don't have to put on a fasade.

Oh Ruf I am so miserable I wish I were dead. To go from such extacy to such anquish is almost more than I can bear. The phone rang a little while ago, and my heart started bursting with joy, but it was for Dennis. I know you're on-line Ruf–I'll send this to you now, but I have to keep the line open, in case he wants me to come to him. I'll call you at midnight exactly if I don't hear from him. PRAY your phone doesn't ring at midnight.

Justin

Subj: Me
Date: 12/27 1:12:01 AM Pacific Standard Time
From: Danzguy@NYAN.net (Joseph Breaux)
To: AndrewTan@wol.com

Dear Andrew,

I know you'll forgive me for writing you, after what happened
today. We can't just leave it that way, with both of us feeling so
much emotion and not expressing it. I've got to say a few things
to keep on living.

Andrew, when I hugged you in the museum today, I felt a
stronger love than I'll ever feel for anyone in my life. For one ecstatic moment I had you back. The past few months have been
so empty and sad for me. I'm like a teenager – every time I open
my mail, I hope I'll find a message from you. When the phone
rings at a strange hour, I think, maybe it's him. There's no use in
saying I'm sorry, it's so obvious after today that I destroyed the
most beautiful thing in both our lives. I would sacrifice
everything I have if I thought I could undo what I've done, to
take away all the pain I've caused you. Of course, these are just
stupid cliches, trying to express sorrow and regret – what can I
sacrifice now, when I've destroyed the most important thing of
all?

Nat looked great – are you two dating seriously? You can't
imagine how much I want you to be happy, Andrew, and if Nat's
the one who can do that, I am sincerely glad for both of you. I
hope you won't be offended if I ask you this, but . . . would you
tell me if you're not serious with him? Please don't think I'm
saying, Gee, I'm sorry, now take me back. Of course not. I'm
not even saying, let's date. Maybe this whole message is crazy
and presumptuous, but I really don't know how I can keep
going on without you. No, that's wrong, without the HOPE of
being your friend, of somehow making up to you what I've

done. If I could just see you again. Just tell me maybe, someday. Make a date with me for one year from now.

Andrew, I love you so much it scares me. Please give me some kind of answer – I'm not asking for forgiveness or a second chance – I don't deserve it. Just for hope, the feeblest hope that you and I will be together again somehow, some way. I must be crazy to write this – it's already the fourth version, and I'll probably stare at the mouse for an hour before I'm brave enough to send it.

Your Joey

P.S. I can imagine what you thought when you saw that kid with us – he's an exchange student from Taiwan who's been sort of "adopted" by Phil and Fritz.

Subj: Joey's message
Date: 12/27 9:35:52 AM Pacific Standard Time
From: AndrewTan@wol.com
To: etan@MIT.edu (Eric Tan)

Hi Eric,

Thanks for calling last night. You're the one person I can always count on. I just got a crazy, mixed-up message from Joey, trying to find out the status of my relationship with Nat, and essentially saying, it can't be as good as what we had, please give me another chance. He said that wasn't what he was saying, but it was. If he only knew how much I want to say yes! But I can't. And I think he lied to me. There was a P.S.: <<I can imagine what you thought when you saw that kid with us – he's an exchange student from Taiwan who's been sort of "adopted" by Phil and Fritz.>> Of course, I don't know . . . it's possible he's telling the truth, but at the time I was certain he was with Joey.

And he really looked Vietnamese to me. What does it matter, Vietnamese or Eskimo . . . the point is, I can never trust Joey again. I want to say yes, maybe, *so much.* And you know what that means . . . I can't keep on dating Nat as a steady boyfriend. That's pretty clear now. So I go from being dumped by the man I love to dumping an incredibly nice guy. What a great Christmas.

Love from your *miserable* brother

Subj: Re: Joey's message
Date: 12/27 4:13:05 PM Eastern Standard Time
From: etan@MIT.edu (Eric Tan)
To: AndrewTan@wol.com

---

hi,

three points:

1. you don't know who that kid was, and you're right, it doesn't matter,
2. you don't have to answer joe until you're ready, and
3. you don't have to say anything to nat before you fly out here except "goodbye, nat, happy new year."

i'm sorry you're miserable, kid. we're going to have a nice time in lenox. andrea is THRILLED that you're coming. i think she has a crush on you. seriously. maybe we'll convert you.

hang in there, kid.

e

Subj: Re: Me
Date: 12/28 10:51:00 AM Pacific Standard Time
From: AndrewTan@wol.com
To: Danzguy@NYAN.net (Joseph Breaux)

Dear Joey,

It's irrelevant whether Nat and I are dating seriously. I love you
too, exactly the way you said, but I just can't do what you ask.
I'm sorry. It kills me to say this, but Joey, it's all over.

Andrew

Subj: HE'S BACK!!!
Date: 12/29 12:21:38 PM Pacific Standard Time
From: Justin777
To: Woofus

Rufus,

Joe came back to me!!! I can't believe it!!! I was so stunned, he
called up and APOLOGIZED, explained how difficult it was for
him when he saw his ex at the museum, and that he just needed
some time alone. He said he MISSED ME, and would I forgive
him! I was so excited I was almost crying, and he laughed and
said, Calm down baby. He asked if my roommates were still
gone, and when I said yes he suggested that he should come over
here, to give Phil and Fritz some privacy. I told him how plain
and sort of ugly the apartment is, but he said as long as there's a
bed it's OK–he's always so sexy. He arrived with flowers and
champane, and brought a video of a movie by Gene Kelly, because I said on Christmas, who is Gene Kelly? I guess he used to
be a big movie star. I made a bubble bath, and we sat in the tub
and drank champane, and I played my classical music tape–it
was so ROMANTIC, like a dream. Then we started watching

the movie wearing bathrobes, he's so big I had to borrow
DeVawn's, but even it barely covered him up. It was pretty
good, about the old-time movies, but a little too much dancing if
you ask me (though of course I didn't tell him that). It didn't really matter because we started making love halfway through.

I know I keep saying this, but every time we're together it's even
more romantic than before. What makes it so exciting for me is
that he is always in control, we do what he wants. He always
tells me what to do, not ordering me around like the guys in
Simon's videos, but gentle and encouraging. And here is the
TOTALLY FOREVER SECRET part, not even little jokes in
front of Simon or Jason–now we've done everything, and I mean
EVERYTHING. Remember the part in that video about the
Latin guys in jail, when we all screamed and said we would
NEVER do that? I did it! It's not gross like you think. It was
wierd at first, but then I started to get excited, and Joe was
moaning so passionately that I couldn't stop until . . . you know.
I don't want to keep talking about sex all the time, but it was so
unbelievably romantic. I still can't believe how strong he is for a
man his age (not that he's that old). He's always so sweet to me,
calls me the cutest names.

Oh Ruf, I am SO DELIRIUSLY happy. I hope it's OK to tell you
all this stuff, but I have to tell somebody, otherwise I would just
burst, and Simon would make jokes about it in front of everybody. You're the only one I can tell EVERYTHING to. He left a
little while ago, and guess what? he said he would buy tickets
for the New Year's Eve party at Celadon. Are you and Jason
coming? It's incredibly expensive, $75 per couple, including hats
and horns and champane at midnight. It would be so great if
you and Jase can come. Joe gets kind of bored there, I think–it's
funny, a dancer who doesn't like to dance. The only sort of bad
thing is that he says we can't spend the night at Phil's too much
anymore. DeVawn is coming back on January 3 and Dennis the
day after, so I don't know what will happen. Also, he keeps talking about going back to Bali. I'm sending you this E-mail instead

of calling, in case he calls (also because I would be WAY too embarrassed to say half this stuff on the phone!).

Justin

P.S. Doesn't Jason have to work at the shop tomorrow? Maybe we can have dinner at Patio Roma, it's free side pasta night. I promise not to talk about Joe the whole time, we can talk about you and Jason or whatever.

Subj: The End, Part II
Date: 12/29 7:02:09 PM Pacific Standard Time
From: AndrewTan@wol.com
To: etan@MIT.edu (Eric Tan)

Hi Eric,

Well, I have to hand it to Nat, he's one classy guy. He just came by, and when I opened the door and he pecked me on both cheeks, the way gay men do, instead of a real kiss, I knew what was coming. Basically he said, "It's obvious that this isn't going anywhere for either of us, so it's better to call it off now, so we can be friends." I don't think I'm being egotistical when I say that I'm *pretty* sure that there was a lot more going on for him than for me, but he didn't want me to have to say the Words of Doom. Very classy. I had been in such a quandary about what to do, that scene at the museum had made it so obvious . . . I didn't want to call him just before New Year's, but on the other hand it's not very nice to drag things out. He realized that and took it upon himself (if my theory is correct, and I'm pretty sure it is). He was very strong and cheery, and we both said a lot of nice stuff, not that it wasn't sincere, but it was awkward. I offered him coffee, but he didn't even take off his coat, saying the time for coffee and a cozy chat will come in a month or so . . . and he was right. So we hugged and said Happy New Year, and that was it. I have to admit, after he left I felt depressed for an hour or two, but then I felt relieved. That shoe had to drop. Nat wasn't Him. It doesn't matter if he fitted all the "specs": I'm not buying a sailboat. I've learned to live on my own, and if another guy comes along, fine. But you can't fake this . . . either it works or it doesn't. As Joey used to say, it's not like horseshoes and pitching pennies: close doesn't count.

So that's my great news. Actually, I'm OK, and anyway I'll be seeing you and the Soph tomorrow night, and that *will* be great.

Love from me

Subj: facts
Date: 1/8 1:23:02 PM Pacific Standard Time
From: Danzguy@NYAN.net (Joseph Breaux)
To: Justin777@wol.com

Dear Justin,

Wow, what a great night! I have been so lucky to meet a lover as passionate and loving as you. Your E-mail messages are so beautiful, and I have saved every one of them in a special file. But Justin, we have to face the facts: you're a student about to go back to classes, and I have to leave for Bali soon. I've become so attached to you and your sweet ways, it's going to break my heart to say goodbye. But I think we both need to face up to the fact that the time is growing near. You have given me so much, and I treasure all the time we have spent together, but there's really no future in our relationship, baby. You need to meet someone closer to your own age, who's interested in the same things you are, the boy bands and video games.

I've been thinking about this a lot, and I blame myself for letting it get this far. I'll never forget how we met at Celadon, the way you clung to me so affectionately on the sofa behind the pool tables. When you asked to come with me, how could I say no? But I should never have let it go on this way. I guess I just can't resist you!

I know you don't want to hear this. You say that the age difference doesn't make a difference, that you want to be with me because you can learn from me, but I'm afraid that one of the most important lessons of life is that you have to accept the inevitable, no matter how painful it is. After a few weeks or months of feeling depressed and blue, you'll wake up one morning and not even think about me. And believe me, with that beautiful face and irresistible personality of yours, you'll have guys swarming all over you.

We have a date for Friday night – let's go to Bacchus, the most romantic restaurant in the city. We'll have champagne and caviar – go out in style!

Lots of love from Joe

Subj: interesting news
Date: 1/9 8:54:10 AM Pacific Standard Time
From: AndrewTan@wol.com
To: etan@MIT.edu (Eric Tan)

Hi Eric,

I should have written you before now to thank you for a great New Year's Eve . . . the first time I ever toasted the new year with Vermont apple cider instead of champagne. Not that I missed it . . . no matter how much Sophie insisted that we open a bottle, it wouldn't have seemed right to drink it without her. It's hard to believe that she still has a month to go. That is going to be a *big* little boy.

Well, I have some interesting news. I've met a new guy, maybe. You'll be shocked . . . he's a carpenter! Not really, more like a

master cabinetmaker. Remember the sketches I showed you for
the kitchen? I was talking to Marnie Steele about it a few weeks
ago, and she told me about the guy who had done her entertain-
ment center, what a great job he had done, so I called him up
and asked him to come over and have a look at the job. When I
opened the door, I couldn't believe how handsome he was, a big
blond hunk with chiseled features, like the heartthrob in a TV
soap opera . . . in other words, totally not my type. Usually men
like that are always showing off their cute little smile and pro-
jecting that "gorgeous me" attitude, but he was completely
down-to-earth, and very smart. We went into the kitchen and I
showed him my sketches. He just sort of nodded and looked
around the room, and then sat down (without being asked, I
liked that) and started talking about a book he was reading
about Japanese gardens, how different they are from Western
gardens.

I made some coffee, and then we just talked, for almost two
hours, about all sorts of things . . . about everything but my
kitchen. Somehow "War and Peace," of all things, came up (you
remember I read it in Bali), and he had such interesting ideas
about it, why "Anna Karenina" is a better book. But he was
completely unpretentious, it's hard to explain. He mentioned
that he broke up with his last boyfriend last summer because he
was sleeping around, as casually as though he were telling me he
was going to Florida for his vacation. I know that sounds weird,
that he would tell me something intimate like that, but it wasn't.
His name is Travis Hardy; even his name sounds like a soap
opera.

So now he's working at the house every day. It's obvious there's
an attraction, but it's so great that it's poking along slowly.
Yesterday, a week after I met him, I invited him to dinner, just
something low-key in the neighborhood, and he said, "Never
mind, I'll cook." When I got home from work, there he was in
the kitchen, cooking up this fabulous Chinese dinner. It's so

strange, I can make killer cakes and pies, and a decent bouillabaisse, but I don't think I could cook a frozen egg roll. Then we watched a video he brought, a hilarious old Peter Sellers movie I had never heard of, and when it was over, he yawned and said, "Well, I better get going." I had been wondering all through the evening, should I make a move? Will he? I think it's unspoken that there shouldn't be any serious dating as long as he's working for me. It was so great to have a date without that pressure . . . that was always the problem with Nat, gentle as the pressure was, it was always there. Actually, last night wasn't a date, it was like . . . you know what.

I can't believe I'm going on so much about this guy. That tells you something right there, I suppose.

Meanwhile, I'm sitting by the phone, waiting for the Big News, waiting, waiting. . . .

Love to the two and half (eight-ninths?) of you from

Andy

Subj: Re: interesting news
Date: 1/12 8:02:45 AM Eastern Standard Time
From: etan@MIT.edu (Eric Tan)
To: AndrewTan@wol.com

hi kiddo,

well, that IS interesting, a cabinetmaker. sounds like a cool guy. but if i can play big brother for a minute, don't have the wedding invitations engraved at tiffany quite yet. you already knew that. frankly he sounds like a more likely prospect than nat, who did seem a little too eager, even if it was a low-key presentation. also, i have to admit i want to see raymond's face when he meets his son's carpenter buddy. mom will just take him up to the third-floor guest bathroom to ask for advice about those falling-down shelves.

swamped with work, sophie just lies on the chaise longue watching videos. she's calm as can be (or so she says), i'm the nervous wreck. mom arrives next week, which will be great. raymond has been talking to sophie's doc daily, no doubt being a pain in the ass. he says he'll be out here "in due course."

you sound great.

e

Subj: farewell
Date: 1/15 11:46:18 AM Pacific Standard Time
From: Danzguy@NYAN.net (Joseph Breaux)
To: Justin777@wol.com

Dear Justin,

I hope this won't come as too much of a shock to you, but by the time you read this I will be on a plane to Bali. I have tried so many times, in every way I can, to tell you that it's impossible for our relationship to continue. I've postponed my trip to Bali for too long, and I can see you're neglecting your studies – you said so yourself on Wednesday night, that you had sketches due the next day but that spending time with me was more important. Justin, I do love you, and that's why I'm going back to my life, so you can go back to yours.

Please believe that I'm only thinking of your well-being when I tell you that when you meet someone new, be sure to use condoms. Our case was special. I really am in good health, but some men will tell a beautiful young guy like you anything to get what they want.

I know this will be very painful for you, and I am sorry that it had to turn out this way. But believe me, someday you will see that there was no alternative. Please believe that you will always be in my thoughts, and that I wish all the best for you. One day we will meet again, and I will give you the big hug I can't do in this message.

Take care,

Joe

Subj: SHATTERED
Date: 1/15 12:12:54 PM Pacific Standard Time
From: Justin777
To: Woofus, GuySimon

Guys,

I'll send you both the same message coz you're my best friends and I would tell you the same thing on the phone if I felt strong enough. He's GONE, this time FOREVER. He went to Bali without me. I'm SHATTERED, all my hopes and dreams destroyed FOREVER. I knew something was wrong on Wednesday night, he wasn't nearly as romantic, hardly interested. And when I said I had saved up enough money for a ticket to Bali, he just sighed, but not in the nice way. Oh god I'm so depressed I wish I were DEAD. DeVawn and Dennis have been nice, but they're not really friends, and anyway I think that Dennis was kind of after him. His message was nice, I guess, but what haunts me is that I think maybe he just used me for sex and never really loved me the way he said. I really need you guys to help me pull through this, but tonight I'm just going to lie under the covers with Mr. Bear and cry, so don't call. I'll call you tomorrow morning. No way I'm going to Introductory Patterns.

MISERABLE ME

Subj: one more chance
Date: 1/15 1:23:54 PM Pacific Standard Time
From: Justin777@wol.com
To: Danzguy@NYAN.net (Joseph Breaux)

Oh Joe,

Your message has left me in a state of total shock. I
COMPLETELY understand that you need to get back to your
choriography, and that you think I should continue my studies,
but my darling my heart is too broken for me to do any
sketches now. I can't even read my textbook, I just stare at the
same page for an hour, crying, remembering all the beautiful
times we had together. I can't eat and barely sleep at all, and
when I do I sleep on the couch because our bed brings back too
many lovely memories. My mind is in total turmoil, wondering
what I did wrong. I tried so hard to be the perfect lover for
you, because I KNOW you are the perfect lover for me. If I
said or did something wrong, please forgive me and give me
one more chance. If you're afraid that I will get in the way of
your work in Bali, I promise I will leave whenever you say, and
sit in a cafe and study. And maybe I can help you, if you need
any errands done. I'll do ANYTHING for you. I can go back
to USF just as easy next year, and actually it makes a lot of
sense if you think about it–in Bali I'm sure I can pick up so
many unique design concepts. I already told you, I still have
the money for this semester in the bank so I won't be a financial burden on you.

JOE, I BEG OF YOU MY PRECIOUS DARLING, PLEASE
GIVE ME ONE MORE CHANCE. I can't live without you. I
pray that after you have been in Bali for a few days, and have a
little space to think it over, you'll realize how precious our love
is. I know I'm young and naive, but I also know deep in my
soul that we were meant to be together FOREVER. I'm ready

my darling, just send the word and I'll be on the next plane to
Bali.

Joe, I will always love you.

your baby Justin

Subj: Returned mail: Address unknown
Date: 1/15 1:24:55 PM Pacific Standard Time
From: Mail Delivery System <WOL MAILSERVER@wol.com>
To: Justin777

The original message was received 15 January 1:23:54 PM PST
from core@localhost

    – The following address had permanent fatal errors –
<Danzguy@NYAN.net (Joseph Breaux)>

Action: Failure
Basis: Host reports address < Danzguy@NYAN.net (Joseph
Breaux)> unknown
Last Attempt Date: 15 January 15:24:49 PM PST

Forwarded Message:

<Subj: one more chance
<Date: 1/15 1:23:54 PM Pacific Standard Time
<From: Justin777@wol.com
<To: Danzguy@NYAN.net (Joseph Breaux)

<Oh Joe,
<
<Your message has left me in a state of total shock. I
COMPLETELY
<understand that you need to get back to your choriography,
and that you

<think I should continue my studies, but my darling my heart is too broken

<for me to do any sketches now. I can't even read my textbook, I just stare

<at the same page for an hour, crying, remembering all the beautiful times

<we had together. I can't eat and barely sleep at all, and when I do I sleep on

<the couch because our bed brings back too many lovely memories. My

<mind is in total turmoil, wondering what I did wrong. I tried so hard to be

<the perfect lover for you, because I KNOW you are the perfect lover for

<me. If I said or did something wrong, please forgive me and give me one

<more chance. If you're afraid that I will get in the way of your work in

<Bali, I promise I will leave whenever you say, and sit in a cafe and study.

<And maybe I can help you, if you need any errands done. I'll do

<ANYTHING for you. I can go back to USF just as easy next year, and

<actually it makes a lot of sense if you think about it—in Bali I'm sure I can

<pick up so many unique design concepts. I already told you, I still have the

<money for this semester in the bank so I won't be a financial burden on

<you.

<

<JOE, I BEG OF YOU MY PRECIOUS DARLING, PLEASE GIVE ME

<ONE MORE CHANCE. I can't live without you. I pray that after you have

<been in Bali for a few days, and have a little space to think it over, you'll
<realize how precious our love is. I know I'm young and naive, but I also
<know deep in my soul that we were meant to be together FOREVER. I'm
<ready my darling, just send the word and I'll be on the next plane to Bali.
<
<Joe, I will always love you.
<
<your baby Justin

X-Mailer: Unknown (No version)

Subj: Bali, baby
Date: 1/18 11:04:16 AM Eastern Standard Time
From: krakatau@indonet.net.id
To: podonnell@sfchronicle.com

Dear Phil,

Aaaaaaaaaah. That was a sigh. It feels so great to be back in
Bali. I got in early yesterday morning, the flight the usual
exhausting nightmare. I'm staying with Angus Gray, my crazy
Scottish friend, until I can find my own place. Phil, I know it
must have seemed impulsive to say good-bye by calling you from
the airport, but I just had to get out of there. Justin was driving
me fucking NUTS. I felt like a naughty scoutmaster at his
squalid little crash pad, where there weren't even enough chairs
for everyone to sit, and the walls so thin, with him squealing
"oh god!" every twenty seconds when we were doin' it. Also,
the little Chinese roommate was clearly interested – there was a
lot of leg-brushing and eyelash-fluttering whenever Justin was
out of the room – and despite all your polite protestations we

had obviously worn out our welcome at your place, on account of the aforementioned nonstop, ecstatic invocations of the Deity.

OK, it was impulsive, but you knew it was just a matter of days. It wasn't irrational – there was no reason for me to return to New York except to pick up what's left at Horatio Street and put it in storage, basically nothing, which the super can easily do for me. I had no idea that it would hit me so hard, running into Andrew like that. Ending that hug was the hardest thing I've ever had to do. I thought I could alleviate the pain with sex, but in the end if just made me feel worse and miss Andrew more. Maybe I was irresponsible in the way I treated little Justin, but you can't imagine how many times I tried to talk to him and prepare him for the separation, and every time he would just dive for my crotch. And the drivel he talks was driving me crazy, always chattering about who's the cutest boy in this band or that television show. He'll get over it. I gave him some great memories.

I don't expect you or anybody else to understand the choices I've made. I'm not sure I understand them myself. Phil, despite the triumphs (and the money), this year has basically been a disaster for me. I need to take a couple of months off to decompress, to do some thinking. Angus's place is a five-minute walk from the beach – yesterday, after I got in, we took a thermos of margaritas to the beach and sat under a palm tree to watch the sunrise. It was glorious. I can feel myself healing already.

I left my laptop in your hall closet, up top – use it if you want to. When I was here before, I spent way too much time writing messages to everybody. This time I'm only going to write to you. Honey, I need you. Don't give up on me.

Love ya forever,

Joey

P.S. You can write back to me at this address – just put my name in the subject window. If you give the address to Justin, I'll KILL you.

Subj: transcontinental suspense
Date: 1/23 10:15:51 AM Pacific Standard Time
From: AndrewTan@wol.com
To: etan@MIT.edu (Eric Tan)

Hi Eric,

The transcontinental suspense is getting intense (sounds like a rap number). Call me the *instant* it happens . . . well, maybe not the exact instant; you may want to have a chat with Sophie and the Little Stranger first. I'll come out as soon as I can, a few days after the baby's born. Problem is, Mattie has set up a big trip to San Diego for me next week, an opera workshop, theater, artists' studios, etc. His father owns a town house in a gated community there (ugh), where I will stay. I'll let you know my itinerary as soon as I do. Anyway, the first couple of days I would just be in the way.

The cabinets are definitely coming along. Last week, Travis cooked here three times, and on the third night, we finally graduated to the cuddling-on-the-couch stage, while we watched an old Kurosawa flick . . . he's very into everything Japanese. Actually, the cabinets are almost done, absolutely gorgeous, much more streamlined than my idea, with grooves carved into the doors instead of metal pulls. I've sort of had the feeling he's dragging it out, which is great on one level, but not the $30-per-hour-level. I was going to ask him about that, but he very casually said, "Oh, by the way, don't worry about the bill for the cabinets. I've put more time into the job than usual. We'll figure something out." Whatever that means. A pound of flesh? I hope so, as long as it's the right cut. Oops!

Andy

Subj: Joseph Breaux
Date: 1/24 1:50:21 AM Pacific Standard Time
From: podonnell@sfchronicle.com
To: krakatau@indonet.net.id

Peripatetic Poppet,

Ta tante will never abandon her darling niece, but she does fret.
You have to look at it from my point of view, petal: you've gone
from a stable marriage and career-building to deflowering college boys and drinking margaritas on the beach for breakfast.
Actually, when I put it that way, it sounds as though you've
made the only sensible choice. Joey, you know I can't stay mad
at you – the Rockies may tumble, Gibraltar may crumble,
they're only made of clay, but our friendship is here to stay.

I'm totally scolded out, but you can forget the "maybe" in
<<Maybe I was irresponsible in the way I treated little Justin>> –
you were a total bastard. She's called here twenty times since
you left, asking where you're staying in Bali. The poor mite has
all her little things tied up in a hanky, all set to wander around
that island until she finds you. I've been as nice as I can be, but I
just don't have time to do all the listening she has in store for
me, and some of what she wants to tell me I definitely do NOT
want to hear – it's nice to know that you're a love god, but I can
do without the details. Finally I told him, as gently as I could,
that you don't want to see him, and that if he keeps calling me,
I'm going to get Caller ID and not answer. We've had a two-day
silence, so maybe he has FINALLY gotten the message.

Fritz and I spent a long weekend at a cute little B&B in Big Sur
run by a stately lezzie couple, ex-stockbrokers. It was pretty
blissful, a little heavy on the caring and sharing over twig tea for
this bitch, but they were actually very nice ladies. Then when we
got home, we had a hissy spat about something, the car rental, I
think. It's becoming a sort of hobby of ours. As usual I groveled

and pretended it was all my fault, and then we ate a pint of vanilla fudge ice cream in bed and watched "Mr. Skeffington." For Fritz, it's like going to church.

Promise me you'll stay in touch. I need you too, Joey.

Phil

Subj: instant life
Date: 1/31 1:24:46 PM Eastern Standard Time
From: krakatau@indonet.net.id
To: podonnell@sfchronicle.com

File: bung.jpg (76231 bytes)
DL Time (32000 bps): <1 minute

Dear Phil,

Thanks for your great message – I'm glad Justin finally left you alone, sorry about that. Also sorry it's taken me a while to get back to you, but I've been busy creating an instant life here. I've got an entire new custom-tailored wardrobe. It's impossible to find anything in my size here – in Indonesia XL is maybe an M at Banana Republic, and I'm a real XL. So I got a tailor to do it all for me custom. It's a little strange, though, because I have basically one shirt and one pair of shorts, in twenty different colors and fabrics. I bought a motorcycle, a big, loud Honda, powerful as fuck. It's dangerous, but it really is the best way to get around here, with the horrific, nonstop traffic jam. And it's FUN. Completing the scenario, yesterday I moved into a nice little furnished bung, in the same compound as Angus. It's a great location, close to the beach and all the clubs. I'm attaching a snap of it I took with Angus's digital camera. It's not as nice as the house I had before, and the garden is tiny, but I pay by the month, so I can leave whenever I want. It's so cheap – $500 a month for a

two-story house, maybe 1,000 square feet, including the maid.
For $2 she makes lunch.

Phil, I feel SO much better now. I can't explain; maybe this is
where I belong. I don't mean forever, but I gotta tell ya, I'm in
no hurry to go back to New York. It's such a relief not to think
one single thought having to do with dance. When the curtain
came down on the last performance at BAM, it was really like
the proverbial toothache going away. I have no idea what I'm
going to do when I grow up, but for now, I plan to have some
FUN.

Love ya,

Joey

Subj: San Diego
Date: 2/4 9:45:25 PM Pacific Standard Time
From: AndrewTan@wol.com
To: etan@MIT.edu (Eric Tan)

Hi Eric,

This has turned out to be quite a busy trip, actually. I just got
back to Mr. Kappan's town house, done up in English
sportsman's style . . . it's so funny, Mr. Kappan is a fat little man
who smokes cigars. I'm sure he's never been near a horse. I love
San Diego, but everyone here is so *cheerful*, and wants to be
my friend (of course, I'm the guy doling out the free green, why
wouldn't they want to be my friend?). I just got in . . . after our
talk last night, it sounds as though the Big Event is about to
happen any minute. I suppose I should rent a cell, but I hate
those things. I don't know what to do, don't want to keep calling, but there's no messaging here. Let's see . . . I'll leave the laptop on-line when I'm out, that way you can send me a message
and I'll see it when I walk in the door. How's that?

I called Travis last night; we talked for an hour about this and that. He said he missed me . . . he has the funniest way of saying the most serious things in such a matter-of-fact way.

Love from the land of sunshine

Me

Subj: Joseph Breaux
Date: 2/7 12:55:22 PM Pacific Standard Time
From: podonnell@sfchronicle.com
To:krakatau@indonet.net.id

Joey,

Honey, I'm so nervous: Fritz popped the question. I feel like Doris Day at the end of the movie, when Rock Hudson finally grabs her and throws her over his shoulder. Last night we were supposed to go out for cheap Mexican, our favorite little joint in the Castro, but instead he took me to Chez Hugo, le trez fancee, and told me all this mushy stuff I can't repeat about how much he loves me, etc., etc., and said, basically, The time has come. I knew his lease was running out on his creepy little apartment on Eureka Street, but I also know that's not the reason. He only goes over there to collect the mail, and half his clothes are here in the Bali Honeymooners Suite as it is. He wants to make it official, Mr. and Mrs. Fritz and Phyllis.

I wasn't surprised, and the truth is, when I say I'm nervous, it's just a habit. I AM nervous, the only time I did the shacking-up thing before was with Steve, and we both knew it was more of a real estate deal than L-U-V. But I'm not really. Nervous, I mean. I have never felt so . . . close to anyone, I mean both physically and in terms of temperament. Fritz is smart, but he doesn't want to sit around talking about plays and books and movies any more than I do. Most of the guys I've dated in my life (if you

count the ones who actually called back, all five of them) seemed
to think that because I'm a critic they were supposed to prove
something, I don't know what – that they were smart or loved
Shakespeare or something. Fritz is NORMAL, and such a sweet
guy. And the thing is, I guess I love him too. I'm not even sure
what that means, except that on the nights he doesn't come over
here – always because I told him not to, out of some idea about
needing space (see what living in California does to you? when
did you ever hear me talking about "space"?) – I really miss
him. It's so nice hearing someone breathing next to you when
you wake up in the middle of the night. So I said yes. Oh god,
what have I done? Actually, I'm fine – I've never felt confident
this way about a fella. And to coin a phrase, I'm not getting any
younger: 50 looms ominously, and I would like to think I'll have
someone to spoon-feed me my prune puree when my senile de-
mentia becomes official.

Write back and tell me I'm not crazy. Of course I know you approve. I just warned him, let me be a jittery bitch for a week,
then everything will be fine. How are you, hon'? I haven't heard
from you in ages. Send news.

Love from Madame X

Subj: Yippee!
Date: 2/8 12:52:21 PM Eastern Standard Time
From: krakatau@indonet.net.id
To: podonnell@sfchronicle.com

Hey Phil,

Yippee! that's great, man. I've been waiting for that news for a
while – you two so obviously belong together. Of course you
made the right decision, though asking me for advice about relationships is a little cuckoo. Yeah, sorry I've been out of touch –
went up to Ubud for a while with Angus, staying at a fabulous

house with some old Swiss queen named Bruno. Sorry to be brief, but it's late here, and tomorrow Bruno is taking us on a cruise on his yacht. Not too shabby for a boy from Covington, Louisiana. I promise I'll check in when we get back.

Congratulations – that's great.

Love ya,

Joey

Subj: TERENCE ANDREW TAN
Date: 2/9 10:56:20 AM Eastern Standard Time
From: etan@MIT.edu (Eric Tan)
To: AndrewTan@wol.com

YOU'RE AN UNCLE! Terence Andrew Tan, eight pounds eight ounces, joined the world at 9:35 p.m. today. andy, this is the greatest moment of my life – i can't believe this is my son. what a beautiful, healthy, LUSTY baby – he hollers like a lumberjack. poor sophie is so exhausted, red as a cherry, dripping with sweat, but so happy, we were both crying. she didn't make up her mind about the name until yesterday, literally hours before she went into labor, and she said just now to be sure to tell you that the "andrew" is just as much for you as for her father. the nice nurse at the desk let me plug in my laptop – I had to bring some work with me to keep from going totally bonkers. obviously, CALL ME, no matter what time. i can't even tell you what i'm feeling – when you call, i'll try. the hell with your opera workshop, get your butt out here. WE LOVE YOU.

eric

Subj: sad and distraut
Date: 2/13 10:52:23 PM Pacific Standard Time
From: Justin777
To: Woofus, GuySimon

Dear guys,

Thanks a lot for thinking of me, but I'm WAY too sad and distraut to go to the party with you tomorrow. I was starting to feel
a little bit better, but every time I think about being alone on
Valentine's Day, it makes me cry. I've been DREADING this for
weeks–I wish we could just skip tomorrow. I have nothing to
live for now, except my memories.

It's OK if you want to call or send E-mails, but I can't go out
into public, with my eyes so red from weeping. Have fun at the
party.

Jus

Subj: the cruise
Date: 2/14 9:54:21 AM Eastern Standard Time
From: krakatau@indonet.net.id
To: podonnell@sfchronicle.com

Dear Phil,

I just got back from the cruise – it was fabulous, we visited some
of the islands way out, where the people are still very primitive,
and a thousand perfect beaches. We went to Komodo and saw
the giant lizards, twice as big as a Louisiana gator. On Lombok
Island, we saw some guys fighting with sticks. It was supposed
to be a ritual of some kind, but it just looked to me like guys
beating the shit out of each other with sticks. I bought a bunch
of batiks and wooden carvings for my bungalow – not my usual
thing, but they were dirt cheap. Bruno's yacht is fabulous – such

good food, and wine flows like water. These guys drink so much, I can't keep up – there they are at 8 a.m., sipping their Australian chardonnay.

Happy Valentine's Day. Every year Andrew and I had the same argument. I would say, Let's go out to some place special tonight, and he would say, Why? It's just another day, Valentine's Day is just Hallmark and candy companies ripping off the kids. And I would say, Well, guess what, babee, your boyfriend is an overgrown kid. Then he would smile that little smile, supposedly in spite of himself, and say, OK, whatever you want, "but no candy." It's no big deal. I'll probably just go to bed early, unless Angus comes banging on my door, as usual.

I'm having a great time here, but to tell you the truth, Phil, I'm starting to feel a little bit like I'm drifting. The thought of creating a new piece is kind of scary. It was the same after "Rodeo" – it takes a while to get the last piece out of your system. Can you believe that I haven't been to a single performance of Balinese dance since I've been here? I guess I got it out of my system. It's strange being back here: what makes it so relaxing is that it has no connection with your real life, but that leaves the interesting question. What AM I connected with?

With you, for sure. Don't worry about me – one of these days I'll be sitting on the beach, and an idea will pop into my head, and the next thing you know, I'll be knocking on your door, wanting to set up my office in your kitchen. It'll be just like the good ol' days on Bleecker Street.

Love ya,

Joey

Subj: home again
Date: 2/14 11:34:55 AM Pacific Standard Time
From: AndrewTan@wol.com
To: etan@MIT.edu (Eric Tan)

Hi Eric,

What a great few days! I've never seen the Tans getting along so
well . . . not just getting along, but jolly. Of course it's all
because of Terry, the jolliest little guy I've ever met. You look
great, with that grin that won't wipe off your face, and Sophie
so . . . blissful, and Mom bustling around, happy to be useful,
and, most amazing of all, Dad acting goofy, talking baby talk,
etc. He looked so crestfallen every time someone took Terry
away from him.

Travis put the final touches on the cabinets while I was in
Cambridge. He just called and invited me to come to his place
tonight . . . a first. He lives in Sausalito, not too far, but way up
in the hills. I'm more curious than nervous about what's going to
happen. I'll let you know.

Well, I love you, guy, and I already miss you and Sophie and
Terry. Why don't you see about getting a post at Stanford?

your sentimental brother

P.S. Happy Valentine's Day. I used to hate it when Joey wanted
to make a big fuss about it. Somehow I don't think Travis is the
type, either. I guess I'll bring flowers. That's always a good idea.

Subj: Joseph Breaux
Date: 2/15 10:25:52 AM Pacific Standard Time
From: podonnell@sfchronicle.com
To: krakatau@indonet.net.id

Oh Joey,

What a totally FABULOUS Valentine's Day. Fritz is the biggest
cornball in the world, or I should say the second biggest. When I
got home from work yesterday the place was simply overflowing
with red roses, I don't know how many dozen. He had dinner
catered for us AT HOME, a dreamy blond child with muscles
bulging under his cheap tux to serve us foie gras and
champagne, then lamb chops (a teeny bit overdone after Tab
Hunter got through with them – he was obviously cast for his
decorative appeal rather than his culinary genius, but never
mind). Platinum-edged china and clunky silverware, and fancy
candelabras with white candles, very Liberace. Then, the piece
de cornballlite, chocolate mousse served in little heart-shaped
dishes. Then the boy poured out the coffee, gathered up the dirty
dishes, and left us to whisper sweet nothings in between belches.
Must have cost him $300. The whole thing was camp as
Christmas, but totally adorable – Fritz can read me like a book.
No one has ever been so sweet to me. I'm starting to feel so attached to him – he's so RELIABLE. He knows what a worry-
wart I am; if he's even half an hour late he calls on his cell.

But sugar, your message left me a little concerned – "drifting"
and "scary" aren't good words. Why don't you come stay here
for a while? just hang out with us? It must seem strange to be
homeless, but you're not – you know you're always welcome
here. Just call ahead, and I'll slip they key under the mat.

Love from Phyllis

Subj: He's back!
Date: 2/16 3:55:54 AM Eastern Standard Time
From: thumbelina@indonet.net.id
To: Erica_golden@IDS.org

Dear Rica,

You're not going to believe this: Joe Breaux is back! Not for
dance or anything like that, he says he's here "just to hang out."
He's really become a mess. I was at Double Six, the popular
disco here, a funky place on the beach. I can't usually stay up
that late, but last night they had a special dance performance by
a group from Jakarta I love, a fusion of jazz and traditional
Javanese you would probably hate. Supposedly for Valentine's
day, which means absolutely nothing to people here, except
what they've seen in American movies. They ran out of hearts
for the decorations, and supplemented them with poinsettias left
over from Christmas. Anyway, there was Joe, with that dazed
Ecstasy-and-booze look we know so well here. When I went up
to say hi, he didn't recognize me – not that we were ever really
friends, but we met each other on a dozen occasions, at least.
Finally he said he remembered me, but I don't think he did, really. We only talked a short while, and he kept looking over my
shoulder at a cute boy the whole time.

He was wearing a very skimpy outfit, to show off his undeniably
fabulous body. He has a little paunch now, but he still looks as
strong and graceful as ever, and brown as a cup of strong cappuccino. I'm afraid he was acting like the worst sort of gay for-
eigner, flirting with all the twinkies and rent boys. He was
patting their bums, had them sitting in his lap. I have to admit, I
sort of spied on him. He was there with Angus Gray, the most
outrageous of that whole group, who was stoned out of his
gourd, and some old German guy laden with gold chains. I
stood behind them for a few minutes while they sized up the
boys as they sashayed by, wiggling their hips. It was really gross,

like a horse auction, Angus giving detailed reports on how they performed in their try-outs with him. Joe slipped away to the dark end of the beach for a while with one lad, then took another one home with him. Classy, huh? Hard to believe it was the same guy who came here a year ago with that lovely Chinese man.

That's my yucky news. It was too late to drive back to Ubud last night, so I stayed at a friend's place in Kuta. When I left, around noon, I saw Joe roaring down Jalan Legian on his motorcycle, bare-chested, the boy clinging to him, trophy of the conquering hero.

This island just eats some men alive.

Big kiss from Pam

ACKNOWLEDGMENTS

I would like to thank friends and readers who encouraged me and made many valuable suggestions: Tracy Brown, Nancy Collins, Vaudine England, Anne Fadiman, David Fratkin, Davien Little-field, Richard Oh, Craig Seligman, Kirk Stirling, and Philip Yong. Also, I'm indebted to Philip Kennicott for use of the lemon zester. Michael Carr made many fine improvements to the text. I am especially grateful to my agent, Katinka Matson, for her loyalty and support over the years, and to my editor, John Scognamiglio, for his sharp, sensitive analysis and many good ideas. Martin Westlake toiled indefatigably against tropical damp and a dull sitter to create the beautiful portrait. John McGlynn corrected many inaccuracies concerning Indonesian life and language, and Rucina Ballinger rooted out a few egregious errors about Balinese dance (though some of the characters in the book say some very silly things because they don't know any better). Finally, I owe special thanks to the book's earliest and most fervent believers, Lindsley Cameron and James Anthony Hull, who read it in electronic dispatches before it ever reached the paper page.